THE END IS HER

Jessica Christ, Book 7

H. CLAIRE TAYLOR

ISBN: 978-1-7330264-2-0 (H. Claire Taylor)

FFS Media, LLC

www.ffs.media

contact@hclairetaylor.com

Contents

THE END IS HER

Jessica Christ, Book 7

H. CLAIRE TAYLOR

"Everything that needs to be said has already been said. But since no one was listening, everything must be said again."

-André Gide

Chapter One

April 1, 22 AGC

Jesus rotated the ladle, allowing the tomato soup to dribble into the homeless man's bowl. "Peace be with you, brother."

The man shifted his shoulders absentmindedly, holding up the long line, and glared from the surface of the soup back up to the face of God's only begotten son. "This smells like shit."

"Be nice to him," Jessica McCloud snapped from beside her half-brother. "It's his birthday."

The twitchy man turned unfocused eyes on her with a skepticism that, for a fleeting instant, caused her to doubt her own existence. "I ain't no April fool." He glared at Jesus. "But you look like one."

Jesus threw his head back, the harsh fluorescent lights

above them illuminating his features. "It is true, my brother! I am quite the fool!"

Not quite what the homeless man was expecting, and he gave one final involuntary shoulder jerk, took his tray, and left. Jesus turned to his sister. "See? Nothing so humbling as serving others."

She wouldn't debate with him on that since it was, after all, his birthday. Had it not been, she wouldn't have even been there, standing shoulder to shoulder with him, hairnet on, subjected to the bubbling vat of soup that did, indeed, smell more like something to come out of a human rather than something to put inside one. If it hadn't been Jesus's birthday, she would have stayed on the couch and continued in vain to brainstorm ways to turn her Father into her second Mother.

"It's your birthday?" the next person in line asked as Jessica handed her a small dinner roll.

Jesus grinned. "It is."

"Not an April Fools' joke?" the woman asked hesitantly. Her voice was both scratchy and mousy, and she was frighteningly thin from head to toe except for a soft ring of bulk around her middle. Jessica didn't get the feeling she was a demon, though, despite the physical similarity to Randy McAllister in the Dallas Zoo so many years ago. In fact, she felt immensely sorry for the woman and couldn't put her finger on why.

Well, other than the homelessness.

I should be homeless right now. I don't deserve a home. I've done nothing to earn it.

"Not a joke!" Jesus declared. "I was born on this day, give or take a few due to the switch from Julian to Gregorian, two thousand and—"

"Twenty-nine years ago," Jessica cut in.

"Ah yes. Twenty-nine years ago."

While the woman's pinched brows indicated that she knew she'd missed out on something, she nodded, forced a grin, and wished the man she knew as Joshua a proper happy birthday.

"I have to say," he began once the line moved again, "it's much better to celebrate in the spring. Nicer weather. And the fact that it is on the most joyous of modern holidays only makes it even more glorious!"

She forced a smile, but she hated April Fools' Day almost as much as she hated her own birthday. That had been true even before Jesus came around and claimed it as his birthday.

"What day do you think my birthday will be celebrated on, centuries from now?" she asked.

Jesus whipped his head around, his lips slightly parted, eyes wide. "Are you telling me that you're finally thinking about your legacy through the ages?"

"I don't really have a choice, do I?" She grunted. "Don't get all worked up about it. It was just a simple question."

Nodding thoughtfully, Jesus greeted the next in line with a preoccupied smile, then said, "Since there's no longer a pagan threat to crush, I suppose your birthday will be celebrated on whatever day is very important to the religious practices of the people your followers eventually want to overpower."

She cringed. "Yeah, that's about what I was thinking too. Anyway, I hope it's in the fall. I like the fall."

"Pride before the fall ..." Jesus muttered.

Jessica leaned closer. "Say what?"

"Huh? Oh, nothing. Just something Jeremy and I were discussing. Austin Pride Week. I asked him when it happened, and he said it was sometime at the end of summer. I haven't been, but it sounds like fantastic fun!"

She imagined Jesus riding a float in the Pride parade and had no trouble with it. Rainbow beads would be such a thrill for him. He would, no doubt, find the whole thing "joyous."

"If you go this year, let me know." Her life may make little sense, but she wasn't completely numb to joy.

In fact, she would have preferred to be a little more numb. But instead, she was alert. Funny how having nowhere to be and no immediate goals other than not starving to death could awaken the senses.

Her brain ran laps around the same scenery of anxieties day in and day out, but there was one particular thing she still couldn't confront head on, one disastrous series of events, the consequences and complicated emotions of which stalked her every move. When would they strike? When would the events of last Thanksgiving be finished with her?

The betrayal.

The smiting.

No, she wouldn't think about that right now. She had hours and hours of time alone in her condo that she'd done nothing to deserve when she could let those fears catch up with her.

"I'm glad you wanted to do this," she said, trying desperately to sound like she meant it.

Jesus met her eyes with his own watery ones, and she prayed—figuratively—that he wasn't going to cry in the middle of the homeless soup kitchen. "I knew that if you just came with me, you would understand why I have been working so hard on my mission."

She looked around the room where four or five dozen homeless sat at cafeteria tables, eating their bread, soup, and chicken.

Jessica had, of course, miracled each of the rolls ahead of time just in case any of the recipients needed that, but during her months off, she'd mastered the ability to minimize the size of her face on them to hardly more than a small burn mark. Not only was the skill handy for keeping a bunch of strangers from ogling her image, but it also served a practical purpose. Last she'd checked with Wendy, Dolores owned the rights to Jessica's miracle brand. And neither of the lawyers Wendy was tirelessly dating had yet found a loophole to get those rights back.

And yes, she felt guilty for Wendy's long hours. She'd even gone so far as to say that she would help bear the burden of sleeping with lawyers if God would let that happen. But, of course, He wouldn't.

That was a shame. She could really use some action.

Her dreams had been so bland lately. Without Chris and Jesus crashing them, all she had to look forward to was the occasional run-in with Moses, who usually looked surprised to see her and had nothing useful to offer insofar as guidance. The last time this had happened, she'd just turned a corner in the halls of Mooremont High, where she was running late for a test she'd forgotten to study for, when she collided with the guy. He was reading intently from a stone tablet, which she sent straight into his chest upon impact.

"Why are you in my high school?" she'd asked.

"Why are *you* in your high school?" he'd replied.

"I'm dreaming."

Moses looked around, taking in the lockers and blur of students passing. "Ah. Yes. Yes, you are."

"Did you want to tell me something?" she prompted, hoping the test didn't start without her.

He looked down at his tablet then back up at her. "Nope. Just got caught up in my reading. Welp. Retirement calls."

And then he'd left. And only after she was already seated in her classroom with the gibberish test on the desk in front of her did the teacher start to take off his clothes and the sexy part of the dream began.

She was shaken from her daydreaming by a gruff voice. "Don't I get a roll?"

"Huh?" She hadn't noticed the newcomer in line.

"You stupid?"

"Huh?" she said, not helping her case.

"I said, are you stupid? Give me my damn roll!"

She tossed one at him like it had scalded her, and he grunted a few more obscenities about her and moved on down the line.

"Blessed day to you!" Jesus said enthusiastically.

Once the man was gone, Jessica waited patiently for Jesus to catch her eye so she could properly scowl at him.

"What?" he said. "Are you unhappy?"

"Did you not hear what he said?" All her sour emotions came flooding back. This was a mistake. She didn't have to put herself though this just because it was Jesus's birthday. He'd had plenty of those already. "I told you they weren't pleasant."

"I never said they were especially pleasant, sister. But that doesn't mean they're unworthy of love. The way I see it, if you can love those who treat you poorly, you can love anyone."

"But why would I want to love people who treat me poorly? I loved Dolores and she turned out to be the Devil. That's worked out *great* for me." She grabbed one of the rolls and took a large bite from it. It was nearly rock solid from sitting out so long.

"It would not kill you to show love for—"

"Don't you say it."

"Fine. I'll admit that it's different when it's Satan. But none of these people are Satan. They're just people who are hurting."

Movement caught Jessica's eyes, and she watched as

one man got another in a headlock and the pair started thrashing around. "Hurting *each other*."

Jesus sighed. "You don't have to understand yet. But someday you will."

She turned to him. "Didn't one of them beat you up recently?"

"Many of them all at once, yes. But it was due to my mistake."

"I thought you were perfect."

"You mean like you are?"

Her mouth fell open. Had Jesus just sassed her?

By the time their shift was done, she was more than ready to get the hell out of there. They had one more place to be, so she had to herd him out of the dining hall where he was blissfully surveying the homeless while they ate. They seemed to like *him* well enough. Or at least they tolerated him. Huh.

As she loaded into the driver's side of her car and shut the door, a waft of stank hit her. She gagged and rolled down the window. "I'll never get this stink out of my nose. It's like BO and old socks just screwed in a Dumpster."

Jesus casually adjusted the air vents to get more direct flow. "It is valuable to acknowledge it. And even more valuable to acknowledge that you can leave it behind."

She was all full up on his wisdom for the day. "Yeah, that's what I'm doing. I'm saying it'll be nice to not have to smell that." She wished she could take a shower before they met up with the others, but there was no time. She hadn't anticipated this part of his birthday plans. "You ready?"

Jesus swallowed hard, grabbed the oh-shit handle above his window and used his other hand to brace on the dash before shutting his eyes in prayer. If she didn't know any better, she'd say he was trying to cast demons out of her engine. But she did know better. Jesus still wasn't used to motor vehicles.

"It's not a long drive," she said.

"Where are we going?"

"You'll see."

Chapter Two

Jessica had initially thought reserving one of the party rooms was overkill, but now that she realized how loud the music in the main gym of Sir Jumpsalot was, she was glad the manager had upsold her on it. It wasn't her money anyway, because she didn't have money. She just had benefactors, and every dollar she spent was an invisible layer of social debt added to the pile that no one would openly admit existed.

"I should probably get out there," said Jeremy Archer, squinting through the large window separating their fifteen-foot-by-fifteen-foot party room from the massive trampoline zone. He was the unofficial sponsor of this event, having insisted that his best friend and roommate deserved to properly celebrate on his *real* birthday.

"Up to you," said Destinee. "Looks like Jesus is havin' plenty of fun without us."

Jessica followed Jeremy's gaze through the observation

window. Jesus, it appeared, had made a couple of new adolescent friends, and the three of them were seeing who could do the best backflip.

It was a shame, really, that probably every parent who saw him would assume he was just your run-of-the-mill pedophile. Jessica hadn't seen joy so pure in a very long time. Maybe not since her high school football days.

"Yeah," she agreed, "Maybe you should go out there." What she didn't say was that Jeremy's presence would likely tip the assumption scales from pedophile to just overly friendly gay. Or maybe the parents would simply layer the assumptions, one of top of the other. "I'll join y'all in a little bit," she said. Maybe that would help.

NOTHING WILL HELP.

Ah, there you are. I was wondering if you'd miss your own son's birthday.

I HAVE NOT FORSAKEN HIM.

Must be nice for him.

YOU CONTINUE TO HOLD A GRUDGE.

Yes, yes, I do.

IF I HAD TOLD YOU WHO THE DEVIL WAS, YOU WOULD HAVE AVOIDED THE CONFRONTATION YOUR WHOLE LIFE.

You're not wrong. Gee, I wonder how a person can get through life without confronting the literal devil. Oh right, everyone does that. Everyone but me.

AND YOUR BROTHER.

She watched Jeremy approach the trampolines and slip off his shoes. It didn't take long for him to climb on and start bouncing. Jesus's eyes lit up and he guffawed with glee when he saw his best friend joining in.

How did Jesus do it? God had hung him up to dry in the most horrifically literal sense, and Jesus could still manage to come to a trampoline park and act like he was the luckiest boy who ever lived.

"So, I guess we gotta wait on this cake?" Rex asked from beside Destinee. Jessica turned her attention away from the mayhem and back to Destinee and Rex, the only two people left in the party room now. Some party.

The cake was compliments of her mother, who'd baked and decorated it in Jesus's favorite colors: all of them. Across it, it said, *Happy 2018th birthday Joshua!!* And below that was a shape that roughly resembled a unicorn's head. When Jessica had first glimpsed the icing design, she would have believed it was a narwhal or a rhino just as easily as she would have believed unicorn. But Jesus had known right away, and he'd become teary-eyed and hugged Destinee tightly and bestowed so many blessings on her that it wasn't long before she'd had to push him away. "It don't feel right, you giving me all those tingles." But then she'd leaned close again and murmured, "At least not in front of Rex."

"I think we need to wait until Jesus wears himself out, then we can cut the cake," Jessica said in response to the inquiry.

"Damn," Rex said. "In that case, I'm gonna go buy another tub of those chili cheese fries."

Outside, an unexpected double-bounce caused Jesus to

under-rotate in one of his frontward flips, and his top half hit the vinyl while his back half continued to rotate. Jessica and Destinee cringed in unison at the scorpion pose, but Jesus was quickly back on his feet and laughing as he shook his finger playfully at the ceiling.

"You got a birthday coming up," Destinee said.

"Not for three months."

"Yeah, well, twenty-three is a big age."

"No, it's not."

"It's bigger than twenty-two."

"Not bigger, just older." She glanced down at the cake again and swiped a finger of icing from a spot that no one would notice.

"I just think you could use a little celebration. Pardon me, but as your mother, I kinda wanna celebrate the life of my child. And you ain't been a barrel of sunshine and bluebonnets lately."

"I have work to do."

"And how's that comin'?"

Before Jessica could answer, Rex returned with his tub of food substitute.

The first whiff hit Jessica's senses, and she was transported back to the homeless kitchen and the vat of soup that smelled like diarrhea. The second whiff didn't smell *much* less like that, but now she was craving the stuff despite it. She didn't wait for Rex's permission before she skimmed a soggy fry off the top.

"I was just asking Jess how her work's coming,"

Destinee said, giving Rex a significant look. Had they discussed this beforehand?

"Oh!" Rex sat up straighter. "Great. Yeah. I fully support working women. How's it coming?"

Outnumbered, Jessica ignored the freshly scalded spot on her tongue and said, "Not great. I don't know how I'm supposed to change God into a woman when I don't even know what it means to be a woman."

Rex nodded gravely. "Gender is a complex subject with a lot of historical baggage."

Destinee also nodded along, then suggested, "Can you, I dunno, give God a vag?"

Jessica grimaced. "Don't think I haven't already considered that solution."

"It's tricky," Rex mused, "because womanhood is just a social construct. One can be any way one chooses and simply call oneself a woman, and suddenly that's it. Poof! Woman."

Jessica treated herself to another one of Rex's fries, considering it Gibberish Tax. "I just need the majority of Americans to start thinking of him as her, then, if he's not full of infinite shit, that should restore peace to the United States."

Destinee shoveled some of the sludge into her mouth and took a quick sip of her Diet Dr. Pepper to counteract the scorching grease. Once she was able, she said, "He might be full of infinite shit, baby."

"I appreciate the support, Mom, but I'm hoping that's not the case."

"If you just need the majority of the population," Rex said, "then why don't you figure out what the majority of the population associates with womanhood? Then you push that."

"That's what I'm leaning toward, but ... I don't know how to get started."

Destinee sat up straighter. "Well, why don't we get started now? You can start by polling us!"

"Um, okay. What do you think makes a woman, Mom?"

Destinee shut her eyes pensively and inhaled deeply, presumably summoning maternal wisdom from the divine source. "What it means to be a woman is to have tits and a hooha."

Before Jessica could respond, Rex was already on it. "You know I respect your opinion, D. But what about women who have had to have full mastectomies?"

"Fine then. Just a vag."

"And what about transwomen? Many of them choose to live as a woman but maintain their male anatomy."

Rather than defend herself, Destinee merely squinted at her lover. "The hell you learn this?"

He blinked. "ESPN."

Jessica jumped in. "What about you, Rex? What do you think makes a woman?"

"Hmm ..." He leaned back in his chair and intertwined his fingers, resting them on his large beer belly. "I'd say it was the embracing of goddess energy, the harnessing of the divine feminine, and the integration of ..."

"You learn that shit on ESPN, too?" Destinee snapped.

Rex nodded.

While Jessica wondered when sports shows had become so woke, she wasn't able to ask the question before the party room door opened and the high-octane music from outside burst in like a thunderclap. Jesus was giddy and drenched in sweat as he led the way inside. Behind him followed Jeremy and two of the kids Jesus had been jumping with. "This is Clint and Garth. We're friends now. I told them we had plenty of cake to go around."

The boys couldn't be older than ten, and yet they were savvy enough to eye the unicorn cake with suspicion.

"Why does it say you're turning two thousand and eighteen?" asked the boy with shaggy blond hair half an inch over his eyes. He shook his head as a tic, but the sweaty hair stayed stuck on his forehead.

"Because I am, Garth!"

The boys didn't ask any further questions, simply took their cake and wandered out.

"Aren't children wonderful?" Jesus said, grinning. He missed the fact that as soon as they were both outside the party room, the blond boy slapped the cake out of the other boy's hands, laughed, and ran off.

Destinee nodded absentmindedly then said, "What do *you* think makes a woman?"

Jesus paused with his fork hovering between his plate and his mouth. "Uh ... I have no idea." His eyes darted to each of them. "I mean, I had very different experiences with women back in my old life. We, um, we thought different things. It was a different time."

Destinee waved him down. "Don't worry, we know what you're talking about. But we're clean now, right, baby?"

Jessica nodded. "I'm menstruating at this very moment, and God wouldn't mind if I touched you."

Jesus nodded cautiously. "If you say so, sister."

Then, before Jessica could stop her, Destinee turned to Jeremy Archer. "What about you? What do you think makes a woman?"

"Heightened levels of fluoride in an area's water supply."

"The fuck?" Destinee ignored her daughter waving at her to not inquire further, but it was too late.

Jessica sighed, cut herself a piece of cake. "Happy birthday, bro."

And as Jeremy continued on about fluoride, Jesus grinned, rainbow icing already staining his lips. "Thanks, sis."

Chapter Three

Jessica scratched the square-jawed mutt behind the ears one last time before slipping out of his kennel and latching the gate. This was always the worst part of volunteering, having to leave. At least, this was the worst part about volunteering *at an animal shelter*. When it came to other types of volunteer work, leaving was usually the best part.

She shuddered, thinking about the vast array of used condoms she'd picked up on the side of the highway the last time she'd naively volunteered for a roadside clean-up.

It had been Wendy's suggestion, the whole community service thing. Until Jessica was officially off the hook for the smiting outside her former bakery, which continued to baffle both law enforcement and the legal system alike, working on her public persona was a must.

Especially since she couldn't work a real job, or rather, was unsure where she should work and where her life was going, and so on. Spending her time volunteering not only helped make the case that she was an upstanding citizen, but it was also a good way to keep her from growing neurotic and prowling circles around her condo like a caged animal.

She hung the shelter leash on one of the hooks leading out from the kennels and went to sign out at the front desk. She would have stayed longer if she could, but they were about to close, and she had a check-in with Cash Monet in half an hour.

Sherri, a lovely woman with large bosoms she seemed more than happy to hide underneath leopard-print scrubs, nodded and smiled at Jessica from behind the front desk. "Everything good?"

"Of course. Are you sure you have enough volunteers for tomorrow?"

Sherri smiled. "All full up for the next two weeks."

Damn. She'd have to go do something no one in Austin wanted to help with, like something human-related. Would it be the government run retirement home, or feeding the homeless again?

She shivered at the prospect of either. The last time she's visited the nursing home, she'd had to press the emergency button for an orderly to rush in after an elderly lady, who she strongly suspected was a demon, cornered her while shouting "Get behind me, Satan!" No matter how much Jessica whispered to her that she was not in fact Satan, but she knew who *was*, the woman continued wielding a Precious Moments figurine over her head, ready to bring it down upon Jessica with all the force of righteous indignation.

The pen in Jessica's hand froze, hovering an inch above where she'd just written her sign-out time. An idea had occurred to her. She went for it before she chickened out. "Hey, Sherri, I know this will sound weird, but what do you think makes a woman?"

To Sherri's credit, her smile didn't falter. "Hmm ... I guess it's the ability to have babies."

Wow. That was so simple. It was completely wrong, of course; however, Jessica couldn't help but admire someone who was able to see things so clearly.

"What about women who can't have children?"

"Oh, I don't know about that." Sherri slid the clipboard back toward her. "I think any woman can have a kid if she just tries hard enough and really wants it."

Jessica waited silently for the woman to laugh at her own perverse joke. But there was no laughter. "Oh. You ... you really mean that."

"Yuh-huh," she said brightly.

"What about after a woman is too old to have children?"

Sherri shrugged. "I just read about a woman who was in her seventies and had her first child. I don't think women are ever too old for it."

"That doesn't ..." Her stomach slowly dropped lower in her torso as it dawned on her that Sherri was no longer someone she could like. "What about women with hysterectomies? They can't have kids anymore. But they're still women."

"I wouldn't agree with that. They've given up their claim to it, haven't they?"

"... No. No, I don't think it works that way." But already, the conviction in Sherri's words was starting to make her wonder.

"The Bible says so."

Jessica paused, felt around in her head ... Yep, there He was.

IT DOES NOT SAY THAT.

"Okay," Jessica said, wondering if there were a way for her to forget this whole conversation. "I'll see you next time."

Minutes later, once Jessica was safely in the comfort of her own vehicle, she exhaled. "Is that it? Is it just babies?"

YOU HAVE NOT ASKED MANY PEOPLE THIS QUESTION YET, HAVE YOU, DAUGHTER?

Not yet.

THEN KEEP ASKING AND YOU SHALL RECEIVE.

Receive what?

YOU'LL SEE.

By the time she made it to the coffee shop where she and Cash held their monthly meetings, the shock of Sherri's response had taken a back seat to Jessica's agony over leaving all the dogs behind in their cages. She'd been well into her daydream about freeing them all with a miraculous wave of her hand and having them follow her into the wilderness where they would enjoy simple yet fulfilling lives as a pack, when she'd found herself turning into the small shopping center.

Cash already had Jessica's triple espresso waiting for her when she entered.

"You smell like you rolled in something," Cash said, crinkling their nose.

"What makes a woman?"

The white-haired pixie arched one transparent eyebrow at her and their lips parted. "Is this, like, a neurological thing? Did you have a stroke? You can tell me if you did. I've found a way to spin worse."

"No. I have to figure out how to make God a woman."

Cash's eyebrow remained arched, but they apparently decided to play along despite concern. "And you think the sole genderless person in your life will have the answers you seek?"

Jessica sighed and leaned forward, "Yeah, and about that... Why can't I just make God genderless? That seems like the better solution."

Cash chuckled, and their eyebrow finally lowered. "If we'd never met, and you were just seeing me for the first time, what gender would you guess?"

"Male."

"There's your answer."

"Huh? Am I wrong? Is female the right answer?"

"No. There's no right answer. My gender is nothing. But even knowing that, you think that there are only two options. Sure, imagining God as a woman is going to be tough for a lot of people, but there are plenty of models for it throughout history. Hell, there's even a word for it: goddess. But you're crossing into uncharted territory when you ask people to make God genderless. And let me just tell you, it ain't gonna happen. I'm standing in front of you right now telling you I'm genderless, and you're still trying to figure out if I'm a man or a woman."

"Am not."

She was.

"So, to answer your original question, I couldn't give a crap less what it means to be a woman."

As unfulfilling as the response was, at least it wasn't outright crazy.

She sighed. "What are we meeting about again?"

Cash steepled their fingers underneath their chin and chewed on their bottom lip in nervous anticipation. Once the drama of the moment had crested, they said, "Great news, Jess. Your Twitter analytics make it clear that the time is ripe for you to take the next step. The groundwork has been laid, and the world is ready to hear it straight from you."

"Hear what straight from me?"

"That God is a woman."

Jessica shut her eyes and wished she was anywhere else. It was an emergent theme in her life, always wishing she were anywhere else but where she was. "I don't even know what that means, though."

Cash scoffed. "Since when does anyone understand what they're talking about before they say it? Come on,

Jessica, get with the times. Knowledge and expertise are dead. Long live the attention economy. Now, I've spoken with Wendy, and I have a campaign of memes that I think will set up this announcement so it's well received ..."

Are you there?

WHERE?

Don't do this right now.

FINE. WHAT DO YOU NEED?

I can't do this. I can't talk about something I don't understand.

THEN MAYBE YOU SHOULDN'T TALK AT ALL.

Will you be this cruel when you're a woman?

ONLY ONE WAY TO FIND OUT.

She sighed, tuned back into the physical world, and tried to follow along as Cash ran through the list of top captions they would use alongside a recent paparazzi photo of her eating a donut on a bench.

God had a point. She didn't understand much about anything.

Chapter Four

It was a beautifully sunny day at the tail end of April, clear skies, not yet so hot that the green grass of the park was flecked with brown despite the city's best watering efforts. Jessica couldn't have asked for better weather, really. Or a better turnout. Of course, almost none of them were here for her, but she would do her best to hijack their attention for a brief time anyway.

She wasn't sure if it was the familiarity or the newness of this situation that made her more nervous. When was the last time she'd held a press conference? High school?

But she'd never participated in one quite like this, so relaxed, unofficial, and with so many off-leash dogs running around.

Wendy Peterman straightened Jessica's collar in the shade of a large oak. "You remember all the talking points?"

"Yes, I remember all the talking points."

"Stick to them. As if your life depends on it. Do not screw this up."

Because the publicist was usually intense and tightly wound, Jessica had always found it tricky to gauge when she was *especially* stressed. But little snips like that were warning flares. This needed to go well, that much was obvious.

"Don't worry, I'll stick to the points."

Wendy stepped back and took her in from head to toe. "Good. Now, are you ready to smile and wave to the crowd?"

"There's a crowd?" The small podium was at the top of a hill, out of sight of where Jessica had spent the last half hour preparing herself in the shade of the oak. When she'd last checked, there hadn't been a crowd so much as a few dozen of uninterested millennials on their lunch break letting their dogs get a good off-leash romp.

"The news started arriving about twenty minutes ago."

"Maria and Gabrielle?"

"Yep, they're among them."

Jessica let the air whoosh out of her lungs. At least she had allies here. She knew all too well how wrong local stations could get a story like this—or like anything —and that was when they *weren't* intentionally twisting it.

She rolled her shoulders back and climbed the hill.

Wendy had insisted that they host the junket somewhere with a beneficial backdrop. Since Jessica no longer owned It is Risen, that parking lot was out. Which pretty much left public parks.

One stood out among the rest, precisely for this hill and the backdrop of the downtown Austin skyline, which the publicist insisted would trigger a sense of Austin pride in anyone watching. That, she said, would remind them that Jessica was theirs, and as such, they would listen to what she had to say.

Or so the theory went.

As Jessica reached the podium, a slobbery Great Dane galloped over, making straight for her.

She tried not to panic, but what was she supposed to do? Wendy had just spent the last thirty minutes making sure Jessica was dressed sharply, rolling her black slacks with a lint roller ("Do you live with thirty cats?" she'd asked testily), and making sure Jessica's boring, lifeless hair had enough body without "looking like you've just gotten lucky in the back seat of a Ferrari," which was obviously a reference to a specific event in Wendy's own mysterious life.

If Jessica pet the dog and the dangling thread of slobber wobbling from the corner of its jowls transferred to Jessica's clothing, Wendy would lose it.

But on the other hand—

THOU SHALT PET THE DOG.

She had never received a better command from her Father.

She turned toward the Great Dane to face it full-on, and gave it a huge two-handed head pet, flopping its ears around. Not only did the act of petting a dog make her feel exponentially calmer, but she heard a few people in the gathering crowd of curious passersby fawn over the interaction. And when she straightened up again and the dog ran off, she realized that, yes, there had been a transfer of drool onto one of her forearms. She cringed and wiped it onto her pants leg, and the onlookers chuckled.

Thanks. That was a good idea. I think it won me some favor.

THE COMMAND WAS NOT GIVEN FOR STRATEGIC PURPOSES. HE WAS MERELY THE GOODEST OF BOYS AND DESERVED A PET.

Well, thanks anyway.

She smiled out at the cameras and found Maria Flores smiling back at her. She couldn't see Gabrielle's face behind her camera, but knowing she was there was enough.

The gathering dog owners watched now with a bored skepticism she rather appreciated. At least it wasn't contempt!

"Welcome. Thanks to everyone who made it out today. I know we didn't give you a lot of information regarding the nature of this event, so I appreciate your curiosity and willingness to take the time to come out." First talking point down. Maybe she could nail this. "For those of you watching at home, who are wondering what this random white girl is doing on TV"—Wendy had written that line for her, and while Jessica had questioned if she needed to bring race into it, the publicist insisted it would loosen up the crowd—"my name is Jessica McCloud. I used to run It is Risen bakery, a locally owned establishment. I'm a former Texas State Bobcat, a native Texan, and, most importantly—" She paused, remembering the words she was supposed to say, that Wendy had pounded into her. But she couldn't say them. Why couldn't she say them? They were true.

She modified it.

"—Most importantly, I've been sent by God to relay a message." There. It expressed the same thing as "I'm the daughter of God" anyway.

"Over the next months and years, my mission is to make it undeniably clear to you and the rest of this country that God as we know him is, in fact, a her." She paused for effect. "That is correct. I've been put on this earth with a message, and that message is that God is a woman."

A fluffy labradoodle ran up to Jessica at that point, but she was too preoccupied with the startled expressions reflecting back at her to notice. Her survival instincts wouldn't allow her to look away from the mass of people who had been on her side only moments before but now appeared ready for a good old-fashioned lynch mob.

Then a male voice rose up from the dog owners, shouting, "Fuck yeah! Lady God!" And Jessica was almost knocked a step back by it. Then the supportive man ran forward, hand raised, and Jessica stepped around the podium for the much-needed high-five.

She was officially off script, and it felt ... right.

She snuck a glance at Wendy to get a handle on how

things were going. The ferocious woman stood straight as a board—that was nothing new—her arms by her side, palms resting on the fabric of her A-line skirt. And she was grinning.

And just like that, it was official. Jessica's ultimate gambit had begun.

Chapter Five

Jessica climbed the stairs of her building, heading for the condo Jameson Fractal still technically owned and stuffing her face with a meatball sub that Chris Riley's NFL contract had paid for. She was officially the moochsiah, but the sandwich was so delicious and her day had been so crappy that the self-criticism bounced right off her.

The last four months since her initial announcement at the park had flown by, hardly more than a blur of volunteering and small public appearances at local events. And though the city's reception of her had warmed enough that she'd graduated from "worrisome religious radical" to "quirky but delusional local celebrity" and might become "revered cultural icon" before long, this morning's highway cleanup under the brutal late-August sun was enough to blind her to all the positive progress she'd made, leaving her with a sour mood and the meatball sub.

As she dug a hand into her purse, searching for her

keys, the door across the hall opened, and Jesus stuck his head out. "Sister! How was your day? Joyous, I hope?"

She used her tongue to cram meatball into her cheek, then said, "Something like that, but much worse."

He frowned. "Oh, but you were having such a good week! Jeremy said footage of you at the Pride Parade has gone viral!"

That much was true, and the various clips of her dancing on a rainbow unicorn float next to a man who, unbeknownst to the crowd, was Jesus Christ in a flower crown, had been well-received and, according to Cash, gained her over twenty-thousand followers on Twitter, and fifteen thousand on Instagram, many of whom weren't bots.

"Right, but that was four days ago," she said. "I just spent the last three hours picking up used condoms and sun-dried squirrel jerky from the side of Highway 71 with a ragtag band of criminal misfits."

Jesus nodded his understanding. "The animal shelter was booked."

"You got it."

Her phone vibrated in her back pocket, and she slipped it out and looked down at the screen. "Um, I gotta go."

"Blessings, sister!"

She juggled the phone as she finally located her keys and hurried inside. She caught the call just before it went to voicemail.

"Hey, Chris." She was out of breath. Out of breath

from climbing a dozen stairs, eating a meatball sub, and hurrying a few steps inside. But she pushed aside thoughts of getting back into shape to focus on the conversation.

"Jess! How's it going?"

He sure was chipper and friendly, considering they hadn't spoken, outside of a few emotionless texts about the logistics of getting money into her bank account, in months.

"Great. It's going great."

"Yeah, I figured it would be. I just saw the video of you and Jesus at the Pride Parade. You know it's gone viral?"

"Yeah, Jesus just told me."

"Hey, listen. There's something I want to tell you about. I was keeping it a surprise, but it goes live today."

The phrase, "it goes live today" sent chills down her spine without her quite understanding why.

"O-kay ... what is it?"

"As you know, the regular season starts this Sunday." She didn't know that, but she let him go on. "So, I've been working with the NFL on a project over the pre-season. There are a lot of eyes on me going into my sophomore year in the league. Outside of the injury at the end of last season, I was doing pretty well, and there's this thing where players who have a great rookie season tend to flop in their second season, so everyone's wondering if I'll do that."

She was having a difficult time following where this was going. "Oh. Um, are you?"

"Ha. I sure as shit hope not. But the point is that

people are watching me closely, and I figure I might as well use that to my advantage. So, I've been working on this initiative."

She squeezed her eyes shut. "Initiative? For what?"

"Women."

"What do you mean?"

"Well, Wendy gave me a rundown of your strategy for this lady God thing—"

"You've been keeping in touch with Wendy?"

"Of course."

"Does she know about this initiative?"

"Eh ... Not exactly. The commercial will be a surprise for her."

Jessica flopped down onto her couch. "Commercial?"

"Yeah. A commercial for women."

She inhaled slowly through her nose and laid her head back on the arm rest. "A commercial for women," she echoed.

"Yep."

"I mean ... are you selling us? What exactly—"

"No, it's like a pro-women commercial. If you want people to believe God is a woman, it stands to reason that you would need people to like women first."

Oh, Chris, what have you done? "Okay. Tell me more."

"I could, but I'd rather show you. Hold on one sec, and I'll send you a link to it."

While he tinkered with his phone on the other line, she closed her eyes and tried to imagine the many ways this would bite her in the ass. What did pro football have to say about God being a woman? What sort of influence did it hold over the masses? She honestly didn't know, although, now that the sports networks were apparently woke, maybe there was something to this. Maybe Chris's initiative *could* make a huge difference. Or maybe ...

"There, just sent it."

"Okay." She pulled the phone away from her ear and saw the new text notification. "I'll watch it once we're off the phone."

"Great. Then I'll talk to you later." And before she could say a proper goodbye, he disconnected the call.

She stared down at her screen for a second, then opened the text and clicked the link.

The video popped up and started playing automatically.

But after a few seconds, she paused it, pulled up her text messages again, and went to the ongoing conversation with Wendy and Cash.

"We have a problem."

Chapter Six

Jessica tossed out the empty microwave meal container and chucked her dirty fork into the sink. It was five till seven, and she settled onto her couch to prepare for her video chat with Wendy and Cash. It had been a long afternoon of panic as she played through the various scenarios where the airing of this commercial ended her attempt to make God a woman before it ever took off.

She'd watched it dozens of times since Chris had called that afternoon, and yet, she still couldn't articulate precisely *why* it was such a horror show.

Was it the corny script?

Was it the execution of the corny script by a rotating cast of semi-literate professional football players staring directly into the camera?

Was it the strangeness of watching men whose notoriety was derived from smashing each other to bits talking about the importance of respecting women?

Or was it all of the above?

ALL OF THE ABOVE.

She opened her laptop.

What was he thinking?

IT WAS NOT HIS DOING. HE STARTED SOMETHING HE COULDN'T CONTROL.

Why would any organization sign off on this?

BECAUSE THERE IS A PROFIT IN IT FOR THEM.

How?

THAT IS NOT YET CLEAR TO THE LORD.

You don't understand it, but they do?

THE LORD IS NOT A PROFITEER.

Tell that to Jimmy Dean.

I HAVE. HE DOES NOT LISTEN.

The cutesy beeping of an incoming call pulled her attention to the physical world, and she answered the chat. Wendy's face appeared. A moment later, there was Cash.

"Can't I go a week without being dragged to a deeper circle of cyber hell?" Cash demanded in lieu of a greeting.

"I guess you watched the commercial already?"

They nodded.

"The question is," Wendy began, "how can we keep this thing from ever airing on TV?"

Jessica cringed. "I believe it's too late for that."

Wendy's face tightened. "Okay, then we're screwed."

"It's not that bad, is it?" Jessica asked, stupidly.

"Of course not," Cash replied. "I think the line, 'You'd better respect women, or else,' really gets the job done."

Wendy piled on with, "And the series of hypothetical questions was great. While I enjoyed 'Remember, that woman you're disrespecting could be somebody's daughter,' I was blown away by the moment when Chris appeared on screen to add, 'or even God's daughter.' "

"Yeah," Cash said. "And the little wink he did was just icing on the urinal cake."

Was the urinal cake reference further proof Cash was born a man?

Stop! Focus! It doesn't matter anyway!

It was about time someone came to Chris's defense. "He meant well. I'm sure he thought this would help."

Wendy sighed. "I know. It's my fault for filling him in and not being completely clear that he wasn't to do this specific kind of thing. I have a feeling he wasn't in charge of the script anyway."

"I had that feeling too," Jessica said. "I can't imagine him agreeing to the line, 'Sexy ain't their fault' or 'Women are people, too.'" But the fact of the matter was that he had watched the finished product, probably multiple times, and had still called her, excited to share it. On some level, Chris had condoned this train wreck of pseudo-feminism.

Wendy bowed her head solemnly, and Cash was clearly already typing away on their keyboard, drafting damage control tweets.

"You know you're going to be dragged into this, right?" Wendy said.

"Yeah, I figured."

"The memes are going to be relentless for a while."

"I can imagine. What I don't get, though, is why it's so bad. I mean, it is. I can tell that with one watch. But it's not like they said anything untrue. Women *are* people. Being sexy *isn't* a woman's fault. And we're all someone's daughter. So why does it rub me the wrong way?"

Wendy didn't mince words. "Because it's fucking stupid, Jessica. Because all the things they say are obvious —anyone with half a brain doesn't need to be told them— and there's nothing more irksome than people shouting painfully obvious things from a pedestal with the hope that it'll make them appear heroes for the little guy."

"But there *are* some men out there who need to hear it, who don't treat women like we're people."

"They still know it, though. This doesn't address the root causes of disrespect. There are people in this world who believe their job is to punish women who don't act the way they want, and that's the long and short of it. But we don't need those people on our side and, frankly, we don't want them. They are the power-starved idiots who ruin social movements. We don't need everyone in our camp. We just need the majority."

"Right, right," Jessica said, remembering their original game plan. "And the majority of Americans are women."

"Not by much, but yes. We just need to get most of the women, a portion of sympathetic men, and a bunch of children. Those are our most likely voters."

"Most likely voters for turning God into a woman," Jessica echoed, hoping to point out the insanity of the topic.

But Wendy missed it. "Exactly."

"So, what are we going to do?" Jessica asked. "How do we—"

Cash interrupted. "I'm already on it. I'm making crossover memes of your first press conference and the NFL commercial as we speak. I'll inoculate social media by injecting it with the virus. It'll flare up for a couple days, then it'll move on."

Wendy smiled proudly, but Jessica snapped, "You're *creating* the memes? You're making fun of me?"

"Yeah, but not as much as other people would. And I'm posting them from your account, so it'll look like you're making them and joking about it."

"And that works *how*?"

"It shows you have a sense of humor. Or at least your persona does, and thankfully that's all that matters. It's not as fun to make fun of someone who is already making fun of themself. Jesus Christ, Jess, how did you even make it through high school without learning this stuff?"

"I suffered for four years straight," she said, honestly. "Fine, I trust you, Cash."

"Your trust is irrelevant. But thanks. Oh, and do me a favor?"

"Yeah?"

"Send Chris a text and give him a heads up that I will be invoicing the everliving testosterone out of his rich ass for all this Photoshop."

She ended the call feeling like she could be hopeful. Cash had it under control, after all.

But could she dare to hope? Could she ever expect the average American to understand the difference between the toxic drivel of this commercial and the message she needed to spread about divine femininity ... especially when she didn't yet understand the difference herself?

Chapter Seven

On more than one occasion, Jessica might have been spared a lot of trouble if only she'd been able to see auras. But that skill was not on her heavenly resume. However, she didn't need the ability to know she was presently surrounded by angels. Sir Pawsington paused on their walk along the narrow strip of dirt behind the shelter to whip his head around and nibble at the place his balls used to be, and she let him. It was probably quite satisfying to gnaw at that particular phantom body part. Also, he had a long day ahead of him locked in his kennel.

As they continued, Sir Pawsington seemed content to simply stare up at her and follow wherever she went, and she reminded herself that she was *not* in any place to get a dog. Nope, nope, nope.

Thankfully, Austin had a strict no-kill policy, which meant, of course, that they only killed a few, and only the especially mean or sick ones at that. At least that was what they told the public.

As she slipped Sir Pawsington a training treat and put him in his kennel, a familiar voice called out, "There you are."

She turned and couldn't quite make sense of who she was looking at. Did he even like dogs? She couldn't remember ever seeing him around one. Why was he here?

"Why are you here?"

Quentin Jones tilted his head back and arched an eyebrow at her. "That's how you say hello now?"

"Hello. Why are you here?"

They hadn't spoken since he'd left her sorry ass on the football field months ago, after she'd sulked too much and, perhaps, said a few things that crossed the line.

"I finished a project early and thought it was high time we talked."

She sighed. "If you want to tear me a new one, I get it. But can you just tweet it at me or send me an email like everyone else? Just don't do it in front of the dogs."

"I'm not on Twitter," he said flatly. "Let's just grab another dog and get a walk in. I'm getting a little pudgy around the middle with all this office work."

"You couldn't be pudgy around the middle if you ate an entire human who was pudgy around the middle." She motioned to the kennels. "Any preferences?"

He scanned the canine selection. "How do you even choose?"

"I usually just go down the line, start where I left off last time."

"Okay, so that one?" He pointed to a short-haired tan thing with a jaw like a cinderblock, sleeping on a ratty blanket at the back of its kennel.

"No can do. It's got a red dot. That means it could be dangerous and we're not allowed to take it out."

Quentin scanned slowly, scoping out their surroundings, then he turned to her. "Looks friendly enough, and who's gonna stop us? You think God is going to let His daughter get attacked by a pit bull?"

She shrugged. "*Her* daughter. And, yeah, I could see that happening. But let's give it a shot. You keep watch."

Getting the leash on the dog was anticlimactic, and the good girl wagged her tail and came with them gladly.

They walked the perimeter, and Quentin said, "About the last time we talked …"

"You were completely right. I was being a sorry sack of crap and I crossed a line."

"I'm not gonna argue that. But what I wanted to say is that I see you taking action. Finally. So I'm back."

A part of her wanted to get mad at him, call him a fair-weather friend, but that wasn't exactly what he was. He'd just gotten tired of her crap. Hell, everyone but Jesus had reached that point during those months.

"Good. I'm glad you're back. You're the sanest person I know, and things are getting progressively insaner by the day."

The dog sniffed his shoes intently, then licked him on

the ankle. He squatted down to get on eye level, and then, as if addressing the dog, he said, "I'm sorry I stayed away so long. I should have come sooner."

"Nah, it's fine." She paused. "Have you seen that NFL commercial with Chris?"

He got to his feet in a hurry. "Okay, I didn't want to be the first to bring it up, but what in your Father's name was that messy shit?"

"It's my Mother's name now, or at least publicly, and I have no clue."

Quentin sighed. "Chris sure does try hard, doesn't he?"

"He does."

"You spoken with him lately?"

"Only when he called to tell me about the commercial. The time before that was just about money. Indulgence." It was the first time she'd spoken it aloud, how she really viewed the money Chris transferred to her each month. She remembered learning about the concept in high school history and had always thought it was a strange thing. Why would anyone fall for that? Paying money to curry favor with God?

And yet here she was, taking Chris's monthly tribute so that he could continue his separate life without feeling guilty for having abandoned his angelic duties to her.

"Did you just say 'penance'?" Quentin squinted skeptically at her.

"Yeah. Why not? That's what it is, isn't it?"

"Damn, Jess, you really are thick sometimes."

"Isn't that a good thing? Don't black guys like thick women?"

He shut his eyes and groaned. "Not that kind of thick."

They continued on until No Name 32 paused to defecate. Once the crap was bagged, Jessica decided to risk it. "You once said you weren't thrilled that I was white, what did you mean by that?"

"Ah, yeah." He stared off at the trees behind the facility, nodding slightly. "I remember that. I probably shouldn't have brought it up."

"But you did. What did you mean by it?"

"I meant what I said. Sometimes it feels like my whole life has been spent answering to and learning to navigate whiteness, and then I come to find I'm an angel and my job is to serve a white messiah? I mean, *damn.* I know you won't want to hear this, but my people have been serving the white messiah for a long-ass time. Way before you and I were born."

"I'm sorry," was out of her mouth before she could stop it, followed closely by, "if I could change being white, I would."

"Then you're even dumber than I thought. Jess, you have to be white. It's just the way it is. And if I couldn't accept that, I wouldn't be here. You wishing you weren't white doesn't help anyone. You gotta accept it before you can make use of it."

"But I don't want to make use of it. I mean, isn't it bad to make use of it? If being born this way gives me a leg up, I shouldn't go around taking advantage of it, should I?"

"Are we still talking about race, or the fact that you're *God's daughter?*"

She tossed the bagged shit in the receptacle as they passed. "I don't know."

"Look, I know this is complicated, and it's not ideal from my perspective, but I have to believe there's a bigger reason for it I just don't see. Don't abdicate your power, though, Jess. We already know what happens when you take one step back. Jimmy Dean takes one step forward. I don't know what the solution to this bigger question is, but it sure as hell isn't giving Jimmy Dean the upper hand."

"You're not wrong. Though, to be fair, I haven't heard much from him since the pigfucking scandal broke. I think he might have his hands full with the cover-up."

They put No Name 32 back into her kennel, and Quentin lingered by it while Jessica returned the leash to its hook.

"You ever think about starting a jail break?" he asked.

Jessica sighed. "All the time."

Jessica and Quentin had just finished up a pub lunch of burgers and beer and were walking back to their cars when she paused by a corner store. "I gotta grab some food for the week." She gestured at the small shop in the middle of town that didn't carry any brands you've heard of.

It was as Jessica had her items on the counter ("No, I didn't bring my own bag. Yes, I'll purchase one.") when she spotted it. Her brain was slow from the beer and burger, and for a moment, it didn't register that the image she was looking at was her own.

She grabbed the plastic wrapped cookie off the rack of impulse buys and held it closer to her face. *Miraculous Macadamia* read the label. She whirled around, shouting, "Quentin!"

He jumped back, holding up the candy bar he intended to buy in self-defense. "Whoa. What? I'm right here."

"Did you see this?" She held up the cookie.

He stared at it, said, "Huh."

She flipped it over a few times in her hand, looking at all the packaging. "How is she doing this?"

"I imagine she custom ordered a brand to toast your image onto the front of things."

Jessica looked through the rest of the cookies on the display and suspected he was right; they all looked exactly the same. "She's merchandising my stuff."

"It's not your stuff."

"How much money is that evil bitch making on me?" She tossed the cookie onto the rack again. "I bet they taste like shit."

The cashier said, "They're not bad, actually."

She rounded on him. "Don't you 'actually' me." She felt Quentin's hand slide onto her shoulder and inhaled to gather herself. "I'm sorry. I didn't mean that. I'm sure they're heavenly." The bitterness wasn't gone, but she was no longer shouting, so she called it a win.

Still seething a few minutes later as they left with their new hemp grocery bags, Jessica and Quentin made for the parking garage again.

"Have you even talked to her yet?" he asked.

"Who, the Devil? No. No, I have not spoken to her. Because if I even so much as see her, I'm going to smite her off the face of the earth."

"Uh, about that." He leaned closer. "Should you be saying that kind of thing aloud? Has that case been dropped yet?"

"I told you, it was never opened. The cops didn't believe in smiting, and neither did the judge they ran it by. My assault charges didn't even stick. They claimed it was self-defense that made me punch that guy after all the stalking."

"Right." Quentin nodded somberly. "I imagine it must be frustrating to be presumed innocent no matter what you say and do."

"It is. But at least now I know that I can smite Dolores without even getting in trouble. When I *do* see her again, it'll be for the last—"

Dolores Thomas appeared around the corner a block up the street from them. Jessica grabbed Quentin by the arm and dragged him into the closest shop.

Quentin looked around the space, confused. "Did you need something leather?"

And now Jessica looked around. Everything was leather. Brown leather, not black, which was an important distinction. Wallets, bracelets, belts, even neck ties were laid out on long tables that ran the length of the narrow shop. "No. I don't need leather. Didn't you see her?"

"See who?"

"The Devil!"

Quentin squinted at her. "Dolores? You just saw her?"

"Yes! She just appeared out of nowhere down the street!"

He nodded slowly. "The same woman you were just talking about smiting appeared, and now we're hiding in a bovine serial killer's wet dream?" He nodded at the cowhide lamp.

The clerk approached. "Howdy folks. Can I—"

"No," Jessica said, cutting him off. "We're just hiding from someone."

He must have heard that often, because he simply shrugged and walked back to his leather chair behind the counter, his overdone spurs clanking with each step.

"Are you sure it was her?" Quentin asked.

"Yes, *Quentin.* I'm sure it was her."

Dolores Thomas walked past the storefront.

"Oh shit, you weren't kidding." He moved behind her and pushed her toward the door. "Well, now's your shot."

She wriggled away. "What the shit are you talking about?! I can't just call her out in the middle of the street like this is the Wild West—" Her argument faltered as she looked around the store again. "I can't do that."

"You can. And you might even win. Smite her in the streets."

"I can't believe you. It's only four in the afternoon."

"Is there a better time of day to smite someone, or are you just pulling excuses out of your ass?"

"Look," she lowered her voice now as the clerk was clearly trying to listen in. "I know you started talking to me again because I stopped wallowing in my own muck and took action, but I ... I just don't have it in me to take *this* action. If that means you want to take off again, fine, but I'm not doing it. I'm not ready to take on the Devil. She outsmarted me, fair and square, and there's really no evidence supporting the idea that I've gotten any smarter since the incident."

"I'm not going to take off. You're right. Taking her on right now probably isn't smart. So at least you're smart enough to know that." He checked out the front windows again, then returned to her side and put an arm around her shoulders. "Let's get out of this creepy place."

"Good idea."

"And then you're going to go home and think of ways to make yourself smart enough to take on the Devil, and I'm going to go adopt No Name 32."

"They won't let you adopt her. She's dangerous."

"Then I'll steal her." He held the door open and let her go out first. "See Jess? When you set your mind to something, you can accomplish anything."

Chapter Eight

Jessica didn't make it to her front door before Jesus intercepted her and invited her for coffee over at his and Jeremy's place. She gladly accepted, not having anything else planned for the afternoon and wanting to get their take on her recent discovery.

Over the months since Jesus had settled in there, the decor, which had previously been so sparse and impersonal it seemed like Homeland Security ought to be informed, had received a few updates.

Now, instead of looking like the home of someone whose weekend plans included not living until Monday, it looked a little like an old-school opium den. Colorful, ornate rugs were scattered on the ground, and floor cushions had replaced the stiff, black pleather couch that she would have sworn Jeremy had pulled right out of a frat house—and not one of the wealthier frats. A low table, hardly more than a glazed cross-section of an old tree, sat in the middle of the circle of cushions, and she suspected it had cost at least a few thousand dollars, which was nothing to a low-key media mogul like Jeremy.

Speaking of him, as Jessica entered, he was relaxing on the floor, propped up on one elbow as he giggled at something on his cell phone.

Jesus whispered, "Memes. I don't get them, but he says they're good."

Jeremy looked up from his phone. "Oh hey, neighbor."

"You done with your three decisions?" she asked. His approach of only making three business decisions a day didn't add up to how he could have the kind of money he claimed to have, but she had long since stopped trying to figure that out; very little about Jeremy Archer added up. And yet, when bills came due, he paid them.

"Yeah. I actually made four, so I'm only going to make two tomorrow. Come here, have you seen this meme?"

"I'll pour you some coffee," whispered Jesus. "Cream and sugar?"

"Please." She walked over and crouched down to look at Jeremy's screen. It was a picture of Jessica petting the slobbery Great Dane at the park with the caption, "She could even be Dog's Gaughter" above it.

Jeremy giggled again. "You gotta admit, that's funny."

She didn't gotta admit. It made so little sense. But as Cash had explained to her just the other day, memes like this one, which was clearly derivative of already derivative content, meant Interest In the subject was wanIng. "Yeah, that's a pretty good one."

He put his phone into the small titanium box he kept around to protect himself from unnecessary radiation and government spying. "How's your day going?"

Jessica located her favorite cushion and settled there across the table from Jeremy. "Good, then great, then not great."

"I heard a funny saying today," Jesus said, popping in from the kitchen with a triangle of steaming cups of coffee clutched between his hands. The contents of each was a slightly different shade, and he handed the lightest one to Jessica before settling on the floor with his legs crossed. "It was, 'Turn that frown upside down.' Ha! Isn't that great? It rhymes. English is great for rhyming."

"Right," said Jessica, body slamming her desire to frown in an attempt to turn it upside down.

"Jessica was just about to tell us about her day," Jeremy said.

"Oh! Delightful! I hope it was a good one."

She rushed through the good part (finally getting her turn at the animal shelter) and the great part (making up with Quentin) and got to the not great part, where she planned on investing most of her storytelling energy.

"She is selling my image in local stores now!" she shouted, having worked both herself and her audience into a lather.

"That meanie!" Jesus spat. "Oooh, boy. I mean, I knew Lucifer was a meanie before, but this just takes it into new territory."

"How does she do it?" Jeremy asks. "How does she get your image on each of them?"

"Maybe a brand? Like, she just custom ordered one and stamps it on there."

"Or"—Jeremy leaned closer over the table—"it's something much more sinister."

She knew there was no reason for him to make this assumption, but she liked it just fine. "Probably. I mean, she *is* the Devil."

Jeremy rubbed the stubble on his chin. "Do you think she would remember what I look like?"

"When was the last time she saw you?"

"At your grand opening."

Jessica thought about it. "That was a while ago. And there were a lot of people there. Probably not. Wait! Are you thinking ..."

He nodded. "It's time for corporate espionage." He paused. "But then again, it always is."

As it turned out, Jeremy's condo had never been as empty as it'd seemed. It was just that all the good stuff was hidden behind a false wall, in a hidden room. And that was where Jessica and Jesus observed the monitor that displayed the livestream from Jeremy Archer's hidden body cam.

They'd spent the evening concocting their plan, and once Jeremy had made his two business decisions the following day, they'd begun the tech setup. It was fairly straightforward, and while Jesus simply sat back and marveled at the modern miracles, Jessica did basic things like holding equipment and speaking into it to make sure everything worked correctly. Jeremy handled the rest, and before long he was all wired up and out the door.

At the moment, he was walking down the block toward It is Risen, and the wobble of the camera was making Jessica seasick, so she allowed herself a moment to look away. "You think this will work?"

Jesus frowned. "Maybe. But it seems dishonest, doesn't it?"

"It's complete dishonesty." She narrowed her eyes at him. "You're just now figuring this out?"

He rubbed the back of his neck. "It was just so exciting at first, I didn't think it through."

"Hey, listen." She placed a hand on his arm. "We're dealing with the Devil here. I think it's okay to use a little subterfuge."

He nodded but continued to appear concerned.

Jeremy's voice came through the speakers: "Okay, I'm about to go in."

Jessica grabbed the handheld microphone that fed into his invisible earpiece. "Then stop talking to yourself."

The jangle of the bell above the door triggered a Pavlovian response in Dog's Gaughter, and for a moment, she forgot that the place was no longer hers. Then, with a jolt, she remembered.

A college-age girl Jessica didn't recognize sat on a tall

stool behind the counter and called, "Welcome to It is Risen, the official bakery of Jessica Christ."

"Yuck," Jessica said. "They're really calling me Jessica Christ there? That's terrible."

Her half-brother nodded morosely. "You get used to it."

From the monitor came the sound of Jeremy clearing his throat. "Greetings! What a kind welcome."

"Is this your first time here?" the girl asked, looking less than thrilled to recite the script.

"Why, yes, yes it is. My very first. Mind if I have a look around?"

She shrugged a shoulder and turned to the next page in her magazine.

The camera panned side to side and Jessica could only imagine what Jeremy looked like at that moment, turning his whole torso rather than his head. Too late, she realized they should have given him a neck brace to explain the strange movement. Next time she needed to commit corporate espionage against Satan, she supposed.

In the course of his movement, she saw that the tables were mostly packed. Granted, it was the tail end of lunchtime, but still. She'd hoped no one would frequent the bakery now that she wasn't there and the recipes had changed.

You only ever got people there through gimmicks. Dolores actually knows business. Or she can manipulate people who do.

But didn't Jessica also do that? Manipulate people who

knew things? That was how Wendy and Cash and Maria always danced around for her.

No, that was different. Somehow.

She leaned toward the microphone again. "Get us a look at the goods."

Jeremy complied, leaning close to the case.

"That's a good angle," she instructed. "Now move slowly to the left … but don't, you know, crab walk or anything weird. Slow down." She looked over the selection. "Do they all look identical to you?"

"Mm-hm," muttered Jeremy.

"Ask the clerk about the ingredients."

Jeremy presumably crab walked back to the counter to speak with the girl behind it. "So, it's all gluten-free?"

"Absolutely."

"What, uh, flours do you use?"

She arched an eyebrow at him. "Gluten-free ones."

"So, they're not made gluten-free through the use of miracles?"

Her exhale closely resembled a laugh. "No."

"But they used to be made that way, right?"

"Again, no."

Jessica whispered, "Lying bitch," just as the camera lurched. Someone had come out from the back, giving Jeremy a start.

"Can I help you?" said Dolores Thomas in a saccharine tone that made Jessica want to smite a few watermelons. But then again, was there a tone Dolores could take that wouldn't leave Jessica feeling a little smitey? She suspected not.

The Devil prowled around the counter so that nothing stood between her and Jeremy but air and, according to him, enough microwaves from cell phones to make a prize stallion sterile.

However, the media mogul stood his ground. "I was just asking this fine young lady about—"

"He thought we used miracles."

Dolores giggled. "Common mistake. But no, unfortunately there was a propaganda campaign by the previous owner to spread those lies. Seems incredibly irresponsible, if you ask me. It was eventually discovered that she was using wheat flour in everything and calling it gluten-free. She could have killed someone. She might even *have* killed someone with celiac without anyone realizing it!"

Jeremy took it in stride. "Ah. New ownership?"

She stared at him for a moment, tilting her head slightly to one side. "Yes. In addition to being reckless with the health of her customers, the last owner also ran the place into the ground financially, until I took over, that is. Have you not seen this on the news?"

"I don't watch the news. Mostly lies."

Dolores smiled. "Too true. Anywho, she was emotionally unstable. I've been rebuilding this place ever since she left."

"You're talking about the daughter of God?"

"Yes, she believes herself to be that. And I will say, it doesn't hurt the branding."

"What's with the faces?" He nodded at the case.

"Just a little holdover. Like I said, doesn't hurt the branding. You'd know an It is Risen cookie the moment you saw it, wouldn't you?"

He nodded. "That's right. I would."

"So," she said, stepping forward. "Can I help you with something?"

"I'll take a dozen of those sugar cookies."

Jessica spat into the mic, "You're not supposed to give her your actual business, Jeremy!"

He ignored her, and Dolores personally selected and boxed up the cookies while the young woman accepted his payment.

After, Dolores handed him the box over the glass display case, and when he reached for them, she grabbed his wrist with her other hand. Her convivial tone was gone now, and her voice cut like a serrated knife. "Tell Jessica that if she sends another angel spy into my establishment, I'll stop playing nice."

Jeremy didn't answer, which was smart enough when it came to self-incrimination. He hurried out of the bakery and cut the feed.

Jessica wandered out into the living room and flopped across the floor cushions.

Jesus was kind enough to join her, plopping himself down near her head. "Sheesh. What a meanie. Just when I think she can't get meaner ..."

"Yeah, Jesus. She's the Devil." Jess shoved her head into the pillow and groaned.

Dolores was not just an obstacle to Jessica owning her own brand, it was so much more than that, *had been* so much more than that since the moment Jessica's phone had gained reception in the middle of nowhere on her way back from Caren Powers' women's retreat in Carlsbad and the deluge of text messages had alerted her to the truth she'd never wanted to see.

The Devil was a woman. How was she supposed to get around that fact? Was there any getting around it? Making God a woman was supposed to change things, to bring peace to the United States, but could she ever hope to accomplish that if word got out that the Devil was also a woman? She had a hunch the public would be much more likely to believe *that* part of the story. Not a far jump from the scapegoat of Eve to a female Satan. More like a half-step for many. And a half-step they would be happy to take.

But more importantly, she still couldn't wrap *her* head around it all.

How can God be a woman if the Devil is?

WE'VE BOTH BEEN MEN FOR CENTURIES.

She's going to ruin everything, isn't she? I can't fully expose her to the world without her making all women look bad.

WHY DO YOU SUPPOSE I CREATED THE DEVIL?

Same reason you created Original Mistake? You were bored? I really don't know. Why don't you just tell me?

OH, NO, I WAS TRULY WONDERING IF YOU HAD AN INKLING. THE LORD CANNOT REMEMBER.

I'm sure it seemed like a good idea at the time.

PROBABLY. I'LL THINK OF IT.

Do you even want to be a woman?

I WANT PEACE.

And you're sure this is the only way to get it?

"Hey," Jesus cut in. "I know you're having a conversation. I can tell by your eyes. Fill me in."

"We're talking about creating peace in the United States."

AND THE DEVIL BEING A WOMAN.

"Ah," said Jesus.

"If Jimmy Dean even so much as gets a whiff that the Devil is a woman," Jessica said, "he'll take it and run. He'll start preaching about 'And so it was that Original Sin took the form of the Devil, and the Devil is woman.' And then all of his followers will get all riled up, and you know what that means, not just for me, but for the local pig population."

Jesus cringed. "Then do not tell Jimmy. Not yet."

AGREED. THERE WILL COME A TIME WHEN YOU MAY NEED TO TELL HIM, BUT WAIT. THINGS ARE ONLY GOING TO GET WORSE FOR HIM.

"Worse than a bestiality scandal?" The excitement in her voice surprised her.

TELL ME, CHILD. HAVE YOU HEARD MUCH ABOUT THAT LATELY?

"No. I guess it's kind of died down."

HAS BEEN COVERED UP. THERE IS A DIFFERENCE. BUT THE LORD SHINETH HIS—

"Her—"

*SORRY, **HER** LIGHT UPON LIES. THE TRUTH WILL GLOW BRIGHT FOR ALL TO SEE.*

"Not to downplay your mighty-and-all-that flashlight abilities, but I don't know if I want to see much more of this one."

FAIR POINT.

Jessica sighed. "I guess I haven't really confronted my feelings about the Devil being a woman."

ADD IT TO THE LIST OF THINGS YOU HAVE NOT YET CONFRONTED.

"Not helping, Dad," Jesus muttered. He turned to his sister. "I hadn't considered this side of the matter, but I imagine it's been difficult for you."

"She was my teacher. She knew me for years. Sometimes it felt like she was the only one who believed in me. How am I supposed to trust women now?"

"You trust your mother."

"Well, yeah."

"And you trust our delightful friend Judith."

"Yeah, she's fine."

"And you trust Wendy."

"... Yeah, okay. But should I? I mean, what do I know? They could be in league with Dolores, playing the long game. How do I know that's not the case?"

Jesus gazed into her face, placing a hand on her cheek. "You can never know that it is not the case."

"*You* knew, didn't you? You knew one of your friends would betray you."

"Yes, I knew he would. But other friends betrayed me along the way that I did not see coming."

She pushed herself up to lean on her elbows. "Really?"

Jesus nodded.

"You mind if I ask who?"

"Not at all. For a start, there was Gunther."

"Gunther."

"Yes. He was a dear friend of mine, and he betrayed me by selling my favorite pair of sandals to buy himself a wife."

HEADS UP, DAUGHTER, THERE IS A LOT TO UNPACK ON THIS ONE.

I don't even know where to start.

BEST IF YOU DO NOT.

But her curiosity got the best of her. "Is Gunther ... is he in the Bible?"

"No." Jesus straightened his spine and lifted his chin. "He was a meanie. I made sure it was clear that he was not to be included."

"But what about the other guy who betrayed you?"

"Judas? He got to stay in. It's ... complicated."

"Getting you nailed to a cross isn't as bad as selling off your sandals?"

Jesus shoulders slumped. "They were really good sandals, Jessica. The point is that we can never know who will betray us, whether they mean to or not. Don't you think the world would be a much better place if there *was* a way to know that? Friendships would be wholehearted with no fear of abandonment or broken oaths. We wouldn't hide behind our many shields when it came to speaking our truths. But the world doesn't work like that. The people we love most hurt us regularly, and the more love you give to the world, the greater the opportunity for pain."

Her top lip curled. "You're really making a case for taking off into the wilderness and never returning."

"Been there."

She paused and gave his words an honest chance to settle in. "You're telling me I should knowingly open myself up to more pain?"

"If it means more love, yes."

"You think I should reach out and try to make things right with Dolores?"

Jesus gasped. "Oh, Heaven, no. That would just be stupid."

"Right, right. So, uh, what are you saying?"

Jesus considered it for a moment, but before he could answer, the front door burst open, and Jeremy stumbled in, out of breath, holding the box of cookies and wearing a wild grin. "I dunno about you guys, but I think that went pretty well."

Chapter Nine

Jessica was thinking about dogs. That was what she usually did while working at Waverly Hills Retirement Center. It was either that or thinking about death, which paced up and down the hallway like a prison guard.

There were a handful of residents who Jessica had taken a liking to in the course of her visits. Jan Bradford was lovely and always had a jar of orange slices ready to hand out to visitors. The woman was also a devout Catholic and thought it was just wonderful what Jessica was trying to do for women. Did she truly believe Jessica was God's daughter? Who gave a shit, really? She was kind, and she had candy.

Then there was Santori Dukas, a Greek man in his eighties who delighted in asking Jessica who her enemies were and then cursing their names for upsetting such a sweet young woman. He didn't have candy, but he offered something even sweeter with his outrage.

But today, she wasn't asked to visit Jan or Santori or any of her other favorites. Instead, the nurse had asked her to go check on Rosemary Heathrow. Rosemary (pronounced rose-mah-REE if you didn't want to set her off) was the absolute worst assignment. Jessica had taken to approaching the white-haired wight with caution after the woman had insisted she was the Devil and gone after her with the Precious Moments figurine.

Why the nurse in charge of volunteers thought she should ever go back into that woman's room, Jessica couldn't understand. Maybe the nurse was a demon. Either way, Jessica would give the nurse's name to Santori next time she saw him.

Jessica approached the door to Mrs. Heathrow's room. The woman was lying in her bed, watching the TV that sat atop her standard-issue dresser. Would it be wrong to just back out and spend the next hour with someone else?

Not *that* wrong, she decided.

But as she tried to inch out without the woman seeing her, she was summoned. "If they sent me the Devil again, then you might as well come in."

"You shouldn't invite the Devil into your room," Jessica advised.

"You would enter anyway. But I don't fear you. I'm a holy woman. I've lived a holy life."

Tell that to the figurines you smashed.

"I suppose you're here to tempt me," Rosemary said without looking away from the television.

"Sure, why not?"

"Then go on."

Shit, this woman was insufferably pious. "How about we just watch the news instead? I can tempt you later."

Finally, Rosemary pulled her focus from the screen to shoot a sharp look Jessica's way. "I don't make a habit of taking suggestions from the Devil, but seeing as how I had plans to watch the news anyway ..."

Thank whoever. Watching two hours of Sanctum News on repeat wasn't ideal, but it was better than the alternative.

After a half hour of it, Jessica thought she might prefer to have porcelain objects chucked at her instead. The news, which she made a point never to watch, was a parading horror show. Suddenly, she found herself unable to really blame someone like Rosemary for thinking the end was nigh.

Three dead in a car accident on I-35 just north of Austin. A bridge collapsing due to flooding just west of the interstate. A school shooting in Dallas. Another school shooting just outside of Dallas. The anniversary of a high-profile kidnapping where bits of the girl's body were found in a swampy part of coastal Texas. A school shooting in McAllen, but not a major one. Continued trial coverage of a mother who drowned three kids in Amarillo. An outbreak of antibiotic-resistant syphilis on the Texas Tech campus. A man and a woman arrested for beating their child to death. A manhunt for three skinheads who beat a gay man into a coma. A school shooting in Baton Rouge on the two-year anniversary of a previous school shooting there. A memorial for three police officers who were run over on the side of the road one year ago today. A protest against police brutality on the one-year anniversary of a black man being shot while taking out the trash. A school bus carrying a championship high school volleyball team T-boned by a semi-truck on I-10, no survivors. An oil spill in the gulf. Two teens abducted from the beach while cleaning up after the oil spill. A law suit against University of Texas for covering up rape-based incentives for high-performing male water polo players. A school shooting in Alabama that was officially the worst in the state's history, with fatalities still climbing. An obstetrician's house wrongfully burned to the ground in protest of abortions she didn't perform. A gunman entering an office building in Oklahoma City and opening fire on his ex and her coworkers. A memorial service to honor the thousands of Texan soldiers killed overseas in the last decade. An announcement of the 6th Annual Waffle Festival next Saturday! A 5,000 acre wildfire just east of Austin displacing nearly thirty-thousand people. Footage of two meth heads driving a car into a liquor store to rob it. A drug bust of five hundred pounds of cocaine coming up from Mexico. An elementary school on lockdown in San Antonio, no casualties reported. An outbreak of flu in border detention facilities. Internet sensation Pookie the Pugnacious Poodle is coming to Austin!

Jessica nonchalantly searched the room until she

located the remote. It was on the bedside table between her and Rosemary. It was her only hope. She had to get to it. She had to.

While Rosemary shouted at the TV about Mexicans, Jessica made her move, grabbing the remote and desperately clicking up a channel.

"What the—" Rosemary whipped her head around, but Jessica had already hidden the remote out of sight.

"I dunno, that's so weird that it just changed the channel like that."

The old woman narrowed her eyes. "Just like the Devil to pull an old trick like that."

Jessica just shrugged. But then she realized how little she'd accomplished, as this channel was showing news, too.

Rosemary yelled, "Not this station! Nothing but lies from the liberal sinners! They *want* us to sin, but you already knew that."

The coverage switched from the weather report to a breaking story. On screen, a news anchor in a startlingly green dress said, *"New videos surfaced online today, reigniting the recent rumors about White Light Church and its role in a spate of recent bestiality involving pigs. Railroad Commissioner Reverend Jimmy Dean, the founder of White Light Church has issued an official statement in response to the issue saying, 'The videos that surfaced recently are undeniably sinful behavior that our church network condemns wholeheartedly. The events are isolated incidents that occurred months back, and we have already dealt with those involved and addressed the issue with our various congregations. We do not expect any further incidents of animal relations to occur.'* ”

“When I get my hands on that boy,” Rosemary said through gritted teeth, “I’m gonna tan his hide.”

Jessica inspected her, taking in how delusional this woman really was. Did she think Jimmy Dean would suddenly waltz into her room and offer up his hide to tan? It would be a cold day in hell before Jimmy came to a place like this, and an even colder day in hell before Rosemary ever got to leave this place in hide-tanning condition.

“He’s really gone and done it,” Rosemary said.

“He sure has.”

“Next time I see him, I tell you, I’m going to let the wrath of God work through me. That’s a promise.”

“See who, Jimmy Dean?”

“Mm-hm.”

Jessica chuckled at the thought. “I hope I’m here for that. Truly.”

But as pleasing as the thought was of Rosemary Heathrow and Jimmy Dean destroying each other in mutual combat, the joy of the fantasy wore thin quickly, and all that was left of it by the time she signed out for the afternoon and stepped out into the parking lot was a thin specter of Jimmy. Jimmy and all of his schemes. Schemes she hadn’t heard about in months and months. But she knew he had them. He always did. The fact that she didn’t know what they were left her terribly uneasy. Because no matter what they were, they would involve her. Of that, she was certain. Unlike Rosemary, Jessica would see Jimmy eventually.

And when that day came, would she be ready?

Chapter Ten

Jessica raised her glass and clinked with Judith, Brian, Jesus, and Jeremy.

Jimmy's scandal was fully back in the news, and she had enjoyed a wild week of guessing how each station would cover such despicable content without violating FCC regulations. The euphemisms varied at first, with "The White Light Church scandal" and "the pig molestation saga" among the most common. But within a few days, when it became clear the ratings for such a thing were only going to get better over time, virtually every outlet began referring to it as "Swinegate."

Wendy had claimed this was a huge victory. Once something got a "gate" tacked on, it was a sure sign it would get coverage for at least a few more months.

It was as good a reason for celebration as anything, and that was how they all came to gather around a high-top table at Smashmouth, Jessica's neighborhood sports bar.

"What exactly are we celebrating?" Jesus asked enthusiastically as he sipped his water.

Judith answered. "Pigfucking."

Jesus let the sip of water dribble back into his glass. "I can't drink to that."

"None of us can," Jessica said. "And that's *not* what we're celebrating." She shot Judith a stern look. She couldn't blame her for enjoying a jab here and there at Jesus's expense—after all, they were exes, and that always made things complicated. But telling the poor guy they were celebrating pig rape, well, if that wasn't crossing a line, it was flirting with it.

"What *are* we celebrating?" Jesus asked hopefully.

"We're celebrating the powers of the mighty-and-all-that flashlight," said Jessica, "who doth shine her light upon us. Sometimes directly in our eyes. We're celebrating the truth about Jimmy and the festering cauldron of hate he calls a religion finally meeting its demise."

"It's not dead yet," Brian warned.

Jessica still experienced strange flashes of unreality when she hung around with Brian Foster. It was like two parallel realities ran so closely together they almost touched but never did. In one, Brian was Judith's live-in boyfriend whose cynicism and analytical mind made them a perfect match. And in the other, he was Mr. Foster, Jessica's former science teacher and college counselor—not a living, breathing, complex person, exactly, because no adults are when you're young. He had even been her favorite teacher for a while, her confidant, but seeing him in a casual setting, considering him her *friend*—those two realities had never truly combined for her; she merely spent most of her time in the second and would temporarily slip into the first like an electron jumping orbits.

Brian, however, did not seem to struggle with the dissonance. "You'd be surprised how resilient cults like his can be."

Since she currently had both feet in the reality where Brian was a cynical realist, the notion that he would understand cults did not surprise her, and she took his word for it.

"It's not looking good for him," Jeremy Archer said. "And I have some guys on it. It's only been a week since those last videos emerged, but we have at least four more weeks of coverage slated, and that's if another video *doesn't* surface. We're not letting this thing go."

The small part of Jessica that still suspected Jeremy Archer was a complete fraud inspected him closely. If a lie was there, she couldn't find it. "Are you doing that for me?" she asked.

He sipped his IPA and cringed. He'd mentioned multiple times how much he hated the taste of IPAs but insisted on drinking them anyway, claiming they were good for fighting Big Ag's mutant microbes in the gut. "No, though I'm glad to hear it might also help you. I did it because there hasn't been a scandal this good in ages. The child molestation thing with all the priests is a bit played out, ratings wise. People just expect it now, and it's pretty rampant. But bestiality is new territory." He chuckled. "You should see the way the writers are scrambling around to give as much detail as possible without incurring fines." He threw his head back and laughed.

"Hold on," Brian said, "people are becoming immune to stories of pedophilia? That doesn't seem good."

"Of course it's not," Jeremy replied after collecting himself. "Nothing about pedophilia is good. And, if it makes you feel any better, people aren't completely burned out on it yet, but its ratings have definitely peaked, and we're only a few high-level coverups away from it being about on par with campus gang rapes. But, *boy*, is sex with animals on the up." His eyes were wild with excitement. "It's like viewers can't get enough of it. The greater the percentage of the population that condemns an action, the richer the moral outrage and their need to retweet the content to publicly show their condemnation. Jimmy's made this rich man an even richer man."

Jessica and Judith exchanged a glance, and Brian said, "I guess we know who's buying drinks tonight."

While most of the mounted televisions around the bar were rotating through the week's sports highlights, the one closest to their table had been changed to the news by request. It was on mute, but closed-captioning displayed the Texas senator's now famous words: *What if it was* your *pig?* The question heard round the country. As it turned out, no one wanted it to be their pig that was victimized. Of course they didn't. The only person who got to victimize their pigs was them when they ripped them away from their mothers too young, raised them in tiny cages, transported them carelessly, then brutally butchered them for consumption.

Nobody, as far as she was aware, had yet addressed the question of how people might feel if it were nobody's pig, if it belonged to no one but itself.

"Hey, I got a question," she said.

"Is it about pigs?" Judith asked.

"No. I already know too much about them. I did a lot of research on them as a kid for Jimmy. But what do you think it means to be a woman?"

Judith shrugged. "I guess it means you don't have a right to your own body, and everyone pretends your right to vote means you should shut up and take whatever bullshit you're dealt."

That was a minefield if Jessica had ever seen one, so she decided against inquiring further and addressed the question to Brian.

"I don't really think in those terms, 'man' and 'woman,'" he said. "I mean, outside of it helping me guess what specific genitalia they might be working with to some degree of certainty—not complete certainty, mind you—I rarely even notice it."

"You don't notice any differences in behavior?"

"Of course I do. Boys and girls are conditioned differently by society. But in my years of teaching, I've seen so many young minds, and the only overarching patterns I noticed were that the girls tended to complete their work more often than the boys. And the boys were more likely to hurt themselves on the science equipment. But like I said, that's very general. There were plenty of each group who didn't follow that trend."

She turned to Jesus. "And what about you? Have you thought anymore about it since I last asked?"

"Oh yes! I've had many long silent moments to think about it."

"And?"

"And in my experience, women are far less likely to be meanies."

She might have accepted that, except for one glaring problem. "What about the Devil?"

He shrugged. "I suppose that's why she got away with so much. It wouldn't have worked as well if she were the type of person more likely to be a meanie. You would have suspected her sooner."

"That's true," Brian said. "Dolores did well to hide behind that maternal facade. Of course, I only ever saw the soft side of her in passing, but it was still enough to make me question whether I was judging her too harshly for all the other behavior. But eventually I just made up my mind, decided to trust that the cruelty showing through was the real version of her."

"And you were right," Jessica said. "I was wrong."

Judith nudged her. "Don't take it so hard. You got outsmarted by the Devil. Who cares?"

"Trust me," Brian continued, "it would have been incredibly easy for me to go on doubting myself for years. The only thing that saved me was my obsessive relationship with data. After one particularly confounding encounter with her, I started keeping a journal. I was curious if she was a good person or not, and I figured she would be whatever the majority of her actions were. So, I wrote down each interaction I had with her or observed her having with others and sorted them as either generous-philanthropic or selfish-malicious. The results were quite astounding."

"What were they?"

"For every generous or philanthropic action I observed, I counted six selfish or malicious actions. Six! I couldn't believe it. I really thought it would be closer to fifty-fifty. I was quite astounded, really. I consider myself a skeptical person. Just goes to show how easily our feelings can steer us off course."

"But," Judith said, "it was a feeling that prompted you to start collecting the data in the first place."

"True enough. My point is, Jessica, that she neither liked me nor needed me for anything in particular, and still, I was fooled. I suspect she made a concerted effort to ensure your ratio of good to bad interactions was heavily weighted in favor of the good so that one day she could blindside you with the bad when it really counted. Considering how forgiving our minds are of malicious behavior, you can hardly blame yourself when you saw almost none of it up until that point."

"I did, though. Well, I didn't see it, but people told me about it. You told me about it. Chris told me. He told me years ago. I saw the way she treated the Wursts, and I went along with it because I didn't like them either. I thought they deserved it, and it only made me like her more. But they were kids. She was terrorizing kids!"

"She's the Devil," Judith said. "I don't know how many more times we have to point that out."

They sat in silence for a moment, then Jessica popped the big question. "How do I make people believe God is female if there's no consensus on what it means to be a female?"

Jeremy shut his eyes and nodded serenely. "Mind control. You need to figure out how to control their minds."

Jessica looked around the group. "And how do I do that?"

"A church would be a pretty good start," Brian said. "You make an official group, give people an identity as part of that group, and they'll do a lot of crazy shit for you. They'll believe anything."

Judith explained, "He's been watching a *lot* of cult documentaries lately."

"He's not wrong, though," Jeremy added.

But Jesus shook his head. "No, I don't like that idea."

Ah, well that made two of them. "I don't either, bro."

Judith glared across the table at Jesus. "How can you say that? You have a two-billion-person faith all about you! Jimmy may have a lot of locations, but you have a hundred different denominations and millions of meeting places spread across the globe."

Jesus slunk down in his chair because nobody likes being scolded by an ex. "I didn't *start* any of them. I thought I'd made it pretty clear that I didn't like big organizations accepting money in return for privileges of the secular or spiritual variety. I mean, sheesh, I let them kill me just to prove that point!"

Judith narrowed her eyes at him. "I thought you died for our sins."

He shrugged. "It was a twofer. And that 'dying for your sins' thing is used rather loosely. It was more like I died *because of* people's sins. There were some *real* meanies back then."

"So, hold up," Judith said. "If you had your way, there wouldn't be Christian churches?"

He considered it. "I don't know. I like the idea of a bunch of people getting together to decide the best ways to be nice and love one another. I like holding each other accountable for not being meanies. And I like it when people get together to go help those in need. Oh! And I like communion."

Jessica cringed. "You like people pretending to eat your body and drink your blood?"

"That part is a little weird, and I believe much got lost in translation, but the part where they provide nourishment to anyone who wants it is nice."

"That's almost never how it—"

But Jessica caught Judith's eye and shook her head. Jesus didn't need to know all the details about communion right now.

"Okay," Judith said, pivoting "What *don't* you like?"

He sat up straighter, appearing glad to finally get his say. "I don't like people getting rich off of it."

"You don't like rich people?" Jeremy asked, looking wounded.

Jesus tilted his head to the side, gazing lovingly at his roommate. "I can't say *that* because I love you, and you're rich!"

Jeremy relaxed. "I am."

Jesus continued, "I worry about money and its effects on a human's ability to find true inner peace, always have. During my time in the Far East—"

The cocktail waitress came around and they each ordered another round.

"You were saying?" Jessica reminded him.

"Right, right. Things I don't like about church. I also don't like people committing violence in my name."

"And the pedophilia," Jeremy supplied. "Remember when I told you about that?"

"Right!" Jesus wagged a finger at his roomie. "The pedophilia. I really don't like that. That's *very* sinful."

"Is there a way to start a church that doesn't do all those things?" Jessica asked. "That doesn't make the leaders horrifyingly wealthy, that doesn't inspire violence and hate, and that doesn't prey on children?" She hurriedly added, "Or pigs."

"I don't see why not," Jesus said.

Judith raised a hand. "I do. People are awful, and those who want power over others tend to get it because those who don't want power over others don't seek it."

Jessica was careful with her next words; the last thing she wanted was for anyone to hold her to them. "But what if someone who didn't want power over others, who wanted nothing more than to be left alone and live a normal life, what if *that* person decided it was their duty to step up? Could it work then?"

Judith wiped the foam off her lips with the back of her hand. "We all know you're talking about yourself here. Maybe, though. But you need to be really careful, Jessica. Starting a church ... you can't go back."

"I know. Of course I'll be careful. Priority number one since I was a kid has always been not to get myself martyred."

"It is ... not super fun," said Jesus. "I will grant you that."

Chapter Eleven

Jessica was a little tipsy by the time she said goodbye to Jeremy and Jesus and made it into her apartment that evening. The conversation about churches had swirled in her mind on the walk back from Smashmouth while Jesus and Jeremy played a game they'd made up called Fact or Fiction. It consisted of Jeremy running his historical conspiracies by his best friend, and Jesus, who had watched the events of the world unfold from his place in the Great Beyond over the last two thousand years, confirming or denying the rumors.

Could she do it? Could she start a church that didn't become something unwieldy and horrifying that no one person could control? For some strange reason, she thought she could. She'd even begun to imagine it as they'd strolled the dark sidewalk. A whole network of churches that spanned the globe—or at least the US—where women were revered and treated as true equals, where love and respect were kept at the forefront of everyone's mind ...

By the time she set down her purse on the kitchen island, she was convinced it not only *could* happen, but would be inevitable if she truly invested herself in the endeavor.

And then the Heavenly Pest spoke up.

MAYBE YOU SHOULD POUR YOURSELF ANOTHER DRINK.

She froze. It was never a good sign when God suggested she get liquored up.

I'm already pretty tipsy. Why do I need another drink?

I'M ONLY TRYING TO SPARE YOU THE STING.

The sting of what?

But he didn't answer.

The sting of what?!

Her phone rang, and she fished it out of her purse, cursing a blue streak. The screen lit up in her hand, and she didn't fail to notice the treasure trove of missed notification icons spread across the top of her smartphone screen. She must not have heard them while she was in the bar.

Jessica answered the phone. "What is it, Wendy? Someone's dead, aren't they?"

"Not this time. But you should check your texts. I sent you a link to a news story you should be aware of."

Jessica put the phone on speaker and pulled up her texts from Wendy. The first one she saw, the most recent, simply said, *Under no circumstances comment on this!*

"Oh boy ... I'm loading the link now." But she didn't miss that the URL was Eugene Thornton's website.

Wendy waited silently as Jessica watched the whole video, her disbelief growing with each false accusation. When it ended, Wendy's voice came through the speaker again: "We're already working on this."

Jessica laughed dryly. "What is there to work on? Dolores Thomas just went on the record saying she'd known me since I was a child and ... she even dragged my mom into it!"

"Don't worry. I already have people keeping an eye on Destinee. And Rex promised he's hidden the shotgun where she won't find it."

"*The* shotgun? You think she only has one?"

No reply.

"Wendy, when she tells people to fetch her shotgun, she just means the closest one to her in the house."

Wendy cursed under her breath. "Okay, we'll continue to manage and monitor that situation."

"If you think for one second she's not going to lock and load and hunt down the Devil on her own like some Holy Rambo, you've grossly underestimated my mom. This story ... who even *were* those guys who said they'd slept with her?"

"Country bumpkins who no doubt are a little richer for it."

"I mean, don't get me wrong, my mom isn't shy about all things sex, and I know she's been with her fair share of men, but once I was born—"

"I know, I know," Wendy said. "The story is ninety percent lies based on just a little bit of truth."

"And the bit about the criminal record? Sure, she beat the ever-living shit out of Ruth Wurst, but the woman deserved it, and she never pressed charges."

"Once your mother blackmailed her a little. I know. Listen, Jessica. I would never characterize your mother as a hardened criminal or a sex fiend, partly because of all those guns you just mentioned. Either way, we're on the same page here."

"And Chris," Jessica said. "Will this ruin his career?"

"About that." There was a tone to Wendy's voice that set her even more on edge. "As much as I hate to say it, the fact that he participated in a hit-and-run in college and left a woman for dead ... He's in the NFL, Jessica. He's a high-profile player. What happened was years ago. I have every reason to believe this accusation will be accepted as the truth ... and bounce right off of him."

Jessica hadn't seen that coming. "Oh, that's good news, though, right?"

"Good news for him, yes. Bad news for society."

"I just feel so ... I dunno."

"Exposed."

"That makes it sound like all those claims are true."

"Not necessarily. You just had a bunch of crap from your past come to light and be distorted to make you look terrible. Worse, your notoriety put those you love in the crosshairs. All you're feeling is shame, and that's never an accurate representation of the truth. That being said, I don't blame you for feeling like you do. I'd be concerned if you didn't."

"That thing makes me look crazy."

"And I bet it makes you feel crazy, too."

"How'd you know?"

"Dolores Thomas has been gaslighting you your whole life. Why would she stop now? And Eugene Thornton is the master of misinformation. No one does it like him. In a lot of ways, he's more dangerous than the Devil because he can be brazenly honest about his intentions and people still buy his drivel."

Jessica scrolled through the article below the video, taking in the recap. "It's just ... so much. There's so much here. When I look at my life in summary like this, yeah, it doesn't look great for me."

"You listen here," Wendy snapped, startling her. "That is *not* a summary of your life. That is a summary of your weakest moments as a child with enough embellishments on top to crush an elephant to death. A real summary would have mentioned that after Chris's mistake, you two stuck around and you brought Ruth Wurst back to life. A real summary would mention all the times you listened to a friend who was struggling or forgave someone who'd betrayed you. And it would show how many ways Chris has sacrificed something he loves to protect you, and it would show that your mom always had your back and never made you feel ashamed of who you are.

"That article isn't a summary, and if you think it is, you need to get your ass back to fifth-grade English class and relearn the definition. Anyone could look bad with the Thornton touch. Hell, I once set an alligator loose in a frat house and it tore the limbs off of two people. I never got caught, but a handful of people know it was me who did it. Any one of them could spill the beans, and it wouldn't make me look very good, would it?"

"No," said Jessica. "It wouldn't. Wait, the gator ate—"

"It ate the limbs off of two people. But it was the right two people. Do I need to spell it out?"

Jessica's stomach dropped as the story behind it clicked. "Nope. Read you loud and clear."

"My only regret is that it didn't eat the rest of them. Anyway, I know this sucks, and you're probably going to feel shame about the truth in each of the accusations. So, all I can recommend is that you spend more time around those who don't make you feel like that and zero time around those who do."

Jessica nodded and swallowed hard. "God was right," she said. "I should've had a drink to take the edge off."

"If you want to call your mom and Chris, do it. But if I see you make a single public statement on this ..."

"Got it. But what happens if I'm swarmed?"

Silence for a second then, "Maybe you should get out of town for a little while. Make yourself scarce."

"I don't have the mon—"

"Chris does, and he'll give it to you in a heartbeat. Stop resisting this and just do what I say. It's easier for both of us, I promise."

Once they were off the phone, Jessica watched

Eugene's video twice more. She'd wanted to smite him plenty of times, but this one was a cut above. He knew so much. Obviously, Dolores had spilled to him, but who else? Mrs. Wurst? Seemed likely. The part about Jessica smoking weed in high school could only be one person, though. How had he found Greg Burns?

Had Dolores given Eugene the names of every single person in Mooretown who didn't like the McClouds?

Jessica grabbed a pen and notepad and jotted down a list of the worst accusations:

Murdered a bird in cold blood while in kindergarten.

Lured a man to his death at the zoo when she was eight.

Smoked pot starting in tenth grade.

Participated in a hit and run as a senior in high school.

Thankfully, most of her college years were a blank, except for the more public moments, like when she obliterated a statue of President Johnson in the middle of the Quad. The article didn't mention anything about her smiting it, and instead spun it as if she had placed some sort of explosive at the base. And that was worse. Much worse. Bombers were psychopaths.

And then there were all the accusations of fiscal irresponsibility at the bakery, culminating with the strange insinuation that she might have killed the man outside her bakery. That part was true, but merely insinuating it left so much to the imagination that it was somehow a worse jab.

Of course, interspersed with all of her worst moments

were descriptions of when she stood up and spoke out in any way, shape, or form that she was the daughter of God.

Yep, she looked like a real fucking maniac. Possibly a serial killer.

And that was just the way *she* was painted. Chris and Destinee, and even Rex, had been dragged through the mud with her until it looked like the four of them formed a little sleeper cell of dangerous lunatics.

WENDY IS CORRECT. YOU SHOULD GET OUT OF TOWN FOR A LITTLE WHILE.

And do what?

DOES IT MATTER? WHAT ARE YOU DOING HERE THAT'S SO IMPORTANT?

She considered it. *You mean a vacation?*

SURE, IF YOU BELIEVE YOU'VE WORKED SO HARD LATELY THAT YOU DESERVE ONE.

You're such an asshole. What do you mean then? A road trip?

COULD BE EDUCATIONAL. THE REST OF THE COUNTRY IS NOT LIKE TEXAS. I DID NOT TASK YOU WITH BRINGING PEACE TO TEXAS ALONE.

You're saying I should get to know the people I'm trying to convince?

INDEED.

And if I do this, you won't let my car break down in the middle of nowhere again?

THE LORD IS NOT A MECHANIC.

God! You better promise

FINE. YOUR CAR SHALL NOT BREAK DOWN.

She hated to admit it, but it wasn't a terrible idea. She'd only been out of Texas twice—once to Chicago for the NFL draft and another to New Mexico to have her life pulled out from under her.

Perspective. That sounded nice. She could get behind a fresh perspective. However, she knew very little about road trips. She did know that one person going across country alone was called "being on the lam," not a road trip. She'd need a companion, someone to help her gain that perspective, someone she wouldn't get tired of on the road. And she knew exactly who that person was.

Chapter Twelve

"Absolutely not," Quentin said later that night. Ruby, formerly No Name 32, lay curled up by his feet, snoring gently.

"What?" Jessica was stunned. This was supposed to be a given. She stared at him across her kitchen island, trying to decide if he was just messing with her.

"I'm not going on a road trip with you, Jess."

"But you just said the other day that you had a ton of paid time off saved up."

"Yeah, for a *vacation*. You know how long I've been single? Too long. I plan on spending my days off on a beach somewhere—not the Gulf, but a real beach. I'll meet a nice young lady and her friend and get laid. Super-duper laid. I need to get laid so bad I can hardly think at work anymore. Guy I share an office with said the word 'insects' the other day and I got a hard-on." He shook his head somberly. "But that's not even the biggest reason why I won't do a road trip with you."

"You think I'd get on your nerves?"

"Of course you would. And I'd get on yours. But also, I have a dog now—"

"Ruby can come with us! She's an easy dog."

"—and black people don't do road trips."

She jerked her head back and narrowed her eyes at him. "That seems a little self-limiting."

He sighed and crunched down on a queso-covered chip. "Maybe so, but it's just not the safest way for us to travel."

"What do you mean?"

He sighed, and inspected her, and it was clear he was weighing whether or not he should bother elaborating. "You've already forgotten about Mooretown, haven't you?"

"I wish I could, but no."

"Well, then you clearly forgot about how the rumor that you and I were dating brought out the racists."

"No, I remember that."

"We're in Austin right now. But between Austin and the next state, there are a hundred little Mooretowns, each with a startlingly similar attitude about a black man and a white woman spending time together. Or a black man existing."

She cringed. "Is it really that bad?"

"Yeah, it really is. Nothing brings out that spare length of rope like a bunch of white bumpkins knowing they're stuck in the same shitty town for the rest of their lives, and having a black dude with more money than them take a *road trip* through. No. You don't want me along. We wouldn't be able to stop at a gas station without getting looks and threats."

"But I *do* want you along. I don't care if people look at us like that or threaten something. I can smite them if I have to."

"I appreciate the offer, but I'd rather spend my vacation in the Caribbean. Having sex."

"Quentin ..."

"I'm sorry, Jess. I don't know what to tell you. A road trip sounds fun in theory. I'd love to be able to go on one without considering these things and worrying about my safety and yours. But it's just not how things are. I can do everything in my power to break the stereotypes, and it doesn't matter to people like that." He paused and when he spoke again his voice was softer. "Remember when we talked about how God sent a white messiah?"

She felt a pang of guilt in her stomach, thinking back on it. She'd been shocked that Quentin had resented her for her race, so she'd quickly stashed the memory somewhere it wouldn't come back. But here it was. "Yeah, I remember."

"God sends the messiah people are ready for. It doesn't surprise me for a minute that the one he sent us now is white."

"I can't help it."

"I know you can't."

"And I don't even think of myself as white."

"Everyone else does, so maybe you should."

"I don't know if—"

"Yes," he said firmly. "Everyone else thinks of you as white because you are. The only reason you don't think of it is because they don't treat you worse for it. But if they did, you sure as hell would think of yourself as white, because you wouldn't be able to escape it, even if you wanted to."

She jerked her head back. "Are you kidding? I want to escape my life *all* the time."

"I know, Jess. But you'd want to escape it even *more* if everything were the same but you were black."

She kept her mouth shut. She wanted to keep protesting, but something about his face told her she was out of her depth and would only make herself look bad if she kept on.

He groaned. "Listen. I hate to even bring this up because I can tell it makes you uncomfortable, but I don't want you thinking it's personal that I don't want to go on a road trip with you. It's not."

"It's okay. You can make me uncomfortable. It's good practice. And, I dunno if this helps, but I'm sorry you have to be black."

"No, that doesn't help. That's ... I love you and I know that came from a good place, but maybe don't ever say it again."

"Ah, okay. I'm trying."

"That's all I can ask."

Chapter Thirteen

Jessica sat at the airport bar, trying to keep her eyes open so she didn't doze off before the flight. At 5:55 a.m. on a Sunday, the bartender couldn't legally serve them alcohol and so had to keep the cash flowing through other forms of price gouging. At present, it was the seven-dollar glasses of orange juice that Jessica was sucking down one right after another to load up on vitamin C for the big voyage ahead.

While Judith and Jesus weren't her first picks for the road trip, they had one thing going for them: they agreed to do it. Quentin's concerns didn't seem to extend to Judith, who was technically Latina, though her skin was roughly the same shade as Jessica's own. And Jesus merely said he loved traveling, and the whole idea reminded him of his youth when he'd journeyed ... was it East? North? She'd stopped paying attention. The important part was that he was on board. There was probably something to having a male traveling with them. Might scare off a certain type of man who got big ideas when he saw two women traveling alone. No one need know that it was Jesus with them, and he couldn't be relied on to save them if it came to any sort of a physical altercation.

But though they weren't her first picks for traveling companions, she could see the unique value in having them along. Already, Judith had made a contribution by suggesting they take a plane to somewhere else to start off. That meant the first eight hours of their trip wouldn't be spent in Texas simply trying to get into another state.

"I wish they'd turn that off," Jesus of Nazareth mumbled, even as his eyes remained fixed to the television above the bar.

"Really?" Judith said. Despite the summer heat outside, she was dressed in black jeans and a long black sweater that Jessica, in her exhausted state, had a strange desire to nest in. Judith sipped her screwdriver, which was part overpriced OJ from the bar, part vodka from one of the travel-size bottles she'd brought from home. "I find it inspirational."

On the screen, coverage of the White Light Church scandal continued silently, the typo-filled closed captions providing the most recent updates:

The bar rage of videos only seems to be getting started and all we can do is wait for more whore fying videos to surface.

While white light crutch claims no responsibility for the inside dents, they say thieves poking to their congregations and will continue to

insist that their central reliefs do not condom sexual contact with pigs

and that "some us omen pork ohs, said de assist a pair" does not imply

that an act of beast reality is holy or godlike.

Since footage of the transgressions had surfaced from three more sources, the story had sprung into the national headlines. Apparently, this was good news for Jessica, but it sure didn't feel like it was really good news for anyone.

"Doesn't really make Texas look great, does it?" she said, trying to broaden her perspective in light of their impending trip.

"No," Judith said. "It does not. But to be fair, Texas doesn't always make Texas look great."

"I like the state," Jesus said, tearing his eyes from the television. "Everyone's friendly and accepting."

"You've only been to Austin," Judith reminded him. "You should try my hometown. Or even Jessica's, from what I've heard."

"What do you think Seattle is like?" Jesus said, borderline giddy. "I heard it rains all the time!"

"Pretty sure they have a huge heroin problem there," said Judith. "Like, every homeless person is on heroin."

Jesus appeared no less excited. "Oh, I know a cure for that! Love!"

"It's too early in the morning for that shit, Joshua."

Jessica changed the subject. "So, Brian is okay staying behind?"

"More than okay. He gets to spend his summer break doing whatever he wants. Mostly, that's waiting tables downtown so he can continue paying his student loans, but you know ... almost like a vacation."

"And your work really doesn't mind you taking this much time off?"

"They don't. Because I quit."

"What?"

"I quit." Judith shrugged. "It was a crappy job anyway. I can be a barista anywhere."

"Maybe if I ever open up another bakery."

Judith pinched the bridge of her nose, "For fuck's sake. Please don't."

"Why not?"

She looked up and met Jessica's eyes. "Because you starting and running that bakery was the most stressful time of my life. Listen, I'm about to tell you something that will not be pleasant to hear—"

"You and everyone else."

"You were *terrible* at running the bakery. I know it's a hard job, but you were especially ill suited for it, and you somehow managed to make it look even harder than it was. Please, just do what you're good at."

Jessica was stunned by the bluntness, but at least it helped wake her up a little. "And that is?"

"I don't know, whatever comes naturally to you."

"Messing things up?"

Judith chuckled. "Yes, actually. If you're gonna convince the country that God is woman, you'll have to destroy a lot of shit that already exists."

Jessica waved her off. "You're no help, and it's too early for this. I need another glass of orange juice."

Judith reached in her carry-on and pulled out another tiny bottle of vodka, and this time Jessica accepted.

"Where's the first stop we're hitting?"

Judith had taken it upon herself to do most of the research for their route, with Wendy's help in contacting the various houses of worship they would be visiting along the way. And while Jessica had done her best to follow along and be involved in the practical planning stages, it felt like a losing battle to focus on anything other than the impossible task of helping Dad become Mom. It occupied her every idle moment and many that should have been dedicated to other things, like moving the laundry from the washer to the dryer, showering, and planning a cross-country trip.

Eventually, Wendy and Judith had just gotten on with it, not bothering to get Jessica's approval on any of their schemes. Everyone was happier that way.

"Small church a couple hours south of Seattle. Looks like we'll get some great Pacific Northwest views there. The website said their beliefs have a strong focus on the divine feminine, so we thought it might be an interesting place to start."

"Oh! Yeah, that's fantastic." *Maybe they'll know what it means to be a woman.* "Great work, Judith. Hey, maybe this trip will be just what I need after all." She raised her fresh glass of OJ and vodka in a salute, and relaxed into the moment.

Chapter Fourteen

"Drive faster," Jessica ground out between clenched teeth.

"This van doesn't exactly go from zero to sixty in three seconds," Judith said. "I'm doing my best."

Tall, dense woods blurred past them on either side of the long, empty road. They were the kind of trees that could leave you in awe of their beauty or feeling trapped and disoriented. It depended heavily on the situation in which you found yourself while you were in them.

Jesus was in the second row of seats but moved to poke his head between Jessica and Judith. "That was strange."

"No shit," Jessica said, craving more, more, more distance between herself and the commune they'd just left behind. No, not left behind, *fled*.

Not only hadn't she learned a single thing about what it meant to be a woman, she hadn't noticed any specific mention of the divine feminine anywhere in that bleak place. Unless the ritualistic swapping of wives had something to do with that ...?

Prior to visiting the Divine Temple of Freedom, they'd spent a beautiful day in Seattle, though Jesus was disappointed by the anomalous sunny weather that the locals wouldn't stop remarking on, having wanted to see the rain he'd heard so much about.

But big cities like Seattle weren't the point of this trip. Or they weren't the *whole* point. If Jessica was to get a true feel of the country's attitude toward women, she would need to get outside of the more progressive and uniform pockets of the population. She needed to meet some good country people, salt of the earth. That's what they'd done.

"I thought communes were supposed to be laid back," Jessica said, her heart continuing to race from the overabundance of adrenaline flooding her system.

"They are!" Judith protested. "I mean, I *thought* so. Even Wendy believed it."

"That one had no chill," Jesus added.

Both women whipped their heads to look at him, and his eyes shot wide. "What? Did I use that wrong?"

"No," Judith said, "you used it *right*."

He nodded once, pleased.

Once they had a dozen miles between them and the horror show, Jessica felt like she could finally broach the details of what had just happened. "I thought only Texans had that many guns."

"Yeah, my eyes are officially open about Washington."

"What even *is* a free-range kid?"

"A wild animal armed to the teeth who could drop down on you from a tree at any moment like you're in the jungles of Vietnam in the sixties, apparently."

"Can we talk about the sleeping arrangements?"

Judith shook her head. "I'd rather not."

Jesus piped in. "It was a little like a slumber party."

"I'll give you that," Jessica said, "except usually you don't have adults sleeping among the children."

"Should we call the cops?" Judith asked.

"Definitely. But let's get a dozen more miles along before we do."

The experience had been bizarre from the moment they entered the reinforced iron gates of the place until the moment they left the reinforced iron gates at first sunlight.

Despite the alarming welcome, Jessica had persevered with her reason for being there and, once she and her companions were escorted to the Central Temple of Elders by armed—presumably feral—child guards, she asked the commune elders what it meant to them to be a woman. Unfortunately, their answer had fallen on deaf ears, because as the shirtless man on the throne of scrap metal provided his response in a thick, grumbling accent she had never heard before, her attention had fallen entirely upon one of her guards, a little boy, who was having a real go at a booger in his nostril, just getting up there, two knuckles deep. And her distraction was probably okay in the end, since nothing about this place was to be believed or, if she was lucky, stored anywhere permanent in her memory.

"Maybe we don't stay overnight at a cult again," Jessica

suggested as they pulled onto a two-lane road with even thicker trees on either side.

"That's the thing, though," said Judith, "it's hard to tell it's a cult until you're already in it."

Ahh, there it is, she thought. *That familiar sense of doom.*

That had only been their first scheduled visit of many. Was this trip truly cursed?

IT IS BLESSED.

Don't tell me that.

WHY NOT, CHILD?

Because your blessings feel more like curses than actual curses do.

YOU HAVE NEVER ENCOUNTERED A TRUE CURSE.

I was born, wasn't I?

"Shit," she said, putting her head in her hands. "Are we even going to make it home from this road trip?"

Judith grunted. "Not if God's only begotten genius back there keeps trying to bless everyone."

"What?" said Jesus. "No one needs more blessing than the parents of child soldiers."

"The parents were the ones who made them soldiers!" Jessica shouted. "And they didn't want your blessings! They literally said, 'We don't want your blessings.'" If she had to pinpoint a moment where it had all gone wrong for them, where the tone of the encounter had shifted from curiosity to animosity, Jesus's unwelcome blessing was it.

He nodded vaguely. "Ah, is *that* what they were saying?"

"Yes. What did you think they were saying?"

"'We'd want your blessings.'"

Jessica said, "Why in the hell would they say that?"

Judith gave him an out with, "Well, the constant gunfire in the background could have accounted for you mishearing them."

"Yes," said Jesus. "There was a lot of gunfire. I didn't like that part."

"Then it's a good thing our next major destination is in California," Judith said.

Jessica's mind jumped immediately to Miranda at the mention of the next state on their trip. Their route would take them not far from where she lived, but Jess hadn't made plans to stop by for a visit, hadn't even considered it until now.

"From what I've heard," Judith went on, "Californians feel the same way about guns as you do. They're level-headed liberal people."

Level-headed liberal people? Jessica didn't know much about how politics broke down, but from what she gleaned from Judith's tone, being liberal meant it was unlikely they would encounter another cult in California. She let herself imagine it, the cult-free haven of California, and breathed a small sigh of relief.

Chapter Fifteen

Almost a week had passed since their narrow escape from the Washington commune, and things hadn't gotten much better as they'd passed through Oregon and then California.

Turns out, California *did* have cults. Lots of them. More than she could count. Cults galore.

But they were in Nevada now, not necessarily safe, just faced with a different flavor of threat. The woods of the Pacific Northwest that had left her feeling trapped had long been replaced by flat desert, and now she felt exposed.

All in all, though, Jessica was grateful for the change, and the simple pleasure of stuffing her face with french fries while sitting on a bench in an air-conditioned tourist trap wasn't wasted on her. At least she was out of the van. And out of California. And in peace. Even if that required spending a little time contributing to the conspiracy theory industry at the National Museum of Extraterrestrials. The small cafe area was clean enough, though. No roaches or crickets or daddy longlegs to speak of, unlike the last two gas station bathrooms she'd used.

"There you are," Jesus said. He was holding a stuffed green alien in a white Elvis suit, and Jessica knew right away he'd already purchased the thing. She knew it in her gut.

He sat across the table from her and grinned. "Man, I wish Jeremy could be here. He would love this place."

Jesus's unimpeachable joy in this conspiracy theory of a "museum cafe" jumpstarted her cynicism that had been put on pause by the greasy food. "He could be if he wanted to. If he's as rich as he says, he could literally jump on a private jet and fly out here to the middle of nowhere to enjoy this so-called experience. Hell, the landscape is flat enough for him to land the plane anywhere."

"I think he would like the alien stuff."

"I know he would, and it's all alien stuff, bro. This sideshow is called The Alien Experience. I literally had to order 'potato probes with extraterrestrial sauce.' I'm not happy about that."

He sighed and continued grinning as he took in the bright colors of the surroundings. "It's just so lovely, the human imagination. And so limited. They speculate that time travel is possible, but it doesn't occur to them that if time travel ever exists on this timeline, the travelers would likely already be back among us. Yet, they see evidence of it, and they call it aliens. Ha!"

Jessica paused, a potato probe hovering in midair in

front of her mouth, and squinted at him. Then she tossed back the bite and spoke around the food in her mouth. "I should probably dig into that more, but I really just want to eat these fries and *not* think about what you just said, so that's what I'm going to do."

Judith appeared from the direction of the exhibits. She was barely containing her laughter. "Have you spoken with the docent yet?"

"No," Jessica said, feeling her big chance to decompress with a heap of starch slipping away. "Should I?"

"Oh yes." Judith bit her lips and shut her eyes for a moment. "Yes, you should *definitely* go ask that guy what it means to be a woman."

"I feel like I'm being set up."

"You are. Set up for a good laugh."

"I'm thinking it will be more upsetting than funny."

Judith grunted. "I guess if you're going to take that attitude it will." She grabbed a seat at the table. "We have a long way to go on this trip, Jess, and you don't seem like you're enjoying it that much."

"I'm sorry," Jessica replied, "I didn't mean for you to interpret my pure terror as we narrowly escaped one cult after another as a sign that I wasn't enjoying it."

"Jesus Christ. No, not you." Judith grabbed one of Jessica's fries without asking. "How have you still not figured out how to enjoy terror and tragedy? It's your whole life. You'd think enough exposure would give you a dark sense of humor at the very least."

Jesus, apparently sensing the tension, stepped in. "Why don't we discuss some of the things we have learned so far? We have traveled many days already and met many... interesting people. I am sure there are lessons to be learned."

"Yeah," Jessica said, "Don't join a fucking cult."

Judith shared a glance with Jesus. "You know those people didn't think it was a cult," she reminded her. "They thought it was a religion. And the right one."

"Despite all the evidence," Jessica added. "That one just south of San Francisco ... Great Father Kenneth had been wrong about the end of the world three times. Three times! Most folks have never even been wrong about it once, and those people still follow him."

"Yeah," Judith said, leaning forward, "and your job is to figure out how to get that level of devotion from people so—"

"One time, and I can see people being like, 'Oh, he just got the year wrong, but otherwise, he's completely right.' But three times?"

Judith was losing her patience quickly. "You heard what they said, though, right?"

Jessica groaned, remembering. "Of course I did. How could I forget? They thought every time the world didn't end when he said it did, it was because they were able to pray it away."

"And each time, they felt more powerful and more committed to the cause."

Jessica threw the soggy fry in her hand down into the

boat. "I'm not starting a cult. That's Jimmy's thing, not mine."

"You gotta start somewhere," Judith persisted. "It's a fine line between a cult and a religion, and I think yours will be more in the former by definition."

"Then I don't want it."

Jesus leaned forward and put his hand on her shoulder. "My dearest sister, if this is the only way to bring peace to the nation of the United States, then perhaps you should consider it." He let go and leaned back, beaming. "I, for one, think you would make a fantastic cult leader precisely because you do not want to be one."

Judith stood. "I'm gonna get a coke. Anyone want one?"

Jess looked down at her fries. She *was* thirsty. "Yeah."

"What kind?"

"Dr. Pepper."

"Joshua?"

"Dr. Pepper!"

Once Judith left, Jesus said, "I can see this is difficult for you. As I have mentioned before, I did a bit of traveling back in my day to learn the ways of the world. It is a trying experience to talk to those who believe so differently from yourself, but it is worth it. For example, coming down to Earth for the second time has been eye opening! Everything is so different."

"Do you wish you could go back to being dead?"

"Not even a little bit! There is infinite time for being dead, and only a moment to be alive. Sure, life down here is mostly suffering, but there are amazing moments, too. Like this!"

Jessica glanced around at the alien memorabilia on all sides. It felt like her brain was being abducted right from her skull. "What's so great and amazing about this?"

He laughed, spreading his arms wide. "Everything! Look around you! What a silly place! They're so confused, and they believe it so strongly. And they sell it to others who then start to believe it. Then there's you and me and Judith—on a road trip! We get to explore and have experiences most others do not, and we have nothing else we should be doing. We have freedom, sister, and that is a precious and rare thing."

"Dammit," she grumbled. "You're right. I know you are. So why am I so grumpy?"

"Because despite today's freedom, you feel like tomorrow is already set. Trust me, I understand."

She thought about it. "You're right. I have freedom now, but it all seems to be leading to the same destination, no matter what I do."

"You know," he said, "I wasn't *supposed* to be crucified."

"You ... what?"

"Oh yes. My whole life I was led to believe my life would end by being publicly crushed to death with stones. Not pleasant, but by no means as bad as what ended up happening. At least it would have been over sooner. But then I realized that I did have some control over the way things would go. Of course my mortal body would die—

everyone's does—but I had control over how that happened."

"And you chose ... crucifixion? I think I'm missing the silver lining of this story."

"We always have a choice."

"And you have terrible judgment. Okay. Noted."

"No, no. I knew that crucifixion would have a greater impact, and yes, it was not fun from what I can remember, but simply knowing I wasn't locked into the single outcome was greatly helpful. You may have a destiny, but it can take many shapes, and you get to choose which one it takes."

Judith returned with the drinks in a cardboard holder.

"He just said he didn't have to be crucified," Jessica said, hoping for a reassuring reaction of solidarity.

"Of course he didn't have to be."

Jesus stabbed his straw into the top of his lid and drank deeply before making a face.

"Right," Judith said. "They only had Pepsi."

He nodded. "Not a problem." Then he shut his eyes and held an open palm over his cup for a moment before taking another sip. "Mmm ..."

Ugh. A useful miracle. Naturally, *he* got it and not her.

She held out her cup for him to do the same for her drink, and as he did, she replied, "What do you mean, 'Of course he didn't have to be'?"

"It's a typical human sacrifice. They never have to happen."

"But he offered himself up."

"So? There's a long history of human sacrifices volunteering for that shit. They thought it was an honor."

Jess looked at her half-brother to see what he had to say on this account, but he was too involved with his drink. She never should've introduced him to sugary drinks.

But once she had a sip of hers, her brain chemistry started to change. Or maybe the fries were finally taking effect. "So, you're saying I have to start a cult. Then I have to turn that cult into a religion."

Judith shrugged. "Something like that."

"How do I do it?"

"You gotta start convincing a few people that God is a woman. Then you convince more people. And when enough people are convinced, people will stop calling it a cult and start calling it a religion."

Could it really be that simple?

"Okay, let's go with that, then. Y'all believe God's a woman, right?"

"No," Jesus said simply. "I can hear Him. He sounds like a man. Also, He's my Father, so."

"Open your mind a little on what that means," Judith said.

"And you?" Jessica asked. "You believe God's a woman?"

Judith chuckled. "No. I pretty much swing wildly between being an atheist who thinks you're completely out of your mind and believing God exists but is a huge dickhead."

Jessica crinkled her nose. "Well, you're right on the second part."

Her half-brother nodded sagely. "He can often present as a meanie."

Jessica stared down at her empty fry boat, a small pool of grease in it reflecting the harsh overhead lighting. "But that means the two people closest to me don't buy what I'm selling."

"Of course we don't. That's why we're on this trip with you. We're your co-conspirators, not your followers. We're here to help *you* figure things out, not the other way around."

The notion of having co-conspirators was strangely calming, and she said, "Okay, so say I want to start a cult. How do I do that?"

Judith already had an answer ready. "What are some commonalities we've seen in the four we've visited so far?"

Jessica considered it. "Charismatic leader."

"Okay, so that one's obviously out for you. What else?"

She didn't bother arguing. "They all believe something ridiculous."

"Excellent point," Jesus said. "Every religion starts by someone saying something most people think is ridiculous."

"And how do you sell it to people?"

They were silent for a moment, then Judith said, "Jeremy Archer."

"We're already using his media connections to—"

"No, not like that. I mean has Jeremy ever believed something that everyone else believed?"

Jesus chuckled. "No. It's wonderful!"

"And it also makes him a conspiracy theorist," Judith added. "You think if everyone started believing something he believed, he would still believe it?"

"Not a chance," Jessica said, catching on. "He would come up with some other conspiracy to disprove it."

Judith wagged a finger at her. "Exactly. We just met a whole lot of people like Jeremy in those cults."

"Ahh ..." Jesus said, smacking his forehead with his palm. "*That* is why I enjoyed them so much. They reminded me of my best friend! I wonder if they, too, believe Jameson Fractal is Bigfoot."

Judith squinted at him. "Wait, he believes that? But he's met Jameson."

He chuckled. "Yes, I know. It seems silly. And yet ... have *you* ever seen the Bigfoot and Jameson in the same room?"

Jessica ignored him. "You're right. They all wanted to believe something that almost no one else believes."

"And the leaders were able to find and gather those people to them."

"How?"

"That's the million-dollar question. But I can name someone who *does* know."

"Who?" Then, "Oh, are you shitting me? No, no, no. Never in a thousand years would I get his help on this."

Judith held up her hands to calm her. "I understand

why you say that, but the man has thousands of people believing that God is a hog."

"To be fair, God *was* a hog for a while."

"And God *will be* a woman if you can pull this off."

Jessica sighed. "His congregations take communion out of silver troughs. I don't want anything like that."

"That's fine. It wouldn't work with what you're selling anyway. But you know I'm right."

"I *don't* know that. Because Jimmy would *never* help me. He might pretend to, but only if he thought it could get him something he wanted. Once he got that he would throw me to the lions. Figuratively."

"Okay. Then you make sure what you need him to do could *also* help him. And the moment before he's about to ditch you, you ditch him."

"If I was smart enough to do that, I would've done it all those times before instead of getting screwed."

Judith rolled her eyes. "You mean back when you were a kid? Yeah, I'd hope you were a little smarter now than you were then."

"It's not happening. Any plan that involves Jimmy fucking Dean is a plan that I won't sign off on."

The sound of Jesus getting to the bottom of his drink interrupted the conversation, and he looked up. "Any chance there are free refills?"

Judith nodded, and the son of God jumped up and raced to the drink fountain.

"There are rules, too," said Judith.

"About the refills?" Jessica asked.

"No. It's practically international waters over at the drink fountain. I'm talking about the cults. Did you notice, they had all these rules for everyone to follow?"

"Yeah, duh."

"People who join cults must like rules. Or maybe they just like knowing there are rules that only they know."

"The rules were always different, though."

"And they were never written down."

Jessica paused. "I didn't notice that. No, they were never written down."

"Because they needed to change and evolve every time the world was supposed to end but it didn't."

"But all religions have rules written down, right?"

Judith nodded patiently. "Yep. Even Joseph Smith had those golden tablets. Before an angel spirited them away ever so conveniently."

"Who?"

"Joseph Smith. The Mormon dude."

"Mormons are a religion, right?"

"Anybody's guess, really. But they sure as shit know how to run things. You'd do good to take some lessons from the Latter Day Saints."

Jessica wasn't thinking about that, though. Her mind had wandered down a different path. "If I write down some rules, that means I'm founding a religion and not a cult ..."

"If you say so. It also means it's going to be a hell of a lot harder to get the early adopters and keep them if you can't manipulate them by changing the rules."

"I don't want to manipulate them!"

"Sure, you just want to convince them to believe something that isn't, in this present moment, true. Maybe even commit their whole lives to it."

"Jesus Christ."

"Yes?" He sat down, his giant drink in front of him.

"Did you write down any rules about Christianity?"

"No. I had friends do that. And Moses had a lot of it covered already." His eyes crossed as he wrapped his lips around the straw.

Jessica's mouth fell open. "You're *that* guy."

"What guy?"

"The one who gets everyone else in the group to do the work while he gets the credit."

"That's hardly fair," he said. "I died for your sins."

"Not mine," she said.

He wasn't deterred. "Writing was never my strong suit."

"It's not mine, either," Jessica said. "But I guess I'm going to have to get used to it."

"Or you could have someone else do it." He jerked his head toward Judith.

"Nuh-uh," she said. "I didn't get an English degree to become a goddamn scribe. I got it to pretend I'd be a writer someday but end up a teacher instead."

"And how's that going for you?" Jessica asked.

"Great, thanks. I've avoided being a teacher by being a barista."

"Not anymore. You quit that job. You're unemployed. I think that makes you a writer."

"I'd have to write to be a writer."

"I don't think that's true. And now you're my scribe."

"I'm not your goddamn scribe!"

"You are. You're my goddamn scribe."

"No! And fuck you for saying it!"

Jessica snuck a quick glance at Jesus, who appeared stunned by Judith's outburst, then said, "I know you don't mean that. I forgive you."

Judith shivered and a small moan slipped between her lips. She blinked and looked around, then focused in on Jessica again. "Don't you start that holy shit with me."

Jessica smiled innocently. "I thought you were an atheist who thought I was insane."

"Not today. Today, I'm a believer who thinks God is a dickhead for giving you that power."

Jessica leaned back on the bench. "And today I agree with you." She stood. "I'm gonna see what that docent thinks makes a woman. You should come with me and take notes."

Judith narrowed her eyes at Jessica. "I'll come with you, but I'm not taking notes."

"Suit yourself."

Chapter Sixteen

They'd just crossed the state line from Utah into Colorado when Jessica said from behind the wheel, "I got another."

Judith was riding shotgun, and she pulled out the notepad from her pocket and said, "Shoot."

"Sex should be consensual, respectful, and not include non-human animals."

Judith copied that down. "That last bit seems like a dig at White Light."

"It does, but I've been saying that since long before they started doing their thing."

"We're calling pig fucking 'doing their thing' now? Good to know."

From behind them, Jesus said, "Utah was beautiful. But I don't like that I wasn't allowed in the temple."

Judith grinned. "Yeah, I wish we could have told them who you really are. The looks on their faces once they realized they'd refused Jesus entry because he wasn't a Mormon? Priceless."

"It makes you wonder what was going on in there," Jesus added.

"That it does," Judith said. "That it does."

"Some people might find that appealing," Jessica said. "The mystery might make them want to convert."

"That's good," Judith said. "I'm writing that down." She read off the words as she scribbled them. "Create ... mystery ... excluding ... Jesus."

"Hey! Why are you being a meanie?"

"I'm screwing with you. Take it easy."

They pulled over for gas, and while Jesus pumped, a process that delighted him to no end, Judith and Jessica went inside to empty their tanks and refuel.

They stacked a small pile of candy bars, chips, Dr. Pepper, and water on the counter, and the clerk stared down at them without saying a word. But he also didn't start ringing them up.

"That's all for us," Jessica said, urging him along.

"What are you two little ladies doing all the way out here?"

Jessica opened her mouth to answer, but Judith said, "That's our business," and it was enough to get him to do what he was supposed to.

As they took the plastic bag from him, Jessica gave him one hard look and asked, "What would you say it means to be a woman?"

"Not now," Judith snapped, grabbing Jessica's wrist, and pulling her away.

"Ouch! What are you—" Then she looked through the windows at the van, saw Jesus, saw the large men shouting at him, and sprinted after Judith through the doors.

A man in thick, stiff blue jeans and a T-shirt with the sleeves cut off punched Jesus squarely in the face, snapping his head back as he only just kept his feet under him. Jessica lifted her hands without even thinking about it, focusing all her shock and adrenaline squarely on the perpetrator who'd just decked her brother.

She felt the ball of heat in her core as it built, swirling out into her shoulders, down her arms—

"Are you out of your mind?" Judith pushed Jessica's hands down toward the ground. "There are fucking gas tanks beneath our feet!"

Jesus took another punch to the stomach and fell to the ground, and when the two men heard Judith shout and looked up to see the two women sprinting toward them, they seemed satisfied and split, the tires of their old Jeep squealing as it darted out into the street.

"Jesus!" Jessica said, helping him off the ground. "What happened?"

Jesus coughed as he stood. "I do ... not know. They called me a pretty boy, which I thought was very nice."

Judith groaned.

"And then when I told them, 'Bless you for that, my brethren,' and told them I thought they were beautiful creations as well, they called me a ... a faggot. I believe that is perhaps where it began."

"No," Judith said, "it began before that."

Jesus looked confused. "Faggot means homosexual, right?"

Jessica dusted off debris from the seat of his pants. "Yep."

"And ... they do not like that."

"That seems like a decent guess," Judith said.

"I don't understand. Jeremy is my best friend and he is a homosexual. How could anyone not like Jeremy?"

Jessica could name five reasons off the top of her head without trying all that hard, none of which had to do with the man's sexual preferences, but that seemed beside the point.

"Let's get in the van," Judith said, "and Jessica will explain it all to you."

Chapter Seventeen

"Look who it is! The J-crew. Come on in!" Chris Riley grinned at them, stepping to the side and holding open the door to his Philadelphia condo.

While the new nickname wasn't exactly an instant favorite of hers, his face was a sight for sore eyes after so many months without.

Jessica, Jesus, and Judith entered his home. For her part, Jessica was both surprised and not by his decor. If she hadn't known Chris so well, she might have expected something a little flashier from this pro-football star, something that instantly reflected his recent ascension to wealth—ice sculptures or colorful inset lighting in strange places or a giant fish tank. But his approach to nouveau riche was so very *Chris*.

Hardly an inch of wall space wasn't covered with football memorabilia from his heroes. Her eyes landed on a signed Troy Aikman helmet under glass and two signed

Deion Sanders jerseys from different teams. Maybe someone ought to remind Chris he was an Eagle now.

The place wasn't exactly tidy, but at least it didn't stink. She remembered his dorm room had always held a faint sour tinge, and now she realized she had been expecting that. Maybe the air circulation was better in this place, and perhaps Chris had changed a few of his habits. But it was probably the air circulation thing.

"Christopher, my brother, how are you?" Jesus held out a hand to receive his host.

Chris took Jesus's hand to shake, then made a quick escape when he realized this wasn't so much a shake as a hand-holding experiment with strong eye contact. "I'm doing great. I'm glad y'all are here."

Jessica forced a tired grin. "Thanks so much for letting us crash a night."

"Of course." He wandered to the kitchen and dug through the fridge. "Drinks?"

Once that was settled, they congregated around the kitchen island with drinks in hand.

"You know they call this 'pop' up here," Jesus said cheerily. "It makes sense! It pops and fizzes! I ordered a coke and they poured me the wrong thing."

Jessica's eyes found Chris's without meaning to, and the two of them grinned.

"How was church?" Chris asked. "That's what you're doing, right? Checking out church services?"

"And asking people what it means to be a woman." Jessica sighed. "It was okay."

Judith shook her head adamantly. "Uh, no. It was *not* okay. I couldn't follow the sermon at all. It's all fucking sports analogies here. The reverend had some extended metaphor about baseball that went right off the rails."

"I was described as the third-base coach!" Jesus said. "I waaaaved people through"—he spun his arm like a pinwheel—"or told them to stop and not advance." He held up his palm and put on his best stern face. Then he laughed. "I do not know what any of that means."

"No one did," Judith said. "Most of the people in the pews were just checking yesterday's scores on their phone."

Chris nodded. "Welcome to Philly."

Jesus tilted his head to the side. "Are the homeless always aggressive here?"

"Pretty much. Did you—?"

Jessica shook her head to discourage any questions on the subject, and Judith went a step further, making a cutting gesture across her neck. Keeping Jesus from handing over all their cash and credit cards to the brazen homeless who asked for them had been a full-time pain in the ass since the moment they'd entered the city limits.

Chris took the hints and changed the subject. "It's late. Why don't I show y'all your rooms?"

They deposited Jesus in a guest bedroom, where he flopped face-down on the full-size mattress and groaned, and Judith had the door shut and locked behind her in another bedroom before Chris could explain that the women would have to share.

"It's been ... a little much spending all day every day together," Jessica explained. "I can sleep on the couch."

"No, no. You can have my bed. I'll sleep on the couch."

The obvious solution hung unsaid between them for a moment until Chris nodded at her Dos Equis. "You're empty."

Pizza arrived twenty minutes later, and once Jessica delivered a few slices to each of the guest bedrooms, she and Chris settled into his living room to relax. She looked around the space as he folded his third slice so he could down it faster.

Philadelphia was a strange town, but maybe she only thought that because it was new. Maybe she could get used to it. And this decor wasn't what she would choose herself, but it did feel like being inside Chris's head, and that wasn't such a bad place to be. She'd been inside his dreams plenty of times, and she'd generally enjoyed it ...

"There's something I need to tell you in person, Jess."

She turned her attention to him and noticed he'd stopped eating pizza. This was serious. Was he thinking about what she'd been thinking about? "Yeah?"

"That commercial. I'm so sorry. I really thought I was helping, but I lost control of the script, and I don't know *what* they did in the editing booth—"

The commercial? Oh right. "Don't worry about that. I know you meant well."

"Wendy, man. She tore me a new one."

"Sorry about that."

"I wish she could've done it to someone else and I could have just watched, ya know? That woulda been hot."

"Is your arm tired?"

He blinked. "Huh?"

"From carrying that torch for so long. You could just hire her as your publicist. You know that, right?"

By the squint of his eyes, he hadn't yet considered it.

"I have something to apologize for, too," she said. "I didn't believe you when I should have. About Mrs. Thom —About Dolores Thomas. The Devil."

"Oh, that." He waved it off. "You don't have to apologize."

"I do. I have to apologize to you and... and so many other people, really. I always took her side. I dismissed so many people's complaints, just explained them away. I don't know why I did it, either. I don't know why I felt loyal to her."

"I do. She was nice to you. She protected you. Jess, you really can't blame yourself for this. I know I don't. Sure, she threatened me when I was five years old and it's always stuck with me, but that's not your fault. She's evil. In the literal sense."

"You told me, though, and I didn't believe you. I thought you were overreacting. I thought Brian Foster was just being his usual cynical woe-is-me self. And I ... I wanted her to be my *mom*. Instead of my actual mom being my mom. How fucked up is that?"

To his credit, he paused to consider this last bit. "Pretty

fucked up. Because your mom is awesome. But again, not your fault."

"That doesn't make any sense, Chris. I did something fucked up, but it's not my fault?"

"Exactly. She got you young. And she was the only one telling you that you didn't have to do this hard, overwhelming thing. Of course you wanted to be her daughter. She was giving you exactly what you wanted. That's not love, just manipulation. But when you're a kid, you don't know the difference."

"I believed in her until I was in my *twenties*, Chris."

He shrugged. "Yeah, I dunno what to tell you. We're still idiots. I'm just a twenty-three-year-old idiot, and you're a twenty-two-year-old idiot."

She laughed and felt the knot of guilt inside her loosen. He had a point. For whatever reason, she'd always thought she should be smart and know everything already. She'd thought that since she was young. But she would never expect *another* teenager to know anything, let alone everything. "I guess some things never change."

"And some do. You have."

She squinted at him. "What do you mean?"

"You're stepping up now. You're not trying to hide away and pretend you're average. You don't want Mrs. Thomas to be your mother anymore. You're doing things."

She sighed. "It doesn't feel that way. It feels like I'm just biding my time until the Devil or Eugene Thornton or Jimmy Dean knock me on my ass again."

"Yeah," he said, "I get that. But have you noticed that

every time you get back up you're smarter and stronger? Nah, of course you haven't noticed that. But I have. I've noticed it."

She clutched her beer bottle between both hands. "You think I can do it?"

"Never a doubt in my mind."

"Do you even know what I mean by 'it'?"

"Not a clue. But if anyone can do it, it's you. You got God on your side. And Destinee's shotgun."

"Thanks, Chris."

He reached for another slice, realized the box was empty, and switched it out with the one stacked beneath it. "Speaking of Jimmy, what's the latest with him? He's awfully quiet lately."

"Probably just busy mitigating the pigfucking scandal."

Chris shook his head. "That doesn't sound like him."

"No," she admitted, "it doesn't."

"Think he's got something up his sleeve?"

"Always."

"He ever marry that girl?"

"Emily?"

"Yeah."

"I don't think so. They're just engaged."

"It's kind of romantic, if you think about it."

She eyed him closely. Was that a joke? It didn't appear so. "It's Stockholm Syndrome, Chris."

"Doesn't mean it can't still be a little bit romantic. I mean, think about it from her perspective." He gestured with his folded slice. "She gets to be with the man she's idolized since she was a *teen*. That's gotta feel good."

She cringed; she couldn't help it. "I guess I hadn't thought about it like that. But those feelings are being influenced by all kinds of manipulations."

He shrugged and took a swig of his beer to aid in his chewing. "Aren't all our feelings subject to outside influence? You remember Romeo from the Mexicans?"

She was vaguely aware that in any other context, this would seem bizarrely offensive. But in this specific context, having played football for the Mooremont Mexicans, it was just the mundane kind of offensive.

"Of course."

"He came down here a couple months ago and we had lunch. He's hitched now, married a woman who looks exactly like his mom. Exactly. Same first name, too. They even wear the same perfume. But he adores her and she adores him. You can't tell me his romantic feelings weren't also *influenced*. But does that make it bad? He's happy."

"Fine, I see your point, but there's no way Emily is happy with Jimmy. Just no way. I can't imagine a scenario where he's *not* cheating on her, and he's a complete fraud—"

"But what if she is? What if she *is* happy?"

The question almost tripped her up, but she found her footing again. "It doesn't matter because she'll eventually be miserable. She'll catch on, realize what's been happening to her, and she'll split. She'll be angry at herself for sticking around for so long and wasting years of her life with him."

"You don't know that."

"I can't live in Philly, Chris, and you can't live in Austin. Nothing's changed about that."

He made the transition seamlessly, only confirming her suspicion that this conversation had never been about Emily. "Will you ever be done? Once God is a woman, once you do that whole peace thing, will your job be done?"

"I have no clue. I don't"—she pulled back, deciding now wasn't the time to mention her doubt of surviving such an undertaking—"I don't know. Maybe."

"And when you're finished," he said, "you could move. Or whenever I retire, I could. I miss Texas so much it hurts. They don't say 'y'all' up here, and their Mexican food sucks ass. And it gets cold in the winter." He exhaled in a rush, deflating and hanging his head. "I'm sorry. We shouldn't keep doing this. I could never ask you to move up here." He finished off his beer and stood. "You sure you don't want the bed?"

And now there was no question of them sharing it. "No, couch is fine."

He carried the pizza boxes into the kitchen, and then a moment later his bedroom door shut behind him and she was left alone.

TALK ABOUT A STRIKE OUT.

Chapter Eighteen

Jessica ran as fast as her feet would carry her. Chris stayed in lockstep next to her despite his ability to outpace her if he wanted. The zombies weren't far behind. And they had guns. Big guns.

"In here!" Chris called, grabbing her hand and banking hard to the right. They hopped over the debris of the picked-apart grocery store at the bottom of the multi-use building—overturned shelves, empty cans, a few decapitated zombie bodies. Then out a back door, dodging another zombie, ducking as the bullets flew, sprinting into a stairwell leading to the apartments, Chris clutching her hand the whole time. He wouldn't lose her.

They reached the second story and pushed open a heavy steel door, finding themselves in a long hallway. Two zombies awaited them, snapping their hollow jaws. Chris produced a small semiautomatic and blew them away in a shower of bullets.

"There's a safe room," he said, and she wondered how he knew. Did he live here?

He kicked down the door, killed two more zombies, hustled to the bedroom, and there it was.

He knew the combination, and in an instant they were inside, the bulletproof door slammed behind them, and they were left in complete darkness. Her heart raced, but she was finally able to breathe.

He flipped a switch, and a dim bulb overhead flickered to life. This small bunker was well stocked, and the cot in the corner was already made.

"Are you okay?" he asked, grabbing her shoulders and pulling her close to inspect her face.

"Yeah, I'm fine. My heart is racing."

He placed a calming hand on her chest. "I'd be concerned if it weren't."

"They were close. So close."

Dust and blood caked his face, only managing to highlight his strong jawline. She stared into his eyes.

This world they found themselves in ... there was no professional football in it. She couldn't possibly hope to restore peace here. There was a new order to things, and God played no part. Now it was just about survival. No greater responsibilities than that.

She reached up and placed her hand gently on his cheek. His eyes flamed bright. They were safe, together.

He crushed his mouth to hers, and she let him. His grungy shirt went quickly, followed closely by hers. Without breaking the kiss, he grabbed her ass and lifted her, and she wrapped her legs around his waist as he carried her to the bed.

"You planned this," she said, but the accusation carried no anger in it.

"I had to. But I'll stop if you tell me to." He paused midway through stripping off his jeans.

"God no, please don't."

Something banged against the door, trying to get in, and she had one guess what it was.

"They can't get through," he said.

"Let's pretend they can," she whispered. "Our time is short."

He groaned and pounced on top of her.

His body was warm, his skin textured with grit. She bared her neck, and he seized the opportunity to devour it.

The pounding outside grew louder.

"Stop making me wait," she moaned. "I don't—" A metallic crash from *inside* the safe room made her yelp, and Chris jerked his head around, his mouth disengaging from her skin with a small sucking pop.

Large cans of food rolled over the ground around sandaled feet.

Jesus blinked and looked around the space, appearing entirely lost.

"Jesus!" she shouted, grabbing a corner of the comforter to cover herself up.

"Sister!" he said, sounding just as shocked as she'd been. Then he smiled. "Christopher! I did not expect to see you here! What an unexpected gathering of fri— Oh.

Ohhh." He held up his hands. "I'm sorry. I should not be here."

"No, you shouldn't," she snapped. "You can talk to me any old time. Now please just let me have apocalypse sex with my ex!"

Jesus bowed his head, averting his eyes. "Forgive me. I did not mean to intrude. I don't even know how I ended up here. Must be the pizza. It was very greasy, and I did not digest it enough before bed." He looked around and spotted the door. "I'll just let myself out."

"No!" Jessica and Chris shouted as he reached for the handle.

"Huh?"

"There are zombies out there."

"Right. Hmm ... Oh yeah!" He snapped his fingers and disappeared in a puff of white powder.

They continued to gape at the space where he had just been before Chris turned to her. Their eyes met. There was no smoldering lust left in either pair.

"Sorry," he said. "I shouldn't have set this up for us."

"Probably not. But I'm not angry about it. If Jesus hadn't popped in, I would have ... well, you know. It's fine. It was fun while it lasted."

"But we shouldn't do it again."

"Right. We shouldn't."

He dismounted from the bed and grabbed her shirt off the floor. "Here."

She caught it and traded it out with the corner of the

comforter. Once both were fully dressed, they sat side-by-side on the edge of the bed.

"I guess we'd better end this, huh?" he said.

"Guess so. But Chris—"

"Yeah?"

"If there's ever a zombie situation in real life, I wouldn't mind ending up here with you."

He grinned and clapped her on the shoulder. "You'll be the first person I seek out, Jess." He sighed and pushed up to standing, heading for the door. "Okay, here we go."

As soon as it was open a crack, the horde pushed its way in, snapping and gasping.

Jessica woke with a start, alone on the couch. One room over, Chris would be awake as well. She could just walk in there ...

But she wouldn't. Not now, in this fully functioning world of enormous responsibility, where the only zombie in her life was currently in a pizza coma in the guest bedroom, snuggling a stuffed Elvis alien in his arms.

Chapter Nineteen

Jessica wasn't too sad to leave the East Coast behind. New York City was hotter than it ought to be in late June, and Philadelphia was worse. And no one would spare the time to answer her questions about what it meant to be a woman.

"Write this down," she'd said to Judith as they left the Burger King. "Y'all is officially a word. Make that shit scripture and *fuck* that dude who corrected me when he took our order."

"I don't think you're supposed to write scripture based on spite." She paused. "No, I take that back. Spite is definitely how it's always been done. Especially the Old Testament."

They passed a sign that said Charlotte was another fifty miles. That meant their next stop was only a few miles on.

Jessica was nervous about what they were doing. But

she couldn't back out. Not after all the strings Wendy had pulled to get them welcomed in. The publicist had been forced to play her black card, and she'd vouched for all three of them, and Jessica didn't want to let the woman down.

And maybe, deep down, she really, really wanted to be accepted by this particular congregation. No reason.

She *was* aware there was a reason this Southern Baptist church was referred to colloquially as a Black Church, and yet somewhere in her mind a little voice had insisted, "There will probably still be a few white people in there."

That little voice had been wrong until the moment she and Jesus stepped foot through the front doors.

Judith, on the other hand, was miraculously stripped of all whiteness the moment she entered the church lobby. Jessica couldn't explain it, but her scribe stood apart from the rest, but not in the same manner that Jessica and Jesus did; she wasn't seen a threat, just an anomaly.

Jessica, on the other hand, had never felt so out of place, and that was saying something.

"This place is incredible!" Jesus proclaimed, and she gave him a swift elbow.

"They're looking at us like we're lost," Jessica whispered to Judith.

"Maybe we are. They probably think you two belong at the Presbyterian church down the street, and I belong at the Catholic one."

A cheery man in full robes appeared from a small

group and made his way over. "You must be Jessica, Joshua, and Judith!"

They must be.

"Minister Roberson?"

He took Jessica's hand in his for a shake but held on. "Indeed. I'm so happy you're here. Wendy speaks highly of you. She helped us out of a bit of a PR pinch a few years back, and we think she's just the greatest. Any friend of hers is welcome under this roof."

Jesus stepped forward. "This space is magnificent."

"You haven't even seen the sanctuary. Follow me."

Parishioners were already filing into the pews inside the sanctuary, which was, as far as Jessica knew, a pretty average space. There was one noticeable difference about the artwork, though, but she decided not to bring it up.

"We're very excited to hear the sermon today."

The Minister grinned. "Would you like me to introduce you to the congregation? I hope you don't mind me pointing out the obvious here, but you three do stick out a bit. You're welcome to be here, of course, but, well, with history being what it is in this country, some folks might want an explanation."

Her mind flashed back to the first time she was introduced in a church, pointed out by the man at the pulpit.

"I don't really want to be in the spotlight," she said.

"Trust me. Introducing you at the first is the best way to keep eyes *off* you for the rest of the service."

She looked at Judith, who nodded subtly.

"Okay, I trust you on this." That wasn't true. But she also knew he had a point. People would be staring at her regardless. That day in White Light Church when she was only eleven years old it had been the red dress that made her stand out. Now, it was something she couldn't change out of that kept her presence conspicuous. She felt like a virus entering a healthy body, and all the white blood cells were ready to eliminate her.

The minister left them to attend to his other duties, and they found a seat by the aisle. Jessica wanted to be able to make a quick escape if things went south.

"I think I look good black," Jesus said, gazing dreamily over the stained-glass windows.

"It *is* a little strange," Jessica conceded. "I mean, you weren't black when you were alive, right?"

He shook his head. "Nope. I was dark, but we didn't really have a notion of race back then. It was more a matter of class and religion. I did meet quite a lot of what you call sub-Saharan Africans. Never this many in one place, though."

"Have you already forgotten Utah, Jess?" Judith said. "Jesus wasn't blond hair, blue eyes, either." She caught herself. "I mean, he wasn't the first time around. And yet, that's the Jesus they pray to. And my family only prays to Latino Jesus. And Latina Mary."

Jessica nodded, understanding slowly dawning. "Everyone needs to see themselves in God."

"Uhh," Jesus said hesitantly, "I hate to beat a dead camel, but God and I are not the same thing."

"I know that," she snapped. "But it's not about what I know. It's about what people believe about you. They think you're the face of God, and they want to see you wearing their face."

Judith arched a brow. "So now he's serial killer Jesus?"

"You know what I mean."

"Only vaguely."

The congregation had grown to a few hundred people by the time the service began, and true to his word, Minister Roberson introduced the guests. "For those of you long-timers here, I'm sure you haven't forgotten about the incidents that happened a few years back with one bad apple of a youth leader."

A chorus of "Mm-hmms" rose up around Jessica, and she had a knee-jerk urge to shush everyone.

"Our little congregation was nearly torn apart by the devil. The media came after us, the community came after us—as if we were supposed to have known that something untoward was happening in the private conversion sessions held by a man we presumed to be anointed by the Lord Himself.

"Mm-hmm!"

"If it weren't for our dear friend Wendy Peterman and the quick mind the Lord blessed her with, we might not have weathered the storm."

Jessica grabbed her half-brother's hand and forced it down when he started to wave in response to a "Praise Jesus."

"Today we have among us three guests Wendy has sent

to us. I hope we treat them the same way we would treat her if she were here in their place. They are welcome, and we'll treat them the way Jesus might." He gestured to where they sat toward the back, but the clarification of who he was talking about was entirely unnecessary. "Jessica, Judith, and Joshua, we're glad you're here."

The suspicious looks from the congregation softened to smiles and generous head nods, and Minister Roberson moved on.

Just like that, it was over. And painless. She was *welcome* inside this church.

She sat quietly, her hands folded in her lap, waiting for the other shoe to drop.

It was a strange thing, though. The welcome had allowed her to relax, but it hadn't made her feel any less out of place.

Was this what Black people felt like when they attended a farmer's market or a rodeo or a rock concert? Was this what Quentin felt like at his tech job? Or when he was basically anywhere else in Austin?

A deep, bruising shame moved through her for never having considered it before, not like this, and she hurried to soothe the supreme discomfort by thinking of all the ways it wasn't her fault that she hadn't felt this way prior to this moment.

Why *would* she have gone to an historically black church in Austin? Or anywhere? She didn't even go to white churches if she could help it, and there just weren't that many black people in her city. Mooretown had had a larger black demographic than Austin, even. Or maybe she was just thinking of the football team. Had there been any black guys in her high school who *hadn't* been on the football team? No, she didn't think there had been ...

How could she be expected to seek out *every* kind of experience prior to this road trip? She was busy. She had things to do. It hadn't occurred to her that she should be the only white person somewhere, and why would it? Demographically speaking, there were way more Caucasians in the US than any other group, so, naturally, the percentages in any room would be skewed in that direction. Just statistically speaking here.

The shame lessened but didn't go away.

What would happen, she wondered, if she went to the stage and proclaimed herself the daughter of God in front of all these people? Besides appearing rude for interrupting, obviously. She tried to imagine it and the mere attempt made her hot and dizzy. The notion seemed so perverse. These people didn't want a white messiah, that was clear enough. But that was all she could give them. It wasn't *her* fault she was born this color ...

Judith cursed under her breath beside her, and Jesus stared at the pulpit looking ashen, so Jessica decided it was time to pay attention again.

"'... with good works. Let the woman learn in silence with all subjection,'" said the minister. "'But I suffer not a woman to teach, nor to usurp authority over the man, but to be in silence. For Adam was first formed, then Eve. And Adam was not deceived, but the woman being deceived was in the transgression. Notwithstanding she shall be saved in childbearing, if they continue in faith and charity and holiness with sobriety.' That's directly from 1 Timothy 2, verses 9 through 15."

"Timothy, no!" Jesus shouted.

Thankfully, his words were lost underneath the sound of others around them praising his name.

Jesus slumped in the pew. "It was a different time, yes," he moaned miserably once Roberson began speaking again, "but even still, I can't imagine Timothy would write such a thing."

"Maybe he didn't," Jessica said. "Maybe the editors got to it or it was lost in transla—"

*OH NO, HE SAID IT. HE SAID IT **A LOT**.*

Jesus slumped further and pouted his bottom lip pitifully; he'd heard God's words too.

"Okay, so maybe he said it," Jessica whispered.

"I trusted him. He was so good to me."

Judith rolled her eyes. "So good to you, a man and the son of God? But *how* could someone be nice to men and horrible to women? It just doesn't make sense."

Jessica leaned closer to Judith. "I thought this church was supposed to be cool?"

She narrowed her eyes. "Cool because ...?"

"I dunno."

"Because they're black?"

"No! Of course not. Cool because Wendy sent us here."

"Wendy sent us here because they used to be her

147

clients and she had a connection. Anyone who was an emergency client of a publicist is likely *not* cool on the whole. You heard what they said about that youth minister. Doesn't take a genius to read between the Bible verses on that one."

Jessica sighed and was about to give up when Minister Roberson began quoting some more.

"'But I would have you know, that the head of every man is Christ; and the head of the woman is the man; and the head of Christ is God. Every man praying or prophesying, having his head covered, dishonoureth his head. But every woman that prayeth or prophesieth with her head uncovered dishonoureth her head: for that is even all one as if she were shaven. For if the woman be not covered, let her also be shorn: but if it be a shame for a woman to be shorn or shaven, let her be covered. For a man indeed ought not to cover his head, forasmuch as he is the image and glory of God: but the woman is the glory of the man. For the man is not of the woman: but the woman of the man. Neither was the man created for the woman; but the woman for the man.'"

"What's hair got to do with anything?" Jessica whispered to her companions. "Wait, is *that* why all the women are wearing hats?"

Jesus had his head in his hands, and Judith just shrugged. "I dunno. But suddenly I have the urge to shave my head. Let's get out of here."

Chapter Twenty

Jessica was tempted to let Jesus take the wheel as they crawled through traffic on their way out of Atlanta. It would be a good opportunity for him to practice. What damage could he do while they were going five miles an hour in gridlock?

She glanced at him in the rearview mirror and reminded herself that he'd gotten himself trapped in a rotating glass door earlier that day, and she and Judith had been forced to coach him for quite some time before he figured out how to exit safely. Maybe she would stay right where she was.

"I knew traffic was bad in Atlanta," Judith said, "but this seems extreme. How does anyone live here?"

Just then, the sound of the emergency vehicles a few hundred yards back met her ears. "I think there's an accident slowing things down."

They all looked behind them, and it was clear that

there was a problem. The traffic, in its impatience to get a move on, had even blocked the shoulder, and none of the emergency vehicles could get past.

"Idiots," Judith said. She whirled around in her seat, leaning from one side to another to try to see what was happening up ahead. "I hope it's not bad."

"If it is," Jessica said, "they're in trouble. The medics would be better off getting out and walk—"

YOU CAN HELP.

Yeah, she'd just realized that too.

This is an awful lot of cars.

YOU KNOW THAT IS IRRELEVANT.

She closed her eyes and breathed in deep. Their van might sustain some minor superficial damage from this, but it was worth it; the thing was rented on "Joshua's" credit anyway.

She felt the van slide sideways and opened her eyes. The traffic had parted down the middle. The ambulances didn't question it and sped through the newly opened gap.

There. I did it.

THE LORD SUPPOSES YOU WANT AN AWARD.

She ignored Him and turned to face her passengers. Jesus clapped. "Well done! Oh, I do love a well-timed miracle!"

Judith, for once, seemed speechless.

And then, all around them, the fighting started.

Two men whose cars had tapped into each other exited their vehicles. One held a crowbar, and the other held nothing but his fists, but that seemed like enough.

"Oh boy," Jessica said. "This didn't happen when I did it before."

"Atlanta doesn't fuck around," Judith said. "Let's get out of here."

She didn't have to be told twice, and she pulled into the opening down the middle of the eight-lane highway, which was now filling in with the trickle of other vehicles whose drivers were most able to take the strange phenomenon in stride and just go with it.

Traffic was still a crawl, but at least it was crawling.

The flashing lights grew closer on their right, and beyond it, the road opened up completely. The crawl, as it turned out, was mostly due to rubbernecking.

Jessica decided to help herself to a dose of it as well. But when she saw the morbid draw, she felt the air leave her lungs.

The minivan was on its side. Or she thought it was. It was almost impossible to tell which side was up on the twisted hunk of metal.

She counted three. Three human-size lumps under sheets.

Without thinking, she pulled over, just past the last fire truck.

Judith shouted something at her, but the words sounded nothing like English as she leaped out of the driver's door and sprinted toward the smallest of the covered lumps. The officers on scene would be an obstacle to this, but, thankfully, the five of them were huddled by one of the cars. She would only have a few seconds to pull this off before they'd stop her.

She hadn't prepared herself for the sight that awaited her under the first sheet. Had she expected everything to be intact? For the child to look like he was merely asleep?

"Shit, shit, shit, shit, shit ..." Did she even *want* to bring him back with his arm in that state?

Stupid. Of course she did. Life with no arm was better than death.

She hovered her hands over his chest and shot the life back into him.

The soul-shattering screaming was almost immediate, and she ran to the next sheet before the responding officers and paramedics could stop her.

This boy *did* look like he was only sleeping. At least what she could see of him when she pulled the blanket down to reveal his top half. Who knew what the bottom half looked like? She resurrected him as quickly as she could, and made for the largest of the lumps as the screaming doubled.

But before she could get there, someone came at her from the side and wrapped her up.

"Please!" she shouted. "I can save them! I just brought those two back to life. I can do it!"

She was promptly forced to the ground and cuffed by the male officer.

"Please!" she begged, "I can bring them back!"

"The woman's dead," he said, lifting her off the ground. "If you'd seen her, you'd agree with me."

"McCarthy!" came a deep, stern female voice as the officer walked Jessica over to his car.

The man turned and looked at the woman, and so did Jessica. This was the kind of woman no one had yet described when Jess had asked them what it meant to be a woman—bulky, eyes like lasers, a gait like a pit bull, hair pulled back into such a tight ponytail that it doubled the size of her forehead.

Jessica noted the name on her uniform: Sgt. Gabriel.

"Yes, Sarge?"

"Uncuff her."

"Pardon me, Sarge?"

"Didn't you see what she just did? Uncuff her, for God's sake, and let her resurrect the mother."

"Resurrect ...?"

"Oh, for chrissake ..." Sergeant Gabriel grabbed Jessica's wrists from Officer McCarthy and gestured for him to hand over the key, which he did. She clicked off the cuffs and said, "Sorry about that, Miss McCloud. Now, if you don't mind ..."

It was ugly business. Officer McCarthy hadn't been kidding about the state of the mother, but the paramedics were already on site and the treatment of her injuries started immediately. With enough morphine, they might all be fine in the end.

Judith and Jesus waited on the bumper of the van, watching from a distance as Jessica finished giving her statement, which was taken personally by Sgt. Angela Gabriel.

A half hour had passed since the whole thing had kicked off, and Jessica's adrenaline was crashing by the time she headed over to join her friends. "Let's get out of here," she said.

Judith grimaced. "You're not getting in the van looking like that."

Jessica glanced down at herself and only then noticed the blood. "How ... I didn't even touch them."

"Blood is like that," Jesus said sagely. "It just sort of gets on everything."

"That was one hell of a show."

Jessica sighed. "I feel like I need to be taken straight to a therapist, except I hate therapists."

"Stay there." Judith got up from the bumper and crawled into the van. When she returned, she was carrying a pack of cigarettes. "Take one of these. It's almost like therapy."

"Those things kill you," Jesus said.

"So does getting yourself martyred," Judith snapped before lighting one up and offering it to Jessica. It was tempting, but she could already imagine Wendy's bewildered anger when photos surfaced of the smoking messiah. "Thanks, but I'm good."

Judith shrugged and kept it for herself.

"Great," she said, spotting the first news van to arrive. "Just what I need."

Judith shook her head sympathetically. "Yeah, it's going to be so hard to get on camera and tell everyone you saved three people. Truly, being a fucking hero is your cross to bear."

"I believe in you, sister!"

Jessica looked at him. "Thank you." Then she inhaled deeply and went to go meet the camera.

"News 7," shouted a petite reporter with pale skin that looked even paler against the electric blue of her suit. The woman charged forward, microphone first. "Are you the woman who reportedly brought a mother and her two sons back to life?"

The reporter and her cameraman angled themselves so that the backdrop of their shot was the emergency vehicles.

What did she say? Yes? Yes, I just performed three resurrections.

YOU DID JUST PERFORM THREE RESURRECTIONS.

But do I tell this woman that?

The reporter took Jessica's silence as an opportunity to jump in with further questions. "I just watched cell phone footage of you hovering over the body of a child who paramedics had declared dead. You put your hands above him, and he appeared to come back to life. Comment?"

"I resurrected him." Boy, was she tired. "I resurrected all of them."

The reporter blinked. What was this idiot expecting? She'd asked a leading question and gotten the answer she'd wanted. And yet ... "Did you administer CPR?"

"No."

"Would you say the paramedics declared the victims dead prematurely?"

"No. They were dead. Very dead. Otherwise I couldn't have *resurrected* them."

"You're claiming that you just brought three people back from the dead without using CPR."

"Right."

"What technique did you use?"

Feeling suddenly on the border of hysterics, she said, "The power of God," and grinned. "I used the power of God. I performed a miracle. Three miracles, actually." She chuckled, and the reporter's face only grew paler.

Another news van had arrived, and she heard the male reporter call to his cameraman, "Jessica Christ! It's her!"

Shit, had they heard about her all the way in Georgia? She'd occasionally made headlines throughout her life, but she'd always assumed no one outside of Texas kept up.

"Miss McCloud," the male reporter shouted, still yards away but closing. He was built more like a linebacker than a TV personality, and Jessica wondered how his cameraman kept all of him in the shot without standing farther back.

He shouldered the pale woman out of the way. "Miss McCloud. Jim Denver, Channel Twelve News. I just saw the cell phone footage online, and can you explain what we just saw?"

"I just resurrected three people."

"Resurrecting three people, some might consider such a thing nothing short of a miracle!"

"And they'd be right. It was a miracle. I just performed three miracles. That's something I can do. I'm ..." She looked around. If she thought traffic was at a standstill before, she had no idea just how still it could get. It looked like the front lawn at a Mooretown family reunion, cars pointing every which way, squeezing in whatever available space they could find. Faces gaped at her from behind tinted windows.

Jim Denver cleared his throat, pulling her attention back to the interview.

Aw, fuck it. Let's do this.

THAT'S THE SPIRIT.

"My name's Jessica McCloud. I'm ... from Texas. And I'm the daughter of God."

The proclamation sent tingles down her spine, but whether they were simply a result of adrenaline as her body urged her to choose *flight flight flight* after proclaiming something so insanely dangerous, she couldn't be sure. It felt a little good.

After a moment's stunned pause, the reporters' questions started flying at high speeds.

"That's enough," came a now familiar voice from behind her. Sgt. Gabriel stepped between Jessica and the cameras and told the news crews in no uncertain terms to buzz off. Then she turned to Jessica and said in a low voice, "Let's get you out of here," and led her with a firm hand on the small of her back toward her van.

"That was brave," said the sergeant. "It's true?"

"Yes, ma'am."

"Good, good. I thought so. Brave of you to say it."

"Thank you."

"Not a compliment, just a fact. I've seen some of the department's best men and woman get killed for that kind of bravery. But it's the right thing to do, anyway. I make sure their widows know it, too." They paused in front of Jesus and Judith. "You'd better let someone else drive. I can spot an adrenaline crash when I see it." She reached in her breast pocket and pulled out a card. "You call me if you get into any more trouble in this state. I know people."

"We're headed to Alabama, but thanks."

The sergeant sucked in air. "Oooh ... Alabama? I can't help you there. No one can. Not even your Father, as far as I know."

"It's ..." Ugh, this was going to sound so stupid. "It's my mother now. God's a woman."

Sgt. Gabriel narrowed her eyes at Jessica for only a moment, then chuckled. "Sounds good. 'Bout time someone showed up to straighten up this mess of a world, and we both know women always end up with *that* job." She looked at Jesus. "No offense."

"None taken! Bless you for thinking of me, though!"

She eyed him skeptically. "He with you?"

"Yep."

"Okay, if you trust him, I'll have to accept that. Seems a little off to me, though." She shot him a warning look. "I'll let you three get back on the road. Be careful. And I have to say it, whether you'll listen or not. Don't stop in Alabama. Just drive straight on through back to Texas."

* * *

A state line later, Jessica sprinted for the van. Jesus, with his toned, lithe body, could have beaten her there if he hadn't insisted on trying to clear up the misconceptions. That was futile, of course, but he wouldn't have been Jesus if he hadn't tried.

And now he was sprinting, too. She risked a glance over her shoulder to make sure Judith, who'd never been big on physical activity, hadn't been overtaken by the shouting mob.

"Queers ain't welcome!" hollered a stout man in stiff blue jeans, a short-sleeve button-down, and a cowboy hat.

"Illegals neither!" yelled another similarly dressed man.

Jessica reached the van and dug in her pocket for the keys. "Shit, shit, shit!" Her hurried attempt to unlock the van door set off the alarm instead. "Fuck!"

Judith reached the passenger's side. "Let me in!"

She found the right button, pressed it, and both front doors flew open without anyone touching them.

"Get in the van!" Jesus cried. "I believe they intend to harm us!"

"No shit." Jessica slammed her door behind her and struggled to get the key into the ignition.

"Gun, gun, gun!" Judith yelled, pointing out the window.

Jessica didn't bother to look. She knew damn well what a gun looked like.

"Fag!" came a deep voice from outside the vehicle.

Judith cursed again. "That was the *pastor*!"

"Filthy illegal! Go back where you came from!"

"My pleasure," Judith shouted back through the closed window.

Jesus was draped over the back seat, clutching his heart as they fishtailed out of the Alabama church parking lot and made it onto the highway. "So much hate and fear," he wheezed.

"They're not all like that, I'm sure," Jessica said, trying in vain to comfort her half-brother. "We just picked the wrong church. That's all."

Jesus nodded and pushed himself upright. "That's wise of you, sister. Most people are good and loving. I've seen it myself. Maybe we should try another church to—"

"NO!" both Jessica and Judith shouted.

The latter added, "Let's just get back to Texas. I feel like we've learned plenty on this trip. Too much."

It was tempting. But they had a plan for a reason, and Jessica intended to stick to it. "Not yet. We still need to stop off in New Or—"

THOU SHALT HAUL ASS HOME.

She breathed a deep sigh of relief. "Never mind. Guess this show's over."

Chapter Twenty-One

"You were absolutely right," Jessica told Quentin. "It would have been hugely dangerous for you to come."

They sat on opposite sides of her sofa, her legs extended as she leaned back against the armrest. Quentin spread out with one arm slung over the back of the couch. Destinee had situated herself on the floor on the other side of the coffee table, and Rex had claimed the stuffed chair, but not without first musing at length on it. On the one hand, he explained, chivalry was at its core chauvinism, and to assume Destinee required a softer spot to sit solely because of her anatomy would be arguably misogynistic. On the other hand, he considered her a goddess-like being, and she could have whatever of his she wanted.

Only once Destinee told him to shut the hell up and established that it felt better on her back to sit on a rug on the floor had he finally taken his seat.

"And how was the black church?" Quentin asked.

"I know you put Judith up to that. It wasn't bad outside of the scripture they read, but it's hardly their fault that nonsense is in the Bible. I just wish I'd been black for it."

He nodded. "I bet you felt like a bit of an outsider, huh?"

"I stood out for sure. Jesus was worse off than me, though."

"How is he?" Destinee asked. "Seems like a big trip for the little guy."

"I think he's sleeping it off across the way."

"And did you find out anything useful about femininity?" Rex said. "Are you beginning to understand the broad spectrum?"

"I thought you weren't supposed to call us that anymore," said Destinee.

Jessica ignored it. "I have no idea what it means to be a woman. If I'm gonna pitch it to the masses, I think I'll have to be vague. I say woman, and they think of whatever that means to them."

"But will that work?" Destinee asked. "Will it make your daddy a woman?"

"No clue. But while we were on the West Coast, we visited quite a few cults. I might've picked up a few tricks."

Quentin nodded. "I always knew you had it in you to orchestrate a mass suicide."

"Not *those* kinds of cults, Quentin. At least ... not yet. They're probably heading that way, but obviously if they were suicide cults, we wouldn't have been able to speak with—" Her phone vibrated on the table, and out of habit, she grabbed it to see who was calling. "Wendy," she announced. "Probably calling to congratulate me on finally stepping up and owning my shit in Atlanta. Hello?"

The voice on the other line was unusually restrained. "Jessica?"

"Hey, Wendy."

"I want to start by saying I'm proud of you. I just heard you're back in town."

"Yep. Resting up."

"Great. You did a good thing in Atlanta. I need you to know that."

Uh-oh. "I know that. Why do I need to know that?"

"Because I'm worried that what I'm about to tell you is going to make you never want to do something like that again, and we are only getting started with you proclaiming yourself the daughter of God."

"Just tell me what's happened." She could feel the rest of the eyes in the room boring into her.

"Dolores Thomas has seen that clip, and since she owns the personal brand of Jessica Christ ... well, I don't know if it'll hold up in court, but she's suing you for two million dollars."

Jessica closed her eyes, waiting for the news to sink in, wondering when the pit would form in her stomach.

But it didn't.

Huh.

"Jessica? You still there?"

"Yeah, yeah, I'm still here. And I think I don't give a damn what Dolores tries to do. I mean, sue me for what? I own nothing." A caustic energy bubbled up inside her that felt a little like death but mostly like life. "Jameson still owns the condo, my personal checking account has three dollars and forty-five cents in it until Chris deposits more in there, and she's already taken everything else. If she goes after my car, I'll wreck it." Something deep inside her snapped, and it felt good, like liberation. "Doesn't she know I'm the goddamned moochsiah? Let her come for me! Everything I have is someone else's! She can't get shit off me!"

She ignored the questioning expressions of those in the room with her. They wouldn't understand, but she did. She was the moochsiah, and, somehow, that dreaded label had just become her greatest weapon.

Chapter Twenty-Two

On first blush, the private office at the co-working space didn't seem like an especially appropriate place to discuss these matters, but once Jessica considered it, she could guess that the Bible had been written in some uninspiring places, too. What was the equivalent of a co-working space two thousand years ago? A town square? A cave?

A MONASTERY.

Cash sat at the conference table with their laptop open, typing furiously as Wendy scribbled notes on the whiteboard. Judith sat across from Cash, her records from the trip spread out in front of her.

"Simplicity is truly our friend here," Wendy said. "A single landing page will be enough to direct traffic and capture data to retarget. But if we only have one page, we need to unify the main message. Judith?"

"Right. While we were on the trip, we came up with five commandments."

Wendy moaned sensually. "That's so good. Okay, hit me with them."

Judith read them off, and Jessica stared down at the hands on the table, listening to her words read back to her.

"Don't be a dick to yourself or others."

Wendy's hand that held an offensively pink dry-erase marker paused above the board for a microsecond before she nodded to herself and wrote that down as commandment number one.

"It could use a little fine-tuning," Jessica admitted.

"Just a rough draft, don't worry about it," Wendy said. "Next one?"

"Sex must be respectful, consensual, and cannot include any non-human animals."

Wendy turned from the board to Jessica, a single eyebrow arched high. "That's a dig at White Light?"

"Not intentionally," Jessica said. "It's kinda always been the rule. Not my fault his people broke it."

"And are still breaking it," Cash said. "New videos keep surfacing."

"Ew. Why? We get the point."

Cash shrugged. "I can only assume people like watching rednecks fuck pigs."

"They like the feeling of superiority when they watch rednecks have sex with pigs," Wendy corrected.

But Cash just shrugged. "Whatever you want to tell yourself, but this latest one dropped two days ago and it's already hit five million views."

Jessica grunted. "I always thought the 'no non-human

animals' thing was unnecessary and went without saying, but ..."

"Nothing goes without saying anymore," Wendy added. "Next commandment."

Judith and Jessica shared a glance. This was easily the one they were least sure about. The language would definitely need some massaging, is all. But ever since Jessica had heard the notion come from Jesus's mouth, it had wobbled around in her skull, and she had yet to fully explain why it *didn't* make sense. And so, it had made the road trip list.

Judith read it off. "Treat each person as if they are carrying a gun on them."

Wendy just stared.

"Admittedly," said Jessica, "it could use some work."

Wendy sighed. "I agree with you there. You know not everyone is treated equal when they're carrying a gun, right? Permit or not."

"They are by Jesus," Jessica supplied weakly.

"Right. How many Jesuses do you know? Okay, that's fine. Um. I'm sure we can work with this ..."

There was a silence in the conference room, broken only by Cash's typing, and then Judith spoke. "What about if you treat everyone as if you're armed and they're not?"

Wendy tapped the capped marker to her lips. "I think we might be getting closer now. What's really happening there, though?"

Jessica considered it. She's never been on that side of the barrel. What would it be like? "You're not afraid of them. You feel like you have protection. You can take more risks, I guess." Then she remembered so many months ago, outside a bar with Brian and Chris, when the man pulled a gun on them and she'd smote the fire hydrant. Who'd been carrying the gun there, really?

"Can we leave guns out of it?" she said. "I'm kind of sick of them."

"Great thinking. We'll circle back to this one, because there's something here, but I don't know what."

Judith looked down at her list again. "Okay, fourth commandment: Claim power over yourself, not others."

Wendy appeared shocked at first but wrote it on the board without any questions.

"What? What is it?" Jessica asked.

"It's just really good, that's all." She turned to them again. "And number five?

"We ... we don't know."

The publicist blinked. "You don't know the fifth commandment?"

They shook their heads.

"Then why five?"

Jessica shrugged. "Seemed like a good number."

"How about this, then: God is a woman."

"Oh, yeah, that's pretty good," said Jessica.

"And maybe," Wendy suggested, "we make it the first one?"

They agreed to that, and she wrote it down at the top, renumbering the list. "Okay, so the landing page will contain the five commandments—once we've ironed them out a bit more—a professional photo of you, and an email sign-up form."

Jessica straightened. "Time out. Why do I have to be on there?"

Wendy put her fists on her waist. "Are we back to this? I thought you were owning this now."

"I am, but who wants to see my face? The nicest thing anyone could say about it is that it's average."

"And it's the face of God. They could say that about it, too," the publicist snapped. "You have the perfect face for this, Jessica. If you were any prettier, you'd give people a reason to hate you for that. If you were any uglier, people wouldn't want to look at you. Your plain, symmetrical, pale face is perfect. I couldn't have picked a better one if I'd been asked to."

"That was almost a compliment."

"Don't be thick. It *was* a compliment."

Judith said, "I like how she serves up compliments."

"With a side of insult?"

"We'll get you a professional photo, don't worry," Wendy continued. "And you bet your butt it'll be touched up. We can't have the messiah sporting a giant chin pimple."

"I ate a lot of gas station food on the trip. It's not like that's always there."

"My point is that you're in good hands."

"And what about the sign-up form? What are they signing up for?"

"Ownership."

Jessica scanned the other two faces in the room to see if that sounded as ominous to them as it did her. "Ownership of what?"

"This idea. We need buy-in right away. We're generating leads. Anyone who signs up for more information is someone who we could potentially tap for money later."

"Now, wait a second—"

"Being the moochsiah protected you this time, but you can't live that way forever, and neither can a church. Trust me. Have I ever led you astray?"

"Probably, but I can't think of when right now."

"No. The answer is no. The only time you get into trouble is when you don't follow my advice to a T."

She was too tired to argue. "What happens when Dolores finds out I have money?"

Wendy capped the marker and joined them at the table. "I ask you, have you heard anything at all about the lawsuit in the last week?"

"I saw a story about it on Thornton News."

"First of all, you shouldn't be reading that. But also, we only care about Thornton News if what happens there doesn't stay there. Let his devoted readers foam at the mouth. We don't need them. The other stations haven't picked up the story because they don't know where their viewers will fall. Will they side with you? Will they take Dolores's side? You're in the wrong legally, but she's in the wrong morally.

"Meanwhile, how many people have texted you in the

last week about the video of you resurrecting a mother and her two children halfway across the country?"

Okay, she was starting to get the point. "Probably two or three dozen."

"Exactly. I think you have the Devil running scared, Jessica. If you start to have your own money and she tries to take it, let her. We'll make it the top story on every station. *Daughter of God Sued for Performing Miracles, Helping Homeless.* Can't you see it? That headline is our ace in the hole!"

Jessica had always thought Angry Wendy was terrifying, but Excited Wendy was something else entirely. She was dangerous, bloodthirsty.

"Okay," Jessica said. "I guess I could accept a little money. But I don't want to be a cult leader."

"Deal. Most of the money will technically be the church's, anyway, so it'll be safe from the lawsuit."

"I don't want the church to be rich either."

"No problem. You get paid enough to buy your own groceries, Cash and I finally get paid for our time, and then we give the rest to charity."

"Um, hello?" Judith raised her hand. "I don't scribe for free."

"Okay, we'll set aside a little for you."

It was really happening. Not just a religion but a church. She would have a church of her own. It gave her a fingerhold in this crazy endeavor, somewhere physical where her teachings (the idea seemed ridiculous) could live. So why did this feel so ... icky?

YOU HAVE NOT HAD GREAT EXPERIENCES IN CHURCHES.

Am I doing the wrong thing here? It sure feels like it.

SOMETIMES THE WRONG THING LEADS TO THE RIGHT ONE.

So, this is the wrong thing? What are you saying?

I AM SAYING YOU MUST FOLLOW THIS PATH.

You promise it won't get me martyred?

The Lord laughed. *I WILL PROMISE NO SUCH THING. BUT THERE ARE WORSE THINGS THAN BEING MARTYRED.*

Like what?

BEING WHIPPED AND STARVED AND HAVING YOUR PENIS CHOPPED OFF AND FED TO YOU AND THEN BEING SET ON FIRE AND ALL FOR NO REASON AT ALL.

Holy fucking shit. What's wrong with you?

YOU ASKED.

"You okay?" Wendy was staring at her with great concern.

She blinked. "Huh?"

"Are you okay? It looks like you're going to be sick."

She nodded. "I'm fine."

"And the website? Are you good to launch?"

She inhaled deeply. There were worse things than being martyred. "Yeah, let's do it."

Chapter Twenty-Three

The waiter made his way around the large, circular table of Rich's Steakhouse, filling each empty long-stemmed glass with the red wine Jessica had selected based on the fact that she thought she could pronounce all the words in it. She'd been wrong about that.

Chris would be picking up the tab for her birthday dinner, even though he hadn't said it outright. He hadn't needed to. He'd flown to Austin for it and it was on his suggestion that they'd picked this restaurant where none but Jeremy Archer could regularly afford to eat.

He was just her friend, though. They'd made that clear, or at least clear-ish, in Philadelphia. Sometimes one friend would fly across the country to celebrate the twenty-third birthday of another friend and pick up the astronomical tab for all of it. No big deal. It didn't have to mean anything. And it definitely didn't have to make the friend whose birthday it was inexplicably nervous. It definitely didn't need to make her mind spin and cause indigestion.

Jessica drank down half her wine then stared at her glass. Was *this* what good wine tasted like? It was like all the wines she'd had before except she liked it. Noted.

Joining her for the celebration were the usuals: Destinee, Rex, Quentin, Judith, Brian, Jeremy, and Jesus. But at Chris's suggestion, she'd also invited Wendy, Cash, Maria, and Gabrielle. The latter hadn't been able to make it, citing a family event, but Jessica thought the woman might just be smart about not mixing work and play.

As the wine kicked in, her inner turmoil diminished, and she felt a dopey smile taking residence on her face. It was her birthday, after all. Lots of people enjoyed their birthday each year, and while hers hadn't always been joyous occasions, it looked like, at twenty-three, her luck was finally changing.

The waiter came back to take appetizer orders, and Jessica leaned forward and addressed her guests. "Remember, nothing with pork. We can't be seen eating that right now."

Wendy nodded enthusiastically. "Exactly right. Looks like you're learning something."

Destinee's shoulders drooped. "So that means bacon-wrapped scallops are out?"

"Yes."

"Well, damn, baby! I really wanted to taste my first scallop. It ain't like I'm gonna *screw* the bacon, I'm just gonna eat it."

Jessica looked up at the waiter, who seemed rightfully perplexed. "Can we get that appetizer without bacon?"

"So ... scallops?"

"Yeah."

"I just need one," Destinee interjected.

So Jessica amended with, "Just one scallop. Can we get just one scallop for her?"

It was no surprise that Chris was flanked by Quentin and Rex, both of whom were ravenous for his latest off-season training stories. He was happy to indulge them.

Meanwhile, Brian listened politely as Jeremy explained in detail how Florida didn't really exist —"Fiction!" Jesus cried in delight, playing his favorite game with his best friend—and Judith leaned close to Cash to gawk at something amusing on their phone. Cash scrolled, Judith laughed. Wendy and Maria, who Jessica suspected went back further than she even knew, whispered conspiratorially to each other before erupting here and there in peals of laughter.

And that left Destinee and Jessica.

"This is a good turnout, baby."

"Yeah, it is."

"I got you a little something."

"Huh?"

Destinee pulled out a small present from beneath the tablecloth. "It's not much."

A lump formed in Jessica's throat as she took the stuffed lioness from her mother. It had a red bow around its neck.

"I just remember you saying your spirit animal when you took those drugs was a lioness, and I thought that was pretty cool. It ain't much, but I've never been good at thinking up gifts for you, have I?"

"It's great, Mom."

Despite all of her favorite people being here, Jessica had the urge to sprint back to her apartment, slip under the covers, and cuddle the animal for the rest of the night.

"I think this is your year, baby. I just got a feeling about it. You been through a helluva lot, but you're stepping up, and that can only lead to good things."

"Do you remember that day when you had to pick me up at the zoo?"

"You bet I do."

Jessica looked down at the lioness. "That was a good day."

Destinee grinned. "You got to see the lions."

"In action."

The waiter interrupted their moment by setting a single wobbly scallop in front of Destinee. "Your appetizer, madam."

Jessica already knew this wouldn't meet her mother's expectations.

Destinee jabbed at it with a fork. "So... is it like flan or something?"

"No, Mom. It's from the sea."

"It is?"

"You didn't know what a scallop was before you ordered it?"

Jeremy's phone went off, blasting AC/DC. "Pardon me," he said, excusing himself from the conversation with Jesus and Brian. "I'd better take this." He got up from the table and stepped out.

A few seconds later, both Maria and Wendy were looking down at their phones, too. They shared a glance then excused themselves as well. Cash was the next and last to go and pulled their phone away from Judith to begin texting frantically as they stood and left without saying a word.

"It tastes like shrimp Jell-O," Destinee said around a mouthful. "Now I see why they add bacon to it."

Meanwhile, the remaining guests shared uncertain glances regarding the sudden departures.

Maybe there's been a massive terrorist attack, she thought hopefully. *Maybe this has nothing to do with me.*

But she knew. It was her birthday, after all, and things were going too well. She clutched the lioness close.

Jeremy was the first to return, and he offered no information, only took his seat and addressed Brian with, "Where were we? Ah yes, arctic Illuminati." ("Fact!" proclaimed Jesus.)

Jessica was torn—did she demand to know what his call had been all about or did she enjoy a few more moments of blissful ignorance.

She chose ignorance.

But when Wendy and Maria returned, she knew it was time for the bad news.

"I'm sorry," said the reporter. "I really hate to leave,

and I do appreciate the invitation, but I have to run and handle some ... work stuff."

Jessica nodded and tried to act like it was no big deal, and Chris thanked her for coming with an overlong hug. Once she departed, Wendy, still standing, said, "Jessica, can I have a word?"

She swilled a fresh pour of red wine in her tall glass because she assumed that was how it was done, and then she took a long drink from it before saying, "Just say whatever it is here. I assume the party is ruined, so you might as well come out with it. I'll tell everyone here eventually."

Wendy's eyes roamed the rest of the guests, then she said, "Your call," and took a seat. "Jimmy Dean has just announced the end of the world."

Jessica closed her eyes to collect herself as the brunt of the news traveled through her.

Of course he had. Of course Jimmy fucking Dean had declared another Doomsday on today of all days. It was her birthday, after all. Why *wouldn't* he announce the end of the world? It was essentially his way of buying her a birthday card.

"That rat bastard!" Destinee spat as Rex nodded along supportively.

Quentin was the first to ask the most obvious question: "When does the clock run out?"

Wendy gazed mournfully at him. "July seventh of next year."

Jessica squeezed her eyes shut tighter.

There was silence at the table as the restaurant clatter took on the feel of protective armor. There was the outside world, and then there was Rich's Steakhouse. She didn't have to leave where she was just yet, but she knew what was waiting for her out there. Maybe that's why the wealthy visited places like this so often. It felt nice to step outside of the real world with all its messiness once in a while. Or maybe even frequently. As much as possible.

Then Chris said, "But it's not ... he doesn't know what he's talking about, right?"

Jessica opened her eyes. Everyone was looking at her. "Um ... God hasn't mentioned anything about that, if that's what you're wondering."

THE LORD DIDN'T MENTION IT BECAUSE IT IS NOT TRUE. THE EARTH IS GOING TO CONTINUE FOR AN EXCRUCIATINGLY LONG AMOUNT OF TIME. YOUR KIND WILL HAVE KILLED ITSELF OFF IN THE MOST SPECTACULARLY UNNECESSARY AND AVOIDABLE WAY BY THEN.

"God just confirmed. The world will go on and, well, it's not going to have a happy ending, but that's a long ways off. Not our most immediate problem."

Chris appeared incredibly relieved, but Wendy didn't find it so comforting, which made sense. The prospect of only having to spend another year working for Jessica definitely had its appeal.

"I know he was far too quiet," Wendy said. "He's been plotting. So now the question becomes what is he really up to? Is this just a way to distract from the church's scandal, or is there some other move he's making? If I know Jimmy, he doesn't stay on the defensive for long. He's the epitome of the adage 'a good defense is a strong offense,' so we need to figure it out."

"Well," Chris said hopefully, clearly trying to lighten the mood. "We have a whole year to do that, don't we?" He nodded, looking around the table for agreement.

"There's something else." And now Wendy cringed, and that was a bad sign.

Jessica motioned for her to come out with it.

"He's forecasted that the end of the world will be brought upon by ... you, Jessica."

Jessica nodded. "Naturally. But I've done the Antichrist thing before. I know the game."

"Not like this," Wendy said. "Not with the clock ticking down toward the end of the world."

"You're right," she conceded. "But I'm a little drunk, so I'm going to pretend it's not a big deal."

"Right, right." Wendy forced a minute smile and flattened the cloth napkin on her lap. "As long as you know that it's happening and you can manage until we figure something out, I don't see why you shouldn't get to enjoy your birthday. The next one will be ... Well, we'll deal with it."

"Perfect." Jessica raised her glass. "I'm a pro at *dealing* with things. Now, if you'd said we'll enjoy it, that would be a problem. But dealing I can do."

Chapter Twenty-Four

361:11:45:12 until Doomsday

The reality of Jimmy's stunt had sunk in quite sufficiently over the last few days. But now it was time for Jessica to make a move, and, boy, would she rather be doing anything else.

She stretched out on her couch, wondering if it was too early for a beer, and addressed the face staring back from the laptop perched on her thighs.

"I don't know, Wendy. Is this *absolutely* necessary?"

"Don't tell me you're getting cold feet. Quentin, will you please remind her that this is necessary?"

Quentin, who had stopped by on his lunch break and was now scrolling on his phone screen from the chair opposite the couch said, "I'm just the moral support. I don't make the arguments."

Her across-the-hall neighbors had spotted Quentin on

his way in and had invited themselves to the party. She didn't particularly mind, though she did wish Jeremy would stop wearing his new 5G protective gear—a hockey mask and thermal blanket cape—every time he stepped outside his condo. The crinkling sounds whenever he moved were grating on her nerves. "I think if anyone's going to be the moral support," he said, "it's that one." He nodded at Jesus, who snapped, "You're not still mad about that, are you? I already apologized for judging you."

"Too little, too late," Jeremy replied, his words muffled by the plastic face covering.

"You promoted a pharmaceutical that is known to cause testicular cancer!"

He tilted up his mask. "Everything causes testicular cancer! Carrying your cell phone in your front pocket, eating legumes, masturbating with your non-dominant hand. Everything!"

Wendy said, "Anyway, it's going live. That's just the way it is. It needs to happen, you already agreed to it, and it's time. We've wasted days after Jimmy's announcement. We need to ride the wave of his nonsense!"

"Fine," Jessica said. "Do it."

On her screen, Cash, whose pale face blended into their white-wall background, glanced up from their phone and said, "Oh, are we finally ready? Great. There it is. All live. Now hit refresh."

Jessica did, and the landing page that had previously only held a picture of her, her five commandments, and a sign-up form now, at the top, had a gigantic PLEDGE button.

A taste like toxic waste crept into her mouth, and she fetched a can of Dr. Pepper from the fridge before returning to the laptop.

"And I just sent out the email about pledges to all your subscribers," Cash added. "Once the IRS approves our new status, we'll notify the list and all the pledges will be charged to the cards on file."

"Oh crap," she groaned. "I just asked thousands of people to give me money." Her mouth went dry and she treated it with the coke. How many donations would she get from thousands of subscribers? Was she comfortable receiving that much money from strangers?

"Not thousands," Cash replied. "One point eight million."

The bubbles from the coke choked her, and she struggled not to dribble down herself. "Shut up."

"No, *you* shut up, bitch."

She looked at Quentin for backup. He flashed her two thumbs up and a cheesy grin. Worst moral support ever.

"Okay, I gotta ... do other stuff. I'll talk to you two later."

Wendy and Cash had hardly said goodbye before she slammed the laptop shut.

"I guess I run a church now. Shit."

Jeremy and Jesus were still bickering about cancer, but when she spoke, they called a timeout to stare at her. Jesus walked over, set a hand on her shoulder, and said, "Bless you, sister."

She flicked it off her. "I didn't sneeze. Save it."

"You are concerned about how this will play out. I understand. But I have faith in you and your ability to handle even the darkest of situations. I truly believe you will find a way to spread your sacred message."

"I love you, Jesus, but can you go away for a little while?"

He pressed his palms together and bowed. "Of course, my sister."

Jeremy took the hint and, with a great crinkling of his thermal blanket, got up as well. As he passed her, he, too, grabbed her shoulder. "Let me know the *moment* you're a 501(c)(3), and my corporation will donate more tax-deductible money than you know what to do with."

She couldn't help but think that sounded like a threat.

Once they were gone Quentin joined her over on the couch but didn't say anything right away.

"Why can't things just be normal ever? Why am I twenty-three and having to sort through emotions surrounding donations from people who believe something I don't even believe myself and a fucking Texas Railroad Commissioner who's just announced I'm going to bring about the end of the world on my next birthday?"

Quentin shrugged. "Everyone's got problems, Jess. Yours are just unique to you."

"And what are *your* problems?"

"I'm single. My boss is a white guy who thinks it's okay

to use the N-word when we're out for drinks, my best friend pretty much lives her life from one self-pity spiral to the next and is always in a state of chaos on a biblical level, and even though I make good money at my job, I'm struggling to amass any wealth because I have an obligation to support my parents and grandparents who never had a chance to build wealth for themselves because of redlining, income inequality, and all the other setbacks of being black in the Jim Crow South."

Jessica narrowed her eyes at him. "Wait. I'm your best friend?"

He sighed, pressing his lips together tightly before saying, "Looks like it."

"Don't sound so down."

"I apologize. Our time together is always uplifting and never emotionally exhausting."

Her mind leaped to Miranda, her archetypal Best Friend. The lithe blonde figure had faded to hardly more than a subconscious specter over their years apart and months without speaking. Jessica hadn't even called her while she was in California on the road trip. That wasn't how best friends behaved.

Who had assumed the title after Miranda, then? Chris, certainly, though she hadn't realized it at the time. He had been something else in her mind while Miranda continued to hold that title, unexamined, of "best friend." But now? Now that her relationship with Chris was over and he was hardly more than her puppy eyed sugar daddy?

Quentin. Quentin always showed up.

"For what it's worth," she replied, "you're my best friend, too."

Vulnerability hung in the air between them, and he cocked his head to the side, eyeing her closely. "Are we ... are we about to make out?"

She rolled her eyes. "Man, you *do* need to get laid."

"You're telling me."

"I'm surprised Chris isn't your best friend."

"He was, but it's sort of a requirement of mine that my best friend is there for me when I need him, and Chris... well, you know."

"I do. I think he was my best friend for a long time, too."

Quentin cursed. "That two-timing son of a bitch. He was best friends with *both* of us and thought we wouldn't find out?"

"Thankfully he's miserable without us, up there in Philly, living out his childhood dreams."

Quentin laughed. "What were your childhood dreams?"

"Ew. Let's not even talk about it."

"Mine was to work at NASA."

"Astronaut?"

"Sadly, no. I was too nerdy for that. I wanted to be in the control room."

"Bullshit. No kid looks at NASA and wants to be in the control room."

"I did."

"Then I guess you're right about everyone having problems."

"Now you gotta tell me yours."

"My what?"

"Your childhood dreams."

She shook her head. "I don't."

"You do."

"Why does it even matter? I'm locked into this whole messiah thing. I'm happier if I don't think about what I want."

"What happens once you do this thing? Once you bring peace to the United States? You could have decades of your life left. What then?"

Her shoulders slumped. "I've always assumed I wouldn't live past that point. That doing what I was put here to do would require dying."

"Jesus."

"Yeah, like that."

"That's grim."

"And true."

"But what if that's not the end? What if you knock it out in the next couple of years? What would you do then?"

"Not a clue."

Quentin's tone softened. "That's really sad, Jessica. Like, I'm genuinely sad for you."

"Don't be." And as he scooted closer to her on the couch, she put her hands out to push him back. "Oh, come on. Don't— You don't need It's not that bad." But too late. She was already wrapped up in his arms, the side of her head pressed against his chest.

She stopped fighting.

She should say something, but what?

IF THIS ISN'T JUST THE SWEETEST THING THE LORD EVER DID SEE. BLESS YOUR PRECIOUS HEARTS.

Jessica jerked back, eyes wide, staring at Quentin.

He held up his hands defensively. "That's a tube of Chapstick, I swear. I always keep it in my pocket."

"No, it's not that."

Say that again?

But the Lord was silent now. Had she misheard?

"What?" Quentin said, more frantically now.

"God just spoke to me. And the voice sounded ... feminine."

His mouth opened slowly. "Do you think ...?"

"It sure sounded like it."

"We should check the website."

He opened her laptop and refreshed the website to check total pledges.

He gasped. She would have gasped, but she was unable to suck any air into her lungs.

Over three hundred thousand dollars. Quentin refreshed. Three hundred and twenty thousand. He refreshed again. Three hundred and twenty-three thousand.

"Holy shit," Jessica breathed. "It's working. They're starting to believe."

Chapter Twenty-Five

354:13:53:45 until Doomsday

The next week of pretending her new church wasn't absolutely raking in the dough was a blur. Wendy had advised her to keep up her normal routine—after all, money never went as far as it seemed like it would, so seven million dollars for a church was hardly more than pocket change.

That was bullshit, of course, and Jessica knew it. Seven million dollars was seven million dollars. It would more than pay for Wendy, Cash, Judith, and Jessica's groceries with plenty left over to start construction and outreach. But what kind of outreach would she do?

She considered that thoroughly during her morning spent at Waverly Hills Retirement Home.

I could hire better staff here for a start. Could she do that? She might have to buy the place outright, but a few more weeks of the cash pouring in like it had been, and she could probably afford to do it. But did she really *want* to?

It'd been a long morning of volunteering made even longer by the fact that only one of her favorite residents had been available to visit. Santorini was napping, and Jan had some distant niece visiting, no doubt to hit her up for money.

But at least she'd avoided Rosemary Heathrow, so the conflict had been minimal.

Jessica dropped her name tag off at the front desk but didn't bother signing up for a future shift. No need to set the date in stone, and there was never a waiting list.

She had just stepped out into the hot summer sun, felt the scorching heat from above meet the sweltering waves from the asphalt below, making her feel a bit like a microwavable meal, when the worst possible thing happened.

A white Rolls Royce pulled into the parking lot. She'd never seen the car before, but her radar for disaster started to ping right away.

Not bothering to park legally, the driver pulled straight into the semi-circular resident drop-off area in front of her and killed the engine. Through the heavily tinted windows, she could just make out his bright white suit.

"Jessica, my dear!" Jimmy shouted as he gracefully exited the vehicle and immediately turned her way. "What a surprise!" He shut the door and walked around toward her.

"You mean to tell me you just happened to be visiting Waverly Hills?"

He chuckled, showing off his teeth, which were whiter since the last time she'd seen him. Any further bleaching, and she'd be able to gaze right through them. "You got me," he said. "I heard you'd be here, and I've been so eager to have a chat."

He reached her and tried to put an arm around her shoulder, but she twisted and karate chopped it away in time.

An orderly passed them, back from his lunch break, and said, "Afternoon, Reverend Dean."

"And a blessed afternoon to you too," he called back before mumbling, "whoever you are."

"How did he know your name?" she asked.

"Everyone knows my name. Come. Let's have a chat."

Jessica searched her memory—surely she'd filed a restraining order against Jimmy Dean at some point, right? But she couldn't recall having actually done it. Gross oversight on her part, then.

"I don't want to chat with you. I can't even stand to look at you. I mean that in the most literal sense. That suit reflects so much sunlight directly into my eyes, I'm fixing to slap those sunglasses right off your head and claim them as my own."

"Oh, my dear, sweet child! You have your mother's sense of humor."

"And you have the Devil's."

That shut him up. He leaned forward, his grandiose

facade evaporating. "I really need to speak with you. I think we could both help each other out quite a bit."

The implication of his words hit her, and she felt instantly giddy. Jimmy would never offer to help her out. Not really. He would, however, try to get her to help him.

Which meant he needed her help.

He was in trouble.

She had the upper hand.

Unfortunately, she had no fucking clue what to do with that.

So, she reached in her purse and pulled out Wendy Peterman's card. "Call my publicist. If you want to talk, she'll arrange something."

She stepped around him while he was still reading the card. As she made for her car, she heard another orderly say, "Welcome, Reverend Dean. We weren't expecting you today but—"

"I'm just on my way out," Jimmy snapped.

And before she even unlocked her driver's side door, the Rolls Royce sped away from Waverly Hills.

Chapter Twenty-Six

351:10:03:02 until Doomsday

"They love you, sister!" Jesus insisted as he led her down the street toward his new favorite homeless shelter.

"I don't believe you."

"It is true! I've been telling them about your mission for months now, and they are excited to speak with you!"

She stopped walking. "So, like, do I need personal security?" She certainly had the money for it sitting in the church's bank account. It wouldn't be ideal to take money away for security purposes, but she *was* kind of important to the continuation of the budding religion, and there were still millions of people left to convince.

"No, no," Jesus assured her. "They promised to be on their best behavior."

She was aware that "best" meant different things to different people.

But when she entered the shelter's cafeteria, she discovered something strange: Jesus had known what he was talking about.

"Hello, friends!" he proclaimed. When those already at the tables saw him, they cheered and waved.

Wow. He'd really made an impression. His hard work was paying off. Jesus, king of the hobos. Good for him.

"This is my sister, Jessica!" He pointed emphatically at her and a slightly smaller portion of the crowd cheered.

She waved timidly. "What's happening?" she whispered.

"They love you! They want to follow you!"

She hoped he didn't mean literally. "But why? Did they donate to the church?"

"Donate? Of course not, sister. What would they donate, a soiled shoe?"

"Then how did you get them to like me if they're not financially invested in me?"

"To be fair, many of them still do not, so if you have anything of value in your pockets, keep an eye on it."

"And for those who *won't* mug me?"

He led her over to the kitchen to glove and apron up and get in the serving line. "It was simple once I got to know them. They struggle with an assortment of issues and demons—not literally—well, sometimes literally—but there was one thing that kept emerging. One need that I could sense in them."

"And that was?"

"I simply asked them to imagine the last time someone

held them. Not restrained them, because that's where a lot of their minds went, but lovingly held them. I asked them who it was. It was always a woman. And I told them that is because God is a woman and following you could give them that feeling."

On the menu was shredded chicken that smelled more like fish, something that looked like creamed spinach, and, of course, some rolls that she'd low-key miracle before serving. "I'm not holding them. I don't mean to sound cruel, but it just doesn't seem hygienic or safe."

"It is neither. But you don't have to hold them, sister. The goal is simply to help them remember that someone, sometime, held them like that. They want to be nurtured. They end up here because when they really needed it, they were not. These are the people we have forgotten. They just want to know someone cares. And you do."

Did she, though? She was here serving them, so maybe that was something. But her need to recoil slightly upon seeing one of the homeless folks move toward her too quickly or catching a whiff of one in close quarters hadn't disappeared. Could she truly care about people who repulsed her like that?

"You care, too," she said. "And one of these days, I'm going to understand how you do it."

He beamed as he slipped on the hair net. "It's not hard. You just look at them and love them."

"I'll give it a try."

They approached the line and a woman came through.

Her blonde hair was in unintentional dreadlocks and one of her eyes was halfway closed.

Jesus was ahead of Jessica in the serving order, and said, "What can I serve you today, Harmony?"

The woman turned her fully open eye to Jesus, then down to the various food vats. "That." She pointed at the creamed spinach.

There was something about the way she said *that* that broke Jessica's heart. It was childlike but full of a deep exhaustion and futility. Who was this woman? What had she been through? Could Jessica love her?

"And what can I get for you today?" Jessica asked a moment later.

"That." The woman pointed at the chicken.

"Harmony," Jesus said, "this is my sister, the one I told you about. The daughter of God."

Harmony nodded slightly, accepted the shredded chicken and a roll, and then carried her plate over to an empty seat.

"She comes from a place called Iowa," Jesus explained. "Her family found out she was a homosexual when she was fifteen and kicked her out. She has been addicted to drugs ever since. I hugged her and she cried. She hadn't been properly held in seventeen years."

"Jesus Christ," Jessica mumbled, feeling a tsunami of unwelcome emotion gathering a few miles offshore.

"Darius!" Jesus proclaimed as a man entered the dining hall and made for the serving line. Darius scratched at his arms and looked around frantically. He wore shorts that exposed dark, cracked skin on his calves with angry red dots speckled around. Bug bites? Injection sites? She didn't let her gaze linger.

Upon hearing his own name, Darius's eyes went wide until he saw who had spoken. He hurried over to Jesus. "They're following me. The cops been following me for the last seven blocks. They gonna kill me."

"I'll make sure that doesn't happen," Jesus said. "Creamed spinach?"

"Yeah, summa that. How you gonna make sure it doesn't happen? They can get away with whatever they want. They're the law!"

"They are the law of the *land*. But look who I have with me, Darius. This is my sister Jessica who I told you about. God's daughter. She can smite evildoers with the power of Mother God."

Jessica struggled to stand her ground against Darius's intense gaze. "That's me," she said.

He took his creamed spinach and moved down the line closer to her. "You're God's daughter?"

"Yep."

"Then your Mother can go *fuck* Herself."

Jessica laughed before she could help it. "I feel the same way sometimes." She slopped the chicken onto the plate. "It's nice to hear someone else be so honest about it."

He grabbed his tray and left.

"What happened when you hugged *him*?" she asked.

Jesus shook his head slowly like a proud father. "He punched me the first few times I tried. But, you know, I've had worse. Finally he let me do it, but only when he was sure no one was looking. I think he liked it, even though he shoved me and called me a name right after it. He has been nicer to me since."

"Hey, what ever happened to your slogan of treat every homeless person like they have a gun?"

"Oh, that was not for *me*. That was for the rest of the world. Nothing I could say would elicit the sympathy they deserve from the public, so I decided the next best thing was simple protection. Besides, in my experience, they do not carry guns. They carry knives." He pulled up the sleeve of his Ratt T-shirt (he still liked to borrow Jeremy's clothes now and again, even though he had his own) to expose a mean scar running down his left bicep.

"Jesus! Did one of them do that to you?"

"Yes." He let his sleeve fall again. "Tommy Twitcher. Right over there. The one in the dark green jacket."

"Which one in the dark green jacket?"

"The one brandishing his spork at that other man."

"He stabbed you and you still come back?"

Jesus chuckled. "I would hardly call it a stab. More a defensive swipe. In his defense, the drugs he was on caused him to truly believe in his heart that I was a zombie."

"Well, he wasn't far off, was he?"

Jesus's eyes lit up. "Ah yes, I hadn't thought about that! Perhaps the Twitch is a prophet!"

Jessica watched the man in question. Could he be a prophet? But she didn't have to wonder about that long, because Twitch dropped the spork, jumped up onto the bench, and whipped out his dick. To what end, she wasn't sure. But it was out.

"Did you ever hold him?" she asked.

"Oh, heavens no. He would have killed me."

Chapter Twenty-Seven

347:09:25:31 until Doomsday

Wendy Peterman had the AC in her Mercedes on full blast as the audio from her phone fed through the Bluetooth. Jessica watched the screen closely. Apparently, whatever Jameson Fractal had organized with his buddies in his free time between projects had the publicist's stamp of approval, so it must be good.

The ad was similar to the NFL PSA Chris had spearheaded, except it wasn't horribly written. The format was much the same, though.

Face after famous face flipped by, each reading from the same sappy script. She even recognized a few of Jameson's friends from the Dark & Dirty franchise, the ones she'd spent a lovely autumn day with at the music festival the previous year. There was Bolt Stevens and Valerie Villarreal and also Jon Damien and a few more she recognized from movies but had no idea Jameson knew. But of course he knew all kinds of famous people.

There was no equivalent of "Women are people, too" in this one, and in fact, the messaging seemed rather bland to her. It didn't even mention God.

Mostly, it was filled with statistics that made an argument *against* men. She wasn't exactly sure how that was pro-women. But she trusted Wendy. This was likely just phase one of a longer process of indoctrination.

When it was over, Jessica had hardly gotten out, "That's great, but will it work?" before an ad began to autoplay.

The sounds of oinking filled the car, and Jessica and Wendy exchanged a confused look before turning their attention back to the phone.

"Oh my ..." Wendy breathed.

The screen showed a happy farmer overlooking his pigs, who snorted and rooted in their pen. In the distance, a vivid Texas sunset. The farmer turned to the camera. "My girls are my livelihood. I want to make sure they live a good life before their time comes." The screen cut to one of the surfaced clips from Jimmy's rogue congregants. The brunt of the image was blurred, and it only stayed on-screen for a second, but the squealing carried on into the next shot: the farmer again, shaking his head. "I don't know about you, but I can't abide that sinful behavior. I don't think most people can."

The farmer's wife appeared in the shot, and he put his arm around her as she said, "And yet, what's being done?"

He pulled his wife closer, planting a kiss on the top of her head before asking the viewer, "What if that was *your* pig?"

It cut to another pig farmer on a sunny day with a blue sky stretching on behind him. "You think it's no big deal until it happens to *your* pig." The shot switched to another pig abuse video and the loudest grunting in this one wasn't coming from the victim. It was hardly more than half a second, but Jessica felt her stomach lurch, like intestinal whiplash, before it cut back to the second farmer again. His face was determined, his jaw firmly set, when he said, "That *was* my pig, and I'm here to tell you, it could be yours next."

"Oh, for fuck's sake," Jessica said, as the commercial ended with a quick announcement that it was paid for by the Coalition for Chaste Farming.

"Who in the hell started that?" Jessica asked.

Wendy opened her mouth to say something else before she looked through her windshield and said, "Oh! He's here."

She spotted Jimmy Dean walking down the sidewalk in front of the tall row of multiuse buildings heading for their designated meeting spot.

"And he's brought Eugene Thornton with him." Jessica groaned.

"That's not unexpected. He'll want an ally. I don't blame him. He's in a tight spot if he's trying to get your help."

They approached Maggie's Ice Cream, Jessica's heart

racing. She hoped it wasn't visible through her cotton V-neck. She didn't want anyone to know how nervous she really was.

When she'd handed Jimmy Dean Wendy's business card outside Waverly Hills Retirement Center, she'd never expected the woman would actually arrange a time to meet and talk. But here they were.

Even though Jimmy had bested and badgered Jessica countless times over her twenty-three years, she found that seeing him now, standing there by the entrance to an ice cream parlor, stirred hardly more than a niggle of annoyance within her. Perhaps it was because Jimmy had always been a fixture in her life. Even before she'd met him as a child, there were the calls to Destinee asking for money and the subsequent blue streaks from her mother's mouth that followed. Jimmy was like a chronic illness that flared up now and again, and perhaps on a subconscious level she'd come to accept that he would always be there, and that allowed her to feel entitled to roll her eyes at him and, if she was feeling in the mood, berate him openly. No matter what she did, he would remain an obnoxious reality, never much better or worse than the year before. Even his Doomsday proclamation, as rudely timed as it was, felt to some extent like business as usual. Once she'd had time to give it a little thought, she was a little surprised he hadn't done it sooner.

But setting eyes upon the loathsome reporter Jimmy had brought with him made her fingertips tingle with wrath. Eugene Thornton was maliciousness embodied. His attacks on her were less personal, and that made them somehow worse. At least Jimmy cared about her in his own fucked up way. Eugene Thornton would only mourn her death once the ratings from his coverage of it started to wane. He was cold, calculated, and, frankly, smarter than Jimmy. And yet the two of them had formed a sort of alliance. She'd never wanted to see a pair destroy itself more.

What if she smote the hell out of Eugene right there in broad daylight? She already knew the cops wouldn't arrest her for it. Her life would certainly be better off without him. Thornton News would be a mess. She'd have taken out one of Jimmy's main allies. It was a good strategic move, and it sure would set the tone for this entente.

She tried to visualize it as they crossed the street, but a flash from the last time she'd smote a person struck her like a stale loaf of bread to the face.

No. Smiting was better in theory than in reality, it seemed.

"Remember," Wendy said, "let me do the talking. We don't want to give them anything they can use against us, and I'm absolutely sure Jimmy is in some kind of pinch he hasn't told us about. We need to figure out what it is."

They came to a halt outside of Maggie's Ice Cream, two women squaring off against the two men. Eugene didn't even bother to smile politely, but that was okay, because Jimmy did enough grinning for the both of them. "Jessica! My dear, sweet—" He went in for a hug, but Wendy stepped between them and put a palm in Jimmy's face, pushing him back. "You do not touch her. Understood?"

A shadow passed across his face, but he stepped back and straightened his white suit. "I see your bodyguard doesn't understand the history we have."

"She does. That's why she won't let you touch me."

Jimmy leaned forward. "Jessica. Come on. It's me! Jimmy! We're just here to get ice cream together like old times!"

No way. He was trying to be Ice Cream Jimmy, but she hadn't seen that man in years. She was pretty sure Church Jimmy had smothered him in his sleep and fed him to the pigs.

"Whatever," she said. "Let's get this over with."

Jimmy jumped forward to hold the door for her, and she sighed, already knowing this was not going to be a pleasant afternoon.

"Welcome to Maggie's!" said a plump, white, brunette girl in a tie-dyed shirt and a Rastafarian beanie. Behind her, a pale and lanky teen boy with painful looking acne helped the customers ahead of them in line, pounding their toppings into a heap of ice cream with two flattened scoops like it had just pointed out his pimple in front of the entire school yard.

Jimmy stepped forward. "Uh, yes, can I sample the vanilla bean, the Mexican vanilla, the French vanilla, and the country cream?"

Jessica held herself rigidly as the four of them watched

the girl painstakingly dip a sample spoon into every kind of vanilla ice cream they carried.

Jimmy sucked off each one, moaning his appreciation with closed eyes, taking his sweet time.

Was this a power move? If so, it was a strange one.

"I think the Mexican vanilla wins," he announced jovially, turning to Jessica as if she would be thrilled to hear it.

"Great," she said, "order it. I don't give a shit."

Wendy elbowed her, and she remembered their discussion about not cursing during this meeting.

Jimmy ordered a large with hot fudge and marshmallows, and Eugene declined any ice cream at all. The girl plopped the giant ice cream scoop on the countertop, sprinkled on the marshmallows, and began pulverizing it.

Maybe I should've opened an ice cream shop. Spend my days pounding on something that can't fight back, that can't even found a church.

When the girl was done, she formed it into a ball, balanced it on the end of the scoop, and then threw the scoop into the air, catching the ice cream in the serving cup on the way down. Jimmy clapped, and Wendy rolled her eyes. She looked at Eugene, who was eyeing Jessica like a hawk would a field mouse.

Wendy practically snarled. "Why don't you make yourself useful and go get us a table?"

"Why? So you can threaten this poor man without it going on the record?"

The girl handed Jimmy his treat, and he took his first bite, a bit of the chocolate fudge sticking to his lip, and said, "You got this, right?" He motioned at the ice cream with his spoon.

Ah, she should have known. Before she could think of a suitable replacement for "Fuck right off, Jimmy," he nodded at Eugene, saying, "She's got this. Let's go grab a seat."

Wendy got a small coffee ice cream with chopped pecans, and Jessica ordered a medium country cream with peanut butter cups. She'd tried to order it with gummy bears, but Wendy'd nixed that, reminding her this was a professional meeting, and that topping wouldn't set the right tone.

Wendy offered to pay, citing the large sum she was earning from church donations, and Jessica allowed it, albeit with a small twinge of guilt.

They slid into a booth across from Eugene and Jimmy, who was almost done with his large serving already.

Jessica knew not to be the first one to break the silence. Granted, she only knew that because she'd been told it explicitly and then reminded of it multiple times since. On the table in front of Eugene Thornton was an electronic voice recorder. Wendy eyed it suspiciously.

"I expect all of this to be off the record."

"Of course. You have my word." He pressed the *record* button with some flourish.

"Mr. Dean," Wendy said.

"Railroad Commissioner Reverend Dean," he corrected as a dribble of chocolate sauce ran down his chin.

"I understand your desire to have someone backing you up at this meeting, but I do believe you've made the worst choice possible by bringing Mr. Thornton." She glared at the reporter. "That can be on the record."

Jimmy shook his head. "I trust Eugene more than anyone. He's always had my back when the mainstream media snubbed me."

"You're a fool, then," Wendy replied. "And that can be on the record, as well."

Jimmy finished the last of his treat, scraping the bottom to get every last bit. Jessica grabbed one of her napkins and handed it to him. He took it without a second thought and wiped his mouth with it, completely missing the dark blotch on the tip of his nose.

When he was satisfied, he said, "I know you think that of me, but guess what? I'm successful. Could a fool be as successful as I am?"

"Absolutely. *Only* a fool can have your level of success. Because only a fool would fail to see the many pitfalls of it."

"There aren't pitfalls to serving the Lord Our God on a mass scale."

"Then why are we here today, Mr. Dean?"

"Railroad Commissioner Reverend Dean." But now he looked less sure of himself.

Jessica scooped a large bite of mostly peanut butter cup into her mouth.

Jimmy sat up straighter in his seat, something Jessica had long known was a bullshit barometer for him. The straighter the spine, the heavier the load of hogwash he was about to serve up.

"I think we can help one another in a way like never before."

Wendy smiled. "You mean you need my client like never before."

"Not what I mean."

"Then go on. How can we help you?"

He glanced down at the recorder then mumbled to Eugene, "This *is* off the record, right?"

Eugene said nothing but nodded emphatically.

"Good, good." And now he addressed Jessica. "As I'm sure you're aware, White Light Church and its affiliated network of churches has been under quite a bit of scrutiny lately for the behavior of a few outliers."

Finally, Jessica spoke. "The pig fucking."

"If you want to call it that. I've had lawyers working on it night and day to calm the hysteria. But the videos just keep coming. I'm starting to believe those in the videos have never set foot in my holy chapels! There are just so many!" He leaned forward and whispered, "I suspect paid actors might be in play, or perhaps some sinful men who have had porcine desires for many years and have simply attended services at my church as a way to validate acting upon those desires."

Wendy said, "If that's not a sign to check in on what you're preaching, I don't know what is."

Jimmy glared daggers at her. "We have never and will never condone that sort of conduct."

Jessica said, "But you fetishize piglike behavior, tell everyone they're pigs, and preach that God is a hog. Where did you think that was going?"

"Certainly not to ... where we are now!"

Wendy cut in, "I don't understand how my client can help you with that. If you think she wants to get her reputation within a thousand feet of that mess, you're an even bigger fool than I thought."

"No, no. I've got the pig thing handled. Or at least I have people who are handling it, and it shouldn't last much longer."

"Not past July seventh of next year, for sure, right?"

Jimmy squinted at Wendy. "July seventh? What's happening then?"

She rolled her eyes. "The end of the world."

"Oh! Right! That. Yes. I almost forgot. It won't last beyond that."

"Then you can easily ride out less than a year of this scandal, can't you? Knowing it's going to be relatively short lived."

"Of course. But there's something else."

"There always is with you," Jessica grumbled.

"I lead a busy life. Conflict naturally arises. But this one is owed entirely to you and your choices, so I think it's only fair that you help me clean it up."

Wendy put a controlling hand on Jessica's knee, and she took the hint and stayed quiet.

"My client owes you nothing."

"Ah, but she does. Because her foolishness forfeited her personal brand to another. When that happened, I was worried how it might affect my church. After all, she plays a key role in the scripture."

"And what *is* that role precisely?" Jessica blurted. "It seems to change day to day."

"The role is irrelevant," Jimmy said. "You represent many things to many people. But you are, and always have been, Jessica Christ."

"I thought I was the Antichrist now, bringing about the end of the world."

"You are. You are Jessica Christ, the Antichrist. The product of Original Sin seducing Deus Aper and spreading your swine-like filth across this great godly nation."

"And you wonder why people are roasting pigs on their special spit," Jessica said.

"When you proclaimed yourself God's daughter in Atlanta, you set off a chain of legal events. Not only did you get yourself sued, but you also provided Dolores Thomas enough evidence to begin suing White Light Church for trademark infringement. Believe it or not, you openly owning your birthright was the last piece she needed before filing suit against me."

Jessica shrugged. "I should've done it way sooner then."

Wendy stepped in. "She's trademarked it?"

"You didn't know?" He smirked. "Ah yes, she has."

"There's no way to uphold that. Your use of it predates her trademark. It's insane her paperwork was even approved."

"Be that as it may, she is also the wife of a congressman, and Congressman Thomas has connections."

"And you're on the Texas Railroad Commission," Wendy said, "you have connections, too. Don't play the victim here."

"Don't you see?" His eyes jumped uneasily to Eugene for a split second. "We know the same people. And, well, they aren't thrilled with me lately. I might have made some promises ... Well, that doesn't matter. The point is that the pig scandal can be managed, but to add this on top of it ... it's stretching my resources a little thin. You know Dolores Thomas, though. This is where I need your help."

Jessica, who had tried but failed to follow along with his insinuations, understood this last bit just fine. She knew about Dolores Thomas, and he needed that intel. "I can't help you, Jimmy."

"But you two go way back. You could talk with her and ask her to drop the suit against White Light Church in exchange for payment. I understand you now have a church of your own that is impressively funded."

Wendy said, "A reality does not exist in which my client would do that for you."

"Then can your client at least tell me what she knows about Dolores that might prove useful in this situation?"

Wendy's nostrils flared almost imperceptibly. "If we knew something about her that could help anything, don't you think we would have used that to fight our own lawsuit already?"

But Jessica did know something.

TELL HIM.

She almost didn't recognize the voice, what with its slightly higher pitch and tone of helpful suggestion rather than forceful command.

Are you sure? If he knows the Devil is a woman, don't you think he'll use that against us?

LET HIM TRY.

The hair on Jessica's arms stood up, and a small shiver ran through her. *Yes, ma'am.*

"She's the Devil."

There was silence, and Wendy sighed and took a rather large bite of her melting ice cream.

"Sorry," Jessica said, "but God suggested it." She turned to Jimmy again. "Dolores Thomas is the Devil."

"Are you speaking as someone who is currently being sued by her or—"

"The literal Devil incarnate. I know you're probably disappointed, because you wanted me to be the bad one, but I'm not. It's her."

Finally, Eugene spoke. "Many would call what you just said slander."

Wendy went to snatch his recorder away, but he was quicker and held it just out of her reach. "It's off the record," she growled. He shrugged.

"You mean to tell me," Jimmy said, a small glimmer in his eyes, "that I'm being *sued* by the Devil himself?"

"Herself. Yes."

"Wow." He slouched over, staring vaguely at a dent in the metal tabletop. "Wow." He straightened his spine. "That only goes to show how important my work is, that the Devil wants to stop it!"

"Oh, get off it," Jessica spat. "She just wants to ruin you because she wants to wipe any chance of people thinking I'm more than an average person off the face of the earth."

He arched a brow, amused. "You think this is about you?"

"Yeah, Jimmy. I do. I think this is all about me. And so do you. You built a whole fucking church around me! Whether you like me or not, you're *definitely* obsessed with me." She wasn't sure if that were true or not, but it sounded true, and his look of repulsion made it worth saying.

Eugene leaned forward. "Just to be clear, you're asserting that you believe the woman who is suing you for infringing upon a contract that you willingly signed and then violated is the literal Devil."

"She's asserting it *off the record*," Wendy snapped.

"On the record or off, it certainly makes her seem a little unstable. Not a great legal defense, either."

"So I made a deal with the Devil!" Jessica shouted. "I didn't know who she was at the time!"

Wendy leaned toward a group of teens two tables over who had halted their Bible study to gawk. "She doesn't mean it literally, don't worry."

They giggled at each other then turned back to their phones, Bibles remaining open and unread on the table.

Jimmy muttered, "You ain't kidding, are you?"

There it was. There *he* was. She recognized him in a heartbeat. Ice Cream Jimmy. "I'm serious. If you stand any chance of taking on the Devil, you need me, because I have God on my side."

He nodded. "All right. What do you say we team up?"

Wendy waved a hand between them to break up the brewing conspiracy. "Why on her Father's green—"

"Mother's green—"

"—Mother's green earth would she team up with you? What can you possibly offer her?"

Jimmy leaned back, lifting his chin to smile gently down at them. "I've only ever been truly gifted at one thing, and it just so happens to be the thing you need help with the most."

Jessica narrowed her eyes at him. "And what's that?"

"Starting churches. You have the resources now, but you completely lack the know-how. Sure, you have some rules, some commandments—yes, I've read them—but that's like assembling a scarecrow out of twigs and saying you've created life. You're lacking the spark, that special intangible something that transforms a building into a church and a few rules into a religion. But I can show you how to find that inside you."

Jessica felt sickened by the truth of it. The magic that the West Coast cult leaders exuded, the exclusivity of the Mormons, the fear mongering of the Midwestern pastors, and the charisma of the southern preachers—Jimmy had mastered it all, and it amounted to a following that grew exponentially, limited only by the rate at which he could open new locations. And that's what she needed if she stood any chance of changing the country.

"Would you give us a moment?" Wendy said, and then she grabbed her client by the arm and tugged her out of the booth and straight toward the ladies' room.

Jessica leaned against a mural of a cow eating ice cream, mostly so she didn't have to keep looking at it and wondering if that ice cream was made with milk from the cow's own udder, and Wendy paced back and forth past the sinks, deep in thought. Finally, she planted her high heels on the black-and-white checkered tile floor and said, "I think it's a good deal."

"Are you serious?"

"Very. You have nothing you can genuinely offer Jimmy that would help him with Dolores, and he has all kinds of knowledge that could benefit your cause."

"That assumes he's good to his word."

"Did you see the fear in his eyes? He now believes that he's up against the Devil. Most people wouldn't, but Jimmy is just narcissistic enough to believe that he's important enough to have the Devil herself come for him."

"But the Devil herself *is* coming for him."

"But only because of his relation to you."

"Ah, true. Does that make *me* a narcissist?"

"It would, if things weren't *truly* all revolving around

you. But you get to be the exception. By all means, let it go straight to your head. You could use the confidence."

Wendy planted her fists on her hips and declared, "We'll accept his offer, but we're going to have to be incredibly careful every step of the way with him."

"As soon as he doesn't need my help, he's going to betray us. He'll probably start the early stages of it right away."

"Of course he will. But because we know that, I can keep an eye out for it. In the meantime, we need to keep holding the Devil over his head to remind him that he needs us."

"This feels dangerous."

"It is. But I think it could also be great." She paused. "Have you ever wondered why God has kept Jimmy's crazy white ass around rather than giving him the smiting he deserves?"

"I always assumed God wanted to torture me."

"You know what happens when you assume."

"I've only learned it again and again."

After Wendy laid out a quick game plan for the rest of the meeting, the women left the restroom and returned to the table. Eugene's recorder was back on the table, and Jimmy was straightening his hair in the reflection of his phone screen.

Without sitting down, Wendy announced. "Okay, you have a deal. A verbal one, not a written one. We're not signing anything. If you tell anyone about this, we'll deny it to the grave."

"Same goes for me," Jimmy replied. "Last thing I need is my congregation catching wind that I'm in league with the Antichrist."

"You can stop calling me that now, Jimmy. No one here's buying it."

Wendy turned to Eugene, who sported a sly grin Jessica wanted to smite right off his face. "And you?"

"What about me?"

She turned to Jimmy. "Your fool ass brought him here. You better make him promise that this deal stays between the four of us."

Jimmy nodded. "Eugene, do we have your word?"

"Off the record?" He paused the tape recorder. "Yes, you do."

"You rat," Wendy spat. "You're going to tell everyone."

"Of course I won't. My word is as good as gold." He slid out of the booth, the grin still plastered in place. "You asked for all of this to be off the record."

"I did."

Jimmy stood as well, straightening out any wrinkles in his suit with two flat palms. The pig hooves at the end of his red stole clattered together. "Eugene has always been a man of his word. I have no reason to doubt him on this."

"Have you forgotten," Wendy replied, "that he's worked with the Devil herself only recently?"

Jimmy froze. Clearly that thought hadn't clicked into place. He turned to his ally. "You did, didn't you? You interviewed her for that exposé."

Eugene nodded unabashedly. "I did. She was very pleasant."

"She was the *Devil*, Eugene! Of course she was pleasant!"

The reporter laughed and tucked the device into his breast pocket. "No need to get worked up, Railroad Commissioner Reverend Dean."

While Jessica did love to see Jimmy's feathers ruffled, she couldn't fully enjoy it this time, since she, too, was feeling terribly uneasy about the way this was unfolding with the reporter.

Eugene made for the exit, leaving the others behind. Jimmy hurried to catch him, grabbing him high on the arm just before he made it through the front door. He slung the reporter around to face him. "Look me in the eye and promise me it was off the record. All of it. I need you to promise me that."

Eugene didn't hesitate. "I promise it was all off the record. Come on, Jimmy, it's me! We've been working together for years. Have I ever led you wrong?"

Jimmy let his arms fall from the reporter's shoulders. "No. No, you haven't."

Approaching the two men with Wendy in lockstep, Jessica said, "And Dolores didn't lead me wrong until she did."

As Eugene stepped out onto the sidewalk, Jimmy turned to the women, his arms outstretched like he was delivering a sermon. Church Jimmy just wouldn't let up, would he? "Fear not, my new partners! Our agreement still stands. All of it will be off the record."

And so it was at that very moment that, through the large front windows of Maggie's Ice Cream, Jessica witnessed a genuine act of God.

Or later she would classify it as such. In that moment, however, it felt more like permanent trauma.

The piano-size decorative typewriter wasn't there one moment, and then it was. It fell from the sky at a terrifying speed, landing with divine aim upon the head of Eugene Thornton. Or what was the head of Eugene Thornton one moment and little more than mush the next.

A violent splash of blood painted the windows, and only then did Jimmy drop his arms and turn toward the source of the crash.

Wendy let out a little squeak, but nobody moved. Somewhere behind them, a scoop of ice cream that had been twirling through the air fell to the floor.

Jessica hurried out to the sidewalk fueled only by morbid curiosity. Eugene's blood and guts were everywhere, but she suspected the bulk of him was still smooshed underneath the decorative typewriter. She looked for the source of the object. Five stories up a man stared off his tiny balcony, hand clasped over his mouth. "Is he okay?" he called stupidly.

Jessica ignored him.

Eugene Thornton was definitely not okay.

As the other two survivors of the Ice Cream Summit carefully stepped outside, Jimmy foolishly covering his head in case another giant object dropped from one of the condos above, Jessica spotted something silver on the ground. No ... it couldn't be. What were the odds?

Slim. But she had to admit that odds didn't seem to be much of a factor here.

Splotches of blood peppered the metallic object, but upon closer inspection, she determined it *was* the voice recorder. It had fallen free from his breast pocket as his breast was pulverized.

Did you do this?

She waited, and just when she was sure there would be no response, one came.

IT WAS NOT OFF THE RECORD.

Jessica nodded, and then, with the heel of her shoe, she stomped the recording device as hard as she could. "It's off the record now."

Chapter Twenty-Eight

340:07:29:59 until Doomsday

The "private room" of Bat-Ass Brew was more of a storage closet and less of a space that would pass health inspection. Spare toilet paper and eco-friendly to-go lids lined the walls in stacks, making the tight space even more claustrophobic. Jessica cradled a hot cup of Guano'nother between her palms and mentally reviewed the explicit rules Wendy had laid out for her prior to this encounter.

Jimmy didn't knock before letting himself in. He slipped inside quickly and, to Jessica's shock, was dressed much like a normal human being. That is, if the human being thought he was a jewel thief in a heist movie. Above his shiny black sneakers, he wore black tailored jeans and a long sleeve, button down, black shirt that was simply too hot for early August. Only once he'd closed the door did he remove his dark sunglasses, tucking them in his breast pocket.

"That was close," he said. "I'm pretty sure the man behind the counter recognized me."

"That's because I told him I was meeting you."

Jimmy's mouth formed a little O of betrayal.

"Easy there. It's just Rebel. I asked him to keep this on the DL, and I resurrected him one time, so he owes me. Also, I'm pretty sure he thinks he has a shot with me."

Jimmy maneuvered in the close quarters to his chair across the folding table from her. "Just like your mother. Using your sinful allure to control men."

"Oh, fuck off, Jimmy. Seriously. You can drop the act here. I assume it'd be a relief for you. Must be exhausting to be so insufferable all the time."

"I wouldn't know." He adjusted his right sleeve to check his wristwatch that was probably more expensive than Jessica's car. "I don't have long. Why don't you start by telling me what your efforts are thus far."

Can I trust him?

OF COURSE NOT.

God's voice was on the deeper side today, but she didn't let that worry her—the pitch varied day-to-day now based on recent donations to the church, which were affected by all sorts of strange factors like day of the week, moon phase, and low pressure fronts. On the whole, God's voice was trending up.

Then what do I do?

TELL HIM THE TRUTH.

That seems stupid.

THIS WHOLE ALLIANCE SEEMS STUPID. BUT ONLY BECAUSE THERE ARE SLIM ODDS THAT IT WILL NOT BE THE END OF YOU.

Thanks for the reassurance.

She filled Jimmy in on the website and the fact that money was still flowing in. She didn't provide specifics.

"So, you're telling me you have enough to pay consulting fees," was his reply.

"If you think I'm putting your name on any paperwork associated with my church, you've officially lost your mind."

"No, no ... of course not. You put it under one of my *assumed* names." He paused, and when she showed little sign of understanding, he added, "Wait, you haven't created any assumed names to help with cash flow?"

"No."

He exhaled loudly and dragged fingers through his salt and pepper hair. It fell back into place immediately. "This is a bigger job than I was led to believe. I don't see how it's a fair exchange without adding some payment to the mix to balance it out."

"You're right. I guess I can just *not* tell you what I know about the Devil and you can go home and deal with lawsuits coming at you from both ends on your own."

He was silent for a moment, took a small sip of his drink. "You can't be everywhere at once. You need to bring on more people. Those who will help spread your word."

"Like ... disciples?"

"Exactly. But more zealous than the ones in the Bible. You need them to step up and spread the gospel *before* you're dead and gone. And, also unlike Jesus, you must pay them."

"So, what, I just stick up a job posting somewhere?"

"No, no. You recruit through established channels. You have a sorority, correct? Start there. Don't mention money. You need people who would do it for free. But then once they're hired, you pay them, and you pay them well."

"Because?"

"Because *nothing's* free, Jessica. Not really. Life is a constant negotiation of power and position, and you *must* maintain power at all costs."

"So, I pay them because it ... gives me power?"

"You're good at math for a girl, right?"

She nodded.

"Think of it like that. Money equals power. But it's not the *having* money than brings power so much as it is the *spending* of it. Labor always converts into money, and since money equals power, labor converts into power. You following along? Good. Now, imagine you have a scale, like the justice ones, right? There's your side and theirs. When you owe someone something—whether that's money or labor—you have a little weight added to your side. The lower your side of the scale, the less power you have. And your debt to certain people, those who have lots of power themselves, will weigh more than debt to someone you could, say, have murdered without much fuss." He leaned closer. "Your side of the scale must always be higher than the person you're dealing with if you wish to maintain loyalty and control. If they give you labor and you pay them nothing, then it's weight to your side. Why, you may ask, when you got something from them for free? Because that's not the case. Nothing is free, nothing is free! They will recognize the imbalance instinctually and feel entitled to more power for themselves. They'll do that by seeking personal ownership of the endeavor. Nothing will lose you your power faster than bringing on volunteers. No, you pay them *twice* what they think they deserve, always. Remember, the spending of money is power. Keep it so that they feel indebted to you. Make sure they truly believe they cannot get from anyone else what they get from you. If you do that, they'll work harder and defend you more fiercely than you can ever dream."

"But don't I *want* people to take ownership of the church, to feel like they helped build it?"

"No."

"Oh, okay."

"I know you'll hate to hear this, Jessica, but your church needs you at the center. Everyone must believe that it will crumble without you. At least at first, when it's still small enough to control."

"And what happens later, when it grows beyond me?"

"You must end it."

"Like you're doing?"

He grinned and leaned back in his flimsy chair. "No, like *you're* doing. My followers don't believe I have anything to do with the end of the world, other than being the messenger of its arrival."

She hated to admit it, but he *was* good at this.

He tapped a pensive finger to his lips. "You're doing the 'girl power' thing, right?"

"We don't call it that, but yes."

"Then you'll need priestesses. Put them in long flowing dresses. Not white, obviously—they'll look like virgin sacrifices, and then you'll have people sacrificing virgins in no time. The menfolk will be able to think of nothing *but* sacrificing virgins after your services. No, put them in muted colors. A soft rose, an autumn orange. But all different colors. Not blue, though. Too calming. You can't let people relax if you want them to follow you. You must make sure they leave every ceremony you perform with more energy and vigor than when they came."

"What if I serve coffee at the services?"

Jimmy opened his mouth, then shut it again and stared down at his own coffee for a moment. When he looked up at her again, there was something not unlike respect in his eyes. "That's brilliant. You'll need to form a ritual and narrative around it, but it's so simple." He narrowed his eyes. "You might be better at this than I thought."

"And these priestesses, how do I train them?"

"Oh, that's easy. Find a threat—that's always a cinch—then you unite them against it. What do you think the biggest threat to your priestesses is?"

She didn't have to think about it. If she were recruiting from Nu Alpha Omega, she already knew. "Men."

Jimmy jerked his head back. "Men? You can't unite against *men*."

"Why not? Religion has been uniting against women for literally millennia. It's just been pretending it's all about protecting us. And if that's the case, it's done a shit job of it."

"No, no. You can't unite against half the population."

"Slightly less than half."

"It's too large, too powerful. You'll be crushed immediately. You must go after a smaller group, and one with fewer privileges. Jews or immigrants or scientists or something fashionable like that. Not blacks, though. That one doesn't work as well as it used to."

"Hmm ... big nope to *all* those. I'm sure I'll think of something suitable, though." There was a thoughtful pause before she changed the subject. "What's happening with the pig sex stuff? Is it really as widespread as the news is reporting?"

He didn't seem especially bothered by the topic. "As bad? It's *worse* than they're reporting. Much worse." He took a sip, then swirled the ice around before enjoying another.

"Will you at least admit that *maybe* your gospel had something to do with it?"

He chuckled. "It had everything to do with it. That's why I told you not to make your girls look like virgin sacrifices. Generally speaking, people only act in despicable ways if they think something powerful supports their behavior, and nothing is more powerful than religious beliefs. I admit that when I founded White Light over two decades ago, I underestimated the power of my message. That was my only fault. But to be clear, I don't think that it turned anyone on to bestiality. I think it simply attracted those who sought moral permission for it and were able to easily pervert my message."

"Pervert is definitely the right word."

"I think I've helped you enough for one day. I need you to tell me everything you know about Dolores Thomas."

"I know a lot. What specifically do you want to know?"

"How did she do it? How did she get your bakery and your personal brand right out from under you?" She didn't appreciate the tone of admiration in his voice.

It was a question she'd rolled over and over in her mind since, until she had managed to boil it down to a simple explanation, an easy one-two punch she never saw coming. "She hit me when I was weak and desperate. I still needed a sizable chunk of money to start the bakery after the food truck burned down, and I ran into her outside a taco shop. It just seemed like a coincidence, but now I realize it wasn't at all. So I took the money she offered. You're right, I guess. It's the spending of money that's power. And she got power over me when she made me that offer and I accepted, and I didn't feel like it would seem very grateful to read the contract closely. It would look like I didn't trust her, but I felt like I owed her my trust. Or that I owed her something, which, now that you've explained it in such an eerily succinct way, I see that I did. I owed her more than I could repay her, and I should never have taken that loan."

He waved his hand impatiently for her to get on with it.

"Right, so then I got a little behind on payments, but I thought she understood because she knew I was behind but still suggested I go to this leadership retreat for women. She even offered to pay. Why would she have done that if she were mad at me? Other than being the Devil, obviously. But clearly I didn't consider that. So, I went to the thing out, way the hell out there in New Mexico, and on the way back from Carlsbad, I—"

Jimmy sat up at attention and blinked like he was waking from a trance. "Wait, you were in Carlsbad?"

"Yeah. The retreat was just outside of there."

"And *who* did you say was the woman who led it?"

"I didn't. But her name was Caren Powers." Jessica scoffed, asking amusedly, "Why, you know her?" There was no chance in hell a galru like Caren would spend even two seconds around a man like Jimmy. Why he was suddenly interested was beyond her.

"How do you spell that?"

"C-A-R-E-N."

Jimmy's hand flew up to his mouth, and he stared wide-eyed at a stack of paper towels along the wall behind her. Finally, he looked at her and said, "I think our paths might be more intertwined than we previously believed, Jessica."

"Ew. I hope not."

"Go on, then, tell me about how exactly the Devil revealed herself."

Jessica told him everything, right up until the moment when her car broke down and Trooper Gabriel Michaels came and gave her a lift back.

"And did you really smite a man?" he asked. "I heard about it, but I understand you faced no charges for it."

"I did. Believe me, I tried to get them to press charges. I still see him explode like a blood-filled balloon when I close my eyes at night."

"Considering I just saw my last true ally crushed to death beneath a decorative typewriter, I can understand your pain."

"You know he was going to screw you over, right?"

"I don't believe it for a second."

"God told me. Eugene Thornton was in league with the Devil. He had our whole conversation recorded. He would have handed it over to her."

"So you smote him?"

"No, not me. That was all God."

Jimmy rubbed his chin. "That sounds like the hog I knew. He threatened to smite me multiple times on the night we met."

"Maybe He should have done it."

"But He didn't. He spared me. And here we are. God's messenger and His daughter uniting at last."

She had a lot to say about that, but one question stood front and center: "Tell me straight, once and for all. Do you genuinely believe that? Do you believe I'm God's daughter? That I can perform miracles and smite people?"

"I'll give you the straightest answer I can, but you're

not going to like it. Here it is: I don't believe in anything outside of my ability to accomplish what I set out to do. Beyond that, belief only exists where there's a lack of solid information. Faith is the hallmark of uncertainty, and if one wishes to remain powerful, one must be certain of things."

"And yet here you are. Asking me for information about the Devil because that uncertainty exists."

"And I believe in my ability to fill in the blanks."

"But you have the information for this! You spoke to God directly the morning I was born and he told you all these things. How do you still not believe I'm the daughter of God?"

"Because I don't have to believe it. I *know* it."

"Oh." She fell silent, scanning his expression for any hint of how that lined up with his past behavior at all. "You know I'm the daughter of God, and yet you tell your congregation that I'm ..." She sighed. "Jimmy, I just don't understand."

"That's because you're letting your emotions get the best of you. Not uncommon with women. But if you think about it logically, it follows as thus: I met God face-to-face. He chose me as His messenger of your nativity. In all His infinite wisdom and with all His foresight of what was to come, He did not smite me. Thus, He saw some purpose for me down the line. So, until that purpose is fulfilled, I'm free to do whatever benefits me the most, and so far, it's been founding a church that generates me more power than I could've ever dreamed possible. And sometimes, yes, that does mean convincing thousands of people that you are the Antichrist, the harbinger of the Apocalypse, and so on. But He hasn't smote me yet, and as far as I'm concerned, the longer I go without serving a clear purpose for the benefit of you or mankind, the longer I live."

"You call that logic?"

"I do, and most men would."

"Are you ... are you trying to make a case against men? Where do morals play into your logic?"

"Morals are and have always been flimsy things presented as fact to control the masses. Right, wrong, it's all the same. It's just actions. How many times have you meant to do the right thing but hurt someone instead? You would say your intentions were good, but we both know that's just to lessen your guilt over the results of your actions. If you stop worrying about right and wrong, you don't experience that guilt to begin with. It clears out a lot of the mental clutter that weighs down the mind and leaves no room for clear thinking."

"Are you sure you want to take on the Devil? I think you and her might get along."

He chuckled. "I only get along with moral people. Much easier to control." And then he finished his drink, got up, and walked out.

Chapter Twenty-Nine

339:21:53:30 until Doomsday

Jessica had stress-drunk three more cups of coffee at Bat-Ass Brew after Jimmy's departure, one of those being the triple-shot threat Bat Outta Hell.

And now it was 2 a.m. and she was nowhere near being able to sleep. She'd thought the phone recap of the conversation with Wendy might have helped her process enough to fall asleep, but not so, even though her publicist did sound quite pleased with the outcome.

During those over caffeinated hours at Bat-Ass Brew, she'd ordered herself a chicken salad sandwich and thrown together a priestess application form. A quick check from Wendy, then it was live on her website and Cash sent it out in a precisely branded email to her entire subscriber list.

Eight hours later, with her eyelids feeling like they might never shut again, she made herself some hot herbal tea, opened up her laptop on the kitchen island, and checked to see if any applications had come in yet.

They had. More than she would ever have time to go through. She would need to hire a team just to sort through the applications. She wished she could forget about it and go to bed, but since that wasn't happening ...

She began randomly clicking on the names, most of which she didn't recognize, and up popped the full application on her screen.

A disturbing trend began to emerge. These people were highly educated. Harvard Divinity School? What would she even do with a person like that? Besides feel inferior, obviously.

What would Jimmy do?

He wouldn't hire especially intelligent or educated people for this, that was for sure. He would make sure his side of the scales was higher.

As she mindlessly scrolled down the spreadsheet with the rundown of each application, a name caught her eye.

But no. Just no way.

Could there be two Courtney Wursts running around? It was possible.

But would the other one be applying for priestesshood?

Would the one she *knew* be applying for priestesshood?

She clicked the name and pulled up the full application. There was nothing spectacular about it, but it was clearly the Courtney she knew. First Nu Alpha

Omega, and now this? Why was Courtney so intent on following her?

She would be an idiot to give a Wurst a position of power within her organization.

Unless ...

Unless she was just thinking like herself. She needed to think like Jimmy. Jimmy would definitely give a Wurst a high role in the church. He already had. Maybe she could repeat his success.

And when she thought about it, the Wursts, every last one of them, were born for this shit. And Courtney was arguably the best of the Wursts. She'd followed the rules in NAO, even gone on, according to Kate, to help found the Sam Houston State University chapter.

Jessica finished reading through the application, and when she got to the bottom, it clicked.

Maybe there was a plan for Courtney Wurst, too. The woman just kept coming back for more, anyhow.

She scrolled to the top of the page, hovered over the green checkmark for only a moment before clicking it.

And so it was that Jessica accepted her first priestess into her church.

GOOD JOB, SWEETIE. SO PROUD OF YOU.

Chapter Thirty

311:12:31:09 until Doomsday

One month and five priestesses later, Jessica was feeling confident about her prospects. So confident, in fact, that the thought of visiting Waverly Hills Retirement Center for her obligatory community service didn't even bother her.

And it was her lucky day, too. None of her favorite residents had received visitors all week, so she was free to check in and enjoy their presence and wisdom. The overpowering smell of stale urine in the hallways became hardly more than an afterthought.

It was after her visits had concluded, as she was on her way toward the front desk, that the day took a turn for the strange. Rosemary Heathrow's room was drawing nearer, and she considered the merits of sprinting by it so that if the bitter woman *did* spot her, she wouldn't be able to make sense of it before Jessica was already out the front door. Unable to find any flaws in that plan, Jessica committed herself do it, creeping closer to the door, ready to spring.

She sprang.

And she ran straight into someone exiting Mrs. Heathrow's room.

The collision knocked her back and she apologized before realizing that the man she had just run into was one of two people on earth who never deserved an apology from her.

Jimmy Dean put his back to her quickly, as if he still stood a chance of going unrecognized. But no. She'd recognize him with her eyes closed. Jimmyness hung all around him like smog.

"What? she said, her mind trying desperately to put together the not-so-subtle clues. Jimmy Dean had just left Rosemary Heathrow's room. "Do you know her?"

Giving up his attempt at veiling his identity, he grabbed her tightly around the arm and dragged her down the hall and around the corner, until they were alone and out of sight next to one of the emergency exits. "You tell no one," he said.

"Tell no one what?"

"You know what."

She didn't know what. Not until that moment, at least. Her top suspicion had been that Rosemary was a member of his church, but if that were the case, he was unlikely to have any problem with people knowing about it. After all, visiting a sick old woman in a stinky retirement home when he had no obligation to would only bolster his reputation as a man of God.

But that clearly wasn't the case here. She knew that now. His shame tipped her off because she recognized that particular brand of it.

"She's your mother."

"My miserable mother, yes."

A surprising rush of sympathy nearly knocked her over, but she adjusted her stance and wouldn't let it happen again.

"You have to promise me, Jessica, that you won't tell anyone about her."

She stared at him silently because every moment she did so was a moment she had power over him. And, yes, it *did* feel pretty good. His side of the scales was almost touching the tabletop.

"Rosemary Heathrow is your mother." She'd read enough of his memoir *Railed to the Cross* to know that he *had* a mother, but that didn't erase her subconscious belief that Jimmy had merely crawled out of the mud one day, a fully-formed adult, spitting out chunks of bullshit and hellfire.

He glanced nervously over her shoulder. "If you could not say that again, that would be much appreciated. I don't think I need to remind you that you need my help, and if this gets out, I'll know exactly who spread it around."

"No one else knows?"

"Well, of course *someone* knows. The owner of

Waverley Hills is aware for next of kin purposes, but to everyone else, she's just a sick member of my congregation ... who believes I'm her son."

"Why don't you want anyone to know?"

"Have you *met* the woman?"

"Ah. Right. She swore I was the Devil and started throwing things at me."

Was that a hint of pride angling the corners of his mouth?

His gaze darted around again. "She could be used against me by my enemies."

"You mean to say you care about her enough that they could leverage her against you?" She chuckled. "What, like, take her hostage?"

"No, no. I'd like to see someone try to take her against her will. Poor sucker."

"Then why are you worried someone will leverage her against you?"

He shook his head. "You're worse at this than I thought. No wonder you need a whole team to help you." He leaned closer. "If word got out that *that* was my mother, it could damage my reputation."

She took a step back. Perhaps it was the part of her that understood that dynamic all too well that left her bubbling with rage for him. "Right. Not coming from a place of concern for her, but a place of concern for your almighty reputation."

"Exactly. It takes years to build a reputation and one moment to ruin it."

"You mean, say, a moment where one of your congregation is balls deep in a pig? A moment like that?"

She hadn't wanted to say it, especially not like that, but she knew seeing his reaction would be worth it. And she wasn't wrong. He cringed.

Then he reached in the breast pocket of his pearl suit, pulled out his shades, and slipped them on. "I'm going to leave now, and I suggest you don't leave right after me. No one should know we were in the same building together, let alone speaking with one another. And remember: tell *no one.*"

She already had a mental list going of a few people she was looking forward to telling. Destinee, Quentin, Wendy ...

She nodded. "Right. Of course. You can trust me."

It was the last bit that gave him visible pause, but then he pressed two fingers to her forehead before she could knock them away, said, "Sumus omnes Porcos," and left.

She watched him go, wondering who she would tell first.

Sooie!

* * *

"I can't stop thinking about it!" Jessica let her flailing arms fall onto the decorative pillow in her lap.

Destinee sat on the other side of the couch in her and Rex's living room, nodding along in a stunned awe. "Yeah, baby. I just figured his mom was dead."

"Killed herself? I would have guessed killed herself."

"His memoir says the last time he saw her was when he was a kid and she left with that Reverend."

"We already know his memoir is mostly lies."

"Maybe the details, but I have a feeling the general idea holds, especially for his childhood. He didn't paint his ma in a great light, and from what you said, she ain't exactly a saint."

Jessica grabbed her longneck Dos Equis from the coffee table. "She's *horrible*, Mom. So bad, it almost makes me feel sorry for him."

"Yeah, life ain't easy for anyone, but it's even harder with a shitty mom."

"To be fair," said Rex, who'd been watching the Texas Rangers play on mute for the duration of the conversation, "while our patriarchal society values women most highly when they subscribe to the role of mother, it doesn't exactly go out of its way to make motherhood easy. We've created a system in which we deprive women of the necessary knowledge of their own bodies to adequately family plan, and then we outlaw any sort of pregnancy termination, thrusting motherhood upon the masses without providing any meaningful assistance or social support, so as to make it an uphill battle to be a mother, let alone a mother and a working woman."

"The fuck?" said Destinee. "Did you just lecture me on how hard it is to be a mother?"

"Sorry, D. I didn't mean to explain your own experience to you. I just wanted to show support."

She nodded slowly, staring horrified at her daughter. "No problem. But maybe focus that support on baseball." Once he was absorbed in the game again, she leaned forward and said, "I'll train that feminism out of him if it's the last thing I do."

"Do you think I've got him all wrong?"

"Who?"

"Jimmy."

"Wrong how?"

"I mean, he's Jimmy fucking Dean, sure. But what if I've been too harsh to him? I mean, my life hasn't been easy, but at least I have a great mom. What if I— Stop. No, that's not—"

"Sorry, sorry." Destinee wiped a tear from her eye.

"I'm just saying, does a person stand a chance with a mother like that? Maybe it's just not his fault?"

Destinee wiped her leaky face on a pillow, sniffled, then said, "What difference does that make?"

"All the difference? No difference? Some difference? That's the thing. I can't decide if it's worth considering."

"It's a good question. But I will say growing up with a ma like mine wasn't exactly the cotton candy at the county fair on a sunny day. But I didn't end up deciding to ruin some innocent kid's life because of it."

Fair point. The last time Jessica had seen Grandma McCloud, she and Destinee had fled the old woman's beach house and not looked back. It had been Jessica's first and last visit to the Gulf Coast, and maybe she'd go back some day once Grandma McCloud was no longer a presence there.

"You know I ain't much of a philosopher, but it seems to me that you can understand why a person does something without givin' them the go-ahead to keep on doin' it."

"You're starting to sound like Jesus."

"Well, he's a smart dude. Weird. I don't reckon hangin' around Jeremy is the best for him, but he knows a thing or two about people, I'll give him that."

"When we work with the homeless, he always gives me their stories. Fucking tragedies, all of them. But knowing their stories doesn't keep them from kicking the shit out of him every so often. And it sure as hell doesn't keep them from jumping on a table and whipping out their junk."

Destinee shook her head. "Man, that fool sure does love the homeless."

"Right! But how? And *should* he? I know he thinks so, but I just can't get on board with it. Should we love people who don't behave right no matter what? Who constantly make the world a worse place for others? And does it matter if they had a rough childhood if they spend their entire adulthood being an absolute piece of garbage? Does a shitty mother excuse it?"

Destinee's eyes were wide now. "Oh, hell, baby. I don't have a fucking clue. I doubt I'm the person to ask. If Jimmy Dean walked through that door right now, I'd put buckshot in him where the sun don't shine. You know, I had myself a damn fine laugh when I heard about Eugene Thornton. No, I'm not the one to ask about all this."

"Then who is? Jesus? God?"

Maybe it's you, baby. Maybe you're the one to answer all these questions."

Chapter Thirty-One

309:08:06:46 until Doomsday

Without a facility to call her own yet, Jessica was forced to find somewhere else to hold her first priestess training. A co-working space seemed like a good place to set up shop, so the only question then became which one? There were so, so many. Did she pick the one with the sleeping pods and free artisan donuts or the one with table tennis, a plasma TV, and hammocks?

In the end, she chose one with none of those things. It had a common area and a few private conference rooms off to the side, and no "bonus features" or "perks." She liked it because it was empty when she'd toured it. That would do nicely as an impromptu HQ when she needed it.

Jessica sat at the head of the table overlooking the five woman who'd made the cut.

There was Courtney Wurst, who Jessica regretted choosing more and more each day at no fault of Courtney's. It was simply existential dread brought on by repeated childhood trauma. No big deal.

Beside her was Tamara Shilongo, Jessica's former sorority sister who she'd wanted to hire for *something* since she'd brought her on at It is Risen only a few short months before she'd been forced to let her go. Tamara had always straightened her hair and pulled it back in a tight ponytail, but sometime in the last few months, she must have gotten tired of suppressing it, and wore it in a glorious afro that Jessica knew better than to touch, no matter how much it beckoned her palm toward it. Tamara had been an easy choice as priestess because Jessica already trusted her implicitly. She'd joined Nu Alpha Omega before it even was that. She'd taken a risk on Jessica, and Jessica owed that trust back.

Next to Tamara was Natalie Goldman, who Jessica couldn't imagine doing this thing without. Jessica had recruited her former sorority sister directly. The process had involved a dogged courting stage, as the notion of priestesshood had seemed to Natalie "limiting and objectifying." That was just that sort of take that solidified within Jessica's mind the need to have her among the elite. The woman was the bluntest advocate for feminism Jessica had ever known, and if this was going to work, she needed someone like that around who would speak plainly about the inevitable fuck ups. Time and energy to guess what someone *really* meant behind their gentle phrasing was no longer a luxury afforded to Jess.

Across from Natalie was, and this one was as big of a shock to her as anyone, Stephanie Lee. Mooretown's single Asian student had come a long way from her dangerous binge drinking and ruthless conniving with Sandra Thomas. Jessica had nearly rejected the application upon registering the familiar name. Though they'd run in the same circle in middle school, high school hadn't exactly brought the two closer, as Stephanie had joined the high school paper and written a handful of less than flattering articles about the daughter of God. Was she just trying to get the scoop now? It'd taken some sleuthing, mostly by Cash Monet, but it looked like Stephanie had satisfied her journalistic impulses back in high school and had since begun more hands-on work. She'd dropped out of college, a move Jessica had to respect on its own, and had busied herself with volunteering internationally.

But this was where it got weird, because Stephanie Lee had spent the last three years in Southeast Asian countries helping with earthquake relief. It was a passion that, and Jessica really couldn't believe this shit, had been passed down from Stephanie's parents, who had died doing the same thing when she was only five years old.

And when Stephanie Lee was five years old, Jessica had already begun asking God hard questions that He would literally move mountains to avoid answering.

So, refusing to make the last remaining mental connection there and risk an avalanche of guilt falling upon her head, she had instead accepted Stephanie's application.

And finally, sitting next to Stephanie, was the only highly educated person Jessica had selected for the position: Dr. Victoria Bell. The woman hadn't applied for the position, didn't even know there was an application process—clearly she wasn't subscribed to the email list—but when Jessica had clicked through her five hundredth or so application, she had begged Wendy to make it stop. Couldn't four be enough?

"No. It has to be five. We've gone over why. If you don't want to keep looking at applications, then you'll have to recruit directly."

And so it was that Jessica had called her former professor. Not to recruit her, though. Simply to ask her for help in brainstorming what kind of person would be right for the job. But in the end, it became clear—Dr. Bell was angling for herself to take the position.

"It's not paid," Jessica had said, following Jimmy's advice.

"That's fine. I'm tenured. I don't even have to show up and I keep this job."

"It would take a lot of your free time."

"I'm single. All I have outside of teaching is free time."

"You really want it?"

"Yep. Sounds like a nice change of pace. Maybe people will listen to what I have to say for once."

"Okay, it's yours."

"Great."

"And it *is* paid."

"How much?"

Jessica told her.

"Fantastic. I'll retire."

"You ... what?"

"You just offered me three times what I'm making. Why would I work two jobs?"

It was a solid argument, and so here she was, her cardigan pulled tightly around her stout body and thick arms, staring expectantly at her former pupil.

"Right," Jessica said, "I apologize about the temperature. It's always cold in here."

Stephanie Lee said, "You could make your churches a comfortable temperature for women."

"Great idea. Judith?"

Judith scribbled it down.

"Okay, where were we?" She looked back at the agenda on the whiteboard behind her. They'd already knocked out "complete introductions" and "talk about religious history," which meant they were at item number three. "Okay, this one's important. We need to discuss the new rites of passage."

"What were the old ones?" asked Courtney.

Jessica frowned and shrugged. "Mostly being sexually assaulted. So, we're going to do something better." She let the suspense build. "Menstruation parties."

"Ew," said Tamara.

"Absolutely not," said Natalie.

"Huh?" Jessica looked around, saw that her excitement wasn't mirrored back to her, and said, "You don't like it?"

"No," said Judith, "Not at all. That's weird and gross."

"Yeah," said Stephanie. "I remember when I first got my period, I thought I was dying. I wasn't in the mood for a party."

Dr. Bell was silent, but Jessica suspected that was due to her agreement with the rest of the group and her lack of desire to take a side.

"Well, shit. Yeah, I guess my first period was pretty terrible, too."

Courtney said, "Right. I remember that. That *was* terrible."

Jessica refrained from shouting, "Fuck you, Wurst!" at her priestess in training, and simply remained silent. "Okay, well, if you think of a better rite of passage, let me know. We definitely need something.

"Okay, next item. Consent. This is important and, apparently, complicated for some ..."

The women gathered their things after Jessica had concluded day one of training. With the exception of the period parties, which had been destroyed so thoroughly not even Jessica could resurrect it, the topics had gone smoothly, especially the part about consent, which everyone seemed to get without much explaining. A more suspicious and cynical messiah might conclude that the concept was, in fact, quite simple and easy for *anyone* to understand but that some feigned confusion so as to justify rape.

Training was scheduled for the next week straight, and then she would have to move to the next stage: figuring out what precisely to do with all these priestesses.

As she was powering down the projector, Courtney approached tentatively. "Jessica, can I talk to you?"

Her knee-jerk reaction of telling Courtney to go die was fading with each interaction. It was still there, and quite strong, but she was making progress. "Of course."

Courtney's gaze darted over to Tamara and Dr. Bell who were chatting jovially as they made their way slowly toward the exit, and only once they'd left did Courtney finally spit it out. "I just feel like I should tell you something. And if you want to kick me out of this because of it, I understand."

Oh no. What had she done?

"What have you done?"

"Nothing! I promise! I know you still don't trust me— no, don't argue, I can tell—so I've been doing everything I can to earn your trust. But I can't say the same for everyone else in my family." She paused, and Jessica held her breath. Was Mrs. Wurst at it again? But no, what could she do, align with Jimmy Dean? Jessica was aligned with Jimmy Dean, so that would make them partners in a sense, wouldn't it?

Courtney said, "It's Trent."

"Oh."

"He, um ..." She grimaced and stared vaguely at Jessica's naval before meeting her eyes. "You know the scandal in White Light Church?"

"The pigfucking, you mean?"

Courtney cringed. "Yeah, that."

"What about it?"

"Trent ... he's caught up in it. There's footage of him with a ... It hasn't come out yet, but it will soon."

Jessica felt the Holy Spirit of Shadenfreude flow through her just before the full implications of Courtney's confession landed. "Wait, that's not great. He had sex with a pig? And it's on camera?"

Courtney nodded.

"For fuck's sake! Are these people *paying* someone to record them?"

"It was the farmer. He heard his sow squealing and came out."

Jessica held up a hand. "Okay, that's enough. I really don't need details. It was more of a rhetorical question." She massaged her temples, trying to work through all this. Could she have a priestess whose twin brother was a pigfucker of White Light Church? Would that association be too close and bring the scarlet letter over to Jessica's cause? Or could this be twisted to her advantage?

She knew what Jimmy Dean would tell her, because she knew what he'd already done in a similar circumstance. He thought his mother could be a liability for his reputation, so he'd dumped her in Waverly Hills and pretended they weren't related.

Did that mean that Courtney had to disavow Trent, or did it mean Jessica needed to disavow Courtney?

Things sure did become complicated quick when people were held responsible for the actions of others.

"When it does come to light," Jessica said, "when the video starts circulating, can you denounce him?"

"All of him?" Courtney asked, looking pained. "I can certainly denounce what he did."

"Right, but he's kind of been a dick his entire life, so are you really losing that much?" One look at Courtney's face, and she backpedaled. "Okay, you probably think he's fine. But—"

"No, you're right. He's an asshole. My mom said he used to punch me in the head when we were in the womb. But he's my brother."

"I'll take your word for it that that matters at all." She inspected Courtney, and it was clear from her expression that she was genuinely struggling. What would Jimmy do here?

He wouldn't make her feel any better. That wasn't really his thing.

So instead, she asked herself a question she never in a million years would have considered asking before, because she was so, so desperate not to walk in this particular person's footsteps.

What would Jesus do?

The answer came immediately. She put a hand on Courtney's shoulder, trying to make a little physical contact without inviting a full hug—after all, she wasn't *actually* Jesus. "I'm not asking you not to love him, Courtney. He's about to get his ass handed to him by the media and all of his undoubtedly shitty friends. The church that he's committed himself to since he was a kid, really gone all-in with, is going to toss him out on his ass in a big, public way. If you ask me, he's about to need your love more than ever. But if you want to stay associated with this group, I'm going to need you to speak out against his actions when the day comes. If you think you can do that *and* still love him, I'm okay with you staying."

Courtney's mouth was lolling open slightly. "You're not kicking me out?"

"Not yet."

Courtney's shoulders dropped away from her ears like they were lowering on hydraulics. "I thought for sure you would."

"I probably should. But I've been spending too much time with Jesus."

"Jesus?"

Oh right. "Figure of speech."

Courtney nodded, but there was a clearly defined crease running between her brows. "Right. Well, thanks."

"And do me a favor. Tell me the minute the story on Trent breaks." She wanted to watch it live and be sure to follow the tweets as they poured in.

Courtney Wurst nodded solemnly, her little snub nose bobbing obnoxiously before she turned and walked away.

Jessica pulled out her phone as soon as she was alone and typed up the message, *Don't tell anyone, but Trent*

Wurst is about to be implicated in pigfucking. It's not even my birthday. That last sentence was obvious enough, because if it were her birthday, only terrible things would be happening. Not great and exciting things like this.

She read it over once more then sent the text to her old childhood friend, Christopher Riley.

Chapter Thirty-Two

205:13:02:55 until Doomsday

It wasn't easy picking out charities to support, especially around Christmas when every charity was behaving like it'd just done three lines of coke before closing the biggest deal of its life.

Then there was also the question of which ones followed most closely with Jessica's mission.

Mission. Ha! They think I have a mission. Cute.

Wendy had already instructed her that it couldn't *all* go to wildlife conservation groups ... but that didn't mean *some* or even *most* couldn't go there.

So far, it was an even split between wildlife, homeless services, animal shelters, women empowerment initiatives, elderly care, and aid for natural disasters in Asia.

When Wendy had asked why that last was so important to her, she'd simply said it was close to the heart.

It was also close to the conscience, but instead of mentioning that, she reminded the publicist that one of the new priestesses had committed most of her life to that cause and had a good knowledge of the best ways to help and make the money go further.

In total, Jessica had donated nearly ten million dollars over the past few months.

It had become a full-time job, since the money needed to go out as quickly as it came in for the purposes of not amassing any wealth the Devil could claim in the lawsuit. While the new 501(c)(3) status of the church only made for murkier waters in ongoing legal matters—the tax exemption and the First Amendment freedoms that went along with it had been righteously bestowed upon her by the IRS after the Devil's suit had already been filed—one thing was clear: this money could burn a hole in her soul if she held on to it too long.

The matter of money management and who was technically attached to which dollars was a complicated dance that, thankfully, Jessica was not in charge of. They'd brought someone new on for that, a specialist Wendy knew, and assurances were made that there were perfectly legal ways to hide large sums of money, since most laws were designed *by* people with money specifically to *benefit* people with money. Money laundering, turned out, was for the nouveau riche, the unrefined.

She tried not to think about any of it.

But this truth remained: Money was no longer an issue. She could get it whenever she wanted it, pay large amounts to all the groups she cared about, and finally pay people what they deserved, or, following Jimmy's advice, double what they deserved.

And yet, nothing felt any easier.

Though, she supposed she hadn't gone without in years. There was Chris and Jameson's generosity, and before that, the scratch-off lottery tickets from God. And before that, she'd lived in Mooretown where the cost of living was easily one tenth of what it was in Austin, meaning even Destinee's pharmacy pay had mostly made ends meet.

Her phone vibrated on the kitchen island next to where she sat with her laptop open. She checked it and found a message from Wendy. The lawsuit was scheduled to go to court sometime after the new year, assuming they didn't settle, which seemed more unlikely by the day, despite Wendy's insistence that such a resolution was par for the course with legal matters involving religious figures.

WOMEN SHOULD NEVER SETTLE. THAT'S WHAT I ALWAYS SAY.

Perhaps it was her morning of sending off massive donations, but God's voice was higher than she'd heard it yet.

What are you talking about? Always say to who? Jesus? Who else are you talking to?

I TALK TO ALL SORTS OF PEOPLE. JUST BECAUSE THEY DON'T LISTEN DOESN'T MEAN I'M NOT TALKING. YOU KNOW, SOMETIMES, THE LORD JUST... OH, NEVER MIND.

What?

NOTHING.

No, what is it?

IT'S NOTHING, OKAY?

Are you ... are you mad at me?

NO.

It seems like you're upset.

I'M FINE. THE LORD IS JUST FINE.

She didn't believe that, but far be it from her to argue with the Lord when She was in one of Her moods.

Her phone buzzed again, and she grabbed it without thinking, expecting another text from Wendy.

But it wasn't Wendy's name on her screen.

It was Miranda's.

The message was, *You home?*

After months of radio silence, after having concluded that her birthday party the year before was going to be the last time she ever saw her old best friend again, suddenly she had dropped back in. Jess knew she should have been happy, but instead, she was livid. How dare she!

She responded with, *Yeah.*

Ooh ... one-word answers. Perfect. That would be her plot for petty revenge.

Miranda: *Great. I'm at the front door. Can you buzz me in?*

"The fuck?"

OH NO SHE DID NOT.

Right? She just assumes whatever I'm doing can wait.

Jessica looked around. The place wasn't exactly tidy.

"Dammit." She rocked herself off the barstool and went over to the intercom to buzz Miranda in.

And then she began the scramble around her apartment to grab anything that screamed "I cannot be trusted to live a basic adult lifestyle" and threw it all into her bedroom closet.

She'd just managed to get all the dirty dishes off various surfaces and into the sink when there was a knock at the front door.

It was eleven in the morning, and Jessica was still in her pj's. Well, nothing to do about that, because she'd be damned if she put on a bra when not absolutely necessary. Some of the lessons she'd learned at the women's retreat in Carlsbad had made a lasting impression, it seemed.

She opened the door, and Miranda stood there, smiling, wearing makeup and, presumably, a bra. Instantly Jessica knew she should have put a little effort into her looks. Being the sloppier one put her at a power disadvantage.

Oh god, I'm spending too much time around Jimmy.

"Heeeey!" she said.

"Heeeey!" Miranda replied.

They hugged.

She welcomed her inside, and Miranda's first words were, "Keeping this place in good shape, I see." Jessica detected no sarcasm.

"Yeah, you know. I figure so long as it still belongs to Jameson, I should take care of it."

"He still hasn't signed it over to you?"

"He tried, but with the lawsuit going on, Wendy wants to limit my assets."

Miranda's face scrunched. "Oh. That sucks. I bet you hate that."

"Very much so."

She grabbed two beers from the fridge, assuming Miranda would want one, then remembered with some embarrassment that it was still before noon.

To Miranda's credit, she didn't even bat an eye, just used her shirt to twist off the top, which she tossed onto the counter.

They settled in awkwardly around the kitchen island. "So, what brings you to the neighborhood?"

"Winter break. I thought I would slit my wrists if I stayed in Mooretown with my mom for a second longer. Not that she's bad company, but—"

"No, I get it. I totally get it."

"Right. You would."

A strained silence, then Jessica said, "So you came to Austin to see ... friends?"

"Yeah, I know a couple people from school who live here, and they invited me to come out with them for a few nights."

"Did what's-his-name come too?"

Miranda arched an eyebrow. "What's-his-name?"

"The guy you were dating."

"Ohhh ... Desmond? No. We broke up months ago."

Jessica wanted nothing more than to ask why they had, but it didn't feel right. Before she could stop herself, different words rushed out. "Quentin's still single, you know."

As soon as she'd said his name, she knew she'd screwed up. Miranda flinched, the skin around her eyes tightening, and the corners of her mouth slanting toward the ground. "I know. But that's not happening again."

"Why not? You two were so good together. Yeah, he messed up, and ... and we all messed up, but hasn't time away helped? I mean, he's amazing. Any girl would be lucky to have him."

"Sounds like you might have a thing for him. He's all yours."

"What? No, no. That's not what I meant."

"It's too late, Jess. I'm not still mad at him *or* you and Chris for keeping it from me. I appreciate the tough situation you were all in. But I just ..." She paused and took a sip from her bottle. "Don't take this the wrong way, but I needed some space. I needed time away from the whole angels and God stuff. It was weird to know my best friend was the daughter of God and my boyfriend and his best friend were angels and I was *nothing*. Just a human. It got me thinking—maybe I don't have an important role to play here. Maybe it's great that God made me a human and not an angel. I have the ability to leave and stay gone like y'all don't have. Maybe it was a gift."

Before she could stop herself, she muttered, "You're doing a great job of staying gone."

"You're doing a great job of making me regret coming by."

"No, no. I'm sorry. I didn't mean to. Go on with what you were saying."

Miranda hesitated, then did. "I realized, though, that leaving and staying away just because I *could* was, in fact, just another form of this whole thing determining my life. Coming and going as I please is actual freedom from it."

It didn't feel fantastic to hear, but it made enough sense. Besides, Jessica could relate. There were moments, plenty of them, when she would do almost anything to get away from herself.

"Either way," Jessica said, "I'm glad you're here. I'm starting a church, and I've been flip-flopping between asking myself what Jesus would do and what Jimmy would do."

Miranda jerked her head back. "Ew. Why would you want to do anything Jimmy would do?"

"We've sort of ... teamed up."

"Jess no!"

"It's under extreme supervision and totally under wraps." And before she knew it, they were on their second round of beer and she had caught up her former best friend about her meeting with Jimmy, the glorious demise of Eugene Thornton, and her quest to start a church of her own.

"You really think starting a church is going to fix the problems that were mostly created by other churches?"

And there it was, the question she'd been asking herself on repeat since the first setting the idea in motion. She still didn't have a satisfying answer, but she had one that served as a Band-Aid. "I don't see any other way. People don't listen to you if you're not a formal institution who claims to have a direct line to God. Sure, individuals have influence, like pro athletes and Hollywood celebrities, but nothing is quite like a church."

"You're trying to beat Jimmy at his own game while he's coaching your team. Not sure how you expect *that* to end successfully. But more importantly, how do you know you're not going to create a monster like White Light?"

"We left out all the pig stuff from our beliefs."

She nodded. "Okay, that's a good start."

Jessica continued to fill her in on what she'd missed, and when she got to the point of the lawsuit, Miranda said, "That's strange, though. You ignore your main purpose for *years*, and you build up this business that makes you happy enough, and you start running around with celebrities and shit, sort of what everyone dreams of doing, and then the Devil sends you out into the desert for a women's retreat to empower yourself, and in the meantime, she takes all that stuff you've built for yourself out from under you so the only option you have left is to pursue what you were put on earth to do. Why would she do that?"

"Um."

"Doesn't that strike you as odd?"

"When you put it like that, yes, it does."

"It's almost like she was helping you."

"Except that can't be."

"So, what is it?"

Jessica paused. She hadn't considered *that* before. Her

natural assumption was Devil = Evil, and Evil was bad and only around to thwart good. Perhaps it was an overly simplistic take, but the nature of good and evil had always been presented to her that way, and she hadn't had occasion to question it.

But now she did. "I think she believed it would crush me for good. That I wouldn't dust myself off and start on this route."

"And was she right about that?"

"Apparently not."

Miranda grinned. "You think the Devil underestimated you?"

"I guess so."

"Jessica McCloud, that's the most self-confidence I've heard from you in your entire life."

"Don't go around telling people about it. They'll start to expect it from me."

"You sound so confident, in fact, that I think you might be ready to confront her."

Jessica inhaled a sip of beer and began coughing around it. "Con—" She coughed some more. "Confront her? Are you out of your mind?"

"No. I think it's time."

"It's not time."

"You have to eventually."

"I do not."

Miranda groaned exasperatedly. "What do you see happening with this? You just avoid her until one of you dies?"

"That sounds like a great plan. Sure. I'll do it."

"I heard you saw her in the street and dodged into a leather store."

Jessica's mouth fell open. "I thought you weren't talking to Quentin!"

"I'm not. But he told Chris, and Chris told me."

"I'm going to have to have a word with Christopher Riley about his gossiping habits."

"Can you blame him? He wants nothing more than to talk with you about all this stuff, but he doesn't feel like he can, so he goes to the next best thing: me."

"You're the best thing, not the next best thing. We've always known that."

"Not to Chris. You're the best thing in the entire world to that poor guy."

She wanted to argue, but she couldn't, not on that point. "I just don't see the benefit in confronting her. It's not going to change her behavior. She's not going to suddenly become not evil."

"It's not about changing *her*. Think about it. If you can confront the Devil, who is going to scare you after that?"

Shit. That was a solid question. "But what if I confront her and she uses the opportunity to screw me even worse?"

"You just said you think she underestimated you. If that's the case, then she probably thinks your success so far is a fluke. She likely assumes this whole church thing is being orchestrated by someone other than you. You can use her low estimation of you against her to get the better of her. Women and people of color have done this for years, and to great effect."

"But she *is* a woman."

"No, she's the Devil. It's not even remotely the same thing. I know we haven't kept up much lately, but I still know you better than just about anyone. That's why I'm here right now. I've seen the shit you've gone through your whole life, and yet here you are, still standing *and building something*. You can do this. I'm sure of it. You can beat the Devil at her own game, and now's the time, Jessica. Now's the goddamned time."

Chapter Thirty-Three

198:15:31:08 until Doomsday

Jessica's hands were shaking as she approached the office building. She cursed Miranda's name over and over in her mind as she walked in step with her attorney, Angelo Samuels, and Wendy Peterman. The tension between them was palpable, which made sense considering Wendy had been casually dating him for years to gain his pro-bono services and now she no longer had to. She could pay him. And if Jessica had learned anything about money recently, it was that adding it into an existing relationship never improved said relationship.

They'd drilled her on what to say and what not to say in this meeting for weeks now, ever since she'd messaged the publicist with Miranda hovering over her shoulders, and said she was ready to confront the Devil face-to-face.

"Third floor," said Angelo. He was just over six feet

tall, had smooth, tan skin, dark hair, and hazel eyes that meant she wouldn't have been at all surprised if he did some Instagram modeling on the side. After having met him, she felt much less guilty about Wendy's long-standing obligation to date men so that she could afford their legal services.

"I'm going to screw it up," she said as they got off the elevator on the third floor.

"No, you're not."

"I am."

Wendy yanked her so they faced one another. "With God as our witness, I'm telling you. You are not going to screw this up. Do you know how much time and energy I've put into you and your life? Do you know how much I've done behind the scenes without ever telling you because I didn't trust that you wouldn't find a way to mess it up? A lot. A whole hell of a lot. So much. You've kept me on because you trust my judgment. So, are you questioning my judgment when I say that you are about to go in there and *slay the Devil?*"

Jessica blinked. "No, ma'am."

"Damn right. Now take a moment, pull yourself to gather, and then let's do this."

YOU GOT THIS, HONEY.

Are you sure?

THE LORD BELIEVES IN YOU.

That seems backward.

But it was nice to know that God wasn't freaking out. Maybe She wouldn't have to drop another heavy object on anyone. Was that possible? Could God simply drop a giant anvil on the Devil? That seemed like an easy solution that should have happened a long time ago, so there must be a rule or universal law forbidding it.

Or maybe God just loved the drama.

Angelo held open the door for Jessica, and she entered ahead of Wendy.

Dolores Thomas sat at the table facing them as they entered, a fissure of a smile on her plump, stupid, evil face. She was flanked by two male lawyers with rigid postures. They looked like they were related, but one was significantly older, so she concluded they must be a father-son team.

Angelo approached and shook hands with both of them, introducing Wendy and "his client." Dolores remained seated, continuing to smile at Jessica unblinkingly.

Jessica did her best to meet the eye contact without breaking it, but she found that if she did that for more than a handful of seconds, a spot behind her eyes began to burn acutely.

Angelo opened his briefcase and pulled out a stack of documents, and the men conversed in civil tones while Jessica did as she was coached and kept her mouth shut.

TELL HER I HATE HER GUTS.

Now's not the time.

NOW'S EXACTLY THE TIME. TELL HER GOD HATES HER

Why don't you just smite her then? Why didn't you do it ages ago before I was born? Before Jesus was born?

BELIEVE ME, I TRIED.

And?

AND IT DOESN'T WORK. EVERY TIME I TRIED IT ORIGINAL MISTAKE GOT IN THE WAY.

Original Mistake kept you from ending the Devil?

YES. I WOULD TRY TO SMITE HER, AND SOMETHING WOULD ALWAYS INTERFERE.

And it wasn't her? She wasn't the one stopping you?

SHE LACKS THE POWER. IT WAS ORIGINAL MISTAKE. I COULD SENSE IT.

But why would Original Mistake want to keep the Devil around?

NO CLUE. NEVER HAD THE CHANCE TO ASK IT.

"Any questions?"

Jessica blinked. She'd been staring at an imperfection on the marble tabletop as her conversation with God had taken place, and now Angelo was looking at her in a way that made it clear he did not have the confidence in her ability to follow the plan like Wendy did.

"Yes," she said. She steadied herself and looked at Dolores. "Why are you doing this?"

This was *not* part of the plan, and while the Devil's advocates began to protest, Satan shushed them, saying it was all right. "I did all of this because I wanted you to face me, Jessica."

"I'm facing you. Are we done? Will you end the lawsuit?"

Dolores giggled. "No. I wanted you to face me so I could see the look in your eyes when I crushed you."

It was as if Jessica had never fully believed it until that moment. A small part of her, well out of range of her intellect, had still clutched to the belief that this was a misunderstanding, that Mrs. Thomas wasn't the Devil. Maybe she was merely hurting from Jessica's financial betrayal. Maybe this was all one big mistake.

But that shit sealed it.

"You're the Devil."

"Yes. I'm glad you're catching on. Only took you, what, seventeen years?"

"Why are you doing this? Why are you trying to ruin me? I've never done anything to you. I was just an innocent kid when you first locked onto me. I was *eight years old* when you sent a demon to molest me at the zoo, for fuck's sake. I'd never done a single thing to you."

Dolores laughed again. "Typical, Jessica. You're right, of course. You haven't done anything to me. Despite your clear belief that *everything* is about you, this has never been. This is between me and God."

"He hates you." *Balls*. "She hates you."

"The feeling is mutual, I assure you. He screwed me. I did everything for him, and he cast me out, vilified me, acting high and mighty and all that. And everyone *believes* it. Everyone thinks he's perfect and wholly good, but you and I know better, don't we? I can see it in your eyes that you don't buy the wholly good nonsense everyone hawks. He's just a blundering fool who lucked into what he has. Unqualified, overconfident, and a danger to all humankind. He thinks he knows best for everyone, doesn't he? But just how well have his plans worked out for you, Jessica? Are you feeling *blessed?* Because if you, his so-called daughter, are miserable, imagine what the rest of the world around you feels. He could make this place Heaven if he chose, he could have created all people with a strong heart and a sense of connection and loyalty to one another, but he didn't. Ever ask yourself why? It couldn't be that his power depends on conflict. Certainly not *that.*" Jessica could feel her certainty slipping and had an impulse to reach out and grab Wendy, or anyone, as an anchor. These were all questions lodged deep in her own soul, and hearing them voiced left her mildly nauseated.

"And yet," the Devil continued, "despite all his self-serving behavior, *I'm* the bad guy. *I'm* the one responsible for every evil of man. I didn't even create them! I'm just the scapegoat like Eve. I won't rest until I expose him for the hypocrite he is." An image of Jimmy Dean in all white with his arms raised toward the heavens as the weighted ends of his hog-hoof stole jiggled and bounced around his waist took hold of her, and she felt like this might be it, that Dolores was just one more sentence away from pulling sympathy, and then the whole game would be over. Everything would be lost.

But that didn't happen, because the Devil made a misstep. "Meanwhile, he sticks it to your slut mother and thinks he has a good shot of redeeming his image through you. His first child almost worked, but things have since gotten a little iffy with his creation. Time to try again!"

"Jesus Christ," Jessica said, causing Dolores to flinch. "Who cares what *he* does? Look at you. You're the Devil! You almost had me, I admit it. I almost felt sorry for you, and if you'd been anyone else, I would have. But you're you. You're the goddamned Devil, and you deserve whatever comes to you, you crazy bitch!"

Dolores's face was tight like a rubber band, and it was unclear whether the downturned corners of her mouth and the taut wrinkles around her eyes were a symptom of fear or merely contempt. Perhaps it didn't matter, since the two emotions were essentially kissin' cousins.

The room was thickly silent. And from that silence:

YOU HAVE SPOTTED THE LIE.

Which one?

THE LIE OF VICTIMHOOD. IT IS DEADLIEST OF LIES, BECAUSE IT IS THE MOST CONVINCING FOR THE GOODHEARTED.

What do you mean?

IT IS THE DEVIL'S GREATEST WEAPON: SYMPATHY. SHE FEELS NONE FOR OTHERS, SO SHE USES THEIRS AGAINST THEM. SHE WAS CAST OUT OF HEAVEN FOR A GOOD REASON. SHE SIMPLY COULD NOT REMAIN WITHOUT CORRUPTING THE REST. YET, SHE PLAYS THE VICTIM AND RALLIES GOOD MEN AND WOMEN

TO HER SIDE THROUGH NO FAULT OF THEIR OWN.

Remind me what she did to get cast out? She betrayed you somehow?

THE BOOMERANG REBELLION.

Shut up.

THE LORD WILL NOT. SO JEALOUS WAS SHE OF GOD'S SKILL WITH A BOOMERANG, THAT SHE DECIDED TO TURN MY OWN CREATION AGAINST ME.

What did she do?

SHE PRACTICED FOR MILLENNIA IS WHAT SHE DID. THEN, WHEN I WASN'T EXPECTING IT, SHE HIT ME WITH A ME-DAMNED BOOMERANG, KNOCKED ME RIGHT ON MY HOLY ASS. THEN SHE TRIED TO CLAIM THE THRONE... FORGETTING, OF COURSE, THE HOLY TENET OF THE BOOMERANG.

Which is?

WHAT GOES AROUND, COMES AROUND.

Like... Karma?

I BELIEVE I'VE ALREADY TOLD YOU THAT SUCH A THING DOES NOT EXIST. THERE IS NO KARMA. ONLY THE HOLY BOOMERANG.

I really hope you're making this up. I don't want this to be part of the creation story.

NEITHER DID THE ORIGINAL SCRIBES. IT DID NOT MAKE IT PAST THEIR EDITORS. BUT IT IS TRUE. LATER, THE BOOMERANG THAT LUCIFER

HATH LOBBED DID COME BACK AROUND AND KNOCKED THE DEVIL CLEAN OUT OF HEAVEN.

I thought you kicked him out.

NO. I JUST LOCKED THE DOOR BEHIND HIM, AND WE MADE A NEW SECRET PASSWORD THAT WE WOULDN'T TELL HIM.

You ... you use secret passwords for Heaven?

YES, AND THE BEST PART WAS THAT THE PASSWORD WAS "BOOMERANG" AND LUCIFER COULDN'T GUESS IT.

Okay. I think I've heard enough.

As Jessica tuned back into the present, the table was still silent as the lawyers looked at one another. Perhaps they were wondering about the legal precedent for a do-over.

Had Jessica's heart ever raced so fast? Someone needed to speak, so it might as well be her. She hurried to remember where she'd left off before the Boomerang Rebellion nonsense. "You want to stop God because He—She—was onto you and your scheming. Stop making this about you being a victim. You're not a fucking victim. You're a predator, just like your minion Randy McAllister. You sent him off with me at the zoo that day to break me before I even got started, but it didn't work. And I bet you were even behind the assassination attempt on Jameson Fractal, though that just occurred to me now and I'm not really sure what your strategy was there. But I *know* you were behind that scathing article about me that Thornton News published. Your name was even in it." So many things, so many wrongs she'd almost forgotten. But remembering them steadied her.

Dolores grinned. "And now Eugene Thornton is dead. People might start to suspect it wasn't a coincidence."

"It wasn't."

Angelo said, "Jessica, as your legal counsel—"

"It was two tons of his own Karma"—*Boomerang* —"catching up with him. But if you want to make the case that I was somehow behind that dumb hipster dropping a giant decorative typewriter on Eugene Thornton's stupid fedora-ed head, go for it."

"No," Angelo said firmly, addressing Dolores's attorneys, "Don't go for it. Might I remind you that's *not* why we're here."

"We're here to settle a lawsuit," Dolores replied. "And I have everything I need to win it."

"Except case law," Angelo replied, and Jessica thought that was an especially brave thing to say. "There's no precedent for taking someone's personal brand as your own. You have an uphill battle there."

"Not if I happen to personally know the judge assigned."

Jessica turned to Angelo. "She probably does."

"It is Risen is mine until the end of time," Dolores continued. "I think you'll find that the contract is airtight, and there's plenty of case law *leaning* in my favor."

"Great," Jessica said. "It's all yours. Keep that pile of yeast. I have better things to do."

Wendy set a hand on Jessica's wrist, right around

where her hand clutched the armrest. Oh right. She wasn't supposed to be talking.

PROUD OF YOU, HONEY.

"I didn't want to sue Jimmy Dean," Dolores said, interrupting the attorney's latest attempt to negotiate. "He does such a wonderful job of making your life miserable, I wish he were one of my own. But compliance was never one of his strengths, so I simply sat back and watched it all unfold. Churches like his are my greatest ally. They start with a spark of personality and turn into a raging fire in the blink of an eye, gobbling up media attention, gaining popularity among the elite through the promise of an executive suite in Heaven. And just when everyone gets comfortable warming themselves by the fire, it spreads. Then everyone remembers that fire destroys, fire harms. Then they stop trusting fire. They stop trusting everything." She giggled. "Jimmy Dean has done more to make God look bad in the last twenty years than I have, truthfully. I hate to put a stop to it, but I can't let you win. If I don't enforce my ownership of your personal brand evenly, it hurts my case."

"I would never ask you to stop torturing Jimmy in any way, shape, or form."

Wendy's grip on her wrists was making the tips of her fingers tingle, so she shut up again and leaned back in her seat. The Devil added no further interruptions as the attorneys went over the terms.

It was another half hour before the meeting came to a close. Angelo looked browbeaten, and Wendy lacked her usual swagger as she stood and smoothed her hand over her A-line skirt.

Dolores's lawyers didn't look much better.

The only person who appeared satisfied was the Devil herself.

Jessica's crew exited the small room first, and as they stood in the elevator, she saw the others approaching. She had never punched a door close button so hard or rapidly in all her life.

Dolores made no attempt to jump on, but as the doors began to close, she managed get one last punch in. "Tell Courtney Wurst I said hello."

SHE'S JUST TRYING TO RATTLE YOU.

I know.

So, before they were completely cut off, Jessica threw her own right hook. "What goes around comes around. Karma's a boomerang."

She may not live to be one hundred, or even thirty-four, but she would savor that brief look of horror on Dolores's face until her dying breath.

Chapter Thirty-Four

190:07:16:47 until Doomsday

The intercom buzzed, and Jessica tore herself away from the copy of the Bible her mother had smuggled her the day before (she couldn't be seen buying it in public for herself). Genesis was really something. And not a single mention of boomerangs. A more fractured mind might have suspected it a conspiracy, but Jessica *knew* it to be one.

She crossed the room and looked at the low-pixel intercom screen that showed the doorstep of the building. It was ... a woman in a black burka? Had the woman meant to ring Jessica's unit? She had no problem with Islam, or not a problem much different from the one she had with Christianity, but she didn't *know* any Muslims.

Or perhaps she did without realizing it.

But she definitely would've noticed if they were the kind to wear a burka in public.

She decided the buzzer wasn't for her and went back to the couch. But just as she found her place, the intercom buzzed again.

Rather than buzzing this unknown person into the building, she spoke into the microphone, "Who is it?"

A strange falsetto voice replied. "I am an admirer of Jessica"—she pronounced it Yessica—"and I have traveled far to ask for a favor."

What the fuck accent is that?

This was a hit, wasn't it? Had the Devil hired someone to kill her?

More importantly, did it matter? God wouldn't let her be assassinated right now, would She?

No matter, if someone saw her turning this woman away, it would undoubtedly make the news that she hated Muslims. There was only one thing to do.

She looked around her condo for something weapon-like before remembering she could smite.

"I'll be down in just a second. Let me get some shoes."

As she stepped out into the hallway, Jeremy peeked his head out of his front door. "Jess, do you have a moment?"

"Not now. I think there's someone here to murder me."

He held up a hand. "Ah. Say no more. I'll talk to you afterward."

She rotated her wrists, limbering them up for a smiting if need be and steadied herself before opening the frosted-glass front door. "What can I do for you?"

She couldn't see the visitor's eyes behind the mesh veil, and that alarmed her more than anything.

But when the woman reached up, grabbed the veil and pulled it back, her alarm turned to annoyance. Those blue eyes. She would have recognized them anywhere. Who knew you could grow to hate blue eyes so much?

"God dammit, Jimmy—"

His hand shot up and covered her mouth. "No one can know I was here." She nodded and he dropped his hand from her mouth, which she wiped off with the back of her hand.

"What do you want?"

"I'm here to help you."

"I doubt that."

He lunged forward, reaching for her shoulders with both hands, but she sidestepped and shoved the door in his face.

"Gah!" He grabbed his nose, glaring at her once she opened the door again. "I promise. You'll want to listen to me."

"Fine. Talk. But no touching."

"Since our fates are now intertwined—"

"They're not."

"—I wanted to advise you that you would do well to find a strong alibi for Thursday evening. The stronger, the better. Use the paparazzi to your benefit on this."

Dread filled her gut. "What the hell are you up to, Jimmy?"

"Nothing. Just trust me."

"I will not."

"You must! Jessica, you absolutely must find a strong

alibi for Thursday evening from, say, seven to eleven. I know I'll have one myself."

She opened the door wider. "*What* are you up to?"

"You have nothing to lose by following this advice. Please take it."

"Just tell me why."

"It's better if you don't know."

And then he replaced the veil, bowed his head, and hurried off down the street.

At least he was gone. Any moment where Jimmy fucking Dean was leaving was a better moment than the one before it.

She shut the door, making sure to listen for the click of the lock engaging.

An alibi? Something was going down. But he had a point: what harm could a good alibi do her?

And yet ... did she trust him? Nine times out of ten not trusting Jimmy was the way to go.

As she trudged back up the stairs, her eyes landed on the drink machine.

God, I could go for a coke.

The machine rumbled, and a bottle fell into the dispenser. She pulled it out. Dr. Pepper.

She twisted off the cap, took a sip, then raised a toast to the ceiling.

As she reached her doorstep, Jeremy stepped out from across the hall. "All done with the assassination attempt?" He sounded out of breath and looked slightly more disheveled than usual, but at least he appeared to have given up on the hockey mask and thermal blanket cape. Maybe 5G signals weren't harmful after all.

"What's up?"

He looked around, scanning for others who might overhear, but she was pretty sure he was the only one who controlled any recording devices in the vicinity. He moved close, setting a hand on her arm, and she wondered if she'd ever made physical contact with him before. She couldn't think of a reason on God's green earth why they would have. "Have you gained your tax-exempt status for the church yet?"

"Yeah, we got that a while ago."

His knees buckled slightly, and he threw his head back and fist pumped the air. "Great. Yes, okay. Would you like some money?"

The physical contact ceased, which she was grateful for immediately. "Yeah, sure. But what's going on, Jeremy?"

He leaned forward conspiratorially, which was the norm for him, and she worried he was going to touch her again. "I just got the yearly projections in. My company has too much money. *Far* too much money. I need to funnel some off over the next few years, and a church would be the perfect place for it."

"If I take your money, that doesn't mean you have any influence over the way things run. Now or ever. Understood?"

His upper lip curled, and he jerked his head back, conjuring a double chin out of thin air. "Of course. You think I want to get mixed up in a *church*? No, no, no. And besides, I already make enough big decisions every day."

"Oh yeah? You moved up from three?"

"No. Moved down to two. Three was too many. I'm not as young as I used to be. So, can I count on you to take the contributions?"

She sighed. "How much are we talking about here?"

"Five hundred million spread over five years."

She sighed again. "Yeah, I guess that's fine."

"Excellent. Thank you, Jessica. I knew I could count on you. Jesus wasn't sure you'd accept, but I never doubted you."

She opened her mouth to ask why Jesus would assume she wouldn't take five hundred million dollars, but then shut it. It was probably better if she didn't question it.

Jeremy retreated back into his lair, and she stared dazedly at his front door.

After all the scrounging and agonizing over not having enough money to start a business, after failure upon failure that led her to signing a deal with the Devil, now this. She couldn't keep money away if she tried. It just found her now.

She took a sip of her stolen Dr. Pepper.

Money, it seemed, wasn't that hard to come by after all. You just had to start a church.

Jessica finished her coke and dialed the first number that

came to mind. If Jimmy told her she needed an alibi, she might as well listen. No harm in it.

Jameson Fractal answered on the second ring. "Hey, Jess! How's it going?"

"Good, good." *I was just gifted five hundred million dollars and it felt like nothing.* "You?"

"Oh, just breaking for lunch on set."

Damn. "Oh yeah? I didn't realize you were working right now."

Voices on the other line piped up and Jameson chuckled and said, "Yeah, back at you, Dwayne! You take care!" Then, "We're filming another Dark & Dirty movie. Turns out, it's been long enough since the first one came out that a whole new generation of viewers is discovering it and it's getting popular all over again."

"That's great." She couldn't have cared less.

"So, what's up?"

"Well, I just called to see what you were doing Thursday, but I think I already have my answer."

"Aw, yeah, sorry. We're shooting in LA and I'll be here for the next couple of weeks. Why? What's happening Thursday?"

"No idea. I was, um, told I should have an alibi. And you know how much attention you draw."

He chuckled. "I do. Well, sorry I can't help. I could hook you up with someone else high-profile who's not working right now, if you want. How strong of an alibi do you need? I can send a married one your way, really get some cameras on you."

Jessica cringed and tried not to make a noise to accompany it. "Alibi, not scandal. But thanks, I appreciate the sentiment. I'm not in the mood to be murdered by Wendy, though."

"Good point. Well, hey, what about Chris? The Eagles got eliminated in the wildcard game, right? He should be free."

Her stomach clenched. "Yeah, good point." She'd already thought of him, of course, but just as quickly dismissed him. "I'll give him a call. Good luck with the filming."

"Thanks, but I don't need it. My stunt double is on screen more than I am, honestly."

They finished the call with Jameson promising to give her a ring next time he was in town.

She squinted at the phone. What were her options? She needed to be out in public with all eyes on her. She was certainly a pro at causing a scene all on her own. But she also didn't want months of fallout from it.

"Hey, hey! What's up?" The familiarity of Chris's voice felt warm in her chest.

"Hey. I know it's a little bit last-minute, but Jimmy just stopped by."

"Fucking Jimmy. What'd he want?"

"He was dressed as a Muslim woman and he told me I needed an alibi for this Thursday."

There was a pause, then, "The fuck?"

"Who knows. Would you by any chance have the

evening free and want to go grab a bite with me somewhere public?"

"Do I want an excuse to get the hell out of Philly in January after I threw an interception that cost us the wildcard game? Big, fat yes to that. You want us to pretend we're getting back together?"

An invisible fist grabbed her stomach and twisted. "Well, I mean, the paparazzi can make of it whatever they want. I just need it to be obvious that I'm in a specific place."

"Right, right. What do you think he's got planned?"

"You mean beside the end of the world?"

"Besides that, yeah."

"No clue. And I don't really understand why he would warn me about it, either. Since when is he my friend? Sure, we have a truce right now, but I hardly consider him an actual ally."

"Jess, I think you could drive yourself crazy trying to guess what Jimmy will do on any given Thursday. What time should I pick you up?"

They made plans, and it all fell into place a little too easily. It felt more like he was going to give her a ride from practice over to Gordon's burgers, not fly a thousand miles across the country to take her to an undoubtedly fancy restaurant where they'd put on a show for the cameras.

"It's a date," he concluded. "I'll get some rumors going that I'm flying back home to win the heart of my first love, and that should bring the paparazzi flocking."

"You don't have to say all that."

"You want an alibi, right?"

"I do. It's just that you don't have to make up some big, romantic drama on my account."

"Don't be mad, but it's more for me. I need to win some hearts here, Jess. Anything to keep these fucking fans from eating me alive."

She grimaced. "Got it. See you Thursday."

Chapter Thirty-Five

184:05:57:01 until Doomsday

Jessica felt her ears perk up before she consciously registered the sound of the F-350's engine. She peeked out the window down at the street and spotted it pull up to the curb. It wasn't his old one, but she'd known that instantly by sound. This was a much newer version. Probably a rental, considering he'd flown rather than driven from Philadelphia.

She grabbed her favorite purse, noted how weird it was to own more than one functional purse at a time, grabbed a light sweater, after all, it was winter and the sun had already set, and then met Chris downstairs.

He held the door open for her to get into the cab, and cameras seemed to appear out of nowhere.

Offering her a goofy sideways grin that lacked even an iota of smoothness, he said, "You look beautiful." She wasn't sure why she'd expected his NFL stardom to make him suddenly a different person, more like Jameson in the way he commanded the crowd with a symmetrical smile and a wink than the reckless boy who'd punched Greg Burns in the jaw at prom, but she was glad it was still the same old Christopher Riley, albeit a more muscular version than the one she'd known as a child.

"Where we going?" she asked as he pulled away from the curb. He'd promised that he would handle all the plans and she just needed to be ready to leave by six.

"Somewhere fancy."

"Oh no. Please don't tell me it's full of cats."

He took his eyes off the road. "Uh, what?"

"Cats. We're not going to cat sushi, right?"

He winced. "Jess, I don't think you're allowed to eat cats in this country."

"No, you don't eat them. They just crawl all over while you eat regular sushi."

He was silent, staring contemplatively at the road ahead. "That doesn't make sense."

"No." She laughed, feeling relieved. "No, it doesn't."

When he pulled onto a side street heading east, she became confused. If they were going to be conspicuous, wouldn't they want to be downtown? That was the other way.

They turned a corner, and she saw a sudden burst of light down an otherwise quiet, run-down road of tiny, ancient houses on cramped lots that were probably selling for a half million apiece. LED light seared into her eyeballs and she blinked away tracers and squinted at the source. It was some sort of a restaurant, mostly outdoor seating. A long line stretched out the door, and underneath large green arches were rows and rows of packed picnic tables. The interior of the restaurant, which she could see through the glass windows that stretched the entire length of it, was also packed.

"There it is," Chris said.

Yep, they could cause a great scene in a place like this. Multi-angle cell phone footage, lots of timestamps. They didn't even need the professionals to harass them.

"What kind of food is— Oh my god." Her eyes finally found the sign. The logo had been jazzed up a bit, but she knew from the smiling burger man that it was the same one. "Gordon's? Are you serious?"

Chris's grin was untamable. "You didn't know he opened a location in Austin?"

"No! How did I not know?" She paused. "Oh wait. I don't get out much and I stay away from the internet. Is it as good as the one in Mooretown?"

He shrugged. "Dunno. Haven't been to it yet."

She felt a strange sense of pride staring at the little burger joint that could. But more than pride, she felt something else, something deeper, smoother, warmer ...

She looked at Chris, who was still grinning even as someone ran a stop sign and caused him to slam on his brakes. They found parking a block down from the restaurant, and he hurried around and opened the door for her, helping her down from the high seat.

Holding out his arm for her: "Shall we?"

She couldn't *not* take his arm in hers, really. The contact felt as natural as it ever had.

They came from around the side of the building where the line stretched out from the door, and Chris slowed down.

So he *did* know how to play this game.

She heard the first gasp, saw the first young woman's eyes go wide before she whipped around to her friend to not-so-subtly point out that an NFL quarterback and the self-proclaimed daughter of God were walking past.

Chris laughed and leaned close. "We've come a long way, haven't we?"

"And yet we're still going to Gordon's for dinner."

"I wouldn't change a thing."

Finally, someone got the balls to step out of the line. "Chris Riley, can I have your autograph?"

"Absolutely, man."

While she paused for Chris to chum around with his fan, someone tapped her on the shoulder. She turned to find herself staring into a round face of a beautiful round woman about her age.

"Sorry," the woman said.

Ah yes, that old feminine greeting.

"Don't be sorry. What's up?"

"You're Jessica Christ, right?"

That name had never had much of a ring to it. But it was hers. She'd claimed it with the rest of her inconvenient divinity. "Yep, that's me."

"I just want to say ..."

With horror, Jessica noticed the girl's eyes filling with tears. "Hey, hey ..." She placed a steadying hand on her shoulder. "Are you okay?"

"Yeah, I'm fine." Emphatic nod. "I donated to your church."

"Really?" For some reason it'd never occurred to her that those throwing so much money at her were living, breathing people she could run into. "I mean, thanks so much."

"I think you're great. My girlfriend is a Nu Alpha Omega at UT. I didn't go to college, so I couldn't join, but if I had, I would've pledged."

Jessica chuckled on an exhale. "That doesn't matter much. People can be NAOs if they want, but it doesn't mean anything one way or another."

That seemed to cheer her. "Can I have a hug?"

"Of course. Of course."

She hardly even noticed the phones out around her, recording it all.

Once the first brave souls had come forward, more followed, and it was another ten minutes before Jessica and Chris even made it to the back of the line.

"You changed my life," said one girl who looked too young to have needed a life change.

And another said, "I can't wait to tell your story to my daughter."

"That's sweet. How old is she?"

The woman had looked down at her stomach. "Negative five months."

Jessica had felt emotion clench her throat at that point, and she nodded, gave the woman a hug, and then hurried to meet up with Chris.

Her head was swimming as she stood there, plastering on a dazed smile while he chatted with the couple in front of them. The two men held hands and spouted more football knowledge than anyone should possess, which was clearly a holy gift to Chris. He met them stat for stat.

Jessica looked around at the outdoor tables. She estimated that one out of every three sets of eyes was aimed in her direction.

Was this smart, or was she leaving herself too exposed?

OH, HONEY. YOU NEED TO CALM DOWN.

Do I? It seems like we're awfully vulnerable here.

THAT'S THE POINT, ISN'T IT?

Yeah, but what if some crazy asshole decides they've had enough of the daughter of God? And let us not forget we're in Cowboys country. Chris is an Eagle.

WHAT DO YOU THINK MIGHT HAPPEN?

Anything! Someone could just shoot us.

YOU REALLY THINK I'M GOING TO LET SOME NUTJOB SHOOT YOU RIGHT NOW? HAVE YOU DIE IN CHRIS'S ARMS?

She considered it. *No, I guess that wouldn't make any narrative sense.*

EXACTLY. JUST ENJOY IT WHILE YOU CAN.

Just once I wish you could not be so damn ominous.

LOOK. SEE THAT GUY OVER IN THE SHADOWS TO YOUR LEFT?

Jessica peered around Christopher and her eyes found the dark silhouette. Creepy.

Yeah, I see him.

HE WANTS TO MURDER YOU. IT WOULD BE A CRIME OF OPPORTUNITY. DON'T WORRY, HE HASN'T BEEN FOLLOWING YOU OR ANYTHING.

That wasn't what I was immediately worried about. Go back to the part about him wanting to murder me.

HE JUST GOT HIS GUN FROM THE CAR. BUT DON'T FREAK OUT. DO YOU TRUST IN THE LORD?

Hell no.

THEN WATCH THIS.

The man's arm was straight by his side, and Jessica guessed that was because of what it was holding. His eyes locked onto hers, and he stepped away from his car and into the street. She readied herself to smite if it came to that, which it looked like it might. She could see the hatred in his eyes but didn't have time to wonder why it was there before the Jeep Grand Cherokee mowed him down.

A screech of brakes too late, a nauseating crunch, and the handgun went spiraling across the street to land only a few yards away from where Jessica stood.

Her mouth fell open, but she couldn't speak. Thankfully, there were plenty of other people around to call the cops.

The unlucky driver jumped out of the Jeep, and her

hand flew up to her mouth immediately when she saw the crumpled body in the road.

"Chris," Jessica said, pulling him out of his own state of shock. "You take the driver. Calm her down. Let her know she's not responsible for hitting him. He just stepped out of nowhere." She looked around until she saw the familiar faces of women she'd spoken with in line. "You, you, and you. There's a gun on the ground. Don't touch it, but don't let anyone else touch it until the cops come."

YOU'RE DOING GREAT, BABY.

There were enough phone recordings of us, you asshole! You didn't need to do this!

DO WHAT, SAVE YOUR LIFE? SO RUDE.

She hated what she was about to do. Hated it more than anything. Would it convert him? Would it make him despise her any less? She doubted it. Resurrecting this murderous piece of shit would probably only piss him off more.

But it sure as hell created a solid alibi.

The foggy dusk light played tricks on her eyes so she couldn't quite see the extent of his injuries until she was right up close.

"Oh, holy fucking hell." She jerked her head back and averted her eyes. That was not the way his knee was supposed to bend, and the arm that had held the gun was MIA from the elbow down. "I can't do this," she mumbled. "He'll be in complete agony if I bring him back."

She heard the sirens in the distance. Okay. That was good. She'd have to time this perfectly, though. And still, would it work? She couldn't keep her mind from jumping back to the bullet-riddled man on her front driveway back in Mooretown.

The flashing lights turned onto the street, and she shut her eyes.

Fuck you for wanting to kill me.

Then she let the miracle of life wash through her and into him.

A moan like he was clearing his throat, and then the screaming began. She gritted her teeth when he gasped for air. "I forgive you."

There. That might work for a little bit of pain relief.

The cops were on him in a heartbeat then, tourniquets already in hand. One pulled her up and away, and she directed him to the gun on the ground.

She felt arms around her and knew they belonged to Chris. She turned toward him. "I'm going to kill him."

Chris's brows pinched together. "What do you mean? You just saved him."

"No, not him. Jimmy Dean. He's the whole reason I'm here. He's the reason God had to kill that guy."

That was not, as it seemed, clarifying information for Chris. She sighed and decided to change the subject to one he could handle. "You think you could eat?"

He didn't skip a beat. "Yup."

"Still after all this?"

"Always."

* * *

Jessica had passed on ketchup with her fries, but otherwise her meal went down fine. The cops had wanted to speak with each of them as witnesses but had taken a special interest in Jessica, for obvious reasons.

She'd half expected Officer Misty McBride, the gruff woman who had responded to Jessica's bakery twice and become fast friends with Destinee, to show up, but not this time. She didn't recognize any of the officers, and none seemed to recognize her. But some of the other witnesses had clued them in, and by the time they'd taken her statement, boy did they have questions.

Which meant it was an hour later before she'd been able to order her food, and she was well and truly hungry by then.

So was poor Chris, and he inhaled his double burger before she'd hardly done more than unwrap her silver paper and poured her fries out on her tray. They weren't as good without ketchup, but they were still better than vomiting.

"God did that?" he said, finally taking a breath before swigging his Dr. Pepper from the clear plexiglass cup.

"Oh yeah. But to be fair, the guy was coming to kill me."

"What?!"

"Shh ... calm down."

"Why, you afraid we'll make a scene?"

Their eyes met and the laughter wasn't far behind. It was the manic variety that made her wonder if she'd lost control completely, and before long they were both in tears.

He wiped his away and caught his breath with a "Woo …"

She required just a little more time before she was in control again, and when she was, she tossed back a pinch of fries. "Thanks for taking me here. I think that would have happened no matter where we went, honestly."

"You think it was predestined?"

She shrugged. "Who knows. It's just a feeling."

He nodded. "I'm glad God's watching out for you. 'Bout time."

God sent me you, didn't she?

The thought surprised her. It sounded like it belonged on a greeting card, not in her mind beside the countdown clock to Doomsday. She chalked it up to the adrenaline crash.

"Can I ask you something, Chris?"

"Of course."

"Being seen together like this, people are going to assume things about us. It's not going to, you know, cause you any problems with someone back in Philly, is it?"

He didn't seem to understand right away. Then, "Oh. You mean like a girlfriend?"

She nodded.

He tilted his head to the side like a confused puppy. "Jess. You serious?"

She nodded again.

"You know ... I tried. Honestly. But who am I gonna date after the daughter of God? No one comes close."

"Sorry."

He shrugged. "Don't be. It's not like I don't have anything else to occupy my time. What about you, though?"

"What about me?"

"You seeing anyone?" He rattled the ice in his cup then took a sip, almost pulling off nonchalance. "Jameson or whoever?"

"Ha!" Then she realized he was serious and maybe she should be a little more delicate about the situation. "No, no. No time for it. And Jameson is ... He's just a friend."

Chris relaxed visibly. "I was honestly surprised you called me for the alibi and not him."

"Mm-hmm."

"You know, dead assassin aside, this has been a pretty good night."

She smiled. "Yeah, dead assassin aside, it has."

"It's nice spending time with you again. I never want to go back to Mooretown, but being with you feels like home in all the right ways."

Oh, come on. What was she supposed to say to *that*?

She figured it out in short order. "Fuck it. You wanna get out of here?"

His eyebrows shot up as he caught her meaning. "Uh, *hell* yeah."

He gathered her trash onto his tray and was hardly out

of the booth before he grabbed her hand and dragged her impatiently toward the exit.

But when they stepped outside, their impulsive plans came to a screeching halt. The path was blocked by a fresh wave of reporters. Was this about the crash? It was a slow response if so. The police had already cleared the scene, though a few cop cars still hung around, lights flashing as the officers conversed.

The frontrunner of the throng shouted her question as she closed in. "Jessica, any comments on the fire?"

Chris cursed as she gripped his hand so hard she felt the bones of his knuckles grind.

But before she could say anything else, another reporter piped up. "Miss McCloud, what do you have to say about the fire?"

She looked at Chris, who shook his head.

And then it all came crashing together. The whole reason for her night out. The alibi.

She recognized one man from the TV. He had a fatherly face, not literally, in her case, and he'd always expressed a deep sense of calm when he reported remotely. She addressed her question to him. "What fire?"

"You haven't heard?"

"No," she said urgently. "What fire?"

"At the bakery. It is Risen. It's burning down."

Chris hauled ass across town in the F-350 to her former bakery.

Both a thrill and white-hot rage swirled inside her. The loss she'd felt when it'd been wrested away from her hit her all over again. But this time it was laced with a subtle sense of victory. If Jessica couldn't own it, no one should.

"No, left!" she shouted.

Chris took the corner quickly, and she felt the wheels of the truck leave the ground.

"It's faster this way," she said, as the intimate routes of the neighborhood she no longer frequented returned to her like old neural patterns of addiction.

She saw the glow on the horizon, and anything she'd thought she felt moments before was thrown into question. This concoction of emotions was too complex to pick out any one ingredient.

They couldn't get within a block of the bakery. Fire trucks clogged the street directly in front of it, and the police had put up barriers to keep everyone away. She jumped out of the truck and ran over to the edge of the closest barrier to watch.

"'Scuse me, Officer," Chris said, waving down the closest one. She approached, her thumbs tucked into her duty belt. "Was anyone in there?"

Jessica hadn't even considered that possibility. Christ on a trampoline! Could Dolores have been in there? Could she be dead?

No, don't wish for that. She probably can't be burned anyway.

The officer looked Chris up and down, and Jessica didn't miss the moment of recognition when she placed his face. "No, no one was in there."

A gust of wind brought the smoke billowing their direction, and Jessica felt a madness well up in her when she got a whiff of fresh-baked bread. Nothing had ever smelled so perverse.

Her mind returned to the soft opening of the place, the party she'd thrown for everyone who'd supported her. But that was really when everything began to fall apart, wasn't it? Quentin and Miranda had broken up. Mrs. Thomas had been there, no doubt plotting to take the place for her own before long.

And still, she felt the loss of it acutely. Her marks were all over it, her history, her memories. They'd never managed to get her stalker's blood stain completely out of the cement by the front door. She'd smote a man right there. Even that brought about a bit of nostalgia. Her first kill ...

But another memory floated up like hot ash toward the heavens. This wasn't the first bakery she'd watched burn. Her food truck had burned, too.

Things didn't just catch fire.

How many times would she have to watch her creations burn to the ground? How much more of this unique blend of pain would she have to endure in her life? The sense of futility, though, was what haunted her the most. She built something, and someone made it their mission to destroy it. Over and over and over. Would it happen with her church? Would she watch that go up in flames, too?

She wouldn't if she could put an end to the fire starter.

Chris put his arm around her. "We should go."

"Jimmy did this," she whispered hoarsely.

"What?"

"Jimmy Dean set the fire." Fuck alliances, if this was where they got her. "He's set all the fires. It's time to make him pay."

Chapter Thirty-Six

183:17:00:01 until Doomsday

Chris picked her up at 7 a.m. sharp the next morning, and she was already waiting by the curb in front of her condo when he pulled up.

"How'd you sleep?" he asked when she hopped in.

"Great. Got a strong cup of coffee in me and I'm ready to murder a reverend."

Chris made a small squeaky sound, then said, "When you say you're going to murder him, you don't really mean it, right?"

"Depends." She turned to look him in the eyes. "Do you consider smiting murder?"

"Okay, Jess." Chris bowed his head and held up his hands. "I know you're pissed. But we've seen this story time and again—NFL player indirectly involved in a premeditated murder—and it doesn't work out well for said

NFL player. I could be out for two, maybe even three whole seasons. So, if I'm going to drive you out to his house, I need you to promise you won't kill him *or* smite him."

Well, damn. There went the revenge fantasies that had kept her hot and bothered all night. But he had a point. She could obviously get away with smiting someone, but Chris might not be so lucky. "Okay," she said, "I'll try not to smite him. Promise."

"You promise you'll try not to or you promise you won't?"

"Isn't it the same thing?"

He shook his head.

She *knew* she should have called her mom instead of Chris. Destinee wouldn't put all these ridiculous restraints on her. "Fine, fine. I promise not to smite him."

"That's all I needed to hear."

"But I will tear him a new one verbally."

"I'd expect nothing less. You got the address?"

Jimmy's house was out in Westlake, which Jessica knew meant it would be annoyingly large and expensive. But it wasn't until they pulled off a public road and onto his private drive that she began to think she'd underestimated the annoyingness of it.

They rounded a corner, Chris's F-350 announcing itself whether it meant to or not, and there it was. The Villa of Jimmy Fucking Dean.

"I didn't think it was possible to hate him more," Jessica said. "And yet, here I am." Never mind that both she and

Chris could probably afford something similar at this point. She knew neither of them ever would.

The mansion sat atop a hill that made it look like it was part of the sky. If the entire estate had been made of uncut cocaine, it would have been less brazen in its design. Tall white marble columns on either side of the paved drive held up an arch that had SUMUS OMNES PORCOS engraved in fake Roman script so that the "U"s were both "V"s. That detail made her hate him a little more.

The driveway curved round, and in the center of the bend was a marble fountain that depicted Jimmy Dean holding a baby skyward while a fat hog looked on from below.

And so it was that she hated him even more than a moment before.

It was her. She was sure. Jimmy had a fountain that included her as a baby. "I'm for sure not leaving here without smiting *that*," she said, and Chris only nodded his consent silently.

"Where should I park?"

"On the lawn."

He shot her a quick glance and a sliver of a grin peeked through before he pulled the truck onto the perfectly manicured lawn and killed the engine.

The sun was only just up, and it shone directly onto the face of the mansion, making the whole thing glow with an aggravating sense of superiority.

Jessica's heart raced. She didn't exactly know what she was going to do from here. Once her smiting fantasies had kicked in the night before, they hadn't let up. But if that was off the table, what was her game plan?

She didn't have one, but too late to back out now.

She climbed down from the truck, wondering if she could isolate the smite. Maybe just blast off one of Jimmy's hands. Smite that dick right off him. He couldn't be putting it to any good use, anyway.

Chris had to jog to catch up with her on her path toward the front door.

DO NOT SMITE HIM.

I'm not planning on it.

LIKE HELL YOU'RE NOT.

Seriously. I'm not planning on—

THOU SHALT NOT SMITE JIMMY DEAN.

"Dammit!"

SEE? IF YOU WEREN'T PLANNING ON IT, YOU WOULDN'T BE UPSET.

Can I smite him just a little?

NO. HIS PART ISN'T DONE YET.

She found herself stumped when she reached the door and wasn't sure of the proper way to announce herself. Pounding on the door like she was the police sounded nice, but there was that damn boar's head knocker that threw her off. And was this place so big he might not hear her? She went with the doorbell instead and immediately regretted it when it emitted a deep, choral "soo-ie!"

Had she descended into Hell without realizing it?

She heard locks turning and steadied herself for the

attack, but when the door opened, she wondered if there'd been some mistake.

A woman with sex-tousled hair wearing a white silk robe with red embroidery around the edges stared back at them from the other side of the threshold.

Jessica had almost forgotten. Jimmy Dean was engaged, wasn't he?

The woman's mouth fell open then quickly bent into a smile. "Jessica McCloud?" She turned toward Chris. "And you must be Chris Riley, the sports player." She held out her hand. "Emily. The reverend's fiancée."

Jessica exchanged a small glance with Chris before shaking Emily's hand quickly, like it was contaminated. "We're looking for Jimmy."

"Of course you are. I didn't know he was expecting you."

"He's not."

"Well, that's fine. You're practically family." She stepped back, allowing them past. "Come on in. He's breakfasting in the conservatory."

Jessica felt that morning's coffee try to make an esophageal escape at the phrase, "breakfasting in the conservatory," but she swallowed it down and stepped into Hell's foyer. Emily padded barefoot along the white marble floors past an ungodly number of highly stylized photos and painted portraits of Jimmy that lined the walls.

Jessica regretted not tracking in more dirt on her shoes.

The conservatory, it turned out, was on the far side of the residence. Emily led them to the entrance of a sunlit room where a glass wall provided a clear view of the lake. Jimmy Dean wore a robe that matched his bride-to-be's and he hunched over a bowl of something hot, reading the paper. He looked up when Emily announced them. "You have guests, light of my life."

A flash of confusion so brief Jessica thought she'd imagined it, and then he straightened up, dropped his spoon, and said, "Ah! Jessica! And Christopher, too! What a surprise! Come in, come in. I'll have Juanita bring you some porridge, if you'd like. It's ancient grain, only farmed in a small valley in present day Iraq, but the seeds are descended from those of the original fertile crescent."

"I'd rather eat my own shit," Jessica said before cringing slightly at the thought. It wasn't as badass of a retort as she'd imagined. Pretty weird, actually. But too late now. "Jimmy, we need to talk." She stepped forward, and Jimmy nodded to Emily. "You won't want to see this, dear. I might have to be blunt with her. Not all women know their place like you do."

"Yeah," Jessica said, "Lady Stockholm Syndrome is a real role model."

Jimmy stood from his chair as Jessica continued stalking toward him on the far side of the overlong table. "You don't seem happy, Jessica. Tell me what's on your mind."

"You set fire to the bakery last night."

He laughed. "Of course I didn't. You think I would do something like that myself? Ha! Look around you? I could pay someone to carry me from room to room if I wanted."

"I think you like setting fires," she said, pausing when she was only a few feet from him. "I think you would do it yourself for the sheer pleasure of it."

He blinked at her and something in his expression cleared. When he spoke again, his voice was devoid of the puckish playfulness. "I thought you'd be happy to see that place burn. It's owned by the Devil. It was no good to either of us. She was tarnishing your brand."

Jessica felt dizzy at the hypocrisy. "*She* was tarnishing my brand? Are you— Do you even—" She felt her fingers begin to tingle, and her biceps tightened like rubber bands.

Chris was there in an instant, his hand around one of her arms to pull her back from the brink. "You have a lot of nerve, Jimmy. No one's done more to hurt Jessica's reputation than you."

"She must not have told you, Christopher. She and I are allies now. All that happened in the past is forgotten."

"Bull*shit*," Jessica spat. Her gaze jumped down to one of the place settings on the table. She could stab him with a fork, and he'd be fine. Plus, it would feel amazing. She went for it, but hardly got more than a twitch in before Chris had both of her arms in his firm grip.

"Jessica, if you and I are to continue working together, we *both* have to find it in our hearts to forgive. I've done the work myself, so I know it's hard, but it's worth it."

"Knock it off with the Church Jimmy shit," she spat. "I know it was you who burned down my food truck."

His eyebrows shot up. "Your ... food truck?"

"You heard me."

He scratched casually at the gray hair around his temple and chuckled gently. "Don't you see? It's all been to help you. You were thinking too small. A food truck wasn't going to launch you to a position of authority and power. And so long as you had that crutch, you would continue carrying on in your small, protected world. I freed you."

The tide rose in her again. "You *freed* me? You expect me to believe that your whole point in trying to destroy me again and again, starting when I was a *child* was to *free me?* Are you fucking serious with that, Jimmy? Are you fucking serious?!" The pull inside her was growing stronger, and she glanced over her shoulder at Chris. "You gotta let me go. I don't want to accidentally hurt you."

He shook his head firmly, but she could see the fear in his eyes.

"Gah!" She tried to shake free. "Chris! Let me go!"

"DON'T let her go, Christopher," Jimmy said, and she heard the fear in his voice. Everyone in this room was afraid of her. Hell, she was afraid of her.

And she didn't love it.

"Jimmy?" came Emily's voice from the doorway. "Everything okay?"

Jessica spared her a glance and that was what did it. That look in the woman's eyes. Genuine concern. For Jimmy.

For Jimmy?

She looked back at the object of all her hatred, and for a moment, she could see the resemblance he bore to his own mother, that horrible witch in Waverly Hills.

She'd never felt so disgusted in all her life, but with what precisely, she wasn't sure.

She stopped struggling against Chris and finally inhaled a full breath, then exhaled slowly. He let go of her, but she knew it was on a probationary basis.

"This alliance," she said, motioning between herself and Jimmy. "It's off. I won't smite you now, but mark my word, if you get in my way, I will destroy you. You understand?"

His voice came out smooth and measured. "Perfectly."

"Your churches could all go up in flames, and I wouldn't ask God for rain. In fact, I hope they do."

She marched toward the exit. Chris's heavy footfalls remained a step behind her.

"You're more like your mother than I thought," Jimmy called after her, his words echoing off the barren surfaces.

Without slowing, she hollered, "Which one?" and, with a middle finger held high, left the conservatory.

Chapter Thirty-Seven

183:15:49:45 until Doomsday

They made out in the truck as soon as Chris had pulled off of Jimmy's property and found a safe shoulder on which to park. Jessica didn't feel like she'd had much of a choice in the matter, so carried on the wave of victorious adrenaline as she was. However, if given a choice, she would have ended up in the same place, arms groping him furiously as she leaned over the center armrest to meet his horny onslaught with equal force.

And she was positive they would have gone farther than the aggressive liplock, if she hadn't suddenly remembered something important. "Oh damn! The fountain!"

Chris understood immediately and untangled himself from her to drive them back onto the Dean estate, where she rolled down the window and disintegrated the cursed fountain in a fit of smiteful glee.

"We're good," she said, rolling up her window. "Let's get out of here."

And Chris did just that, but not before spinning a few donuts in Jimmy's lawn.

Once they were on the road again, Chris asked, "You hungry?" And before she could answer added, "Because I'm starving."

They agreed that honey butter chicken biscuits were in order and stopped in at an overly posh Whataburger. The long line provided a still moment to think, and she felt the awkwardness settle in between them post-makeout. Did they have to have "the talk" now? Whataburger didn't seem like the right place for...

Then it struck her that Whataburger was, in fact, the exact type of place where people had "the talk."

Regardless, she didn't want to, and she set her mind against it.

And as they sat in their hard booth in silence, devouring their orders, Jessica's adrenaline finally took a hard downward turn. She could sleep for days, and she was tempted to give it a shot. But she had too much to do.

"Wah-ha gig om feel olls?"

Chris turned to her, his mouth equally stuffed to the brim. "Uh?"

She held up a finger while she chewed. "Wanna kick some field goals? Well, I kick them, you hold?"

He held up a finger too, now, until he could speak. "Hell yes, I'll hold for you."

She thought they would have to swing by her condo for the ball, but Chris already had a few in the rental.

Twenty minutes later, they were at the high school. Because she usually came out here in the evenings with Quentin, it hadn't occurred to her that the field might already be in use by, duh, the school. "Well, dang," she said as they pulled into the parking lot.

"What?"

"They're using it for PE or whatever. So we can't go out there." It was the first week of school after the holidays, and it showed. Teenagers were dropping like flies around the track, some bracing themselves on their knees, others with their hands raised over their head, gasping for air, and others flopped on the grass, refusing to move. Ah, she remembered it well.

He squinted at her. "You know I'm a famous athlete now, right?" He rolled his eyes and opened the driver's side door, and once she understood his point, she climbed out, too.

At first, as they opened the gate and entered the practice field, they received glares from the more world-weary of the students. Good for them. Adults had no business wandering around on school grounds like this, not even pretend adults like her and Chris.

But the suspicion faded to incredulousness quickly once the teens recognized the interlopers. After Chris cleared it with their PE teacher, who seemed as enthusiastic to be back in school as his students, the two of them were set. And not only that, they had plenty of willing volunteers to shag the balls for them. Anything to keep from running the track.

They started from the thirty, Chris going down on one knee, his finger pinning the top of the ball, laces out. All of it, every movement, every angle, felt right. Two steps back. One to the side. Set and kick.

Easy stuff. The ball soared through the uprights, and a girl caught it on the other side and held it up like a trophy.

Jessica met Chris's eyes, and they both laughed.

"Move it on back," he said, getting to his feet and holding out his hands for a throw from the girl with the ball.

By the time they were on the twenty-yard-line of the opposing side of the field, making it a ninety yarder when she finally split the uprights, they looked at each other and nodded. That was probably enough. The students were at a fever pitch with excitement seeing something live they'd only ever seen on YouTube clips that by now looked old-timey to them.

Chris wanted to stick around a little while longer and toss the ball with some of the kids, and since Jessica had literally no football skills outside of her miracle, she took a seat on the bleachers to watch.

"How'd you do that?" a boy a few feet down the row from her asked. He had to be in high school, but with his size, he could have easily passed for sixth grade.

"It's a miracle," she said. "Don't you recognize a miracle when you see one?"

He scooted closer. "I don't believe in all that."

"Then how do you explain what you just saw?"

He shrugged a single shoulder. "I dunno. That's why I'm asking you. Come on, you can tell me the truth."

"I did. It's a miracle. I'm the daughter of God. I can do weird shit."

He blinked. "The daughter of God can say 'shit'?"

She looked around for an adult, remembered for the tenth time that day that she was one, and then leaned toward him. "I can say whatever the fuck I want." She straightened up. "Well, some of my words have consequences. I can still say them, but I have to accept the outcome of them."

He nodded sagely. "That makes sense. Words do have consequences."

"Oh, right. I see what *you're* saying, but I just meant when I tell someone 'I forgive you' or 'damn you.' Those two things in particular." She waved it off. "But you're right, too. The way you're talking about is way more applicable."

By the time Chris jogged over, red faced and grinning wildly, she was ready to hit the road. The sun was scorching overhead, and, as far as she knew, she possessed no miracles that protected against UV-A and UV-B.

Only once they were in the truck and had the doors closed did she realize he stank to high heaven. Grass and sweat and dirt—she would have rolled in it if she could.

The smells brought her back to the glow of Friday night lights, the steam rising off bodies in the huddle, even the oppressive musk of the locker room. She was nostalgic for it all.

Me. Nostalgic for high school. Who woulda thought?

"Burgers?" Chris said, cranking up the AC. She hit the button to change it from recycled to fresh air.

"It would seem wrong not to."

And so, fifteen minutes later, they pulled up to Gordon's burger joint.

She was both pleased and a little horrified to discover that within twenty-four hours of seeing a man ripped open by a motor vehicle just yards from where she was, she'd regained her ability to eat ketchup without issue, and she'd slathered it over her fries.

She hadn't gotten so much physical movement in a long time, and when she paused in her eating to take a breath, she found Chris staring at her. "What?" She dabbed at her face with a napkin in case that was it.

"I think we should get back together," he said.

She set down her burger. "We've been over this. I'm starting a church, Chris. The first service is less than seven months away."

"I know," he said, undeterred. "But when we do have time, I want to spend it together." He looked down at his tray for a moment, and she thought he might lose his train of thought and simply continue eating, but instead, he looked back up at her. "I'm never gonna find anyone else who can compare to you. I've had women come through my life and they're just ... women. You're more than that."

"A demigod?"

"Well, yes, I guess, but I also mean as a person. I've loved you since I can remember. When I think of what a girlfriend, or, hell, even a wife looks like, you're all I can think about."

It was all very flattering, but there was one fat detail nagging at her. "You're forgetting that you're an angel, Chris. These feelings you have for me, they're mostly due to the fact that you're wired to protect me and do what I say."

He reached across the table and took her hand, mustard and pickle juice and all, in his. "Is that so bad? I was predestined to love you, Jessica, and maybe you're predestined to love me. But would that be so bad? We could live our lives knowing the other was made for us. I thought that was the dream."

Jessica found herself in a mild state of shock. Besides never having guessed that Chris knew the word "predestined," he made a solid point.

"I do still love you, Chris. Of course I do."

"But?"

"But the thought of giving into my dad's—sorry, *mom's* —plans just makes me uncomfortable."

"How do you know God planned this?"

Shit. Was he secretly an atheist too? "Because ... that's what God does."

"Does She plan the earthquakes in Asia?"

"No, pretty sure that's Original Mistake."

"Does She control the Devil?"

"She better fucking not."

He nodded. "So maybe there are forces outside Her control."

Since when did Chris know just what to say? "Yeah, maybe."

"And of all the things She *has* planned for both of us, being together isn't so bad."

Finally, she squeezed his hand. "No, it's not so bad. In fact, it's good."

"I want to be with you for the long haul, Jess. I want to retire from the league at a solid age thirty-five, brain still mildly functional, and I want us to be together for the years to come."

"Are you ... are you proposing to me?"

He scrunched up his nose. "Huh? No! I mean, not right now. Maybe someday. Do you want me to propose?"

"Right now? No."

"Okay. Like, I don't have a ring or anything ..."

"No, no," she said, lamenting how quickly she'd demolished the mood. "I just ... never mind. We're good. Long term, mild brain injuries. Got it." She smiled, allowing him to relax again, too. "I'm in."

Chapter Thirty-Eight

157:13:48:26 until Doomsday

Jessica couldn't remember a time when she had sat in front of a mirror for so long. She hardly recognized herself now, and while a part of her rejoiced at how good she looked after an hour of hair and makeup, mostly she felt disappointed in herself for not putting a little effort into both more often. She could have been attractive this whole time. How would her life have been different?

Wendy tip-tapped up to the makeup station in her stilettos and indicated to the woman perfecting Jessica's curled hair that she needed a moment with her client. "You look beautiful."

"Isn't that bad?"

"Huh?"

"You said before it was good that I wasn't beautiful because people wouldn't like me."

"Oh, no, it's different now. You're rich. You're allowed to be pretty without people hating you. It's expected. Now, if you *don't* look sharp enough, don't glow and appear put together, everyone will assume you don't deserve what you have."

Jessica frowned, caught sight of the unflattering expression in the mirror, and let her face go slack.

"You remember our talking points, right? You're going to stick to the talking points?"

"Of course I do," Jessica said.

"No mention of God being a woman. This is just to get people to like you and find out more about you. They'll go to the website, read our expertly crafted copy, and that will do the heavy lifting. You just want people to know you're the daughter of God. That's enough for now."

"I *know*," Jessica replied, feeling self-assured and in control now that she was pretty. "It'll be fine. No one wants to knock this interview out of the park more than I do."

She didn't, in fact, remember the talking points. But she remembered a few general rules that she'd gleaned from watching hours and hours of *Helen in the Morning* prior to this booking: laugh with your teeth, get the audience involved, say nothing of substance, and thank Helen profusely for having you on the show. If you had a book to push, even better, but she didn't have one of those yet—though Judith claimed to be working diligently on it.

Her hair had never been so voluminous. She hoped Chris got to see this and tried to capture a clear mental image of it in her mind so she could recreate the look later on when she met him in their dreams. He would go nuts for it.

Wendy narrowed her eyes at her client. "You look calm and confident. Did something happen?"

Jess inhaled deeply through her nose, feeling the over oxygenated air of the studio fill her lungs. "Maybe. I just have this strange sense I can do this. That this is the easy part."

The publicist nodded slowly. "Okay, that's good, but let's not get too confident, right? This appearance is important. She owns a demographic we need to convince. It's not everything, but winning the hearts of her viewers is a good start. They'll help us spread the—"

Jessica raised a hand to stop her. "I know. You've done well preparing me. I don't know why I'm calm, but I am."

Wendy leaned close, staring into Jessica's eyes. "Are you drunk?" she whispered. "High?"

"No! I'm just beautiful!"

Wendy didn't buy it. "It's Chris, isn't it? You two getting back together must be giving you that glow." She straightened and smoothed her palms down her A-line skirt. "Fine. Whatever works. Just don't let him get you pregnant. That's not the glow we need." Then she forced a smile and added, "I know you'll do great."

Jessica decided not to ask why she'd just interrogated her if that were the case.

But by the time an assistant producer had her lined up backstage, waiting to be called out, presumably to applause, she was lost in the same questions Wendy had asked her. Why *was* she feeling so good? Could she have, without meaning to, discovered her own competence? God knew she'd handled enough sticky situations to have earned a little confidence in her ability to take whatever life threw at her. But she thought it was more than that. Things were starting to come up all Jessica. She thought it might have started when that typewriter fell on Eugene, though yelling at Jimmy Dean in his own home had sure felt amazing, and that man who'd wanted to assassinate her turning into quite a vocal advocate for her cause helped, and, yes, getting mega laid in her sleep by Chris every night for the last couple of months had definitely brought a little color to her cheeks.

She heard Helen introduce her, using her real name, as instructed by Wendy, and suddenly it was showtime.

She stepped out, felt rather than heard the applause, and swallowed down the swell of emotion bubbling up in her.

Damn, acceptance from strangers felt good.

Wave, don't trip, hug Helen, then chair.

She found herself seated without remembering how she'd gotten there. Perhaps she'd simply ridden the wave of applause. She discovered quickly that laughing with your teeth was a natural result of having so many soccer moms cheer for your mere presence at once.

"I'm so excited to have you on the show," Helen said, her sweet voice showing no signs of forced excitement. The host wore similar middle-age white woman regalia to her audience, but *her* peach-colored boatneck tee and seafoam green capris had clearly passed through the deft hands of a tailor and had never seen the inside of a department store. "I've been following you since you were in high school, you know."

"Really?" Jessica's genuine shock elicited a wave of laughter from the studio audience.

Helen laughed too. "It does sound a little creepy when I say it that way, doesn't it? But seriously, when I heard there was a girl down in Texas kicking hundred-yard field goals, I had to watch the video. Speaking of which, I think we have that, don't we, Lenny?" She addressed the producer standing to the left of the camera in front of them, and he gave her a thumbs up. A moment later, it was rolling on the screen behind them, and Jessica had nothing to do but watch her young self kick the field goal that won the Mooretown Mexicans the state championship that year. There were far worse things to watch in front of a crowd.

People cheered as the ball passed the uprights and Jessica saw herself for the first time grab the younger version of Christopher Riley and kiss him in front of everyone.

Helen's audience didn't mind that part one bit.

Jessica wondered briefly if her plane from Austin to LA had crashed and this was Heaven—sitting here, looking pretty while an influential celebrity played back the best moments of her life for strangers to cheer. Or maybe this was just the result of finally being able to pay Wendy on a bonus system.

"Now, if I'm not mistaken," Helen said, "that boy you're kissing in the footage is Chris Riley, the starting quarterback for the Philadelphia Eagles."

Jessica felt her face heat up, but she was pretty sure it was hidden beneath the overdone blush. "Yeah, that's him."

"And the two of you were seen together a couple months ago at a burger joint in Austin. Is it too much to assume the two of you still see a lot of each other?"

She could feel the repressed sexuality of the audience pulsating in anticipation. *Draw it out,* a tiny, unfamiliar voice inside her said.

So she nodded slowly. "Chris and I dated for a while through high school, college, and we tried to make it work once he moved, but it was tough, you know?"

Helen nodded along sympathetically.

"But yeah, we went out for burgers recently, and we decided that we would rather be together than not, no matter how far apart we lived."

Helen's hand flew to her heart. "Does that mean you're back together?"

"Yeah, we're back together."

And now the audience's applause simply mirrored what Jessica had been feeling for the last two months.

"My heart can't take that," Helen said. "That's really fantastic." She paused. "Now, a lot has happened since that state championship, correct?"

"Oh yeah."

"I would be remiss if I didn't mention that you claim to be the daughter of God."

"Yes, Helen, that's true."

The audience was silent, and she remembered Wendy's instruction to tread lightly—most of the audience identified as Christian, regardless of whether they attended church, and nothing brought out the fight in people quicker than a threat to their identity.

"I have to be honest, as someone who's followed the highlights of your life since you were young, I'm inclined to believe you."

Jessica blinked, refrained from sputtering, "Really?" and instead went with, "Thank you." A talking point sprang into her head. "It's nice, as a woman, to be believed."

Helen turned to the incredulous audience. "Seriously. I mean, has anyone here been following along?" She indicated for a show of hands, and Jessica saw two women in the back raise their hands. Her eyes nearly popped out of her head when she realized one of the women was Miranda. "I know her!" Jess said before she could stop herself, and she waved.

"Oh yeah?"

"Yeah, it's my best friend Miranda!"

Helen laughed mirthfully, then said, "Right. Maybe she'll make some of these highlights, then."

Jessica was pulled back to reality when her life began flashing before her eyes, literally. She stared at the screen as the images flickered by. She had to be dead. This had to be heaven.

Miranda didn't make the highlight reel, but Rebel, the barista she'd resurrected at Bat-Ass Brew, did. So did the former statue of LBJ in the middle of the Texas State University Quad when she blasted him to bits. And then there was plenty of footage from multiple angles of her latest resurrection outside Gordon's. To cap it all off, a clip of her interview in Atlanta after she'd resurrected the mother and her children and publicly pronounced herself God's daughter.

By the time the reel ended, she felt drained, and the mood in the studio was palpably subdued. Helen responded accordingly with a somber recap. "Now, I understand those were just some of the resurrections you've performed."

Her mind leaped immediately to the bullet riddled colander of a human in her driveway and Jameson's bloody jaw as he lay dead in his sister's arms outside Midland Memorial Hospital and the horror in Chris's eyes when he realized he'd killed Ruth Wurst just before Jessica had discovered her least favorite miracle. "Correct."

"These probably aren't fun moments to relive, but I have to say, they're compelling."

"Yeah," Jessica echoed, staring at the blank screen. "They're not fun to relive."

"There's one we didn't show due to the graphic nature of it."

"Jameson Fractal?" Jessica said on reflex. The tension in the space tightened.

Helen nodded. "I understand you and Jameson became friends after that."

"Not till years later, but yes."

"And the two of you are still on good terms?"

"Oh yeah. I love Jameson. He's great."

A sly smile spread over Helen's face until she could suppress it no more. "That's good news. Because guess who decided to drop in today. Jameson, come on out here!"

And just like that, the audience lost its collective shit. Jessica turned in her chair, saw the radiant, familiar face of her friend, and knew that no matter what happened from here on out she had this thing in the bag.

Wendy really was a magician.

She didn't remember everyone getting to their feet when she'd entered, but they did it for him, and she couldn't blame them. He entered like a firecracker. His mere presence was a refractive thing, sending rainbows in every direction. He waved with both hands, blew two-handed kisses to the audience, and then spread his arms wide for Helen like hugging her was the only thing in the world he could ask for. He lifted her off her feet briefly, and the crowd ate it up. Then he turned to Jessica, who'd stood with the rest of the room upon his entrance, and after a firm hug, he grabbed her shoulders and planted a quick peck on her lips. Nothing salacious, nothing she couldn't easily explain away to Chris later, but enough to transfer some of his status to her. It was his way of telling her he had her back, and she was grateful for it.

He settled in the chair next to hers, bouncing with hardly contained energy, and patted Jessica on the knee. "I'm so happy to be back on the show, Helen. And with one of my favorite people, no less."

When Jessica met his eyes, she saw only safety, trust, and confidence.

And the rest of the show went up from there ...

Jessica crawled out of the rideshare, her feet crying out for freedom, her heavy eyelids rebelling, and her serotonin levels at a lifetime high.

After the show, Jameson had insisted on taking Jessica and Miranda out to celebrate with some of his celebrity friends, and who was she to refuse?

But fourteen hours later, she understood why LA was fueled by cocaine and Starbucks, only one of which she'd ingested over the course of her long but terrific day.

As she shuffled toward the hotel entrance, she assigned a fat tip on her phone to the driver, who had seen her on Helen that morning and was now a fan.

"Evening, Miss McCloud," the doorman said, nodding at her.

"Oh, hi. Evening." She paused, looked back at him. "How did you know my name?"

"I'm an Eagles fan."

"Ah. You think they have a chance next season?"

He grinned. "Depends on whether Riley can stay healthy. But with the way the offensive line is shaping up, it might take a miracle." He winked at her.

Her eyes flew open despite the weight of her lids. "I'll look into it."

As she rode the elevator to her room on the seventeenth floor, she had her first real moment since that morning's grand victory to sit with herself and reflect. People—strangers—in a state she didn't live in, where famous people were a dime a dozen and hard enough to keep track of, knew who she was now. Many of them, it seemed, even believed she was capable of miracles. Whether they were ready to accept that she was God's daughter was another thing, but it wouldn't be a far leap.

This was it. She was doing it!

The elevator doors opened, and she stepped out into the long, silent hallway.

Oh shit. This was it. She was doing it.

She was doing the thing that she always feared would get her killed, and she was going full-force into it.

The lock to her room flashed red when she slipped her card in. "Dammit!"

YOU SEEM UPSET, DAUGHTER.

Ya think?

She tried it again, and this time it flashed green, and she was facedown on the airy white comforter before she knew it.

"I can't do this," she moaned.

YOU JUST DID. YOU'VE BEEN DOING IT ALL DAY.

She rolled over onto her back and stared at the ceiling. "That wasn't me! That was some other woman who took over my body, who made me friendly and open and—fuck, did I have *charisma*? I mean, I certainly know *I* didn't. But whoever possessed me today might have. And if that's who they think I am, it's only a matter of time before they're let down, before *that* woman decides not to show up on time for my morning show appearances, and the whole country realizes that I'm just ..." She struggled for the word. "Just me."

YOU ARE TALKING LIKE A CRAZY PERSON, SWEETIE.

"Thanks a lot."

NO ONE TOOK YOU OVER. THAT WAS YOU.

"What if I can never reproduce it?"

YOU DID IT ONCE, YOU CAN DO IT AGAIN. HAVE FAITH.

"You know I have faith in nothing."

I'M NOT ASKING YOU TO HAVE FAITH IN ANYTHING BUT YOURSELF.

"Faith that I'll get myself killed."

AND SO WHAT?

"And so ..." So what? That was a good question. "And so I'll be dead."

HATE TO BE THE ONE TO TELL YOU THIS, BUT IT'S COMING FOR YOU NO MATTER WHAT

"But there are better and worse ways to die."

NO, IT'S ALL KIND OF THE SAME ON THE COSMIC SCALE.

"But ... pain."

DYING USUALLY HURTS, YES.

"I just want to die peacefully in my sleep when I'm old."

YOU AND EVERYONE ELSE, DAUGHTER. BUT HAVE YOU EVER THOUGHT THIS WHOLE THING ISN'T ABOUT YOU AND WHAT YOU WANT?

"Are you kidding? Of course! I think about how I don't want this life every single day."

NOT LIKE THAT. YOUR PURPOSE. THE REASON YOU EXIST. IT ISN'T ABOUT YOU. JUST LIKE YOUR MOTHER'S LIFE ISN'T ABOUT HER, AND CHRISTOPHER'S LIFE ISN'T ABOUT HIM.

"Wait. You did this to *everyone*? You made it so that *no one*'s life is about them?"

DUH.

"What *is* my life about, then?"

THAT'S THE REAL ME-DAMNED QUESTION, ISN'T IT?

It sure was.

She continued staring at the speckled ceiling, and as she did, a new tally began in her head. Not the days until her thirty-third birthday or the total donations her church had received or how much longer until Jimmy's bullshit doomsday, but something with much more appeal—all the things her life was, or could be, about.

Chapter Thirty-Nine

72:13:22:18 until Doomsday

"Do you swear to tell the truth, the whole truth, and nothing but the truth, so help you God?"

This was the moment. Clint Daniels, her new attorney since Wendy's ugly breakup with Angelo Samuels, had coached her through this part. He'd been very explicit: Do not scoff at the last four words of the oath. Just say yes and let it go.

Jessica didn't scoff, but she definitely smirked. "So help me God, yes."

For a civil matter, this hearing had amassed quite the media turnout. She'd known her response would play well with the cameras, and indeed she saw a few reporters struggle to suppress their grin. No cameras had been allowed into the courtroom, and that was a real shame;

she'd dressed up, and she was feeling like this could have been *Helen in the Morning* all over again.

She took her hand off the Bible and sat.

Jesus grinned at her and shot her a thumbs up. Would people one day swear on her biography, even if it was riddled with as many inaccuracies at her brother's?

She didn't know why she felt so confident today. Wendy and Clint didn't seem to share her enthusiasm. The only way she could describe it was that some act, some force had been set in motion sometime in the past, and she was pretty sure it would reveal itself today. For once, she thought it would work out for her.

Had Rebel slipped something extra in her Nosferabrew this morning? Or was this what faith felt like? Or was there something more substantial that made her feel this way?

Clint Daniels was the first up. "Miss McCloud, would you please state your full legal name?"

"Jessica McCloud."

"No middle name?"

"No, sir.

"And I understand you now answer to, at least publicly, Jessica Christ. Is that correct?"

"Yes, sir.

"Do you like that name?"

"Not even a little bit."

Daniels faked a playful chuckle as if they hadn't rehearsed this. "Okay. Noted. How, then, did you come by that name?"

"Jimmy Dean started it." And couldn't that statement apply to so much?

"Jimmy Dean? The man who was present at your birth? The one most people know as Texas Railroad Commissioner Reverend Jimmy Dean?"

"Yeah. That one."

"And he began calling you that at a young age, correct?"

"Yes, sir."

"Why do you think he began calling you that?"

"Because I'm the daughter of God."

"That makes sense."

Nothing could make less sense, she thought.

Daniels continued, "Will you state what your relationship is with the plaintiff, Dolores Natasha Thomas?"

"Nothing now. But I've known her since she taught me in kindergarten." *And she's Lucifer.*

"Kindergarten? Wow, that's a long time. And how would you describe your relationship with Mrs. Thomas for the majority of the time since you met?"

"It was good. I sort of thought of her as a mother figure. When I was younger and had the normal teenage angst, I sometimes wished she was my mother." She found Destinee's eyes in the crowd. Her mother didn't appear hurt by the statement—she probably already knew it. But in the end, Destinee had won, hadn't she? Jessica had bet wrong, bet on Satan. Whoops.

"Did you have any reason to believe she was going

after your personal brand of Jessica Christ, daughter of God?"

"No. None whatsoever. She always encouraged me to explore life and be whatever I wanted to be. Whenever I'd tell her I was God's daughter and needed to follow that path, she would encourage me to consider if it was really what I wanted to be, and of course it wasn't. She was one of the only people telling me I didn't have to be a messiah if something else would make me happier."

"And you appreciated that?"

"Of course. You know what happened to Jesus, right? I'm not exactly in a hurry to follow in his final footsteps up to the cross."

Jesus laughed loudest of all at that from his seat beside Destinee, and she thought she heard him say, "Good call."

"Do you have any reason to believe, Miss McCloud, that Mrs. Thomas would have wanted to prevent you from moving into the public eye as the Daughter of God?"

"I do. When I finally stepped up, even just a little bit, by opening a bakery and showing off one of my miracles, she did everything in her power to thwart it."

"Including?"

"She inserted herself into the process under the guise of helping me. When my first bakery burned down—the truck, that is—I was desperate for money to start a brick and mortar one. When I ran into her one day, she insisted that she give me the rest of the money I need, and I would start paying her back once I made a certain amount of profit for a certain number of months in a row."

"I believe you're referring to the contract in question in this suit, yes?"

"Yes, sir."

"And did you read the fine print at the bottom?"

"No, sir. I was about to, but it was small, and she assured me that it was nothing, just a formality. I was stupid not to, but I was also very young and, as I said, I trusted her after years of a close relationship. I had no reason to believe she would include anything potentially threatening to my personal brand."

"Why do you think Mrs. Thomas is so eager to own that brand?"

Because she's the motherfucking Devil.

"Objection. Speculation."

Jessica glanced at Dolores's attorney, careful not to look straight at the plaintiff herself.

The judge agreed with the objection.

"What benefits do you see going to the person who owns your personal brand?"

How many hours had she considered this in the isolation of her condo? How many circles had her mind completed around the mental track, coming up with nothing, nothing, nothing ...

And then, only in the last few days, something.

"The benefits for me to own it are freedom of speech. I believe everyone has a right to state who they are and be able to claim that without fear of litigation. If I don't have that first amendment right, guess who does? Everyone else. The press, Jimmy Dean, Dolores Thomas, and anyone else with an internet connection. If this trademark is enforced, it's stripped me of my right to tell my own story, and everyone else will tell it for me. I only have one story of who I am and why I was put on this earth. A person's story is everything. Who has the right to control it for them? Who has the right to twist it around, to crush an individual and twist every bit of good I do into something bad?"

"The press, Miss McCloud."

"Exactly. And I deserve to defend myself from that without fear of being sued."

He nodded. "Going back to the original question, what benefits do you see for someone else who owns your personal brand?"

"They own my story. They own my life. They're able to keep me from fulfilling my calling."

"Which is?"

What? He hadn't told her he would ask that. *Shit.*

"Which is ..." she said, swallowing hard, and looking from one familiar face in the audience to another. Jesus flashed her the peace sign and an encouraging smile.

"Which is bringing peace to the United States." She thought she might throw up. Reporters scrambled to write that down verbatim, and she could practically feel Dolores silently laughing at her. It was so pretentious, so futile, and to many, so unnecessary. The United States wasn't in a civil war. It didn't need peace. And she was no Abe Lincoln.

Then she remembered that Abe Lincoln was a little bit

of a closet racist, according to God, and she felt a sudden strange sense of superiority to the Great Emancipator.

She was brought back down to earth by the sound of the gavel, and though her head still swam, it felt like she'd just thrown up something that had been making her ill since she was fifteen. Jesus shot her an enthusiastic two thumbs up.

Well, Jesus approved. That was something, she supposed.

"Do you have further questions for Ms. McCloud?" the judge asked Daniels.

"Just one more." He turned to Jessica. "And I only ask this because I have a feeling Mr. Lindgartt is planning to ask it. Where were you on the evening of Thursday, January tenth, twenty-nineteen, between the hours of six thirty and nine thirty p.m.?"

"I was at Gordon's Burgers in Austin with Chris Riley."

"Can anyone verify that besides Mr. Riley?"

"Yes," she said. "Yes. A lot of people can. I believe I was caught by multiple cell phones resurrecting a man who had just been struck by a car outside the restaurant. You can check YouTube. I believe there are close to a hundred individual recordings of me spanning the duration of that time frame."

Clint Daniels grinned up at the judge. "That's all, Your Honor."

Now it was time for Patrick Lindgartt to question her. Daniels had warned her about him. He played dirty. And when an attorney says another attorney plays dirty, it's smart to believe it. She'd prepped for this, though. He would grill her relentlessly until she slipped up. That was his favorite trick. So, she had to not slip up.

"Miss McCloud, when did you first publicly declare yourself the daughter of God?"

She thought back to the date in Atlanta and provided it.

"And what day did you sign the contract with my client for financial backing of your bakery?"

"I ... I'm not sure."

"Can you give a month and year?"

She gave it her best shot.

"So," he continued, "you admit that you didn't publicly brand yourself 'Jessica Christ' until after you signed the contract with my client?"

"No."

"No, you don't admit it?"

"No, I didn't brand myself ... What does that even mean?"

Patrick Lindgartt nodded and looked to be enjoying none of this.

"When you signed the contract, were you drunk or otherwise intoxicated or impaired?"

"No."

He addressed the judge now. "It's not the place of the court to decide someone's divinity. It is the place of the court to enforce intellectual property rights. This doesn't have to be complicated. She signed a contract, didn't deliver on her part, and so the consequences agreed upon in the contract took effect. Now she's breaching the agreement and infringing upon the brand of It is Risen and Jessica Christ. We're obligated to take the necessary legal action to enforce our trademark or else it becomes void. The defense can paint my client in a negative light, but that's irrelevant to contract law. Miss McCloud wasn't coerced into anything, and she was of a clear and sound mind when she signed. Yes, she might have felt like she had no other options, but if that voids a contract, then we ought to forgive every loan in existence to the peril of the nation's economy."

The judge listened, her head tilted to the side, but appeared about as disinterested as Patrick Lindgartt himself. "Do you have any other questions for Miss McCloud?"

"No, ma'am." He turned and walked back to his seat, and, for a moment, Jessica felt glued to hers. That was it? It couldn't have lasted more than two minutes. Clint Daniels caught her eye and nodded for her to get off the stand. She jumped up and returned to her seat next to him.

He didn't look at her, and that told her everything she needed to know about how things had just gone.

Then the judge announced, "Next, we'll hear from Dolores Thomas."

Chapter Forty

72:12:57:02 until Doomsday

Never in her life had Jessica seen Dolores Thomas dress in the fashion she wore in court today. She looked like a little old church lady, and were hats allowed in the courtroom, Jessica was sure the Devil would have been wearing one. Maybe a little round boxy thing with a bit of lace around the edge and a broach pinning a silk flower to it.

Jessica wondered if anyone else noticed that her hand hovered just above the cover of the Bible as she was sworn in.

"Mrs. Thomas," Daniels said, "how long have you known my client?"

"Since she was five years old. I believe that's seventeen years ago, now."

"From what you know of her, does she strike you as the type to expect the best or worst of people?"

"You can hardly blame her for it, but she always expects the worst. Projects it onto people, I think. Self-reflection isn't one of her strengths."

Jessica blinked, stunned by the sudden accusation. She should have expected it, perhaps, but she hadn't, and she thought that sort of disproved the Devil's claim.

"You'd say she's a suspicious person?"

Dolores pretended to think about it, chewing her lip. "She has moments of intense suspicion that I've seen. It's not all the time. Consistency isn't one of her pronounced traits, either. She's very hot and cold."

"Can you provide an example?"

"Oh yes. She confided in me quite a lot growing up. As she said herself, she thought of me as a second mother. Anyway, for years she suspected her best friend of trying to steal her boyfriend. She even went so far as to sneak over to her boyfriend's home to watch him and make sure her best friend wasn't there."

Daniels clearly wasn't expecting that. But neither was Jessica. What in the hellshit was this bitch talking about? She'd never suspected Chris and Miranda!

She shut her eyes to steady herself against the lie, and a flash memory of Destinee beating the snot out of Ruth Wurst on the Wursts' front lawn flashed into her mind. Except now Jessica had Dolores by the hair, and Sandra and Fischer were forced to look on.

Ahh … that felt good. It was too bad these things couldn't be settled in her mother's preferred court of two-fisted justice.

Satan was speaking again. "I did think of her like a daughter. I gave to her selflessly over the years, helped her out when she needed it, provided guidance, kept her out of harm's way throughout her school career. I did all that even though she never once showed gratitude, never once changed her behavior. I don't do the things I do because I need praise or a thank-you. I do them because they're the right thing to do. That's why I offered her the money in the first place for her bakery. She seemed truly passionate about the culinary arts, and I wanted to encourage her to follow her passion after such a rough and neglected childhood. But at the same time, I recognized that she had a certain pattern of behavior, so I wrote those clauses into the contract at the bottom just in case. Having boundaries and limits to the abuse you'll take isn't malicious, Mr. Daniels. It's called self-love."

"I'll show her where to shove that self-love," Destinee murmured a few rows back.

Daniels said, "Sounds more like martyrdom to me."

"Objection."

"Upheld. Let's not opine, Mr. Daniels."

"Knowing what you claim to know about my client, why did you believe it was a good idea to get into business with her at all? Did you believe she had a chance of success?"

Dolores tilted her head to the side and said softly, "I always believe my students can succeed. If I didn't, I would leave education. Perhaps I'm a fool for believing in her after I'd been burned so many times, but a contract is a contract."

"Did you go into it with the belief that my client would not be able to uphold her end of the bargain and you would be able to seize her personal brand?"

"No."

Liar! Jessica's gut felt like it was on fire, and she wanted to scream and probably not stop for a good long while. But what could she do about it? Smite Dolores?

Could she smite the Devil? Did the laws of the universe even allow for such a thing? If Dolores suddenly exploded, would anyone genuinely be able to point a finger at Jessica? Maybe she could do it real sneaky-like. No big show with her hands. Just direct the force under the table ...

Daniels took his seat next to her. This was her chance. A clear shot. Then it would all be over, right?

UH NO. SATAN JUST KEEPS COMING BACK.

Damn. Another metaphysical boomerang. Okay then.

Lindgartt nodded at his client and then began, and Jessica knew she was in for a world of hurt.

"Would you say Ms. McCloud is spoiled?"

"I don't know about that, but she does seem to feel very entitled to things. I mean, she claims to be the daughter of you-know-who. Can you blame her?"

"Do you believe she's the daughter of God?"

Dolores did a good job of feigning sadness and met Jessica's eyes directly, causing her to jerk back before she could stop herself. "No. I don't believe she is. How could she be?"

"So, when you encouraged her to pursue a life outside of being God's daughter, you were trying to protect her?"

"Yes, exactly. Her mother has raised her with the delusion that she was immaculately conceived. I didn't want to outright contradict that notion—far be it from me to refute what's taught in the home—but I wanted her to know that there were other possibilities for her besides this delusion. It's quite an unhealthy thing for a child to be raised believing about him or herself. I always felt for her. So much pressure. The weight of the world on her shoulders. It's really no wonder she acted the way she did —entitled, paranoid, and so on. She was raised to believe she would follow in Jesus's footsteps. I mean, you heard her. She's still worried about being crucified. It's no way to rear a child."

"What did you think when you heard that her bakery was based on the premise that she was the daughter of God?"

"Well, I wasn't all that surprised, let me tell you. But I thought it was a start, you know? Maybe her love of baking would be the thing that steered her away from the grandiosity. But I soon realized that was unlikely to be the case."

"Mrs. Thomas, did you include that clause in the contract with the hope of saving her from herself?"

She tilted her chin up, rolling her shoulders back. "Yes.

Yes, I did. If the bakery failed, I wanted to make sure that she did not fall into old patterns. That's why I wrote in the clause about her personal brand going to me. It's also why I paid for her trip to the women's retreat in Carlsbad. I wanted her to explore herself more, to step out of her old ways and see the vast possibilities of life. It's not easy for children to break away from the beliefs of their parents, and I could already see that she was struggling to make that space between herself and her overbearing mother."

The holes in this story were excruciatingly obvious, but Jessica knew it was too late. The narrative only had to make emotional sense to stick. If Dolores had thought the retreat would help, then why didn't she wait to hear the results before pulling Jessica's life out from under her? That simple question could unravel everything.

But no. The damage was too severe. Jessica was watching her character be assassinated in real time. But unlike with Jameson, she wasn't sure she could resurrect it.

"Everything I've ever done has been to protect Jessica from herself and her mother. I see the potential in her. I always have. But if she keeps down this road, I'm afraid it will become a self-fulfilling prophecy, and she *will* follow in the footsteps of Jesus. All the way up the cross. She seems set on it. Preventing her from continuing this psychotic charade was the only thing I could think to do to help her. If I don't enforce this trademark, it could cost a young, troubled woman her life."

"I'm not gonna do nothin'!" Destinee hissed, and

Jessica glanced over her shoulder in time to see her mother smack Rex's hand off of her as she sat back down on the wooden bench.

Good man, Rex.

"One last question, Mrs. Thomas. Who do you think was behind the recent fire that destroyed It is Risen bakery?"

"Objection. Speculation."

"Upheld. Please drop the speculation, Mr. Lindgartt. This is a trumped up civil suit, not a criminal matter."

Dolores bowed her head briefly, and Mr. Lindgartt acquiesced. But then suddenly, Dolores was speaking again. "I know Jessica has a solid alibi. But I believe she paid someone to burn down the bakery. She certainly has the money to do it."

"Objection!"

"Upheld. Please strike that from the record."

But it couldn't be stricken from the minds of everyone present. The accusation was out there.

She'd never thought much about Hell, presuming she couldn't end up there, but she bet it felt a little like this. The sound of the reporters' pens scratching on paper, the eyes of the Devil upon her, all those she cared about listening on while her entire life was spun so that she appeared credibly awful.

She even believed it herself. She *was* entitled. She *was* ungrateful. She had always suspected she was those things. A little voice inside her had been telling her so for most of her life.

She had to face it: nothing the Devil could say would have bothered her if she hadn't already known it was true all along.

Chapter Forty-One

72:12:41:50 until Doomsday

The judge declared a recess and Jessica hurried out into the hallway, Clint Daniels following after her. But she didn't wait up. She needed air, not legal counsel.

As a habit, she checked her phone, which had been on silent. Five missed called from an unknown number and a voicemail.

Obviously, she wasn't about to listen to a voicemail. Life was too short.

The pattern didn't fit a robocall, so she keyed up the number and hit dial.

On the second ring, "Hello? Jessica?"

She recognized that voice, but the sense of urgency was like a foreign body to it, a virus that had snuck in. "Yeah?"

"It's Caren Powers."

"What do *you* want?" *You were supposed to be my galru, and all you did was keep me in the desert while the Devil screwed me!*

"I didn't … Are you upset with me?" came the woman's smooth voice.

"For being in league with Dolores Thomas? Yeah, just a little."

"We're old friends, but I'm not 'in league' with her."

"Bullshit."

"Jessica, there's something you should know. Something I need to tell you."

Oh, this ought to be good. "Go for it."

"Is this call being recorded?"

Caught by surprise, Jessica chuckled dryly. "No."

"Well, you'd better record it. Do you have an app for it?"

Now she was really confused. "You want me to record our conversation?"

"You'll need a record, and it will be less of a conversation and more of a confession, I'm afraid. Download a call recorder app and call me back."

The line went dead, and Jessica was left staring at the screen with her eyes mildly crossed.

But she downloaded an app, called Caren back, and hit record.

"Are you recording?" the galru said.

"Yes."

"Okay. Good. This is Caren Powers. Here's what you need to know. I just had a vision, but I'll get back to that.

On December thirtieth of last year, I received a call from my friend Dolores Thomas with a request. She'd long been aware of my previous relationship with Jimmy John Dean, and asked if—"

"Nope! Hold the hell up. *What* did you just say?" Jessica shut her eyes as her brain threatened to short circuit. "You had a *relationship* with him? Not, like, a romantic one, right?"

"It was a passionate and taboo love affair, yes."

"Ew! What's *wrong* with you?"

"I was in a loveless marriage with three awful children. He swooped into my life, showed me the divine in more ways than one and—"

"Rhetorical," Jessica spat. "It was a rhetorical question." She looked around the front steps of the courthouse, where she hunched over her phone, shielding the microphone from the wind, and saw Daniels motioning for her to wrap it up. She waved him off harshly. "So you and Jimmy had a thing, and Dolores wanted you to do something?"

"Yes. She offered me money. Money to convince Jimmy to burn down her bakery. I wasn't to let him know it was her idea. I was just supposed to plant the seed."

"Why did she want him to burn down the bakery?"

"She said it was a nuisance. A money pit. But if it burned down, she could collect insurance on it and move on."

"It would also make her look like a victim. But go on. I

assume you convinced Jimmy, based on the fact that he burned it to the ground."

"Yes, I'm afraid I paid him a visit and struck up a conversation that would lead us down that road. It didn't take much prodding."

"You know this is a crime. I mean, probably. I don't know exactly what it's called, but I can't imagine it's legal."

Caren sighed heavily into the phone. "It's a crime against good conscience if nothing else."

"Is that why you're calling? To lighten your conscience? I just mean, this happened a while ago. Why now?"

The woman sounded excited for a chance to tell that story, and her voice took on a new vibrance. "The burden of the act has been weighing heavily on my heart since. I would have done it for free, I think. Dolores has always been my friend. But this morning I awoke to the fiery New Mexican sunrise with a heavy heart. So, I went into my tent and commenced a spirit journey."

"You tripped balls."

"Commenced a spirit journey. And on that spirit journey I found myself on the precipice of a yawning hole in the earth. I looked over the edge and into a writhing, bubbling bath of lava. It was like looking straight into hell. And then I heard movement behind me and turned to find a regal lioness. She told me her name was Asha."

"Wait. Was this lioness especially foul-mouthed?"

"Yes. Very much so. But not at first. At first she simply came to stand next to me and stare into the gaping chasm of hell. And from that chasm I heard a voice. A familiar one. It was Dolores. She was telling me to jump. To jump! Into the scalding pit of lava! And, Jessica, I must tell you that I considered it. She told me that I had walked the long path to get here, and all I need do to complete my journey was take that final step. This was my destination the whole time. She claimed the fire would purify me as it did her, and that it was the only way to true enlightenment.

"I almost did it. I almost took that final step."

"Why didn't you?"

"Because of Asha. She said, and I'll do my best to quote verbatim, because I believe the wording is important to the message, but forgive me if I'm not entirely correct. She said, 'Bitch, if you're even considering that shit, you're even more fucknuts than I thought. That voice speaking to you? That's the motherfucking Devil! You've been doing all this spiritual bullshit out here in this dry as fuck desert, hoping for some sort of breakthrough, and your dumb ass can't even identify Satan when you look her in the eyes. What kind of a bitch-ass guru are you?'"

"Is that," Jessica began, feeling slightly embarrassed on the part of her spirit animal, "is that all she said?"

"Essentially, yes."

She let out a heavy breath. "I guess you didn't jump."

"No, I came back to reality with a start! It took me a minute to understand what the message was trying to tell me"—*dumbass*, Jessica thought—"but then I realized. I think ... I think it was trying to tell me that Dolores might be a negative influence in my life."

A gabby group came up the stairs toward Jess, and she stuck a finger into her free ear to drown them out. "No, Caren. It was telling you that Dolores Thomas is Satan. Literally the Devil incarnate. She has ruined my life with your help, which I think makes you a minion of Satan. Maybe that's what the vision was telling you. Either way, I've got good news for you. Your timing is impeccable, and you might have gone and redeemed yourself slightly."

"Have I?"

"Maybe. I gotta go, but might I suggest never speaking to either Dolores or Jimmy ever again? And if you see Asha in another trip, tell her I said hi. Then do whatever she says." Daniels set a firm hand on her shoulder and she shrugged it off. "Before I go, can you confirm one more time that Dolores Natasha Thomas paid you to convince Jimmy Dean to set fire to It is Risen bakery?"

"What the hell?" muttered Daniels.

Jessica ignored him, waiting for the response that could fix so much in her life. So, so much.

"Yes," Caren said. "Yes, she paid me five hundred dollars to convince him."

"Five hundred?! That's it?" It was too bad Asha hadn't smacked Caren around a little when she had the chance. Put those big-ass paws to good use. "Okay, that's beside the point. Thanks for calling. Consider your conscience clear." Caren attempted a goodbye that had the word "blessed" in it, but Jessica had her finger on the red phone icon before she could be subjected to any more nonsense.

She looked up at Daniels, whose mouth was hanging slightly open, his eyes wide. "What was *that*?"

"That," Jessica said, "was great timing."

Thanks.

YOU'RE WELCOME, SWEETIE.

Chapter Forty-Two

68:03:48:09 until Doomsday

The cool night air ran fingers through Jessica's hair as she stood on the rooftop of the McConaughey Hotel and soaked up her victory. A sweeping view of downtown met her on all sides, and she felt something delicious flowing through her veins. What good chemical was that? Serotonin? Or perhaps just a lack of adrenaline?

THIS SEEMS A BIT EXCESSIVE.

I couldn't stop him from doing it. He insisted. Something about taxes.

*YOU MEAN **EXCESSIVELY** AVOIDING PAYING THEM?*

Can't you just let me have this one? I finally defeated the Devil. Thanks for the help, by the way.

Jeremy Archer, whose finances were covering this elaborate reservation, sat at a bench in the far corner of the rooftop deck, hunched over, the glow of his phone lighting his bored expression as he scrolled, scrolled, scrolled.

"I think that toilet's malfunctioning," Destinee said, coming back outside to join the rest of the group. "Tried to flush it and it squirted water all over my boots!"

Rex headed over from the small bar, two freshly mixed drinks in hand, and passed one over to his live-in girlfriend. Destinee stared down at it. "What's this?"

"Mojito. I found a great recipe for it on one of the mommy blogs I follow, and I've been wanting to give it a try."

She eyed it suspiciously. "There's not breast milk in this, is there?"

He grinned and slipped an arm around her waist. "No. Not in the mojitos. Maybe someday I'll make you the white Russians, though." He addressed both mother and daughter as he explained, "You know, the microbiome of breastmilk is unmatched. It's much more compatible with our immune system than cow's milk. I tell you, the female body is really a thing of wonder."

"My drink's not strong enough," Destinee said.

"You haven't tried it."

"Don't need to. Either make it stronger or stop talking about titty juice."

They walked back to the bar, leaving Jessica alone again to take in the scene. In a far corner of the rooftop, Judith and Brian made out shamelessly, and in another, Quentin was playing phone photographer for Chris, who had mentioned earlier that he needed a sweet shot for his Insta. Which left one person unaccounted for ...

"Sister," Jesus said from behind her, causing her to jump. "Sorry, sorry."

"It's okay. Are you having fun?"

He nodded. "I have never been up this high before."

"But what about ...?" She nodded skyward.

"It's not ..." He narrowed his eyes at her. "It's not really in the sky."

"Right. I knew that."

He moved to stand beside her, gazing out over the rooftops and twinkling electric lights. "I think if I'd been this high in my first life, I might not have proceeded the same way."

"I guess it's good you were never up this high, then."

"I suppose so." But he didn't look so sure.

"Hey, grab yourself a drink. I'm feeling in the mood for a toast."

He nodded, his brows still pinched with the afterglow of deep introspection.

"And if Rex offers you anything with dairy, don't take it."

Chris and Quentin finished up their shoot, and a moment later, she had a citrus-y smelling drink in her hand, and the others gathered round (Judith and Brian required a little extra prodding).

"I'd like to raise a glass to everyone here tonight. Thanks to Jeremy for these swank accommodations, and to Chris for fixing me this drink, and to everyone else who's helped me on this just plain stupid journey. God told me when I was eight years old that I'd have to take on the Devil, and it's been hanging over my head ever since. But now that I've beat her at her own game, I feel like a huge weight has been lifted. I finally have a win, and with months to spare before the first service at Church of the Girl Christ. So, here's to all the help you've offered me. I'm glad to say it wasn't all for naught." She lifted her glass, and the rest followed suit. But as her gaze momentarily passed Jesus's, she felt a jolt run through her at his downturned expression. Why did he look so glum?

She shoved it from her mind, focusing instead on Chris's jubilant grin right before he and Quentin saw who could chug their drink fastest.

"That was beautiful, baby. I'm so damn proud of you." Destinee wiped a tear from her eye and told Rex, "This mojito thing is good. Don't tell Dos Equis I said that."

"I'll get you another one, my goddess."

"Imma watch you make it this time. Maybe I can learn something."

"You know what muddling is?"

"No fuckin' clue, but sounds dirty."

Jesus stepped forward and took Jessica by the arm, leading her away from the rest. "A word, sister?"

They paused by the glass door to the elevator as two bats swooped out of the night air and then disappeared just as quickly. "I don't mean to detract from your celebration with what I'm about to say. After all, you *did* best the Devil this week, and that's no easy feat."

"But?"

"It's not a one-time thing, I'm afraid. She's not going to lose this round and forfeit. She's the Devil, Jessica. Doing evil is all she has. She's not going to give up and retire to Florence."

"Florida," Jessica corrected halfheartedly. "That's the place old people go."

"She won't go there, either."

"But I thought you battled with the Devil in the desert and that was that?"

"It worked out for story purposes to write it that way, but the Devil confronted me pretty much constantly, even when I was on the cross. No, especially when I was on the cross. You don't battle with the Devil once. You battle with it constantly. Nonstop. Death is the only relief. And the stronger your power for good, the more relentless the Devil becomes. She'll have fixated on you, Jessica. I just want you to be prepared."

"She threw everything she had at me, though. What does she have left? She made her move, and I outsmarted her. I won. Nothing she can throw at me can compare to stealing my bakery and trying to take my personal brand."

"What about stealing your church? Or destroying it?"

She opened her mouth to speak, found no words, and filled the thing with alcohol instead. "I'd like to see her try."

"No," he called after her as she returned to the rest of the group. "You would not like it."

Chapter Forty-Three

05:17:55:34 until Doomsday

Jessica had heard more than once that women didn't even need to have periods anymore. There were pills and procedures that could stop it, apparently. As she stepped out onto the sidewalk in front of her condo that morning and saw the firefighters working tirelessly to extinguish a lightning-struck car parked right down the street outside the boutique candy store, she wondered if she should look into such a thing for herself. On the one hand, it would be nice to not be kept awake by raging storms when she was at the point of lowest estrogen and progesterone in her cycle and could really use the sleep. But on the other hand, the world could do with fewer pedophiles. Her cycles had eased up and regulated significantly since her teen years anyway, and now they were manageable and only one or two pedophiles were struck down each time she began spotting.

What would it be like, she wondered, to make decisions for her body without having to consider her social responsibility to others?

It was a shame that she was on her period today of all days. It was a big one (the day, not the period). The biggest of her life, perhaps. And, as would naturally follow, the one most likely to end in her assassination.

And who will resurrect me? It was a desperate thought she kept circling back around to.

And close on its heels, *Oh right. Jesus could probably do it.*

Man, it was handy to have another demigod around.

He would be there, of course. As would pretty much everyone she knew and then some. The grand opening. The inaugural service.

She breathed in the fresh air, choked on the toxic smoke from the burning vehicle as the wind brought it toward her, and eventually managed to get her senses about her again.

It was July first. Six days until the end of the world.

Considering, it was a pretty nice day.

Destinee and Rex pulled up to the curb, and Jessica jumped in the back seat of the old truck.

"Any idea what the hell happened there?" Destinee nodded at the infernal sedan.

"Pedophile."

"Ah. You got enough tampons to last you then, or you need us to stop somewhere?"

Jessica patted her purse. "I'm all set."

Rex turned to look at her over his shoulder. "You look powerful today, McCloud. You're absolutely radiating the divine feminine."

"Thanks."

With the Devil out of her way, and Jimmy Dean wrapped up in his apocalyptic theatrics, Jessica had been able to focus all her attention over the last two months on the construction, landscaping, and design of this goliath undertaking. And as of last week, the very first Church of Girl Christ was complete. And it was perfect.

She'd spent every day since reveling in it. It was her home. It was everything she thought a church ought to be, and not even Wendy Peterman could tell her how to decorate this time. This was *her* church.

The dome was northeast of downtown, and as it came into view down the street, Jessica's heart raced. Everything about it made her feel lightheaded, from the stone archway that resembled two Nubian giraffes necking to the wild, abundant vegetation surrounding the grounds—vines already crept up the legs of benches she'd scattered around for people to sit and daydream. The more hidden benches would be key make-out spots for teens, and she even loved that idea. Making out at church! How fun!

Indoor plants were non-negotiable for her, though no one tried to talk her out of it, and as she stepped through the threshold, it was like she'd entered the Amazon.

Natural light streamed in through the surrounding windows and skylights, making the inside feel almost identical to the outside. With the exception of the restrooms, a changing room, two meeting rooms, and an office, it was all a single space, large, open, with not an uncomfortable pew to be found. Long, arced pillows spread out from the center of the room like sound waves, each one sewn out of rich, vibrant colors—purples and golds and reds and greens. When she stood in the center of the room and looked around, only one word came to mind: celebration. And not of her, thankfully. No, not a celebration of her life or anyone else's in particular. But everyone's celebration of being together. Celebration of being allowed to leave at any time, no questions asked.

She was alone in the dome now, letting her imagination run wild with images of people settling in on the pillows, feeling the sunshine overhead, feeling like they were in nature, like they *were* nature.

"And so the humans gather," spoke the voice of Sir David Attenborough in her mind, *"to celebrate surviving one more dark night and to welcome the safety of another warm day."*

It *was* a warm day, but it was pleasant inside.

Nothing lasts.

The truth of that had lived with her for her entire life. In her happiest moments, the ones of victory, of friendship, of joy, it had been there, tapping her on the shoulder, whispering its name. *Nothing lasts.*

It was always strangely quiet when she found herself

in the midst of things she wished would pass, but perhaps she'd heard it after all. Perhaps her misery had simply drowned out its quiet voice. *Nothing lasts.* But she must have heard it, or else how would she have carried on? There had been so much struggle, so many lows. Yet here she was.

And it wouldn't last. It couldn't. The good didn't last and neither did the bad. *Nothing lasts.*

She was prepared for it this time. She was ready for things to rise and fall. And she was determined for it to happen on her terms this time.

The mauve carpeting kept her from hearing the footfalls until they were right behind her, and she turned to find Jeremy Archer only a few feet away. He had his hands on his hips and nodded as he looked around. "Yeah, I suppose this will do." He looked down at her. "You've done a fine job. The extraterrestrials will be impressed. They've always enjoyed a good dome."

"Thanks."

"Oh!" He pointed at her. "Right. Jesus sent me. He says the homeless buses will be arriving soon, and he'll lead them straight to the medical care and showers before letting them inside."

"Right." She forced a smile. The homeless guests were already arriving?

What if they were the only ones who showed? What if all the other promises fell through and her grand opening was seen only as some sort of grand HoboCon? Homeless people would travel from all over the country to come sleep in her dome ... on her hand-sewn pillows.

She dug her fingernails into her palms to snap herself out of it. "And he just got the ones who don't want to be homeless anymore, right?"

Jeremy shrugged. "Beats me. I can't account for what Jesus does."

"Right. No one can. Thanks for the heads up."

She waited until he was gone to talk herself off the edge, and then she checked the clock on her phone. Nearly eight in the morning. The service was scheduled for noon.

Chapter Forty-Four

05:12:23:33 until Doomsday

"I still don't understand why the scribe has to wear this shit," Judith said, adjusting her dress. "I'm a writer, not a virgin sacrifice." She stood beside Jessica who greeted the VIPs as they arrived, the sun's brutal July rays overhead. On the other side of Judith the priestesses stood in a line leading down the path to the front doors, a sort of a welcome committee gauntlet everyone had to pass through before entering the Church of Girl Christ.

"We don't use that word anymore," Jessica reminded her.

"What, virgin or sacrifice?"

"The first one. But also the second. Don't jinx this."

Jessica happened to think Judith looked more like a goddess than a sacrifice in the voluminous pale blue dress and her dark hair pulled back at the sides, tumbling in tendrils down her back. She was the one to whom villagers would offer their sacrifice.

It made Jessica feel frumpy by comparison, as far as deities went.

"Well, if it isn't the woman herself."

She followed the source of the overconfident voice and spotted a familiar face. But how was it familiar? Where did she know this man from? He had maybe ten years on her, and he was deathly handsome, but she couldn't put a name to the face. "Welcome," she said, forcing a smile as she took his hand.

"When Jameson invited me, I thought he was on drugs. But this is all pretty remarkable."

Jameson. Okay, so this guy was probably someone famous. It was starting to come to her. James-something? No, no, David-something?

"I'm glad you're here," she said. "It's not exactly intended to be a spectator show, but I understand that's why most people are here."

He didn't let go of her hand yet. "Don't worry." He winked. "I'll be respectful. But I do feel obligated to mention that I'm a devout Satanist, so you probably won't change my mind."

Oh, for fuck's... a Satanist? "Not a problem. When we say all are welcome, we mean it."

EXCEPT FOR THE SMELLY.

Don't start on that again. If we don't require the homeless to shower before they join, no one else will show up to the next service.

I'M NOT JUDGING.

Of course you are.

OF COURSE I AM.

The homeless showers had been hotly contested among her trusted confidants. Clint Daniels had been adamant that nothing good happened in church showers and that her liability might not cover the claims that would inevitably emerge. But Judith had brushed that off as a minor detail compared to the smell of dozens of homeless in a single dome with the sun shining directly on them.

It was Jesus who made the best point, though. He'd said allowing people to bathe was an act of mercy (when Judith accused him of having a thing for washing feet, he denied it), and that asking a thing of another person before you got close to them wasn't cruel—love can only be preserved with basic boundaries intact.

With Jesus on Jessica's side, Daniels relented and they set out to design low-liability showers with individual stalls and a process for allowing only one person into each one at a time and installing high-tech locks on the doors so nothing untoward could happen in them after hours.

God, meanwhile, was critical of it. She had been critical of a lot of this process, but most of the criticism came in a deeper voice.

The transition wasn't always easy for Her. God, it seemed, was still hanging on to vestiges of "the good old days."

There was, however, one thing that caused She-God to voice serious concern. And Jessica only had the vaguest notion of an answer to it, even though she herself had been considering the possible moral tarpit during most of her waking moments.

The animals. Everywhere. Could she keep from making the same mistakes Jimmy had made with his introduction of the God Hog? Or would her beautiful church, her life's work, as it were, accidentally turn into the most famous encourager of bestiality of all time?

She had a plan for it, though, and, holy fuck, did she hope it worked.

The time came for Jessica to disappear for a while. She graciously excused herself from the receiving line and retired to her private office within the church.

Where she promptly began hyperventilating. "Stupid, stupid, stupid," she said on each forced exhale.

It was an animalistic fear response, which should have comforted her, she supposed.

The thought shifted her focus from the high stakes of the day and how easily everything she'd been working toward could come crashing down on her to the inaugural sermon she was scheduled to deliver in just over twenty minutes. This would set the tone for the rest of the church's existence, and she couldn't screw it up. As long as she kept to the carefully practiced script, she could, at the very worst, stumble her way through the words. Those, at least, she could recite in her sleep. Wendy had made sure that was the case. As far as the publicist was concerned, this was the big one. All or nothing. She had said as much countless times, despite Jessica having developed a habit of covering her ears when one of Wendy's pep talks was clearly ramping up to that proclamation. "This is the big one! It all comes down to this! This is your moment. All or nothing!"

There was a small knock at her office door, and she asked whoever it was to come in. Just short of it being Jimmy Dean, she would take whatever company she could just then. Any distraction.

Courtney Wurst poked her head in. Against Jessica's better judgment, she'd begun to trust Courtney over the last few months, and her desire to shout, "Shut your fucking mouth, Courtney!" every time the Wurst tried to speak had diminished *almost* entirely.

"Hey, sorry to bother you. But Joshua sent me. He said to tell you some of the more famous guests are griping about being so close to the homeless."

Shut your fucking mouth, Courtney!

"Okay. Did he say what he wanted to do about it?"

"No, he just thought you should be aware of it."

Jessica bit her tongue. "Thanks. I'm aware now."

Taking the hint, Courtney shut the door silently, and Jessica was left with one more thing to "be aware" of. Her eyes felt as big as an ocelot's, her ears as sensitive as a barn owl's. But she had to do this. It was the only way to bring peace to the United States, and that was an important thing.

Could anyone else do it? Jesus could probably manage it. Maybe she could just disappear and let him handle things. He had way more experience. Who was she, anyway? A twenty-three-year-old nobody from West Texas with no college degree, a tepid high school GPA, a trigger-happy mom who was practically the same generation as her, and an absent father in the throes of a gender transition.

I'm a nobody.

Perversely, that thought helped.

She checked the clock. Showtime.

In a moment of weakness, she did the thing she promised herself she wouldn't do and imagined she was Jimmy Dean. Rolling her shoulders back, she inhaled deeply, filling her chest with delicious oxygen. No one captivated a crowd like Jimmy.

And talk about a nobody. He wasn't God's child. He wasn't the Devil. He wasn't even a demon! He was the ultimate nobody from The South with a terrible mother he hated and kept in a prison-like retirement home. And yet, what he said, the masses believed.

If she could channel some of that bullshit confidence right now, she'd take it. She didn't have a hog-hoof stole, but if someone had offered her one in that moment, she might have taken it, too.

A few minutes later, she waited in an anteroom just off the sanctuary and listened for the crowd to settle down. If she peeked out, someone might see her, so she was unable to satisfy her curiosity regarding the state of affairs between the homeless and the rich and powerful. She'd done her best to organize the seating so they weren't near one another. After the showers, the homeless guests should have been tolerable to the refined, or possibly cocaine-ravaged, noses of the wealthy and influential on her guest list.

She listened for clear signs of discontent but couldn't make out much of anything outside of the general murmur of conversation.

As that began to settle under a blanket of anticipation, she hooked on her headset mic, thinking once again of Jimmy Dean, and took that first agonizing step out of her hiding place toward the center of the room.

Chapter Forty-Five

05:11:56:21 until Doomsday

Each step was slightly less agonizing than the one before it. The applause helped, she had to admit. She grinned widely, flashing her teeth, before reining it in. Humility. Smiling too widely showed no humility. This wasn't *Helen in the Morning*.

Without meaning to she thought, *What would Jesus do?* And when her eyes found him in one of the front rows, she saw that his mouth was open wide, his teeth flashing white as he grinned unabashedly.

Well, shit.

His smile quickly faded when the man next to him tried to light a cigarette, forcing Jesus to quickly lean close and humbly request he not. The man put his cigarette out on the seat cushion next to him. She felt her left eye twitch.

This isn't doomed. This isn't doomed. This isn't doomed.

Reaching the center of the sanctuary, she cleared her throat and then flipped on the mic. "Welcome! I'm so glad to see each and every"—*holy hell, how did Dolores Thomas get inside?!*—"one of you here today." Okay, this was bad. The Devil had managed to slip inside her church.

SHE WAS WEARING A HEADCOVERING.

For fuck's sake! These head coverings would be the death of her. She was determined not to turn people away based on simple matters of religion, but what was she supposed to do about an entire culture so well dressed for espionage?! Had she no recourse?

The Devil stood at the very back by one of the emergency exits, her arms folded across her chest, a shit-eating grin nestled between her fat cheeks.

Should she interrupt the service to request Dolores be removed? Should she cause a scene to expel the Devil? What would that lead to? Surely, people would assume it was all staged ...

What do I do here?

CARRY ON.

Jessica let her eyes roam over the hundreds of faces looking at her in this theater-in-the-round and pretended to take in a single one while her mind was fixated elsewhere.

Would the Devil do anything? What would she try? Could she have them all killed? Could she cause the doors to lock and set the place aflame?

You could smite your way out.

FOCUS. DO NOT CARRY OUT THE WORK OF THE DEVIL FOR HER. DO NOT SABOTAGE YOURSELF.

Fine. The Devil could stay for now.

"Today has been years in the making, as I'm sure you all know. I want to start off today by telling you a little bit about myself. Because by now, you've all heard things about me, but most of them did not come from me. They came from Jimmy Dean. He hijacked my story from the moment of my birth, and today I take it back.

"I am and always have been God's only begotten daughter. I know this is hard enough to believe, and only made harder by the fact that I'm telling you that God is a woman. So, allow me to clarify: God was not always a woman. When they crucified Jesus, God was a man. During the bloody Crusades, God was a man. When the first European explorers landed on the shores of what we now call America, killing and raping and enslaving the indigenous people, God was a man. When we enslaved millions and brought them to our shores from Africa in the name of industry and freedom, God was a man. When women were beaten and jailed for demanding the right to a vote, God was a man. When World War II killed over seventy million people, and we dropped the atomic bombs on Japan to end the deaths by creating horror, God was a man. During the Cold War of egos that threatened to end the world as we know it, God was a man. When the Klan, a self-proclaimed Christian organization, was murdering our brothers and sisters for the color of their skin, God was a Man."

She paused to let it sink in. Dolores was still staring straight at her.

For all of those stains upon humanity, the Devil had been a man, too. All kinds of things were changing now.

"God has been a man for long enough. Millions of people have been tortured, starved, raped, and murdered in His name. You may say none of that was the work of God, but it was work done in the name of God, done with the notion that it might please Him. And when His son spoke out against those behaviors, the God-fearing murdered him. It doesn't take a genius to see the state of things while God is a man does not work." The atmosphere around her felt flammable. She could practically feel the particles around her vibrate with frenetic energy. And yet, all around her, those in attendance didn't move. Whether they were waiting for the final bit of information to validate killing her or whether she had finally said something worth considering, she couldn't be sure. But she had their attention.

"I didn't ask to be born. But I'm part of a plan, as are all of you here today and those who will join us in the coming months and years." *If I have that long.* "I was born to an unwed mother, conceived in the backseat of a car. My mother gave birth to me on her hands and knees on the same living room floor where I learned to crawl. The same floor where I watched hit piece after hit piece about myself on our old TV and where I learned to hate myself for who I was.

"When I was eight years old, God told me I was destined to confront the Devil." She looked at Dolores and felt a sudden confidence rush through her. The grin broke through before she could stop it. She inhaled deeply. The oxygen went straight to her head. "When I was eleven years old, Jimmy Dean called me the embodiment of Original Sin. Not even a teenager, and my identity was already determined by men. I was Jessica Christ. I was Jessica Antichrist. My life wasn't my own, and I couldn't win no matter what I did. I was stuck in a web of contradicting identities. It took me years to realize that even though I heard all these things spelled out plainly for me, I wasn't the only young woman with this burden on my shoulders. I wasn't the only one under the false belief that I was responsible for fixing the evils of this world, even while the world told me I was too broken to ever do so. It was my Sisyphean task, my punishment for being Original Sin. But not just mine. Never just mine, even on the days when I felt completely alone in it.

"Because so long as God has been a man, women have been both the clean-up crew and the scapegoat. And now that God is a woman, what will we—any of us—be?

"When I wanted to run away from my purpose in this world, there was one person who never let me. My mother, Destinee, always told me I could be whoever I wanted to be, so long as who I wanted to be was the daughter of God. It was in my nature. How could I accept that, though, when so many people told me that my nature was evil or that of a servant of my Father's bidding? Who wants *that* nature?

"For as long as I can remember, I've been obsessed with nature shows. They brought me peace in this crazy world, though I didn't understand why when I was younger. But I know now. Everything has evolved to fit perfectly where it is. Only through human interference do things fall terribly out of balance. Otherwise, it all works in harmony. Everything has a reason for being just like it is."

She'd broached the subject of animals, and it seemed to be turning on lights behind the eyes of her rapt audience. Perfect. This next part would be tricky. She would have to nail it or else this whole costly experiment could go off the rails from the start.

"So, what I propose when I say that God is a woman is that we all return to our natural state, to the personality and passions deep within us. Let us return once and for all to Nature."

And this next part was exceptionally crucial, because if she didn't address sexual consent immediately—

A hoarse holler went up from somewhere behind her, and she looked over her shoulder, unsurprised to find her attention drawn to the section reserved for the homeless.

What *did* come as a shock, though perhaps it shouldn't have, was the glint of the brilliant sunlight off the metal of a homeless gentleman's knife.

SHANK, God corrected.

Jessica gasped, and what little attention hadn't already

moved to the source of the yelling did so then. Jesus jumped up and dove right toward the conflict, and that's when the real shoving started.

"I got him!" cried a man nearby, and he held up a thick baseball bat.

"They're so armed," Jessica muttered, staring helplessly from a distance that kept her safe from immediate danger, so long as no one produced a gun, but made it impossible for her to offer help.

She turned her attention to the Devil, but she was gone. This was her handiwork, then, and the damage was already done.

As the streak of black clothing rushed the conflict, Jessica was forced to admit that Wendy's idea of a police presence—resisted in equal parts by both Jessica and Jeremy, though not for remotely the same reason—had been sound.

She scanned the room. Most everyone was off their cushion and on their feet now, just in case the mood called for a good old-fashioned stampede. Would it be possible, once the troublemaker was extracted, to restore calm and continue the service?

Jesus dusted himself off, requested that the officers be kind with the beknifed man, and then hurried over to his half-sister. "That was a close one." He appeared in good spirits.

She flicked off her mic. "A *close* one? Just because nobody's dead?"

He nodded succinctly.

"Someone just pulled out a knife in church!"

"And a baseball bat," he added. "Don't forget about that. And I think Janice was about to pull out something she calls her 'defensive dildo.'"

"No."

Jesus chuckled. "It's a funny word, is it not? And you should see the thing. Quite intimidating. It rattles like a snake. Don't know how she thought of it. Mind of an inventor, that one."

She took a deep breath as all of her misgivings from the last few months danced circles around her, naked and chanting, "We told you so! We told you so!"

"This was a terrible idea."

"Huh?"

As the action died down, the congregation began to look around for guidance on what to do next.

"I never should've believed I could make all these groups work together. I *wanted* to be loving and inclusive, but I just *knew* the homeless would cause problems."

Jesus blinked. "Of course. They are on *drugs*, Jessica."

"They're— You knew they were on drugs and you brought them anyway?"

"Of course. Who needs community and acceptance more than those addicted to drugs?"

She pinched the bridge of her nose. "I can't deal with you and your love right now. Can you just ...?" She waved him away, and he shrugged and obeyed, going at once to speak with the restless transients whose pecking order had been disrupted.

YOU MUST KEEP GOING, CHILD. God's voice was deeper than it'd been of late, and it was that which dealt the hardest blow to her. She'd failed to tip the scales, but more than that, it seemed that fewer people believed God was a woman now than earlier that day. Had the chaos, the open act of violence, reset the defaults?

Must I? She looked around. She'd have an easier time wrestling 200 greased pigs into a pen. *It's too late. I've lost the crowd.*

She shoved her palms into her eyes despite the damage it would do to her makeup.

What would Jimmy do here?

He'd cause an even bigger scene, is what he'd do.

But she didn't have it in her. She wasn't Jimmy.

Inhaling deeply, she opened her eyes, rolled her shoulders back ...

And found the parishioners leaving through the exits in droves.

"Wait!" Her voice was drowned out completely, and she clicked on her mic again. "Wait!"

A few people halted. "The service—" The service *what?* Was this really the best time to introduce the gluten free offering? Could she capture the attention of her congregation fully enough to be clear about consent? Would any of these people sit still while she read them her commandments?

Not a chance. But she remembered Jimmy's annoyingly wise advice. They needed to leave feeling better than when they came. She could do that with three simple words—"I forgive you"—but sharing the bonds of forgiveness with so many strangers not only felt disingenuous, but dirty.

Thankfully, she already had something planned to end on a high note. "The service is now concluded. We, uh, we like to keep them short. Please help yourself to the coffee stations out in the courtyard, and I invite you to stick around to get to know your fellow humans."

She would put her faith in coffee.

Chapter Forty-Six

05:11:25:19 until Doomsday

Not even five minutes after the conclusion of the service, the coffee station more closely resembled a soup kitchen line than the mingling place of the classes that she'd hoped it'd be.

"Don't be mad," Judith said, taking a seat next to Jessica on one of the tucked-away make-out benches, "but that went way better than I expected it to."

"It started so strong."

"There were no fatalities."

Jessica looked up from her feet to inspect the face of her friend. "I can always count on you to find the silver lining."

A small rustle through the dense plant growth, and the grinning face of Jesus appeared. "There you are!"

"You know there are sidewalks built in," Judith said.

"Oh, sure, but it is so much more fun to cut through! I pretend to be in the jungle! Like a panther!"

He knelt in front of Jessica and took her hands in his. "Sister. You look disappointed."

"Uh, no shit. I just had to end the service early so the whole place didn't devolve into a gambling arena for bum fights."

He tilted his head to the side. "It was only the first service. It takes a lot of practice to love all."

She wanted to slip her hands free of his grasp, but she didn't want to hurt his feelings. "Or maybe some people make it impossible to love them."

"No, no, no." He shook his head firmly. "Not true. I take it you mean the homeless, and you should know that *I* love them."

Judith said, "But do you like them?"

"Not always. Sometimes when they call me names or beat me up I do not feel especially charitable toward them. But I always love them."

Jessica squinted at him. "*How?*"

"More importantly," Judith added, "why?"

"There are few things on this planet that you truly *should* do, but trying your best to love everyone is one of them, and you do it by making the choice that you will."

"Even the impossible-to-love ones?"

"Especially them. You cannot fully love yourself until you learn to love everyone else you share this world with. Do the homeless smell? Undeniably. But it is not on purpose. Are many of the homeless pumped full of a toxic concoction of chemical substances? Clearly. But no one ever chooses to be an addict ahead of time. They simply make poor choices with the best information they have. Do the homeless carry around improvised weapons? We should all know the answer to that by now. But they do it because they are so vulnerable out on the streets. They know the world does not value their lives equally with the homed and that when something happens to them, they cannot expect anyone to come to their aid. They are terribly alone. I cannot imagine. Even when I was being crucified, I had friends and family around me."

And she'd had the same. Through all the tough times, she'd had the same, even when she'd done her best to drive them away.

"That's how you love them?"

"It is. I want to cry for them daily. And I want to cry for those who cannot look upon them and feel compassion. Compassion does not mean you cannot ask the homeless to bathe or that you have to accept that they will die of an overdose, and it does not forbid you from calling the cops when they become violent. You do all those things, *and* you figure out how to show them love and acknowledge their humanity. It is the lack of acknowledgement that has landed them where they are. The hard-to-love people cannot see themselves in God. You must learn to do it for them."

She squinted at him. "You mean 'see themselves in God' figuratively, right?"

"Yes, of course. Our heavenly parent is ... well, you know."

"Not a great role model."

"Right."

Though she wasn't totally sold on what he was saying being possible for her, she felt like she might be starting to get it.

She'd have to continue pondering it later, though, because, she had somewhere else she needed to be, as she remembered the moment Wendy Peterman and Cash Monet appeared around the bend in the path.

"It's time?"

Wendy frowned sympathetically and nodded. Cash, not usually one to have their head out of their phone, had the device nowhere in sight. Instead, they hugged themself tightly as if a bone-chilling breeze were blowing through.

Doom settled in around her. Jesus's message was strangely comforting, but not even Jesus could save her now.

She was a dead woman walking, and everyone knew it. Her inaugural service had been an irreparable disaster. Her message had been incomplete. And she knew what that meant; someone else would pick it up and finish it for her. She would do whatever it took to keep that from happening, but it may not be enough.

The Devil had bested her again. Jesus had been right. It wasn't a one-and-done with Satan.

As she got to her feet, so did Jesus and Judith. "We'll come with you," Judith said.

"I love you, sister. Remember that."

She nodded, realized she was still wearing her headset, and yanked it off, tossing it aside into a fern. "Okay," she said, "I'm ready."

This press conference wouldn't hold itself.

Chapter Forty-Seven

05:11:17:41 until Doomsday

Wendy led her to a quiet place out of view of the cameras, which had been swarming the parking lot for hours, and brought a small powder compact from her pocket. She dabbed at the sweaty creases around Jessica's nose and chin and gave a little extra attention to the spot below her eyes. As she dabbed the summer shine away from Jessica's forehead, she said, "You'll do fine."

"And if not?"

She expected a dark and gloomy doomsday type response, but that wasn't what she received.

"We've survived worse. Just do your best."

"What if I forget the talking points? What if they ask me something we didn't anticipate? What do I say about the homeless violence?"

Wendy let her hand fall to her side, and she sighed and

looked her client in the eyes. "Listen closely to me now. I've been coaching you for years, and I'd give you a solid C-plus on following my directions and sticking to the script. But the moment you stepped into the middle of that congregation today and began telling your truth, that part of our relationship ended. Don't you see? The moment you arrived in *your* house as the messiah you are, you took back your story. All these years, I've been doing the same thing to you as everyone else: telling your story for you. I considered myself a steward of it until you were able to take it upon yourself. And today you did that. I can't tell you what to say anymore. It's all you." She paused. "I will leave you with a little parting advice, though, and that's this: you're a female religious figure now. You can't win their game no matter *how* you play. So don't play it. Create a new game."

As Jessica approached the small microphone stand, the semicircle of cameras and mics shuffled restlessly. But in the crowd, she found her mother's face, and next to her, Chris. She twisted to look behind her and saw Judith and Jesus waiting a few feet back, out of the shot. Jesus made a heart shape with his hands.

She hurried through with the prepared bit, but the words felt like a sweater tailored to a much smaller body—awkward, restricting. She pushed through them, though, speaking clearly into the microphone as if she didn't know she was about to get a verbal lashing from the muckraking media. How could Wendy just abandon her like that in her moment of need?

And when it came time to describe how the inaugural service had gone, she paused, considered honestly, but opted to continue with the script as planned.

The service was a huge success! A victory for love and compassion!

She concluded with the phrase she'd said so many times already, it made her want to scream: "Because God is now a woman."

It was a lie.

She had failed. Her one path toward bringing peace, the one thing she was put on this earth to do, and she had failed. Despair made her blood feel thick in her veins.

Gloria Tatum from Channel Nine got the first question in. "Many know you as Jessica Christ. Does that mean you consider this a Christian Church?"

A planted question. Coordinating this was one of Wendy's final acts of help, and Jessica hadn't even known it. "That's a nickname I've received over the years, yes. As most know, my legal name is Jessica McCloud. So, to answer your question, yes and no. Yes, it is a Christian church because if you look at the meaning of the word Christ, it refers to the messiah, and that describes me. I'm a female messiah. But if you look at what many Christian churches have become today, overrun by bureaucracy, structured in such a way that allows for the egos of men to hijack the message of Jesus, and, most importantly, worshipping a God with male pronouns, then no, we're nothing like that."

Gloria Tatum nodded, satisfied.

"What are you going to do about the bum fights?" came a booming male voice from the throng. She wanted to ignore it and take a question from the polite Lou Mann with Channel Thirty-Seven, but no one else tossed a question her way. They were all clearly wondering the same thing.

Fucking bum fights. She had no prepared answer for this one. "Besides offering continued financial support to resources for the homeless, we're already brainstorming ways to ensure the safety of those who come to worship without exclusion."

She blinked, and a soporific part of her perked up. Hey, that wasn't half bad. And it was mostly true.

But the same voice, which she now identified as Todd Basserfield from one of the 24-hour news stations, followed up with another question: "Sure, but what are you going to do?"

"We're still considering it."

"But how can you keep responsible people safe while also allowing drug-addled miscreants in the same space?"

She glared at him, feeling a slight tingling down her arms to her fingertips. "Sounds like you've already made up your mind that it's an impossible task. I guess it's a good thing you're not in charge of the effort. As I just said, we're going to discuss solutions that serve everyone, not just those who can afford the outrageous cable TV fees to enjoy your network." Oh boy. Probably too harsh. She shouldn't have come at him like that.

Instinctively, her eyes searched the crowd for Wendy's,

and when she locked onto her target, she found the publicist ... stifling a laugh? No. Certainly not.

Finally, Lou Mann chimed in with *his* pre-planned question. "How is yours different from other religions?"

She felt her shoulders unclench the smallest bit. "How are we different from other religions," she mused, relaxing back into her rehearsed words. "For one, we're the only mainstream religion that believes God is a woman. I don't think that will last for long, though. I think the rest will start to come around. I have a good feeling about Judaism, especially." A small, unexpected chuckle rose up from the tightly wound crowd, and she allowed herself to wonder if she was actually being charismatic.

She went on, "But another important difference is that no one who attends these services is required to call themselves anything in particular. In fact, we discourage it. Rather than saying, 'I am a Christian,' we want people to say, 'I attend this particular church.' The wisdom behind that distinction is that once people feel comfortable labeling themselves, they also feel comfortable dismissing harmful behaviors by saying, 'But I'm a whatever.' We won't tolerate any harmful acts in the name of this religion."

Todd Basserfield shouted, "What about the hobo showers?"

She glared at him. "What about them?"

Before he could formulate a coherent question that would mask his vile classism under a veil of concern for, say, women and children, Fiona Abernathy from the public station jumped in. "Is God a white woman?"

The rest of the reporters fell silent.

"Um, beg your pardon?"

Fiona Abernathy was not a white woman herself. She had umber skin and wore her hair closely shorn to her scalp. Jessica guessed her age at roughly late fifties, and the reporter had a calm air about her that brooked no argument and refused to be ignored. "You've stated in previous interviews that the reason God had a daughter and not another son is so we could begin to see God in the female persuasion. Is that correct?"

Swallowing desperately to wet her suddenly dry throat, Jessica croaked out, "Yes, that's right."

"Then following that logic, there was also a reason God made you white, is there not?"

Shame kept her from a firm answer. "I suppose so."

"So, when you say God is a woman, it might follow that God is specifically a white woman."

Jessica's eyes darted around for Wendy, then for Quentin, then for Tamara before she realized why she was looking for those three specifically for moral support. The unnameable shame intensified.

The reporter Maria Flores broke the silence. "Well, she had to be *some* color, didn't she?"

A few of her white colleagues laughed tightly, but Fiona wouldn't be deterred. "Exactly. If God was so intentional about gender, why would She be *unintentional* with race?" Though the question was a response to Maria's comment, it was addressed directly to Jessica.

She didn't have a clue. She'd managed to avoid asking this question in earnest for so long, but it looked like she couldn't avoid it any longer.

Why am I white?

BECAUSE I MADE YOU THAT WAY.

No help then.

Why was she white?

Well, because her mother was white, biologically speaking.

But why hadn't God impregnated someone of a different race?

Wait, wasn't Jesus's mother Middle Eastern or something?

Her mind continued to run circles, but her mouth opened anyway, and from it, came words she probably shouldn't have said.

"Yeah, I guess God wanted me to be white. She works in mysterious ways."

And there it was. That thing so many people were afraid to name was out in the open. She had a brand-new almighty problem on her hands.

Chapter Forty-Eight

05:08:43:25 until Doomsday

"But it *is* a good question!" Jessica paced back and forth across her living room while Wendy and Cash shared a meaningful look from their spot on the couch. "Why am I white?"

Wendy reached out and grabbed Jessica as she made another lap, forcing her to stop. "You think I haven't asked that a thousand times?"

Jessica blinked. She had been living in a dizzying fog in the hours since Wendy had stepped forward to the mic, said, "We get the Messiah we deserve," and ended the press conference.

Jessica had remained in that haze as Chris and Destinee loaded her up into the rented F-350 and carted her back home.

And now, finally, after Wendy, Cash, Jesus, and

Jeremy had joined them in her condo for a debrief, she felt like she'd just woken up.

Jessica glared down at her publicist. "You shouldn't have hung me up to dry right before I went up there."

"I didn't. You've been avoiding this question for too long. Someone had to ask it."

A bolt of betrayal ran through her. "Did you *plan* that with Fiona?"

"Of course not. Don't be dense. It's simply an inevitable question for anyone who's not white. The timing wasn't ideal, but I knew it would come eventually. Frankly, I'm surprised it didn't come sooner."

"Then why didn't you prepare me for it?"

Wendy let go of her arm. "Because I don't have a good answer for it. I only have deflections. But it demands to be answered fully. Only you can do that."

Jessica threw her hands into the air. "I don't know the answer! I don't know why I'm white!"

"Have you considered asking your Mother?"

Jessica had not.

But she shifted her attention that way.

"Huh?" Destinee perked up from her spot on the stuffed armchair once she realized all eyes had turned to her. "Oh, that's easy. You're white because both me and Ross Hawthorne are white."

Cash looked up from their screen. "Who the hell is Ross Hawthorne?"

"The guy God looked like when we banged. Don't tell

me you're too young to know who Ross Hawthorne is. Shit."

Wendy steered the conversation back on track. "Not *that* mother."

"Oh, you mean God? Yeah, already asked her. She said I'm white because She made me that way."

Wendy sucked in a deep breath and let it out slowly in a way that indicated she might be asking Jessica's Mother for patience at that very moment. "And then did you ask *why* She made you that way?"

"Uh ... no. I guess I didn't."

But before she could ask the question, God spoke. *YOU ARE A WHITE WOMAN BECAUSE, FOR NOW, I AM A WHITE WOMAN. I AM THE ALPHA AND THE OMEGA. I AM THE OPPRESSOR AND THE OPPRESSED.*

What the actual fuck are you talking about? No, never mind. Why did you make me white?

THE SAME REASON I GAVE YOU THAT GOLDEN FOOT YOU NEVER USE ANYMORE.

Just say what you mean for once!

(Cash waved a hand vaguely in front of her glazed over face, but Wendy knocked it away. "Stop. She's praying ... or whatever.")

WE'VE TALKED ABOUT THIS BEFORE, DAUGHTER. WHY DID I GIVE YOU THE MIRACLES THAT I DID?

Because they were the ones people needed. Because they were the most likely to convince people that I was for real.

EXACTLY.

But you could have made me black if you'd wanted to, right?

YES.

So you didn't want to?

I VERY MUCH DID WANT TO.

Then why didn't you?!

There was no response, but she didn't need one. She understood, or at least she was starting to, and it left her breathless with a hollow aching in her chest.

She let her vision refocus on the publicist in front of her, and her gut roiled. "Wendy, if I'd been black and claimed to be the messiah, from a publicist's perspective, what would you say my odds were of anyone listening to me?"

"Anyone *white* listening to you?"

Jess cringed and nodded.

"Let me put it this way: I wouldn't have taken you on as a client if you'd come to me and said you wanted white people to believe a black woman was a messiah."

"And that's because?" She braced herself.

"That's because I can hardly convince people that I'm a college graduate, and I have my masters and fifteen years' experience running my own firm. When I answer the phone for Peterman Public Relations and say, 'Wendy Peterman speaking,' people ask me if they can speak with my boss."

Jessica grunted and dropped down onto the ottoman next to Chris, her arms flopping limply into her lap. "I don't know what to say. I believe you, but … This is painful."

Wendy leaned forward and tapped Jessica's knee in what was clearly intended as consolation. "I can't believe I'm the one comforting you right now, but … it's not your fault."

"Quentin brought all of this up before, and I just didn't get it."

Wendy nodded. "To be fair, you still don't. But you're trying, and you're making progress."

Jessica put her head in her hands, trying to think as Chris rubbed gentle circles on her back.

She'd started this conversation looking for reassurance that the reporter's question had been unjust, an unfair attack on something Jessica couldn't help, possibly even a racist jab. Yet now it was clear that not only was there no reassurance to be provided, but she herself had some serious reckoning to do. She couldn't avoid the question any longer, and every answer that felt true also felt like a knife turning in her heart.

After a few silent minutes of the new perspective churning, she looked around the room at the faces she trusted the most to give her honest answers. "Have I been promoting …" What was the word? Then it came to her, and a bitter taste blossomed on her tongue. She'd heard it used before, but only in relation to swastikas and white hoods. Was there a milder version of it for what she might've done? She wasn't lighting crosses, after all

But she was exhausted, and these were people she

trusted, so she let the rest of the question tumble out. "Have I been promoting white supremacy?"

Chris and Destinee hurriedly reassured her that it was not the case, while Jesus, from his lounging spot on the rug, asked what white supremacy was, and Wendy, Cash, and Jeremy nodded compassionately. The two camps looked at each other in confusion. And Jesus looked at *everyone* in confusion.

"Just 'cause she's white—" Destinee began.

And Cash said, "Exactly, she's white."

"You're the whitest person in this whole room," Chris snapped back.

"But I'm not claiming to be the messiah."

Jeremy, leaning against the wall by the window, put an end to the fragmented conversation with, "To be fair, white supremacy serves as the foundation for everything that has happened in this country since the ancient alien race landed on the shores of what we now call Alabama and injected their DNA into the local indigenous populations."

And the room fell silent.

"I didn't mean to," Jessica said miserably.

"I know you didn't," Wendy assured her. "You had to play the game, though. At least for a while."

"But I thought you said I couldn't win this game, that I shouldn't even play it. Wait, how many games are there?"

"So many. And I did say that. You had to play the game to get to where you are, and now that you're here, it's time to change the rules."

Jessica craved a beer, but now seemed a racially insensitive time to get one.

However, reading her daughter's tell-tale signs, Destinee jumped up and headed to the fridge, and as she returned with a long-neck, Jessica said, "Won't I be a hypocrite if I change now?"

Destinee offered the Dos Equis to her daughter, but Wendy grabbed it first and took a long swig. "No, Jessica. Learning to be better and changing your behavior accordingly is never hypocrisy."

"It's not, I dunno, too late?"

It was Jesus who eagerly replied, "It's never too late in the day for a laborer to arrive."

Wendy eyed him skeptically. "I ... wouldn't have said it that way, but he's not wrong. Better late than never."

"Ooh!" Jesus said. "I like the way you put it. Much simpler."

"Is this why I haven't succeeded yet?" Jessica asked. "Why I haven't brought peace to the United States? Because I've only convinced white women?"

Wendy nodded. "Our recent polls certainly support that assumption. But white women are a powerful group of people to lead. The most privileged of all the oppressed."

"Huh." It was Destinee who'd spoken. "Well, I'll be damned. Ain't never heard it put like that."

"I can't do this without all women, though," Jessica said. "So, how do I get all the non-white women on board?"

Wendy opened her mouth to reply, then shut it. Her square shoulders sagged. "Honestly? I don't know that you can." She paused. "I always knew we were heading straight toward this, but I just told myself I'd figure it out when we got to it. And now we're to it, and I still don't know."

The rest of the group remained silent. Jesus watched with rapt attention, his eyes wide, Destinee stared at her hands in her lap, Chris looked on the verge of speaking without having any clear idea of what he might say, and both Cash and Jeremy were already buried again in their phones.

The front door swung open, hitting the springy door stop with a bang, and Rex stepped through carrying a large cardboard stack. "I got pizza!"

"Not now," Destinee snapped. "We're talking about race!"

The blood drained from Rex's face as the door swung closed behind him. Then he blinked. "Intersectionality," he whispered reverently before rushing to drop off the pizzas on the kitchen island. "One second! I'm ready to listen! I want to hear you!" He scrambled over to sit on the floor by Destinee and next to Jesus, where he settled in cross-legged, his belly hanging over his belt to take up most of his lap as he stared wide-eyed at the only person of color in the room.

Wendy arched an eyebrow at him.

The smell of pizza acted as a familiar swaddle, taking the edge off of Jessica's frayed nerves. A few more deep inhales, and she felt something shift. She could be brave. She could ask the hard questions. And if it all blew up in her face, there was always, *always* pizza. "Should I apologize?"

The publicist tore her eyes from Rex's disconcerting attention and shrugged. "Eventually, sure. But I think we both know actions speak louder."

She could practically feel Chris's self-control stretching to its limits as he refrained from defending her. Or maybe he was refraining from answering the pizzas' siren song. Either way, she was grateful for his discretion. She needed to think.

"How much damage have I done?" she asked.

"Nothing you can't undo."

"How can I undo it if I don't even know what exactly I did?"

"You listen, for a start."

Rex nodded emphatically.

Jessica shot him a sideways glance before asking, "To who?"

"To the ones you haven't heard yet," Wendy replied. "The ones who don't have microphones, the ones who don't own the networks." Then to Jeremy: "No offense."

His face remained buried in his phone as he replied, "None taken. My kind are vultures."

"And," Wendy concluded, "listen to the ones who are punished for speaking."

"I've been punished for speaking," Jess said, sliding comfortably into that familiar role of the oppressed like it was a warm bath after a chilly day. "What about that?"

The publicist didn't appear especially impressed. "Yes,

you have. So you should keep speaking. But you could have been punished *more*. Or they could have simply ignored you, which is often worse."

Her shame surged again. "I just wish you would have told me sooner! You let me go out there totally oblivious to any of this, and I've made a complete ass of myself. I've been promoting ... *bad things* without meaning to."

Wendy's voice became that of a strict teacher who had been through this routine before. "It's not my job to educate every white person about this. But also, I've definitely brought this up in so many words before. You just didn't hear it. By the sounds of it, Quentin's brought it up *directly*, and you still didn't hear it. You weren't ready to hear it, and that's the hard truth of it. But now you're listening, so I'm *telling you*."

"Okay. You're right. You're right!" She held up her hands in surrender, then took a deep breath as her control returned to her. "So, how do I fix this?"

"First, you have a whole lot of learning to do, and it's going to be uncomfortable, challenging, and there will be mandatory reading. And then you're gonna need an audience. I hate to be the bearer of bad news, but I don't think you're going to pull much of one on your own. Not after that lackluster showing today."

Jessica winced. Was reminding her of the day's almighty flop *really* necessary?

"However," Wendy went on, a small smile creeping onto her face, "I do happen to know someone who is already positioned to draw *quite* a crowd next weekend."

Ah yes. Jessica got to her feet to face her publicist, already feeling supremely out of her depth but pushing onward anyway. "Then we'd better get—Chris!"

He'd crept over to the kitchen and was folding a giant slice in half to better torpedo it into his mouth. He froze. "What?"

"This is an important moment!"

He didn't move, but his eyes darted around, no doubt looking for support. "And what better way to celebrate than with pizza?"

Jessica turned to Wendy for a cue on how to proceed, but the publicist just shrugged. "Can't fight systemic racism on an empty stomach."

And as it turned out, that was truer than Jessica could have imagined, because as she started on her third slice, thinking about all the ways it would be impossible for someone who looked like her to bring peace to the United States, the seed of an idea dropped through the fresh cracks in her cemented worldview ...

She paused, the mushy lump of pizza going temporarily unchewed. If she so much as breathed, she might lose the thread.

So she held onto it gently, following it, asking *What next?* and *Then what?* Her heart raced, and in her soul, she knew this was it—God didn't have to tell her. It was like she'd been born with this answer inside her and only now had she accessed this secret wisdom. She didn't understand it yet, but she would if she kept asking the right questions.

God's wisdom from years ago surfaced in her mind, hardly more than a whisper: *THERE IS ALWAYS A LOOPHOLE.*

Indeed. And she was pretty damn sure she'd just found it.

Chapter Forty-Nine

00:01:05:01 until Doomsday

The vast parking lot of White Light Church was set up like a carnival of doom, lit up against the dark backdrop of the night sky. Its original purpose, to house cars, had been usurped, and all those who believed the end was nigh were being asked to park on the shoulder of the frontage road nearby—what was it to them if their cars were towed once the world was over?

And that freed up space for the many horrors that Jimmy Dean had arranged, including, but by no means limited to, rows upon rows of shiny silver troughs full of communion wine that sparkled bloody under the bright lights; confession circles, where a guilty party would stand, surrounded by all of his closest friends, and confess to his worst transgressions publicly (no going back now!); and, for the children, a pin-the-tail-on-Original Sin wall that depicted the mother of Christ delivering her child on all fours.

Jessica split a rideshare over with Destinee, Rex, and Chris to avoid the parking nightmare. Their meager disguises, which were more camouflage than anything else, were already in place by the time they got out of the cramped Toyota, thanked their driver, and gave him a rating of five stars in advance for not snitching on social media about who he had just transported to this event.

"I've always wanted to be a redhead," Destinee giggled, straightening her wig as they slipped between two parked trucks on the frontage road.

It was hardly what anyone would call a "natural" shade of red. More like the inside of a grapefruit. And it stood out boldly against the blank canvas of her white clothing.

"You look great, my goddess," Rex said. "Of course, you know your looks are always secondary to your true essence for me."

"Just say I look hot, Rex. Jesus."

The high school football coach wasn't especially disguised, but that was because he looked like so many people without even trying. Despite knowing him for years now, Jess was pretty sure that if he grew out a beard, she wouldn't be able to pick him out of a lineup of middle-age white men who hadn't listened when their doctors told them to cut back on red meat. He had opted for a white pearl-snap shirt, white Wranglers, which she didn't even know existed until the hunt for camouflage had begun, and cowboy boots to further allow him to fly under everyone's radar.

Jessica had always believed her appearance to be forgettable, which was why, even after so much press coverage during the course of her life, she could still go most places without being recognized, so long as she didn't have any accompanying context with her like the pro footballer Chris Riley or the movie star Jameson Fractal.

Or, as the case may be, White Light Church.

She was so closely associated with the damn institution that she would be fresh in everyone's subconscious—the product of Original Sin, the one who would bring about the End. She was an archetype here. The shadow. The *she*dow.

Sunglasses and a baseball cap just weren't gonna cut it this time.

It had been Chris who'd suggested the thick-rimmed glasses, and because she didn't have the heart to tell him that she wasn't Superman—so there was no way eyewear would be enough—she'd decided to give it a shot and had ordered a decorative pair off the internet. White rims, of course. All she needed then was a wig (thankfully Destinee had gone hog wild at Party Palace and purchased plenty to share), and now she was basically unrecognizable.

Chris, however, had been a conundrum. How to disguise the starting quarterback of the Cowboys' biggest rival? His face had been emblazoned into the consciousness of so many people as they struggled to maintain the tension between pride for one of their own and hatred for the other side.

It was Rex who'd finally cracked it. "How about a mustache?"

And so the four of them were ready for the apocalyptic shitshow awaiting them at Jimmy's Austin church.

Or so they'd thought.

"What's that smell?" Destinee said, scrunching up her nose as they passed between two long rows of communion troughs. A sea of white clothing enveloped them, and Jessica felt immediately sure their disguises would hold for as long as they needed. No one seemed to be noticing anyone else. Self-absorption for the win! "It's like a moldy ham sandwich bumped uglies with moldier bale of hay."

She wasn't far off, as they discovered once they moved closer to the main stage, which was situated in front of the obligatory *Sumus Omnes Porcos, Sed Deus Est Aper* archway with a statue of Jimmy on top.

"Are those things *wild*?" Destinee said, expressing the alarm each of them felt when they spied the corralled hogs.

"They don't look like any domesticated pigs I've ever seen," said Rex, holding out a protective arm in front of his girlfriend.

"I told you I shoulda brought my gun," Destinee grumbled. "Who the hell thought they could keep two dozen wild hogs in a fence? It's just sheer luck they haven't got the urge to get out yet, or else they would've." She turned to her daughter. "You remember when Mable Cornbaucher's yard was overrun by 'em and Harrison Pibil had to come out with his AK?" Jessica did remember that. She had been seven years old but could still hear the squeals as the bullets tore through the swines' thick flesh. "Bastards killed both of her cats and two of her cows before he put 'em down." She shook her head. "If anyone ends up dead here tonight, it'll be from those little shits."

"I'll be rooting for the little shits," Jessica mumbled.

On a stand at the back of the stage was a giant digital countdown clock that cast a strange red glow over the empty space below it. They still had just about an hour to kill before it ran down to zero. *Happy birthday, Jessica, I got you the end of the world!*

"If you had an hour left," Chris asked as they passed by one of the confession circles where a fight was perhaps seconds from breaking out between two large, red-faced men who Jessica might have confused for Rex if she were a few drinks in, "what would you do with it?"

"Probably take a nap," she said honestly. "I've always wanted to die in my sleep. You?"

"If you were taking a nap, I'd take a nap, too." He slipped an arm around her waist, grinning lustfully.

It quickly became clear to everyone in their small group that, sometime between when they'd gotten in the rideshare and when they'd entered into the mindfuckery of Jimmy's Apoca-palooza, Destinee had crossed the line into hangry. This was not a variable they needed, so Jessica herded them toward the row of food vendors.

Is all this food poisoned? Is this a mass suicide?
DEFINE POISON.

Will it kill us?

NO. BUT IT MIGHT MAKE YOU SICK.

Not my mom. She's got a stomach of iron. I once saw her eat five-day-old fast-food tacos after microwaving them for only fifteen seconds.

"The fuck's with all the pork!" Destinee yelled as she looked over the menu. Rex tried to calm her with gentle rubs on her back. Didn't work. "I'm so sick of pigs! So goddamn sick of *pigs*!"

"It sounds like you're sick of pigs," Rex said.

"Course it does! I just said I was!" She threw her hands into the air as she put her back to the vendor and looked around at the lit parking lot. "They think God is a Hog and then they eat hogs and fuck 'em and stick them in a pen. What the everloving hell is wrong with these people?"

The language was beginning to draw eyes, and Jessica hurriedly turned her mother away from the crowd and back toward the vendor. He was a small South Asian man whose eyes were probably not normally that large. He blinked at her. "We have bottled water, too."

"She'll have the fried pork rinds," Jessica said, hoping an exception could be made this one time to the wrongness of eating pigs. She turned to her mother. "It's not that you don't have a point. We all agree with you. It's that we need you to zip it so you don't blow our cover. You know what's at stake."

"Mmm ... Now there's something I could go for. A genuine Texas steak."

"Mom."

Destinee took the paper bucket of rinds from the vendor and tossed one into her mouth. "Yeah, I know, I know. It just gets to me sometimes. And I'm hangry."

Jessica's eyes involuntarily flickered to the nearby pin-the-tail-on-Original Sin wall, which she was absolutely sure her mother hadn't yet noticed. "Yeah, I get it."

They'd hardly made it three steps away from the food truck when Jessica spotted the one person who might be even more uncomfortable to be here than she was: Courtney Wurst.

Courtney had not originally been part of this plan. But after the girl had shown up at Jessica's doorstep three nights prior, begging to help with something, anything, there was no way to exclude her. Besides, when taken into account how deeply the rest of the Wursts, who had stopped speaking to Courtney months ago, were intertwined with White Light, Jessica had a strange feeling that perhaps it was less a matter of Courtney having an important part to play in Jessica's story and more that Jessica had an important part to play in Courtney's.

Then there was the ticking time bomb of Trent's involvement in Swinegate. And if ever there was a time and place for something like that to explode, it was here, with just under an hour to go before the End.

Jessica nodded at Courtney through the crowd.

An agonized wail rose up a dozen yards to their left, and Jessica didn't even bother to look. The wailing from the confession circles was frequent enough that she was already growing numb to it. Jessica's mind jumped back to her eighth grade English class where Ms. Cantos had taught about Dante's *Inferno*. Standing amidst all these lost souls as they waited for the arrival of a God who wouldn't come felt a little like Divine Comedy cosplay.

And where was Jimmy? When would he make his grand entrance? It had to be soon. The clock was ticking.

Someone clipped her shoulder in passing, and before she could get a word out, he was already apologizing. "I am so sorry, friend!"

Jesus looked horrorstruck at the accidental contact, and then his eyes traveled up to Jessica's wig. "Your hair is *fantastic!* I have never seen anything like it."

"It's a wig."

"Ah. Well, I am certain your real hair is fantastic, too."

She squinted at him. "Jesus, it's me."

He squinted back at her. He blinked. His eyes shot open wide. "Wow! It *is* you! I did not recognize you in those glasses."

"How're you liking this?"

"Oh," said Jesus Christ, "it is one of the worst places I have ever been. I cannot wait for it to be over."

"I think that's the whole point." She searched around. "Where's Jeremy?"

"Having a discussion with a gentleman whose hat asserted that God does not like gays."

Her hackles rose immediately. "Jesus. Jeremy's about to get his *ass* kicked." She turned to her mom. "Will you go with him to find Jeremy? The idiot is out there trying to change someone's heart and mind."

"Oh," Destinee said, looking from her daughter to Jesus and back, her expression tightening. "He's gonna get his ass kicked."

"Exactly."

Rex stepped forward. "I'll come with you, honey, but not because I don't think you're capable of handling this without me."

Nervously, Jessica watched them go. Or maybe she was misattributing the nervousness. That could easily be the case. The air around them vibrated with anxiety. At least she knew her mother could hold her own in a fight, and that might be the difference between a narrow escape and hospitalization for Jeremy Archer.

At this point, it was just about surviving the inevitable chaos. The people around her did not, she suspected, feel especially concerned for their own safety with the apocalypse only—she checked the clock above the sea of heads—forty-three minutes away.

Jimmy would take the stage any minute now. Nowhere had that been announced, and she had no intel on it, but she knew Jimmy. She'd studied under him for a time, after all. He wouldn't let the clock simply run down to zero without giving some sort of fevered speech to bolster his own ego and rile up the masses. But then what? What would he do when the clock ran down? She had a few guesses, and none of them was exactly good news for her or anyone else in this overcrowded parking lot.

But she had no intention of allowing him the mic that long.

Chris leaned close. "It's gonna work."

"I know."

He jerked his head back. "You do?"

"Yeah. Because it has to or else we're all fucked, aren't we? I don't know what Jimmy has planned, but it's going to be big, dangerous, and then he'll be gone. He's smart enough not to stick around once all these staunch supporters realize he's a fraud, and then I won't get another chance like this to make things right. So, it has to work, and I don't see a point in considering other possibilities."

It was only a short time later when, as predicted, Texas Railroad Commissioner Reverend Jimmy Dean took the stage. There were twenty-five minutes and twelve seconds left until midnight.

Chapter Fifty

00:00:25:12 until Doomsday

How many people in the crowd were, at that very moment, questioning the logic of the end of the world at midnight in the central time zone specifically? It seemed a little perverse that those in Australia might be enjoying a chilly July eighth afternoon when the end came. Or perhaps the apocalypse would roll slowly from one time zone to the other, pausing at the artificial dividing lines until the clock struck twelve and Doomsday was allowed to proceed.

It was all so very stupid.

Those were the thoughts occupying Jessica's mind as Jimmy paced across the stage to stand silently at the very front of it, the toes of his white snakeskin boots practically hanging off the edge.

He had donned his usual attire—white suit, red hog-hoof stole—but added a few flourishes to mark the occasion

—a white-gold watch that caught the artificial light from the parking lot, and a disturbingly bloodred tie that draped down toward his giant hogshead belt buckle like a deep gash.

Why dress up for the End of Days? It wasn't like there would be anyone around to remember what he'd worn. It was this detail, if nothing else, that baffled her. How could no one here see it? How could they not pick up even the slightest whiff of Jimmy Dean's pungent bullshit?

A part of her could have, dare she think it, respected him for doing the insane things he did if he'd believed in them, even a little bit, but now he was telling nothing but hollow lies, she couldn't have loathed him more.

As she built her ultimate case against him, she collected further evidence from his hair. The grays had long been salting and peppering his coif, but nothing quite to this degree. In the few weeks since she'd last seen him on the news, his hair had lost all color; not a gray was left as far as she could see. Now, his perfectly styled 'do was as white as his suit, with only a few brushstrokes of darker gray painted tastefully in. It was a professional job, and she wondered who he'd hired for it and how much he'd paid for the hairdresser's silence.

His snakeskin boots appeared newly shined, glistening like pearls in the spotlight he stood in. He pressed his hands together in a prayerful pose and shut his eyes, pious as all get out for the audience.

Nobody breathed.

A hog squealed then another snorted.

Jimmy Dean lifted his head and opened his eyes, staring vaguely into the night sky above their heads.

"You have all joined me on this sacred and momentous day. Praise be to Hog."

And from those surrounding her in the crowd: "For the Hog is good and filleth our slop bucket full."

She shivered, and Chris pulled her close against his side.

"And God said, 'When the pretender from the womb of Original Sin turns four and twenty, the conclusion will come, churches will fall, and the apocalypse will reap all the righteous, for the end is her.'" Jimmy paused, let his words hover in the hot July air. "The Lord told me this just one year ago today. He spoke to me directly, just as He's done before, and relayed the message of the End Times. And now, as the day of our Judgment swiftly approaches, we're left to face all of our sins. Bring forward the sinner!"

Jessica tensed, half expecting someone to grab her and wrestle her on stage. Chris appeared to be of the same mind as his arm tightened around her.

But when seconds passed and no one laid a hand on her, she was able to relax.

Someone else approached the stage at Jimmy's beckoning, flanked on either side by none other than his own parents.

Jessica gasped, and a small bit of empathy she didn't know she had for him twisted in her chest.

Trent Wurst couldn't bring himself to look at the audience, though it was clear he thought he should. So instead, he stared, eyes unfocused, at the very edge of the stage. His hands were clasped in front of him as he marched forward.

Jessica was both surprised and not at all surprised to see Ruth and Chief Wurst up on that stage with their son, each holding one of his arms, though it was clear he would make no attempt to flee. After all Jimmy had put this family through—his affair with Ruth and his subsequent abuse of her as the church's scapegoat—the Wursts had remained miserably married. They'd disowned their only daughter over the church, marking them as the pathetic parents of a single twin: Trent, the porcophile, the worst of the Wursts. And now they were leading him to slaughter. Sooie.

The procession stopped in the center of the stage, and Mr. and Mrs. Wurst stepped away, but not before she nodded proudly at her son. Chief Wurst seemed unable to look at anyone in particular and stared vacantly but determinedly over the heads of the spectators.

"Run, Trent," Chris whispered. "Just run and don't look back."

Despite never having been friends with him like Chris had been for so many years, Jessica couldn't help but agree. This was a setup.

Sure, Trent had been caught on camera raping pigs, but whatever was about to happen to him wouldn't just be unpleasant for *him*. If she knew Jimmy Dean, the spectacle would also be unpleasant for everyone watching, too. They were all well within the splash zone of Trent's shame. So it was, perhaps, more for her own sake that she wanted him to make a break for it.

"Please step forward." Jimmy motioned his loyal parishioner closer then held up a hand. Trent stopped right in the middle of a tape circle on the stage.

Oh damn. This *was* about to get ugly.

"And now, with the clock ticking, I believe it's time to finally discuss the specter that has been haunting my pure and holy church for years now, the seed of sin that has sprouted. It's a behavior that must unequivocally be condemned, and that's what we're here to do. Trent Wurst has been a member of White Light Church since the early days. He attended at the flagship location in Midland every Sunday for years. And when he went to college in Lubbock, he was central in creating a White Light College Ministry on campus. In short, he was one of our most promising members. Emphasis on *was*." Jimmy scowled at him, and Trent's posture would have deflated had it not already been completely so.

"When I discovered that not only had a small group of my parishioners been engaging in the ultimate sinful act of bestiality, but had selected *hogs* as their target ..." He pressed his steepled fingertips to his lips and shook his head somberly. "Well, you can imagine how my heart broke for us all. It's heresy of the highest degree. Among the worst sins imaginable."

IT REALLY MUST BE THE END TIMES, BECAUSE I AGREE WITH HIM THERE.

Where have you been?

JUST WATCHING. THERE'S A LOT TO TAKE IN HERE. BESIDES, IT SEEMS LIKE YOU HAVE IT UNDER CONTROL.

Could something like this be under control?

FAIR POINT. HEY, I GOTTA RUN, BUT I'LL CHECK IN WITH YOU LATER.

"Never once have the teachings of White Light encouraged or condoned this foul behavior. Nothing about our way of life says to engage in husbandly relations with a hog. Yes, Sumus Omnes Porcos—"

"—*Sed Deus Est Aper.*"

"But that doesn't mean that as pigs we were intended to engage with actual pigs. Blood of the Hog! Know a metaphor when you see it!" This last bit he shouted at Trent, who flinched but remained in his shame circle.

However, it wasn't the flinch that captured Jessica's interest. Instead, it was the last few words Jimmy had spoken. They hadn't sounded like Church Jimmy at all. They'd sounded an awful lot like Ice Cream Jimmy.

Was he coming unraveled?

Jimmy took a step away from the tainted to allow himself more space to extend his arm and point at said tainted. "Trent Wurst. Now is the time. Confess your sins and be clean!"

Looking around, Jessica noticed that everyone in the crowd seemed about as excited for this spectacle as Trent himself. Grimaces galore. This was group punishment if she ever saw it, and she had a feeling the gory details wouldn't go down smoothly with all the pork products everyone had just consumed.

Trent began to speak, but she couldn't hear the words from this distance, and Jimmy quickly cut him off with, "Upp-upp. Hold on. You're not—?" He nodded at someone off stage. "He's not even miked up! I told you." As he waved impatiently, a scrawny and pale man in all black hurried onto the stage with a tiny headset in his hand. He hooked it over Trent's ear before scurrying off.

Jimmy scowled at the stagehand before turning back to Trent. "Okay, now."

Trent, having been adequately knocked off his shame spiral by the technical interruption, blinked and said, "You want me to talk about the pig stuff?"

"Yes," Jimmy hissed through his teeth. "Go."

"Uh, okay. Well, um. I don't really know where to start. I didn't always have a thing for pigs ..."

Chris groaned, and Jessica couldn't help but agree.

"But I've spent basically my whole life thinking about how God is a Hog. And then when the Pretender started talking about how God was supposed to be a woman, I just got to thinking, ya know? I'm a straight guy, as the Hog intended, and I like women. Nothing wrong with that ..."

Oh wow. This. *This* was something Jessica had not foreseen, mostly because the timelines were so mismatched that the story shouldn't have held any water. Members of White Light had been caught fucking pigs *long* before her recent campaign to turn God into a woman.

But she should have known. She should have known

that if she turned God into a woman, men would use God as their scapegoat for all their disgusting behavior. And here it was. As the logic went, if God was a Hog and God was a woman, then it made perfect sense for men to stick their dicks in hogs, who were just asking for it, really.

She tried to muster up a little anger, but she found herself suddenly too exhausted.

It was a rehearsed statement, no doubt about that. This twisted testimonial had Jimmy Dean's signature all over it.

Trent continued, "She looked at me, and because I was so mixed up, wondering if God was a woman like the Pretender kept saying, I could have sworn I saw the face of God on her. I thought I heard the voice of God, too, telling me that it would be all right if we ... well, you know."

"Yes, please spare us the details," Jimmy said. "Your confession makes it clear enough that you were made mentally ill by the falsehoods of the Pretender. This is increasingly common as she spreads her heresy." He addressed the crowd. "Heed this warning! For I do not bring this disgusting man before you solely to punish him. Let his punishment save your souls and awaken you from any confusion you might be containing inside your soul. It was *not* my teachings that led him and so many like him down the road of temptation and into sin, but the lies of *Jessica*. The lies of the one who has tricked us into believing she could be born of Original Sin and yet be the child of Hog Himself!"

The clock had ticked down, and only eighteen minutes

remained until Jessica's birthday officially began (in the central time zone).

"You, Trent Wurst, have confessed your sins. Will you commit them again, if given the opportunity?"

There seemed little chance of that happening, according to Jimmy's narrative, unless Trent hopped right off the stage, undid his belt, and jumped wiener-first into the wild hog pen.

"No, I repent for my sins and see the error of my ways. I was so confused by the sexual implications of a female God that I lost my mind temporarily."

"It's not your fault," said Jimmy.

"It's not my fault!"

"You were weak, but so are we all."

"I was so, so weak!"

"And nothing in White Light's teachings encouraged you to act in such a way. The church is faultless."

"The church is faultless! Oh, Hog! Forgive me!" His knees gave out, and he crumpled into a ball, remaining within his shame circle all the while.

"And for all of you out there," Jimmy said, "take note. He was blessed with an opportunity to confess his sins before the end. Some of you have not yet done so, despite your access to the confession corrals. So, I will leave you with a few minutes before your time runs out to relieve yourself of your burden so that you might receive Hog's grace within you and ascend to Heaven upon death."

Chris muttered, "What are the odds that he'll record every one of those confessions?"

"One hundred percent."

"It seems appropriate," Jimmy announced, as Trent continued to sob, "that on this occasion we revisit the night when this all began, the night when God spoke to me in the body of a Hog and sent me to view a lowly birth that would show me the way until the Final Moment." He nodded at someone on the side of the stage, and Ruth Wurst climbed the few stairs back up into the spotlight. Only now, she was wearing different clothes from the whites she'd previously worn. Those had included a thin white cardigan over a white blouse that hugged her neck so tight it seemed likely to strangle her.

Now, however, in horrifically clingy tights and a leopard-print shirt that exposed her middle-age belly, which flopped over the waistline of the zebra-print tights, Ruth Wurst closely resembled someone Jesus would spend a lot of time with.

Makeup like a clown in the rain completed the look with stringy and overly gelled hair.

And yet, the self-righteous woman held herself with dignity as she approached Jimmy across the stage. Jessica wondered briefly if anyone else noticed the reverend's slight eyebrow arch, the twitch at the corners of his lips, and the flare of his nostrils.

Tucked beneath an arm, Ruth carried something white. Only when she handed it to Jimmy and he shook it out did it become clear that it was a bedsheet.

The charade came into sharp focus like a slap to the face.

No, no, no …

Jessica shook free of Chris's arm to free herself up. She scanned the audience urgently, looking for the shock of red wig. Where was she?

HAVE FAITH.

Are you kidding me?

I KNOW WHAT YOU PLAN TO DO. CONSIDER HOW THIS COULD AID YOU IN IT.

You know my plan? Of course you do. But you're okay with it?

No reply, so she was forced to consider God's suggestion. Maybe She had a point. In fact, this whole thing was starting to play out like perhaps it had been orchestrated from the start by a single—

"Are you okay?" Chris was staring down at her.

"Yeah, I'm fine."

"I think maybe we should get out of here. The crowd is turning ugly."

"The crowd's been ugly, Chris." She looked back at the stage where Ruth Wurst was slinking from one side of the stage to the other, sticking her tongue out and rubbing herself suggestively while the crowd, and her wide-eyed son, looked on.

Jeers issued from the crowd, and Jessica heard a man yell, "SLUT!" followed closely by a chorus of female voices parroting the insult.

Jessica's fingers tingled. Did Destinee see what was taking place on stage? And if so, had it clicked for her yet?

Of course it hadn't. Because once it had …

Destinee's moment of epiphany occurred not long after Ruth Wurst went down on all fours and began grunting, and Jimmy set the scene: "Away in the mobile home, on the dirty shag carpeting, a sow birthed a baby girl ..."

Destinee's footsteps on the stairs to the stage were thunderous, and for the first time in her life, Jessica felt no moral obligation to step in and prevent her mother from kicking the ever-living shit out of Ruth Wurst.

It was liberating. Exhilarating.

The years her mother had spent watching football with Coach Rex had clearly improved her form. She got low, bending at the waist, and with one final push of her powerful thighs, leaped straight into her impersonator.

Ruth, still grunting on all fours, didn't see it coming. Destinee came at her from behind. Jimmy was smart enough not to get in the way of the bulldozer.

Destinee flattened Ruth facedown beneath her, and kidney punches followed in short order. The crowd gasped and screamed, in delight as much as judgment, as the two women went at it. Ruth managed to twist around to face her attacker directly but made the crucial mistake of going for the hair. The red wig, which was already half off, yanked free completely, and in the wake of it, Destinee managed to sneak in a loud slap to Ruth's right cheek and ear.

"Behold! The sows squabbling!" Jimmy announced, and Jessica thought, *Now's my time.*

It was eight minutes until midnight.

She squeezed Chris's hand to get his attention. "You don't need to save me on this one, okay?"

"Huh?"

Grabbing his face, she pulled him toward her, planting her lips on his. But before he could respond, she let go and slipped through the crowd.

It was time to make things right.

Chapter Fifty-One

00:00:08:49 until Doomsday

No one had yet attempted to break up the catfight on stage as Jessica snaked her way through the tightly packed bodies toward it. But that was to be expected of a crowd full of cowards who got off on the novelty of open female aggression. Or perhaps, Jimmy's unexpected mention of metaphor earlier had confused his followers just enough to make them wonder if they should be taking this as a literal brawl or if there was a deeper meaning they were supposed to glean from it.

Ruth's ground fighting skills had improved somewhat since the women's last brawl, or perhaps she was simply channeling her opponent through the ridiculous costume she wore. Either way, it looked to be an even fight, and Jessica thought someone ought to intervene. Would it be a fight to the death, otherwise? Or would Destinee get the upper hand, force Ruth to cry uncle, and then walk away? She wouldn't make it far in that scenario before the mob turned on her.

There didn't seem to be a good end to this, but that was the theme of the hour, wasn't it?

Unless ...

Perhaps if there was a distraction big enough, it would make the onlookers forget about the brawl completely while serving the secondary purpose of getting all eyes on Jess. And she was about to need *all* of the eyes.

Before she resorted to that, she would attempt to get attention the old-fashioned way.

She approached Jimmy, who gave her a quizzical look.

Oh right. The disguise.

She pulled off her wig and discarded it, immediately realizing that it meant her hair would appear unfavorably smashed for the duration. Damn.

Jimmy cocked his head to the side, processing the strange new development.

But when she pulled off her thick rimmed glasses, he gasped, at first in shock but quickly in delight. "I had a feeling she would come. She was there at the beginning, so of course she's here at the end. My friends, the Pretender, Jessica."

But not even Jimmy with his charisma of mass destruction could wrestle away the undivided attention of his congregation from the brawl, and with the attention split, faint lines of frustration appeared in thin parentheses around his mouth.

She checked the clock over her shoulder. Six minutes left.

She turned to the crowd. "Is no one going to stop them?" She pointed to the tangle of woman still grunting and squealing on the stage. Nope, no one was going to stop them.

Well, someone would.

She marched over, grabbed her mother's right arm—the odds of the other fist whipping around to knock her away were high, and she'd prefer her mother's non-dominant hand for that—and by the grace of God alone, when Destinee did as Jessica had predicted, the swing went high and she was able to duck under it. One hard tug, and she'd pulled her mother away and onto her ass.

Ruth, wheezing, readied herself to spring, but Jessica planted her feet in front of the bloodied woman. "I didn't bring you back from the dead just to have you act like a fucking fool, Ruth." The words felt silly as they slipped from her lips, but she'd had an intended result in mind, and she got it.

Ruth blinked with the one eye that wasn't already swollen shut and used her arm to wipe away a stream of blood from her nose. It looked broken, and if it *looked* broken, that meant it would have to be professionally set later. That seemed punishment enough.

"Get out of here and take your son with you, you pathetic excuse for a mother." This part, she didn't have to fake, the anger came easily, flowing through her arms. *Hold onto that,* she told herself.

Ruth did as she was told, scrambling to her feet and limping pitifully across to the shame circle, where she grabbed her son by the arm and tried to lift him.

"No, Mom! I belong here!"

She muttered persuasion at him, but he shook her off.

"This is my punishment! I need to see it out before the end of the world!"

Jessica groaned. "For fuck's sake, Trent. Get out of here! Go take care of your mother, you idiot."

He glared at her but didn't move, and it was something about that dead-eyed stare, the contempt *he* deigned show for *her,* that pulled the pin from the grenade.

Jimmy commanded, "Stay there, Trent, if you care about your soul and that of your slut mother!"

Trent's face contorted. "Huh?"

Not used to hearing your mom called that, huh, Trent?

But her gratification was short-lived if the spark of life ever inhabited it at all.

Jimmy grinned. "She's a slut, your mother. I've seen it firsthand."

"Huh?"

Jessica didn't have time for this. "They slept together, Trent! A bunch. Come on, you didn't know that?"

"I was confused!" Ruth howled, cheating outward toward the audience. "I'd spent too much time in the presence of the True Slut"—she pointed, of course, to Destinee—"to know right from wrong anymore!"

Destinee slipped free of Jessica's hold, and charged forward for round two.

But before she even got close to her target, the statue of Jimmy Dean and the archway below it exploded into a spray of rock and sand.

Yelling, screaming. Even Jimmy, the ever unflappable, ducked and covered. And slowly, once the thick dust settled, the charlatan turned to face the only person who *hadn't* flinched at the explosion.

Jessica.

She couldn't keep from glaring at the panicking crowd, not with contempt, but out of sheer disappointment. She'd had to show might before they would listen.

Snatching the mic off Trent's head, she held it to her mouth. "Do I have your attention yet?"

It was three minutes and forty-one seconds till midnight.

As it turned out, she did have their attention. All of it. Her mother's gasping attempts to catch her breath, the occasional passing car on the highway, and the contented snorting of the hogs were the only sounds wafting through the night air of the parking lot.

She scanned faces in the crowd for ones she knew and found Chris and Rex right away. Jesus was easy enough to spot next, since he was waving at her. Then there was the horrified face of Courtney Wurst, watching the humiliation of her estranged family happening in real time, and, next to her, Judith with a steadying arm around her shoulders. Somewhere out there would be the rest of her priestesses and Jeremy and even Quentin, dear Quentin, whose response to her End of the World invite had simply been, "I can't explain it, but I have to see this shitshow through."

But, before she could locate the rest, something else caught her eye. One of the hogs had its front hooves braced on the top of the fence. It stood on its hind legs and stared straight at her. Then it waved.

"I'm here to bring you, everyone, an important message, and it's this: Jimmy is right. The End is coming. But it's not the end of the world. It's the end of many other things that never should have happened in the first place." She gestured at Trent and his mother, both huddled together now in the shame circle. "You look at them and presume to see so much—their sin, their imperfection, their weakness. But the one thing you can't see is the most important part of them.

"I thought that the key to peace was for everyone to see themselves in God. I believed that was why I was born, so that women could finally see themselves in God and stand up to the people who want to keep us down. It's why black churches have a black Jesus and why Mormons have a white Jesus. But that was never the problem. Women have never seen themselves in their professed messiah. So, they've found other avenues to self-love. They've had to." She returned her attention to Ruth. "Well, not all of us. Some of us have ingested the poison, haven't we? But it's not just Ruth.

"No, the key is, and has always been, that there can be no peace until we see God in everyone around us. But we're pretty stupid animals, all told. As Jimmy pointed out, metaphors don't work that well for us. We need to see a literal child of God who looks like those we oppress before the oppression has any chance of ending. I mean, we are truly dumbasses in this department. But it's how things are.

"When I was fifteen years old, I was assigned a mission to restore peace to the United States. I know now that I was never intended to see that moment. I've only ever been able to start the process, and I can't do it by myself.

"Because while I'm the daughter of God, I'm still the *white* daughter of God. There's no getting around it. I tried to pretend it didn't matter, that it was just luck of the draw, that the odds simply favored it based on demographics. But I can't pretend anymore. God made me white for a reason.

"She spoke to me recently. She always does. But this conversation especially changed me."

DID IT? WOW. NICE TO KNOW YOU'RE LISTENING FOR A CHANGE.

"She told me that her next child would be here soon."

WAIT, WHAT?

"In fact, she could already be among us. Yes, God is having another daughter. And this one will be black."

WHOA, REALLY?

"There will be no peace until we can learn to see God in her, no hope for our future until we learn to love her more than we love ourselves."

HEY, SO, I LOVE THE DIRECTION YOU'RE GOING WITH THIS, I REALLY DO, BUT ...

God downloaded a short history lesson into her mind.

Jessica cursed, then quickly added, "Oh, and, this *should* go without saying, but like I already mentioned, we're all a bunch of fucking idiots, so if you go around trying to kill black baby girls to avoid the next coming, I promise it won't work. Also, you'll be smote to shit. God thought I ought to mention that."

Good call.

I DO LEARN FROM MY MISTAKES.

You truly have *changed, then.*

Jessica paused, looked out over her audience, taking the temperature of the crowd. They were still listening, so that was something, and the cameras continued to roll, so maybe the viewers at home could hear her words and understand.

"I've spent my whole life trying to learn this simple lesson. But it was Jesus who finally taught me that until we can love the ones society has ignored, cast aside, and devalued, our love is cheap. Until we can—"

A loud buzzing came from behind her, and she turned just in time to see the clock at zero before another deafening explosion knocked her to the ground.

Chapter Fifty-Two

The glass front doors of White Light Church were blown clean out in a rain of glass, but thankfully they were far enough away to keep from causing deadly injury.

When Jessica finally looked up from her prone position on the stage, she saw flames bellowing from the front of the building.

Jimmy. The bastard.

He lay facedown on the stage, spread out like a starfish and not moving at all. She would deal with him in a minute.

The stampede had begun, but whether the hogs had kicked it off with their inevitable escape from the shoddy corral or not, she might never know.

Courtney emerged from the sea, hoisting herself up onto the front of the stage. She wasted no time, sprinting to the shame circle to grab her mother and twin under their arms, attempting to lift them to their feet. Each only stared up at her blankly, though. "Get the hell up," she ordered, and with an effortful shout, she deadlifted Trent until he got his feet under him.

Ruth continued to flop. "Leave me."

"Oh, you wish." Destinee grabbed the woman's ankles and nodded for Courtney to take one of her arms. "You're no one's fuckin' martyr." And then Destinee and the Wurst twins carried Ruth across the stage toward safety.

The contingency. Jessica had almost forgotten about it. But Courtney's efforts jogged her hazy memory. It was why all the priestesses had been asked to attend this hellish spectacle, and surely it was still in place. They hadn't known what kind of crazy Jimmy had in store, but they knew it would be something. Even as she stood there, the blast from White Light ringing in her ears, her friends would be guiding the most frightened and vulnerable to a secure place.

And that left Jessica free to handle the one thing she'd needed to handle for her entire life.

Jimmy bled from the cheek, no doubt from shrapnel of his own creation. Perhaps his age was catching up with him, because he was slow to get back on his feet. The effort appeared painful, and he grimaced as one of his knees buckled on his initial attempt to put weight on it.

They locked eyes for only the briefest of moments.

And then he sprinted for the stairs. The sole of his snakeskin boot found the asphalt an instant before a rampaging hog swept both his legs out from under him. With a pearly flash, he involuntarily somersaulted over the hog, who carried on as if it hadn't even noticed, and grunted sharply when his back collided with the parking lot.

She felt the heat from the burning church on her back as she rushed forward. She may not have Miranda's speed in a 90-foot sprint, but she had the wrath of God inside her. Jimmy Dean wouldn't slip away this time.

He was almost to his feet again, gasping, holding his side, when her fingers curled around his suit collar and yanked him backward onto the stairs.

Dirt spoiled his suit, and the thin red stole twisted tightly around his neck, the hoof on the end dangling over his shoulder and down his back.

"Not this time, Oscar Meyer," she said, stepping over him. "I know about Hatch, Utah, the centurion bunnies in the clouds, the way it all burned down. And *everyone* knows about John Sonville and the underage brothel you had in Elbow. Your fraudulent ass is not getting away again. This time, you get to stick around and deal with the mess you've made."

He yanked at the stole, loosening it around his neck. "I could kill myself right now, and you'd have to bring me back."

"I wouldn't."

"Oh, but you would. Otherwise, you clearly can't see God in white men."

"Shut up, Jimmy!"

"You know I'm right. But don't worry. I won't do that."

"You won't?"

"No. I don't need to. Everything I've been working toward, you've just completed."

"I've ... What?"

He seized upon her moment of confusion and pushed himself up. Around them, the rushing crowd began to thin, and the first distant echo of sirens could be heard. "You've done it, Jessica. You've planted the seed, and it will grow. Trust me, I know a thing or two about that." He was grinning now. She wanted to kick the smug expression from his face.

"Hold on," she snapped. "I know what you're trying to do here. No, Jimmy. Absolutely not."

"Just because you don't want to face the truth doesn't mean it's not real. I created the crowd you need. I built the church that drove you to build your own. If it weren't for me, you never would have come forward to claim your story. You would have hidden your whole life." He cackled, and it wasn't the voice of any Jimmy she'd met before. "You've succeeded in what you set out to do, and you couldn't have done it without—"

"Suck my knucks, asswipe!" Destinee's fist came out of nowhere, smashing into Jimmy's jaw and knocking him out cold.

"Mom!"

Destinee looked like she'd recently seen the underside of a few stampeding hogs. She shook out her wrist and snorted in what Jessica could only assume was a steady flow of blood from her nose before looking away from Jimmy's limp body to her daughter. "I know, I know.

Shouldna done that. But it was just too good to pass up. Besides, we got no idea when we'll get another chance to hit him without anyone carin'. Hell, he probably won't even remember who did it when he wakes up. Free pass!" She glanced down again at the unconscious Jimmy Dean. "Happy birthday, baby."

And from behind Jessica: "YEAH. HAPPY BIRTHDAY, BABY."

She whirled toward the source, and the giant sow trotted forward.

"Damn, the whole family's here," said Destinee, taking the talking pig in stride. And why not? It made about as much sense as anything that had transpired in the last ten minutes. "The three of us oughta make ourselves scarce. Those sirens are close, and he ain't waking up anytime soon."

And so, as their first act as a flesh-and-blood family, the McClouds fled the scene of multiple crimes.

Chapter Fifty-Three

January, AGC 24

There was a time when Jessica would've said that the only way she'd see Rex in a Philadelphia Eagles jersey would be if she unknowingly walked in on him and her mother in some kinky humiliation role-play. But here he was, not only wearing one, but wearing one openly, outside the bedroom, hosting an NFC Championship blow-out party. It was like he'd lost a bet with himself.

This would never have happened if the name Riley weren't emblazoned on the back of the jersey. But as it was, she sported a matching jersey (underneath a midnight green hoodie). So did most people at the party, except for those who were only there for the food, not the football.

Speaking of Judith, the scribe made her way over from the elaborate snack table on the patio, a beer in her hand, and stopped just shy of where Jessica was parked in a canvas chair on the lawn. "The center is all locked up. Found a couple teens messing around on one of the benches in the garden. I let them be."

"Good. Thanks. Were they students of ours?"

The McCloud-Archer Community Center, formerly the Church of Girl Christ, had, in conjunction with Dr. Fractal, begun hosting free sex education classes for anyone whose school program had taught them nothing of any use. As it turned out, that was twelve hundred students over the last four months alone. Plans were in the works to expand to adult classes as well.

"Yeah, I recognized them. Keira Flannery and ... I don't know the boy's name."

"Keira?" Jessica said. "Must have been Forester."

"Nope, not him."

"But I just caught her with him last week."

Judith shrugged. "Dunno what to tell you. He must not have been any good."

On the big-screen out on the back lawn, a singer Jessica was pretty sure she'd met through Jameson once before belted out the national anthem. After holding "brave" for much longer than was warranted, the singer grinned up into the stands, waved, then added into the mic, "She is good!"

Judith cast Jessica a curious glance, and she wasn't the only one. A few gazes set on Jessica, and she could only shrug. "I didn't tell her to say that."

Jameson. Or maybe the singer truly believed it.

It was a phrase heard round the country. Started as a

hashtag following the melodrama on the last of days, it was a simple yet precise way of pronouncing that you believed God was a woman.

In the seven months since her birthday, multiple news outlets had theorized the origin of the hashtag, but none of them had come to a definite conclusion. It was like the thing had been immaculately conceived in cyberspace. An internet miracle!

Except it wasn't, and Jessica had paid Cash Monet a hefty bonus for their covert effort.

Yes, the revolution was gaining momentum, and she couldn't wait to ignore all the think-pieces that would follow this singer's ad lib at the end of the National Anthem. She was sure "Jessica Antichrist, Anti-American" would be included in its fair share of headlines.

She didn't care anymore, though. The movement had started. More and more people were openly supporting the idea of a She God and eagerly awaiting the next in line. And more than that, they were living it with their charitable donations.

But though her job has stopped being about her, it was far from over. Someday, perhaps soon, perhaps years from now, the real work would begin.

On the back porch, out of earshot of the TV, Destinee held court with the former priestesses, now community liaisons. Jessica couldn't tell what they were talking about, but she did overhear her mother say, "limper than a jellyfish on muscle relaxers," so she had a pretty good guess this was one of Destinee's legendary high school stories.

While preliminary plans were to invite all kinds of folks from Destinee and Rex's jobs, friends from the community center, and even some of Jeremy's exec buddies, in the end, that hadn't felt right. Destinee had been the first to mention it. "Ya know, Rex, I kinda feel like Chris is the son I never had, and I'd like to celebrate with just the people who know him."

Rex had become immediately teary-eyed and agreed, heaping praise onto his girlfriend for her generous emotional insight and the courage to speak her truth.

So it was that the guest list whittled down to fifteen people, but they were the people Jessica most wanted to have around her in this world while cheering Chris on in his championship debut. Win this, and it was off to the Super Bowl.

The odds had the opponent favored by twenty-four points, but Jessica had called in a favor with her Mother and had received confirmation that things would go Chris's way. The best part of the exchange was that she didn't feel the need to specify that she didn't want Chris to win at the cost of his opponents suffering life-threatening injuries, not because she was callous to the health of others, but because God wasn't. God, as it turned out, had more compassion than ever.

Standing by the refreshments, the former priestess Stephanie Lee cackled with glee at the conclusion of Destinee's tale, and then took over as storyteller.

Jessica needed a drink, and for once it wasn't because

she wanted to forget anything. This one would be celebratory.

She approached the drink bucket where Quentin stood with his back to her. On the other side of him, Miranda raised her longneck at Jessica. "One hell of a party."

DON'T SAY IT.

I wasn't going to.

YES, YOU WERE. JUST ACCEPT THAT THEY MIGHT END UP FRIENDS AND MOVE ON.

But they're meant to be together!

THEY ARE NOT. IF THEY WERE, THEY WOULD BE.

Miranda and Quentin shared a curious look. "God," he said. Miranda nodded, and they returned to their conversation about neuroreceptors.

"KICK OFF!" came Jesus's excited shout from near the TV. "THEY ARE ABOUT TO SPAR!" He'd stood from his chair to make the announcement and clapped his hands in frenetic excitement.

Rex shushed him as those partygoers who'd been milling around descended upon the lawn chairs gathered round the TV. Jessica did the same.

The smell of barbecue was stronger over here, and the wind changed suddenly, flooding them with smoke, but she didn't care.

The ball sailed through the air, sparking a strange pining deep inside her for her own kicking days. Fair catch. Whistle blown. Commercial break.

"Look away!" Jeremy hollered from his seat. "Don't watch the commercials. I happen to know they all contain subliminal Soviet propaganda! Don't allow yourself to be exposed!"

"This is a toothpaste commercial," Rex pointed out.

Jeremy leaned forward, furrowing his brows darkly. "I *know*. I own the parent company. Believe me when I say they cannot be trusted."

"But why—" Miranda began, but Quentin placed a hand on her arm and shook his head, and she dropped it.

A series of grunts from the back fence caught Jessica's attention fifteen minutes later, after the Eagles' first drive had ended in a punt. "Mom, I think Aper wants some grub."

With a similar grunt, Destinee lifted herself from her seat "Course she does. She probably smelled the barbecue from a mile away."

Theirs was a temporary arrangement with Aper, she knew. The wild hog whose body her second Mother had inhabited for End Times stayed in the area for now, rooting up the creek bed behind Rex's property. She'd taken a shine to the McClouds after they'd scooped her up and tossed her in the back of the XL rideshare, fleeing the fiery shindig before the cops arrived.

Of course they couldn't keep her, she was feral, so they'd cut her loose in the brush behind Rex's property. But she'd turned up at the back fence daily for whatever leftovers she could get and sometimes a head scratch.

It wouldn't be long until someone shot her. It wasn't technically legal in the city limits, but the local government had a way of turning a blind eye to that sort of thing.

God had assured her that whoever *did* carry the bullet with Aper's name on it would *not* be damned to Hell for killing one of God's former outfits.

Destinee approached the sow, it jumped up onto the fence and waved. God enjoyed an occasionally romp like this. Helped Her feel grounded, apparently.

It was halftime and the Eagles had a two-score lead when the chain-link side gate flung open, swinging all the way until it clattered back on itself. The sound was like a small bomb going off, and everyone's attention turned away from the pharmaceutical commercial aimed at those suffering from occasional nervousness and toward the source of the sound.

A stout woman stood just across the threshold and appeared surprised to find everyone staring at her. "Oops! I didn't expect it to be so flimsy."

Jessica jumped to her feet and felt the ground lurch beneath her.

The rest of the party: silence.

The television: *"Consult your doctor if you experience sexual disfunction, suicidal or homicidal thoughts."*

Dolores Thomas held up her hands defensively. "I'm sorry, I realize I'm not exactly welcome here, but I just wanted to talk."

Jessica whirled at the sound of the shotgun rack. "Mom, no!" Where had she even gotten that thing from so fast?

But Destinee kept the butt of the rifle against her shoulder, sights on the Devil. "Get off my lawn, Dolores. I have every right to shoot you this very second."

The Devil pursed her lips impatiently. "I'm well aware of Texas laws, Destinee. And it's only if you can claim self-defense. You have quite an audience watching right now. Are you sure every one of them would lie for you?"

Destinee shrugged her free shoulder. "Pretty sure, yeah."

Jessica inched closer to her mother as she addressed the Devil. "Why are you here?"

"I wanted to apologize."

That was obviously bullshit.

"I know what you believe me to be," Dolores said, "and I think for a long time, I *was* that. But it's left me now. I'm just ... me."

She thought of Aper, the way God could jump in and out. Could the Devil do that, too?

NO. IT'S ANOTHER TRICK, BABY!

Jessica addressed her mother now. "Don't do it. This is another play of hers. She wants you to shoot her so you'll go to jail."

"How do you know?" Destinee murmured, the tip of the barrel lowering a fraction of an inch.

"I don't know exactly what her plan is, but why else would she be here if not to screw us?"

Destinee adjusted her aim again. "You get the hell off my property, Satan!"

"Jessica," pleaded Dolores, and Jess felt a nauseating wave of sympathy wash through her.

"Mom, please put the gun down. We'll just call the cops and have them deal with it."

For a moment more, nobody moved, then, with a muttered string of cursing, Destinee lowered the shotgun. Rex was there in an instant, taking the weapon from her and setting it safely out of reach against a keg.

Jesus set a comforting hand on Destinee's shoulder. "That was the right thing to do. It's not our job to kill the meanies, even the ultimate mean—"

"Die, you atrocious bitch!"

Stephanie Lee grabbed the shotgun and marched straight for the Devil.

"You think I forgot the things you used to say to me? The threats, the abuse, the implications that nobody loved me?" It was clear by her slurred speech that she was already a few drinks deep. "You knew my parents died in an earthquake in the Himalayas when I was young. You knew it and you made that our science lesson the first week of kindergarten just to hurt me. All the years of it. Did you make Sandra befriend me just so you could torture me? All the horrible things you said to me, all the quiet comments to make me feel unloved. I can't believe I ever confided in you! You used me as a punching bag because you knew I wouldn't say a word! Well, I'm saying something now, you bitch! Even if I didn't *know* you were the Devil, I'd have guessed it."

"Stephanie," Dolores said sweetly, "I had no idea. I never—"

The shotgun blast took the Devil off her feet, and she didn't move again once she landed in the grass.

The party fell silent again except for the TV announcers and a distant squeal from a satiated Aper.

Destinee was the one to break it. Her voice came out hoarse. "She ... had a gun. Dolores was reachin' for a gun! Y'all seen it, right?"

"No," said Jesus. "I didn't see any such thing."

Rex barked at Jeremy, "Get him out of here. Now. Don't let him talk to any cops."

Jeremy gasped, offended. "I would *never* let him do *that*." Then he rushed over and scooped up his roommate, whisking him away into the house.

"Holy boomerang," Jessica breathed, staring at Satan's unmoving body.

Destinee turned to the rest of the partygoers. "Anyone *else* not see her reach for a gun?"

Heads shook en masse.

Destinee was really getting excited now. Her pupils were large, her nostrils flared wide. Not scared, but in her element. "Don't forget, that bitch was the Devil. The literal Devil. She had it comin'."

"Sh-shouldn't we make sure she's dead before we just ...?" Miranda's shaky voice faltered.

"Good thinkin'," Destinee agreed.

The shotgun hung loosely from Stephanie Lee's hands.

"Here, hun," Destinee said, gently disarming her. "I'll take that."

Destinee McCloud marched over to the Devil and fired a shot right between her eyes. "There. I'm sure she's dead now."

Chapter Fifty-Four

26 AGC

Jessica met with Jimmy Dean in the library. It was just the two of them, if she didn't count the prison guard.

He looked up from his reading, and she felt a useless twinge of pity for him. His dyed gray hair was naturally gray now, a darker, muddier shade than when he'd gotten it professionally done—was that already two years ago now?

In that time, his strong cheekbones had become hollow trenches, and when he looked up at her, the clear blue eyes were faded like a polluted lake. The only thing that remained the same about his appearance was that he still wore all white. Only now it was the fashion of the Texas Correctional Institutions.

"You came," were the first words out of his mouth, and she immediately questioned her decision to visit him.

"Don't act like you prophesied it, Jimmy. If ever there was a time for you to cut the bullshit, it's now. You've lost. No one is going to follow you to the end of the world. You've been found out."

He shut the book in front of him, and she saw the word "Siddhartha" across the cover.

"Jesus. Don't tell me you're planning to hijack another religion."

He didn't respond. Instead, he merely gestured to the bench across the table from him, the seat she was going to take *anyway*. It was the only seat around. She wasn't following his orders.

She glared at him across the table, wondering how to even start. She knew what she'd come to say, but did she just dive right in?

Deep creases formed around his eyes as he smiled at her. "You look like a real woman now, Jessica."

"How do you do it?"

"Do what?"

"How do you make sure that everything you say is creepy, sleazy, or insulting?"

He chuckled, an Ice Cream Jimmy-like sound, harsh, scratchy, and leaned back in his chair. "It's easy when the person I'm speaking with is perpetually insecure and guarded."

"There you go again. How's Emily?"

It was a cheap shot, she knew. That was why it was so fun. His fiancée had taken off once it was abundantly clear that Jimmy had planned to pull another Judgment Day Irish goodbye on her. She'd become famous on daytime talk shows since.

Before he could load Jessica up with more bullshit, though, she said "Look, I didn't come here to listen to what you have to say about anything. I came here to tell you something. And to give you something."

Now he was listening.

"That night at White Light. The very last one. You told me I wouldn't be what I was without you. That I never would have risen to the occasion without you challenging me." Those words had haunted her for more sleepless nights than she cared to admit. "I came to tell you, you were right. I never would've claimed my own story if you and the Devil hadn't kept trying to steal it."

He narrowed his eyes skeptically. "I appreciate you admitting I was right, but it's not necessary. I already knew that. But go back to the part about the Devil. It sounds like you spoke of her in the past tense. Has she stopped trying to steal your story?"

The coverup for Stephanie Lee had gone so smoothly, Jessica had long since stored the memory at the back of her mind with all the other disturbing moments that were not immediately relevant. "Oh, right. She's dead. You haven't heard?" It was clear from his shocked expression that he had not. "Yep. Blown away with a shotgun." Leaving off *who* had done it was intentional. The word "shotgun" was so closely associated with her mother that she'd leave

Jimmy to chew on the notion that Destinee had put a hole through the Devil the way she'd threatened to do to Jimmy on multiple occasions.

"She'll be back," Jimmy warned in low tones. "She won't stay dead."

"I know. But it's been a nice couple of years without her. I'm not here to talk about her, though."

"You're here to tell me I was right all along."

"Yes, that. You *were* right. But also ..." She leaned across the table, locking eyes with him. She'd dreamed of this moment for months and months. "Fuck. You. Fuck you for everything you ever did to me."

Before he could rebound from his mild shock, she set his gift on the table between them with a thump.

His eyes flickered down to the volume, giving it a quick exploratory pass before meeting her eyes again. She slid it over to him, and with a vague, bored, expression, he rotated the book around to read the cover properly. "After Girl Christ?" He smirked. "What's this?"

"It's my story, Jimmy. It's done. All my own words and experiences collected in one place. The gospel according to the woman who fucking lived it, not some train-hopping narcissist from Alabama. *My* story."

"It says it was written by Judith Magdalena right here on the cover."

"She helped me," Jessica spat. "She's my scribe. But she got all the information straight from me."

"Mm-hm ..." His smirk widened.

She slapped the table. "God damn you, Jimmy!"

He gasped and clutched at his chest.

"No, I didn't mean that. Don't have a heart attack. You don't get to die." She glanced over her shoulder at the security guard who was busy staring wistfully out a small window at the cloudy, gray sky. When she returned her attention to Jimmy, he appeared to have recovered from the jolt but was still breathing heavily.

"Anyway," she said, careful not to apologize to him, "that's your copy. I thought you ought to know how wrong you are."

His eyes flickered to the security guard, and then he cracked open the cover. But he didn't linger on the first page. Instead, after sneaking another furtive look at the guard, he took the thick book into his hands and flipped rapidly through the pages until he reached the back cover. He glanced up at her in confusion. "It's just a *book*."

"It's ... of course it is."

"You brought me a *book*?" He leaned forward urgently. "With no contraband inside?"

Her mouth fell open. Was he serious?

"Can't you tell I have plenty of *books*? We're in a library, for chrissakes! I don't need another goddamn book!" He threw his hands into the air. "Who brings a fucking *book* to a prison? There's not even a fucking bobby pin inside this thing! How the *hell* am I supposed to escape this place with a goddamn *book*!"

She leaned back and would have gotten up from the

bench seat, but she didn't want to take her eyes off him. She'd never seen this kind of rage in him before. He'd lost it. He'd completely lost it. "Why would I help you escape?" she asked.

"Because you're *nothing* without me. You wouldn't have amounted to more than a fat slut's fat slut daughter if I hadn't shown up at your birth and proclaimed you the child of God. You and your cheap lay of a mother would still be in that filthy double-wide, counting your bills from the day's work on the corner. You'd never have left Mooretown, never have discovered any of your miracles, and never, *never* have founded a church if I hadn't blazed the way for you. Now you have the audacity to come in here and tell me that I've been right all along, but then not do a single fucking thing to help me after all I've done for you? God *damn* you, Jessica McCloud! God damn you to hell!" Spittle had formed sticky pools at the corners of his mouth. "Your mother might be a slut, but you're something even worse. You're a tease. A worthless, meek, TEASE!"

He was on his feet as he flipped open the book and began tearing pages from the center of it, crumpling them in his fists before throwing them at her. "If God exists, He's lost his mind sending a woman to do a man's work!"

She caught her heel on the bench as she tried to back away and landed hard on her tailbone on the concrete floor right as the security guard managed to pin Jimmy's wrists behind his back and slam the side of the prisoner's face down on the metal table.

When she left, she didn't look back. Her heart continued to race, and a loud hum like a tuning fork continued in her ears, even after she was safely in her car.

And then she began to cry—big, thick tears that felt like rebirth.

Chapter Fifty-Five

By the time the last animal expert left the dome of the McCloud-Archer Community Center, the sun had long-since fallen below the skylights. Once Jessica powered down the rest of the interior lighting, she would be able to see at least a few stars in the night sky.

The beautiful hand-sewn cushions she'd once laid around this space for her doomed idea of a church had long since been replaced by standard folding chairs where participants of the various educational programs and community discourses could gather round and learn. Tonight it had been wildlife education with a local rescue organization. There had been squirrels and snakes, coyotes, deer, and even a wild hog, and the place smelled like it.

She inhaled deeply, savoring the earthiness.

"And so it is that another day comes to an end, and the humans disperse to their own homes after a full afternoon of gathering and sharing their hard-earned wisdom," Sir

David Attenborough's voice crooned in her mind. It was, by far, her favorite of the two voices she most often heard there.

She cherished her solitary moments here at night. It was the only place where she didn't feel the least bit afraid to be alone in the dark. It wasn't that she felt nothing could harm her here, only that she was fine if this was the last place she ever saw, and that brought her a sense of peace. She could, for once, let go and let God.

Where was She right now? Her Mother's divine intervention had become much sparser in the last couple of years, and she often wondered if there had been an uptick in genocides on the other side of the globe, and She was needed there. Or, maybe, She trusted that Jessica had things under control on her end, and now She could finally give Original Mistake the kind of attention it needed.

Or maybe She was taking a little time off for Herself.

Jessica went to lock up her office but paused by another door that she knew to already be locked. It would remain locked until the right person arrived. Her half-sister. Would she be the peacemaker? Or would she just be the next in line to clear the way?

And would she arrive before Jessica died? Had she already been born? Should Jessica be out looking for her? God, on Her rare visits, wouldn't say. So, for now, all she could do was hold this space for God's second daughter and help pave the way as best she could.

As much as she often daydreamed about fading into obscurity whenever the Third Coming did arrive, she knew better. She would support her half-sister the way Jesus had supported her. When the next of the Christ family arrived, the real work would begin.

Her phone rang just as she slipped the key into her office lock.

"Sister." Jesus sounded fabulously out of breath on the other line. "I have just learned of a festival where you can travel back in time!"

"Uh-huh?"

"Jeremy tells me there are all kinds of fantastic games and food at this event. And knights! He also informed me that you could wear a costume to obscure your identity so you can fully enjoy the celebrations without harassment. Would you like to join us next weekend?"

She double-checked her office door to make sure it was locked. "Assuming you're talking about a renaissance festival and not a weird sex party, sure, I'm in."

And as Jesus continued gushing about all the spectacular fun he was sure they would have while visiting an epoch he'd only been able to observe from Up There, she turned off the last of the lights, locked the front door behind her, and made for home.

Epilogue

33 AGC

Jessica McCloud startled awake from a deep sleep. Adrenaline surged through her arms and legs, and she felt like there was someone in the room watching her.

Because there was.

WAKE UP, BABY.

I'm awake.

The sandpaper sounds of light snoring from the warm body beside her did exponentially more to calm her racing pulse than the presence of God Herself.

Christopher Riley McCloud turned over in his sleep.

PUT ON SOME CLOTHES.

Don't you try to shame me. I get to be naked in my own bed with my husband. That was the deal.

I AM NOT SHAMING YOU FOR THE TEPID SEX YOU ENJOY ONCE EVERY OTHER WEEK. I AM

MERELY TELLING YOU THAT YOU NEED TO PUT ON CLOTHES.

Why? She looked over at the clock. Just after one in the morning.

BECAUSE IT IS ILLEGAL TO DRIVE NAKED.

Jessica struggled to connect the two disparate concepts of nakedness and driving while her body was still so ready to sprint and her brain felt like a lead weight.

What should I wear?

Even she wasn't sure why that was the question she'd come up with.

YOUR SUNDAY BEST. ARE YOU KIDDING ME? I DON'T CARE WHAT YOU WEAR. JUST COVER YOUR NAKEDNESS TO THE MINIMUM REQUIRED BY LAW AND RISE FROM YOUR BED.

Is there an emergency? Is everything okay? Oh no, is my mom—

*YOUR MOTHER IS FINE. BUT THERE **IS** AN EMERGENCY.*

The fog of her brain cleared as she pushed her palms into her eye sockets and she flung her legs over the side of the bed.

THERE IS A MESSAGE I NEED YOU TO PERSONALLY DELIVER TO A WOMAN. BUT IT'S GOING TO BE A LONG DRIVE. YOU NEED TO LEAVE RIGHT AWAY.

And now Jessica understood what she was being asked to do. Another wave of adrenaline surged through her.

Now? Today?

NOT TODAY. IT IS A LONG DRIVE. YOU WILL ARRIVE ON THE DAWN OF THE THIRD DAY.

Jessica rolled her eyes. *Always with the fucking theatrics. Can't I catch a flight instead?*

There was no answer. Fine. She knew what came next, anyway.

Her work, the real reason she was put on this earth, was only just beginning.

THE END

Keep reading for a final word from the author...

Author's Note

Back in late 2018, when I set out creating the ultimate book of this series, I just had this *feeling*, call it female intuition if you must, that we would be ovaries deep in a pandemic when I released *The End is Her*. And I also suspected that such conditions would be the perfect landscape for a powerful anti-racism conversation to finally take root in mainstream discourse.

"Really, Claire?"

No, of course not. Not a clue about any of it. I thought the big upheaval of 2020 would take place on November 3rd, not over the course of the whole fucking year.

Anyway, I won't wax philosophical here because I just said what I wanted to say in the story.

However, one thing I'm sure you folks will (understandably) ask me through email and social media is this:

Will there be any more Jessica Christ books?

The answer is a resounding no. But, my goddess, am I going to miss these characters! Destinee and God, Chris and Rex, Judith and Jameson, Jesus and Jeremy—even Jimmy!—and, of course, Jessica.

(Will I ever start another character's name with a J? I would rather die.)

The year of 33 After Girl Christ is the end of the line for Jessica's narrative. It's time for her to stop being the center of attention and instead step out of the spotlight so another messiah can step in. Jessica must become a supporting character.

The Third Coming isn't my story to write. But it's my great hope that someone will. Someone who has the lived experience of Jessica's half-sister, like I had the lived experience of being a young, straight, white girl growing up in Texas. I don't know when or if this wish of mine will ever happen, but I'm holding space for that person to show up and say, "Hey, I want in on this intellectual property because I *know* how to tell this one." And if that day comes, I'll do what I can to support her as she makes us laugh our asses off. And if it doesn't come, no big deal. I'm here to amplify, not dictate.

So, thanks for coming along for the wild ride. Jessica Christ is a series that, by all accounts, shouldn't have made it this far. Suffice to say not everyone in my life when I started publishing it was super thrilled with the premise. Writing this series has caused me grief, anxiety, insomnia, depression, migraines, indigestion, a complete mental breakdown or two, and has been, far and away, my most rewarding creative project to date. Although I'm still young. I turn 33 in November.

Any success these books enjoy is all thanks to people like you who took a chance on a series you'd never heard of from an author you'd never heard of who claimed she could write something funny. As a reader myself, I'd never bother, but I'm sure glad you did.

I have a shitload more funny books coming your way, assuming I survive the switchblade armadillos or giant syphilis meteor or homicidal land dolphins or whatever insanity the following months have in store for us. And I hope *you'll* humor *me* by giving the next series a shot.

Awomxn.
-H. Claire Taylor
7/7/2020

About the Author

H. CLAIRE TAYLOR has lived in Austin since the eighties (it's her hometown) and hasn't yet found a compelling reason to move away.

She shares a home with her husband and two black-and-white mutts.

Casually stalk her:
www.hclairetaylor.com
contact@hclairetaylor.com

facebook.com/authorhclairetaylor

twitter.com/claireorwhatevs

instagram.com/claireorwhatevs

bookbub.com/authors/h-claire-taylor

goodreads.com/hclairetaylor

Books by H. Claire Taylor

The Jessica Christ Series

The Beginning (Book 1)

And It Was Good (Book 2)

It's a Miracle! (Book 3)

Nu Alpha Omega (Book 4)

It is Risen (Book 5)

In the Details (Book 6)

The End is Her (Book 7)

The Kilhaven Police series

Shift Work (Book 1)

Same Old Shift (Book 2)

Shift Out of Luck (Book 3)

Wimbledon, Kentucky

A Single's Guide to Texas Roadways

See all at www.hclairetaylor.com

Find more funny books at www.ffs.media

Made in the USA
Columbia, SC
10 May 2024